CANDIDE
or Optimism

A   NEW   TRANSLATION

BACKGROUNDS

CRITICISM

A NORTON CRITICAL EDITION

VOLTAIRE

CANDIDE
or Optimism

A NEW TRANSLATION
BACKGROUNDS
CRITICISM

Translated and Edited by

ROBERT M. ADAMS
UNIVERSITY OF CALIFORNIA AT LOS ANGELES

W · W · NORTON & COMPANY
New York · London

ISBN 0-393-05327-X Cloth Edition
ISBN 0-393-09649-1 Paper Edition

W. W. Norton & Company, Inc., 500 Fifth Avenue, New York, N.Y. 10110

PRINTED IN THE UNITED STATES OF AMERICA

3 4 5 6 7 8 9 0

Contents

74096

vi · *Contents*

Preface

When Candide first set forth into the world, in January, 1759, he did not do so under the aegis of M. de Voltaire, the well-known poet, tragedian, historian, philosopher, and friend of Frederick the Great. As illegitimate as its hero, the book *Candide* proposed itself as the work of "Dr. Ralph"; and if it had not been signed extravagantly between the lines with another and better-known autograph, would doubtless figure today only in Barbier and Billard's labyrinthine listing of anonymous literature.

The little book made its way, in other words, on its own—was read because it was amusing, and for that reason alone, and has only lately started to appear on assigned-reading lists and enumerations of "the world's great books." Now that it is a classic, I suppose the first thing the startled student must be told is that it is still funny.

The other things about the story, and there are a good many of them, come a long way after this first article.

Candide is a cruel and destructive book as well as a funny one. Funny and cruel: the qualities go together more easily perhaps than we like to think. But they would not suffice for the peculiar vitality of *Candide*, unless something else were added. If all it did was demolish a long-outdated system of German philosophy, its fun might feel as antiquated and its cruelty as gratuitous as Shakespeare's puns or Pope's malignant hounding after dunces. But *Candide*'s cruelty is not sour, and its fun remains modern and relevant. Dozens of heroes in modern fiction are Candides under one disguise or another,* as our standard heroine is a reworked Madame Bovary—who herself has more than a touch of Candide in her complexion. Why Voltaire's little book feels so modern clearly has something to do with the things it destroys and the way in which it carries out that work of destruction. But it is neither necessary nor possible to be peremptory in defining its targets, for satire generally works more widely than even its creator realizes. There's something in it for everyone. So the book's exact import is evidently up to the decision of the duly informed and sensitive reader—for whose individual responses to the actual work of art there neither is nor can be any substitute.

---

* For example, all the Evelyn Waugh and Aldous Huxley heroes, as well as Augie March, Holden Caulfield, Huckleberry Finn and all his multitudinous descendants, not to mention the "étranger" of Camus, good soldier Schweik and an infinity of other battered innocents.

Though its action scampers dizzily around the perimeter of the civilized world, *Candide* is an essentially European book in its passionate addiction to, and scepticism of, the reasonable life. It could easily have a number of subtitles other than "Optimism"; one good one would be "Civilization and Its Discontents."

The present translation has aimed to be neither literal nor loose, but to preserve a decent respect for English idiom while rendering a French intent. It was made from the old standard Morize edition, still a classic despite its age, and especially useful for the dry, neat erudition of its notes. But in its late stages, the English text was read against, and modified to conform with, M. René Pomeau's 1959 edition, which introduces a few recent textual modifications. The text of *Candide* contains little that is problematic; it is clean, clear, and relatively uncluttered with afterthoughts. As for Voltaire's prose, it is late in the day to pronounce in its favor; a translator, however, may speak with special feeling of its lucidity, lightness, and swiftness of tonal variation. It is a joy to translate.

The editor wishes to express his acknowledgments to John Bender and Dennis Prindle for looking up necessary items in the library and sending them across necessary oceans; to an editor whose professional modesty keeps him anonymous; and to Mlle. J. Dubuis of the Musée et Institut Voltaire at Les Délices in Genève, for permission to use the collections there and for five-o'clock tea on raw winter afternoons.

ROBERT M. ADAMS

The Text of
Candide
or Optimism

translated from the German of Doctor Ralph
with the additions which were found in the Doctor's pocket
when he died at Minden in the Year of Our Lord 1759

Translated by Robert M. Adams

Candide

CHAPTER 1

How Candide Was Brought up in a Fine Castle and How He Was Driven Therefrom

There lived in Westphalia,[1] in the castle of the Baron of Thunder-Ten-Tronckh, a young man on whom nature had bestowed the perfection of gentle manners. His features admirably expressed his soul, he combined an honest mind with great simplicity of heart; and I think it was for this reason that they called him Candide. The old servants of the house suspected that he was the son of the Baron's sister by a respectable, honest gentleman of the neighborhood, whom she had refused to marry because he could prove only seventy-one quarterings,[2] the rest of his family tree having been lost in the passage of time.

The Baron was one of the most mighty lords of Westphalia, for his castle had a door and windows. His great hall was even hung with a tapestry. The dogs of his courtyard made up a hunting pack on occasion, with the stableboys as huntsmen; the village priest was his grand almoner. They all called him "My Lord," and laughed at his stories.

The Baroness, who weighed in the neighborhood of three hundred and fifty pounds, was greatly respected for that reason, and did the honors of the house with a dignity which rendered her even more imposing. Her daughter Cunégonde,[3] aged seventeen, was a ruddy-cheeked girl, fresh, plump, and desirable. The Baron's son seemed in every way worthy of his father. The tutor Pangloss was the oracle of the household, and little Candide listened to his lectures with all the good faith of his age and character.

Pangloss gave instruction in metaphysico-theologico-cosmoloonigology.[4] He proved admirably that there cannot possibly be an effect

---

1. Westphalia is a province of western Germany, near Holland and the lower Rhineland. Flat, boggy, and drab, it is noted chiefly for its excellent ham. In a letter to his niece, written during his German expedition of 1750, Voltaire described the "vast, sad, sterile, detestable countryside of Westphalia."

2. Quarterings are genealogical divisions of one's family tree. Seventy-one of them is a grotesque number to have, representing something over 2,000 years of uninterrupted nobility.

3. Cunégonde gets her odd name from Kunigunda, wife to Emperor Henry II, who walked barefoot and blindfolded on red-hot irons to prove her chastity; Pangloss gets his name from Greek words meaning all-tongue.

4. The "looney" I have buried in this burlesque word corresponds to a buried nigaud—"booby" in the French. Christian Wolff, disciple of Leibniz, invented and popularized the word "cosmology."

without a cause and that in this best of all possible worlds[5] the Baron's castle was the best of all castles and his wife the best of all possible Baronesses.

—It is clear, said he, that things cannot be otherwise than they are, for since everything is made to serve an end, everything necessarily serves the best end. Observe: noses were made to support spectacles, hence we have spectacles. Legs, as anyone can plainly see, were made to be breeched, and so we have breeches. Stones were made to be shaped and to build castles with; thus My Lord has a fine castle, for the greatest Baron in the province should have the finest house; and since pigs were made to be eaten, we eat pork all year round.[6] Consequently, those who say everything is well are uttering mere stupidities; they should say everything is for the best.

Candide listened attentively and believed implicitly; for he found Miss Cunégonde exceedingly pretty, though he never had the courage to tell her so. He decided that after the happiness of being born Baron of Thunder-Ten-Tronckh, the second order of happiness was to be Miss Cunégonde; the third was seeing her every day, and the fourth was listening to Master Pangloss, the greatest philosopher in the province and consequently in the entire world.

One day, while Cunégonde was walking near the castle in the little woods that they called a park, she saw Dr. Pangloss in the underbrush; he was giving a lesson in experimental physics to her mother's maid, a very attractive and obedient brunette. As Miss Cunégonde had a natural bent for the sciences, she watched breathlessly the repeated experiments which were going on; she saw clearly the doctor's sufficient reason, observed both cause and effect, and returned to the house in a distracted and pensive frame of mind, yearning for knowledge and dreaming that she might be the sufficient reason of young Candide—who might also be hers.

As she was returning to the castle, she met Candide, and blushed; Candide blushed too. She greeted him in a faltering tone of voice; and Candide talked to her without knowing what he was saying. Next day, as everyone was rising from the dinner table, Cunégonde and Candide found themselves behind a screen; Cunégonde dropped her handkerchief, Candide picked it up; she held his hand quite innocently, he kissed her hand quite innocently

---

5. These catch phrases, echoed by popularizers of Leibniz, make reference to the determinism of his system, its linking of cause with effect, and its optimism. As his correspondence indicates, Voltaire habitually thought of Leibniz's philosophy (which, having been published in definitive form as early as 1710, had been in the air for a long time) in terms of these catch phrases.
6. The argument from design supposes

that everything in this world exists for a specific reason; Voltaire objects not to the argument as a whole, but to the abuse of it. He grants, for example, that noses were made to smell and stomachs to digest but denies that feet were made to put shoes on or stones to be cut up into building blocks. His full view finds expression in the article on "causes finales" in the *Philosophical Dictionary*

with remarkable vivacity and emotion; their lips met, their eyes lit up, their knees trembled, their hands wandered. The Baron of Thunder-Ten-Tronckh passed by the screen and, taking note of this cause and this effect, drove Candide out of the castle by kicking him vigorously on the backside. Cunégonde fainted; as soon as she recovered, the Baroness slapped her face; and everything was confusion in the most beautiful and agreeable of all possible castles.

CHAPTER 2
What Happened to Candide Among the Bulgars[7]

Candide, ejected from the earthly paradise, wandered for a long time without knowing where he was going, weeping, raising his eyes to heaven, and gazing back frequently on the most beautiful of castles which contained the most beautiful of Baron's daughters. He slept without eating, in a furrow of a plowed field, while the snow drifted over him; next morning, numb with cold, he dragged himself into the neighboring village, which was called Waldberghoff-trarbk-dikdorff; he was penniless, famished, and exhausted. At the door of a tavern he paused forlornly. Two men dressed in blue[8] took note of him:

—Look, chum, said one of them, there's a likely young fellow of just about the right size.

They approached Candide and invited him very politely to dine with them.

—Gentlemen, Candide replied with charming modesty, I'm honored by your invitation, but I really don't have enough money to pay my share.

—My dear sir, said one of the blues, people of your appearance and your merit don't have to pay; aren't you five feet five inches tall?

—Yes, gentlemen, that is indeed my stature, said he, making a bow.

—Then, sir, you must be seated at once; not only will we pay your bill this time, we will never allow a man like you to be short of money; for men were made only to render one another mutual aid.

—You are quite right, said Candide; it is just as Dr. Pangloss always told me, and I see clearly that everything is for the best.

They beg him to accept a couple of crowns, he takes them, and offers an I.O.U.; they won't hear of it, and all sit down at table

7. Voltaire chose this name to represent the Prussian troops of Frederick the Great because he wanted to make an insinuation of pederasty against both the soldiers and their master. *Cf.* French *bougre,* English "bugger."

8. The recruiting officers of Frederick the Great, much feared in eighteenth-century Europe, wore blue uniforms. Frederick had a passion for sorting out his soldiers by size; several of his regiments would accept only six-footers.

together.

—Don't you love dearly . . . ?

—I do indeed, says he, I dearly love Miss Cunégonde.

—No, no, says one of the gentlemen, we are asking if you don't love dearly the King of the Bulgars.

—Not in the least, says he, I never laid eyes on him.

—What's that you say? He's the most charming of kings, and we must drink his health.

—Oh, gladly, gentlemen; and he drinks.

—That will do, they tell him; you are now the bulwark, the support, the defender, the hero of the Bulgars; your fortune is made and your future assured.

Promptly they slip irons on his legs and lead him to the regiment. There they cause him to right face, left face, present arms, order arms, aim, fire, doubletime, and they give him thirty strokes of the rod. Next day he does the drill a little less awkwardly and gets only twenty strokes; the third day, they give him only ten, and he is regarded by his comrades as a prodigy.

Candide, quite thunderstruck, did not yet understand very clearly how he was a hero. One fine spring morning he took it into his head to go for a walk, stepping straight out as if it were a privilege of the human race, as of animals in general, to use his legs as he chose.[9] He had scarcely covered two leagues when four other heroes, each six feet tall, overtook him, bound him, and threw him into a dungeon. At the court-martial they asked which he preferred, to be flogged thirty-six times by the entire regiment or to receive summarily a dozen bullets in the brain. In vain did he argue that the human will is free and insist that he preferred neither alternative; he had to choose; by virtue of the divine gift called "liberty" he decided to run the gauntlet thirty-six times, and actually endured two floggings. The regiment was composed of two thousand men. That made four thousand strokes, which laid open every muscle and nerve from his nape to his butt. As they were preparing for the third beating, Candide, who could endure no more, begged as a special favor that they would have the goodness to smash his head. His plea was granted; they bandaged his eyes and made him kneel down. The King of the Bulgars, passing by at this moment, was told of the culprit's crime; and as this king had a rare genius, he understood, from everything they told him of Candide, that this was a

9. This episode was suggested by the experience of a Frenchman named Courtilz, who had deserted from the Prussian army and been bastinadoed for it. Voltaire intervened with Frederick to gain his release. But it also reflects the story that Wolff. Leibniz's disciple, got into trouble with Frederick's father when someone reported that his doctrine denying free will had encouraged several soldiers to desert. "The argument of the grenadier," who was said to have pleaded pre-established harmony to justify his desertion, so infuriated the king that he had Wolff expelled from the country.

young metaphysician, extremely ignorant of the ways of the world, so he granted his royal pardon, with a generosity which will be praised in every newspaper in every age. A worthy surgeon cured Candide in three weeks with the ointments described by Dioscorides.[1] He already had a bit of skin back and was able to walk when the King of the Bulgars went to war with the King of the Abares.[2]

How Candide Escaped from the Bulgars, and What Became of Him

Nothing could have been so fine, so brisk, so brilliant, so well-drilled as the two armies. The trumpets, the fifes, the oboes, the drums, and the cannon produced such a harmony as was never heard in hell. First the cannons battered down about six thousand men on each side; then volleys of musket fire removed from the best of worlds about nine or ten thousand rascals who were cluttering up its surface. The bayonet was a sufficient reason for the demise of several thousand others. Total casualties might well amount to thirty thousand men or so. Candide, who was trembling like a philosopher, hid himself as best he could while this heroic butchery was going on.

Finally, while the two kings in their respective camps celebrated the victory by having *Te Deums* sung, Candide undertook to do his reasoning of cause and effect somewhere else. Passing by mounds of the dead and dying, he came to a nearby village which had been burnt to the ground. It was an Abare village, which the Bulgars had burned, in strict accordance with the laws of war. Here old men, stunned from beatings, watched the last agonies of their butchered wives, who still clutched their infants to their bleeding breasts; there, disemboweled girls, who had first satisfied the natural needs of various heroes, breathed their last; others, half-scorched in the flames, begged for their death stroke. Scattered brains and severed limbs littered the ground.

Candide fled as fast as he could to another village; this one belonged to the Bulgars, and the heroes of the Abare cause had given it the same treatment. Climbing over ruins and stumbling over corpses, Candide finally made his way out of the war area, carrying

1. Dioscorides' treatise on *materia medica,* dating from the first century A.D., was not the most up to date.
2. The name "Abares" actually designates a tribe of semicivilized Scythians, who might be supposed at war with the Bulgars; allegorically, the Abares are the French, who opposed the Prussians in the conflict known to hindsight history as the Seven Years' War (1756–1763). For Voltaire, at the moment of writing *Candide,* it was simply the current war. One notes that according to the title page of 1761, "Doctor Ralph," the dummy author of *Candide,* himself perished at the battle of Minden (Westphalia) in 1759.

a little food in his knapsack and never ceasing to dream of Miss Cunégonde. His supplies gave out when he reached Holland; but having heard that everyone in that country was rich and a Christian, he felt confident of being treated as well as he had been in the castle of the Baron before he was kicked out for the love of Miss Cunégonde.

He asked alms of several grave personages, who all told him that if he continued to beg, he would be shut up in a house of correction and set to hard labor.

Finally he approached a man who had just been talking to a large crowd for an hour on end; the topic was charity. Looking doubtfully at him, the orator demanded:

—What are you doing here? Are you here to serve the good cause?

—There is no effect without a cause, said Candide modestly; all events are linked by the chain of necessity and arranged for the best. I had to be driven away from Miss Cunégonde, I had to run the gauntlet, I have to beg my bread until I can earn it; none of this could have happened otherwise.

—Look here, friend, said the orator, do you think the Pope is Antichrist?[3]

—I haven't considered the matter, said Candide; but whether he is or not, I'm in need of bread.

—You don't deserve any, said the other; away with you, you rascal, you rogue, never come near me as long as you live.

Meanwhile, the orator's wife had put her head out of the window, and, seeing a man who was not sure the Pope was Antichrist, emptied over his head a pot full of ——— Scandalous! The excesses into which women are led by religious zeal!

A man who had never been baptized, a good Anabaptist[4] named Jacques, saw this cruel and heartless treatment being inflicted on one of his fellow creatures, a featherless biped possessing a soul[5]; he took Candide home with him, washed him off, gave him bread and beer, presented him with two florins, and even undertook to give him a job in his Persian-rug factory—for these items are widely manufactured in Holland. Candide, in an ecstasy of gratitude, cried out:

—Master Pangloss was right indeed when he told me everything

3. Voltaire is satirizing extreme Protestant sects that have sometimes seemed to make hatred of Rome the sum and substance of their creed.
4. Holland, as the home of religious liberty, had offered asylum to the Anabaptists, whose radical views on property and religious discipline had made them unpopular during the sixteenth century. Granted tolerance, they settled down into respectable burghers. Since this behavior confirmed some of Voltaire's major theses, he had a high opinion of contemporary Anabaptists.
5. Plato's famous minimal definition of a man, which he corrected by the addition of a soul to distinguish man from a plucked chicken. The point is that the Anabaptist sympathizes with men simply because they are human.

is for the best in this world; for I am touched by your kindness far more than by the harshness of that black-coated gentleman and his wife.

Next day, while taking a stroll about town, he met a beggar who was covered with pustules, his eyes were sunken, the end of his nose rotted off, his mouth twisted, his teeth black, he had a croaking voice and a hacking cough, and spat a tooth every time he tried to speak.

CHAPTER 4

How Candide Met His Old Philosophy Tutor, Doctor Pangloss, and What Came of It

Candide, more touched by compassion even than by horror, gave this ghastly beggar the two florins that he himself had received from his honest Anabaptist friend Jacques. The phantom stared at him, burst into tears, and fell on his neck. Candide drew back in terror.

—Alas, said one wretch to the other, don't you recognize your dear Pangloss any more?

—What are you saying? You, my dear master! you, in this horrible condition? What misfortune has befallen you? Why are you no longer in the most beautiful of castles? What has happened to Miss Cunégonde, that pearl among young ladies, that masterpiece of Nature?

—I am perishing, said Pangloss.

—Candide promptly led him into the Anabaptist's stable, where he gave him a crust of bread, and when he had recovered: —Well, said he, Cunégonde?

—Dead, said the other.

Candide fainted. His friend brought him around with a bit of sour vinegar which happened to be in the stable. Candide opened his eyes.

—Cunégonde, dead! Ah, best of worlds, what's become of you now? But how did she die? It wasn't of grief at seeing me kicked out of her noble father's elegant castle?

—Not at all, said Pangloss; she was disemboweled by the Bulgar soldiers, after having been raped to the absolute limit of human endurance; they smashed the Baron's head when he tried to defend her, cut the Baroness to bits, and treated my poor pupil exactly like his sister.[6] As for the castle, not one stone was left on another, not a shed, not a sheep, not a duck, not a tree; but we had the satisfaction of revenge, for the Abares did exactly the same thing to a

---

6. The theme of homosexuality which attaches to Cunégonde's brother seems to have no general satiric point, but its presence is unmistakable. See Chapters 14, 15, and 28.

nearby barony belonging to a Bulgar nobleman.

At this tale Candide fainted again; but having returned to his senses and said everything appropriate to the occasion, he asked about the cause and effect, the sufficient reason, which had reduced Pangloss to his present pitiful state.

—Alas, said he, it was love; love, the consolation of the human race, the preservative of the universe, the soul of all sensitive beings, love, gentle love.

—Unhappy man, said Candide, I too have had some experience of this love, the sovereign of hearts, the soul of our souls; and it never got me anything but a single kiss and twenty kicks in the rear. How could this lovely cause produce in you such a disgusting effect?

Pangloss replied as follows: —My dear Candide! you knew Paquette, that pretty maidservant to our august Baroness. In her arms I tasted the delights of paradise, which directly caused these torments of hell, from which I am now suffering. She was infected with the disease, and has perhaps died of it. Paquette received this present from an erudite Franciscan, who took the pains to trace it back to its source; for he had it from an elderly countess, who picked it up from a captain of cavalry, who acquired it from a marquise, who caught it from a page, who had received it from a Jesuit, who during his novitiate got it directly from one of the companions of Christopher Columbus.[7] As for me, I shall not give it to anyone, for I am a dying man.

—Oh, Pangloss, cried Candide, that's a very strange genealogy. Isn't the devil at the root of the whole thing?

—Not at all, replied that great man; it's an indispensable part of the best of worlds, a necessary ingredient; if Columbus had not caught, on an American island, this sickness which attacks the source of generation and sometimes prevents generation entirely—which thus strikes at and defeats the greatest end of Nature herself—we should have neither chocolate nor cochineal. It must also be noted that until the present time this malady, like religious controversy, has been wholly confined to the continent of Europe. Turks, Indians, Persians, Chinese, Siamese, and Japanese know nothing of it as yet; but there is a sufficient reason for which they in turn will make its acquaintance in a couple of centuries. Meanwhile, it has made splendid progress among us, especially among those big armies of honest, well-trained mercenaries who decide the destinies of nations. You can be sure that when thirty thousand men fight a pitched battle against the same number of the enemy, there will be about twenty thousand with the pox on either side.

7. Syphilis was the first contribution of the New World to the happiness of the Old. Voltaire's information comes from Astruc, *Traité des maladies vénériennes* (1734).

—Remarkable indeed, said Candide, but we must see about curing you.

—And how can I do that, said Pangloss, seeing I don't have a cent to my name? There's not a doctor in the whole world who will let your blood or give you an enema without demanding a fee. If you can't pay yourself, you must find someone to pay for you.

These last words decided Candide; he hastened to implore the help of his charitable Anabaptist, Jacques, and painted such a moving picture of his friend's wretched state that the good man did not hesitate to take in Pangloss and have him cured at his own expense. In the course of the cure, Pangloss lost only an eye and an ear. Since he wrote a fine hand and knew arithmetic, the Anabaptist made him his bookkeeper. At the end of two months, being obliged to go to Lisbon on business, he took his two philosophers on the boat with him. Pangloss still maintained that everything was for the best, but Jacques didn't agree with him.

—It must be, said he, that men have corrupted Nature, for they are not born wolves, yet that is what they become. God gave them neither twenty-four-pound cannon nor bayonets, yet they have manufactured both in order to destroy themselves. Bankruptcies have the same effect, and so does the justice which seizes the goods of bankrupts in order to prevent the creditors from getting them.[8]

—It was all indispensable, replied the one-eyed doctor, since private misfortunes make for public welfare, and therefore the more private misfortunes there are, the better everything is.

While he was reasoning, the air grew dark, the winds blew from all directions, and the vessel was attacked by a horrible tempest within sight of Lisbon harbor.

CHAPTER 5

Tempest, Shipwreck, Earthquake, and What Happened to
Doctor Pangloss, Candide, and the Anabaptist, Jacques

Half of the passengers, weakened by the frightful anguish of seasickness and the distress of tossing about on stormy waters, were incapable of noticing their danger. The other half shrieked aloud and fell to their prayers, the sails were ripped to shreds, the masts snapped, the vessel opened at the seams. Everyone worked who could stir, nobody listened for orders or issued them. The Anabaptist was lending a hand in the after part of the ship when a frantic sailor struck him and knocked him to the deck; but just at that moment, the sailor lurched so violently that he fell head first over the side, where he hung, clutching a fragment of the broken mast.

8. Voltaire had suffered losses from various bankruptcy proceedings, which lend a personal edge to his satire here, besides diverting its point a bit.

The good Jacques ran to his aid, and helped him to climb back on board, but in the process was himself thrown into the sea under the very eyes of the sailor, who allowed him to drown without even glancing at him. Candide rushed to the rail, and saw his benefactor rise for a moment to the surface, then sink forever. He wanted to dive to his rescue; but the philosopher Pangloss prevented him by proving that the bay of Lisbon had been formed expressly for this Anabaptist to drown in. While he was proving the point *a priori*, the vessel opened up and everyone perished except for Pangloss, Candide, and the brutal sailor who had caused the virtuous Anabaptist to drown; this rascal swam easily to shore, while Pangloss and Candide drifted there on a plank.

When they had recovered a bit of energy, they set out for Lisbon; they still had a little money with which they hoped to stave off hunger after escaping the storm.

Scarcely had they set foot in the town, still bewailing the loss of their benefactor, when they felt the earth quake underfoot; the sea was lashed to a froth, burst into the port, and smashed all the vessels lying at anchor there. Whirlwinds of fire and ash swirled through the streets and public squares; houses crumbled, roofs came crashing down on foundations, foundations split; thirty thousand inhabitants of every age and either sex were crushed in the ruins.[9] The sailor whistled through his teeth, and said with an oath:

—There'll be something to pick up here.

—What can be the sufficient reason of this phenomenon? asked Pangloss.

—The Last Judgment is here, cried Candide.

But the sailor ran directly into the middle of the ruins, heedless of danger in his eagerness for gain; he found some money, laid violent hands on it, got drunk, and, having slept off his wine, bought the favors of the first streetwalker he could find amid the ruins of smashed houses, amid corpses and suffering victims on every hand. Pangloss however tugged at his sleeve.

—My friend, said he, this is not good form at all; your behavior falls short of that required by the universal reason; it's untimely, to say the least.

—Bloody hell, said the other, I'm a sailor, born in Batavia; I've been four times to Japan and stamped four times on the crucifix[1]; get out of here with your universal reason.

9. The great Lisbon earthquake and fire occurred on November 1, 1755; between thirty and forty thousand deaths resulted.
1. The Japanese, originally receptive to foreign visitors, grew fearful that priests and proselytizers were merely advance agents of empire, and expelled both the Portuguese and Spanish early in the seventeenth century. Only the Dutch were allowed to retain a small foothold, under humiliating conditions, of which the notion of stamping on the crucifix is symbolic. It was never what Voltaire suggests here, an actual requirement for entering the country.

Some falling stonework had struck Candide; he lay prostrate in the street, covered with rubble, and calling to Pangloss: —For pity's sake bring me a little wine and oil; I'm dying.

—This earthquake is nothing novel, Pangloss replied; the city of Lima, in South America, underwent much the same sort of tremor, last year; same causes, same effects; there is surely a vein of sulphur under the earth's surface reaching from Lima to Lisbon.

—Nothing is more probable, said Candide; but, for God's sake, a little oil and wine.

—What do you mean, probable? replied the philosopher; I regard the case as proved.

Candide fainted and Pangloss brought him some water from a nearby fountain.

Next day, as they wandered amid the ruins, they found a little food which restored some of their strength. Then they fell to work like the others, bringing relief to those of the inhabitants who had escaped death. Some of the citizens whom they rescued gave them a dinner as good as was possible under the circumstances; it is true that the meal was a melancholy one, and the guests watered their bread with tears; but Pangloss consoled them by proving that things could not possibly be otherwise.

—For, said he, all this is for the best, since if there is a volcano at Lisbon, it cannot be somewhere else, since it is unthinkable that things should not be where they are, since everything is well.

A little man in black, an officer of the Inquisition,[2] who was sitting beside him, politely took up the question, and said: —It would seem that the gentleman does not believe in original sin, since if everything is for the best, man has not fallen and is not liable to eternal punishment.

—I most humbly beg pardon of your excellency, Pangloss answered, even more politely, but the fall of man and the curse of original sin entered necessarily into the best of all possible worlds.

—Then you do not believe in free will? said the officer.

—Your excellency must excuse me, said Pangloss; free will agrees very well with absolute necessity, for it was necessary that we should be free, since a will which is determined . . .

Pangloss was in the middle of his sentence, when the officer nodded significantly to the attendant who was pouring him a glass of port, or Oporto, wine.

2. Specifically, a *familier* or *poursuivant,* an undercover agent with powers of arrest.

CHAPTER 6

How They Made a Fine Auto-da-Fé to Prevent Earth-quakes, and How Candide Was Whipped

After the earthquake had wiped out three quarters of Lisbon, the learned men of the land could find no more effective way of averting total destruction than to give the people a fine auto-da-fé[3]; the University of Coimbra had established that the spectacle of several persons being roasted over a slow fire with full ceremonial rites is an infallible specific against earthquakes.

In consequence, the authorities had rounded up a Biscayan convicted of marrying a woman who had stood godmother to his child, and two Portuguese who while eating a chicken had set aside a bit of bacon used for seasoning.[4] After dinner, men came with ropes to tie up Doctor Pangloss and his disciple Candide, one for talking and the other for listening with an air of approval; both were taken separately to a set of remarkably cool apartments, where the glare of the sun is never bothersome; eight days later they were both dressed in *san-benitos* and crowned with paper mitres[5]; Candide's mitre and *san-benito* were decorated with inverted flames and with devils who had neither tails nor claws; but Pangloss's devils had both tails and claws, and his flames stood upright. Wearing these costumes, they marched in a procession, and listened to a very touching sermon, followed by a beautiful concert of plainsong. Candide was flogged in cadence to the music; the Biscayan and the two men who had avoided bacon were burned, and Pangloss was hanged, though hanging is not customary. On the same day there was another earthquake, causing frightful damage.[6]

Candide, stunned, stupefied, despairing, bleeding, trembling, said to himself: —If this is the best of all possible worlds, what are the others like? The flogging is not so bad, I was flogged by the Bulgars. But oh my dear Pangloss, greatest of philosophers, was it necessary for me to watch you being hanged, for no reason that I can see? Oh my dear Anabaptist, best of men, was it necessary that you should be drowned in the port? Oh Miss Cunégonde, pearl of young ladies, was it necessary that you should have your belly slit open?

He was being led away, barely able to stand, lectured, lashed, ab-

3. Literally, "act of faith," a public ceremony of repentance and humiliation. Such an auto-da-fé was actually held in Lisbon, June 20, 1756.
4. The Biscayan's fault lay in marrying someone within the forbidden bounds of relationship, an act of spiritual incest. The men who declined pork or bacon were understood to be crypto-

Jews.
5. The cone-shaped paper cap (intended to resemble a bishop's mitre) and flowing yellow cape were customary garb for those pleading before the Inquisition.
6. In fact, the second quake occurred December 21, 1755.

solved, and blessed, when an old woman approached and said,
—My son, be of good cheer and follow me.

*How an Old Woman Took Care of Candide, and How
He Regained What He Loved*

Candide was of very bad cheer, but he followed the old woman
to a shanty; she gave him a jar of ointment to rub himself, left him
food and drink; she showed him a tidy little bed; next to it was a
suit of clothing.

—Eat, drink, sleep, she said; and may Our Lady of Atocha, Our
Lord St. Anthony of Padua, and Our Lord St. James of Compostela
watch over you. I will be back tomorrow.

Candide, still completely astonished by everything he had seen
and suffered, and even more by the old woman's kindness, offered
to kiss her hand.

—It's not *my* hand you should be kissing, said she. I'll be back
tomorrow; rub yourself with the ointment, eat and sleep.

In spite of his many sufferings, Candide ate and slept. Next day
the old woman returned bringing breakfast; she looked at his back
and rubbed it herself with another ointment; she came back with
lunch; and then she returned in the evening, bringing supper. Next
day she repeated the same routine.

—Who are you? Candide asked continually. Who told you to be
so kind to me? How can I ever repay you?

The good woman answered not a word; she returned in the evening, and without food.

—Come with me, says she, and don't speak a word.

Taking him by the hand, she walks out into the countryside with
him for about a quarter of a mile; they reach an isolated house,
quite surrounded by gardens and ditches. The old woman knocks at
a little gate, it opens. She takes Candide up a secret stairway to a
gilded room furnished with a fine brocaded sofa; there she leaves
him, closes the door, disappears. Candide stood as if entranced; his
life, which had seemed like a nightmare so far, was now starting to
look like a delightful dream.

Soon the old woman returned; on her feeble shoulder leaned a
trembling woman, of a splendid figure, glittering in diamonds, and
veiled.

—Remove the veil, said the old woman to Candide.

The young man stepped timidly forward, and lifted the veil.
What an event! What a surprise! Could it be Miss Cunégonde?
Yes, it really was! She herself! His knees give way, speech fails him,
he falls at her feet, Cunégonde collapses on the sofa. The old

woman plies them with brandy, they return to their senses, they exchange words. At first they could utter only broken phrases, questions and answers at cross purposes, sighs, tears, exclamations. The old woman warned them not to make too much noise, and left them alone.

—Then it's really you, said Candide, you're alive, I've found you again in Portugal. Then you never were raped? You never had your belly ripped open, as the philosopher Pangloss assured me?

—Oh yes, said the lovely Cunégonde, but one doesn't always die of these two accidents.

—But your father and mother were murdered then?

—All too true, said Cunégonde, in tears.

—And your brother?

—Killed too.

—And why are you in Portugal? and how did you know I was here? and by what device did you have me brought to this house?

—I shall tell you everything, the lady replied; but first you must tell me what has happened to you since that first innocent kiss we exchanged and the kicking you got because of it.

Candide obeyed her with profound respect; and though he was overcome, though his voice was weak and hesitant, though he still had twinges of pain from his beating, he described as simply as possible everything that had happened to him since the time of their separation. Cunégonde lifted her eyes to heaven; she wept at the death of the good Anabaptist and at that of Pangloss; after which she told the following story to Candide, who listened to every word while he gazed on her with hungry eyes.

CHAPTER 8
Cunégonde's Story

—I was in my bed and fast asleep when heaven chose to send the Bulgars into our castle of Thunder-Ten-Tronckh. They butchered my father and brother, and hacked my mother to bits. An enormous Bulgar, six feet tall, seeing that I had swooned from horror at the scene, set about raping me; at that I recovered my senses, I screamed and scratched, bit and fought, I tried to tear the eyes out of that big Bulgar—not realizing that everything which had happened in my father's castle was a mere matter of routine. The brute then stabbed me with a knife on my left thigh, where I still bear the scar.

—What a pity! I should very much like to see it, said the simple Candide.

—You shall, said Cunégonde; but shall I go on?

—Please do, said Candide.

So she took up the thread of her tale: —A Bulgar captain appeared, he saw me covered with blood and the soldier too intent to get up. Shocked by the monster's failure to come to attention, the captain killed him on my body. He then had my wound dressed, and took me off to his quarters, as a prisoner of war. I laundered his few shirts and did his cooking; he found me attractive, I confess it, and I won't deny that he was a handsome fellow, with a smooth, white skin; apart from that, however, little wit, little philosophical training; it was evident that he had not been brought up by Doctor Pangloss. After three months, he had lost all his money and grown sick of me; so he sold me to a jew named Don Issachar, who traded in Holland and Portugal, and who was mad after women. This jew developed a mighty passion for my person, but he got nowhere with it; I held him off better than I had done with the Bulgar soldier; for though a person of honor may be raped once, her virtue is only strengthened by the experience. In order to keep me hidden, the jew brought me to his country house, which you see here. Till then I had thought there was nothing on earth so beautiful as the castle of Thunder-Ten-Tronckh; I was now undeceived.

—One day the Grand Inquisitor took notice of me at mass; he ogled me a good deal, and made known that he must talk to me on a matter of secret business. I was taken to his palace; I told him of my rank; he pointed out that it was beneath my dignity to belong to an Israelite. A suggestion was then conveyed to Don Issachar that he should turn me over to My Lord the Inquisitor. Don Issachar, who is court banker and a man of standing, refused out of hand. The inquisitor threatened him with an auto-da-fé. Finally my jew, fearing for his life, struck a bargain by which the house and I would belong to both of them as joint tenants; the jew would get Mondays, Wednesdays, and the Sabbath, the inquisitor would get the other days of the week. That has been the arrangement for six months now. There have been quarrels; sometimes it has not been clear whether the night from Saturday to Sunday belonged to the old or the new dispensation. For my part, I have so far been able to hold both of them off; and that, I think, is why they are both still in love with me.

—Finally, in order to avert further divine punishment by earthquake, and to terrify Don Issachar, My Lord the Inquisitor chose to celebrate an auto-da-fé. He did me the honor of inviting me to attend. I had an excellent seat; the ladies were served with refreshments between the mass and the execution. To tell you the truth, I was horrified to see them burn alive those two jews and that decent Biscayan who had married his child's godmother; but what was my surprise, my terror, my grief, when I saw, huddled in a *san-benito* and wearing a mitre, someone who looked like Pangloss! I rubbed my eyes, I watched his every move, I saw him hanged; and I fell back in a swoon. Scarcely had I come to my senses again, when I saw you stripped for the lash; that was the peak of my horror, consternation, grief, and despair. I may tell you, by the way, that your skin is even whiter and more delicate than that of my Bulgar captain. Seeing you, then, redoubled the torments which were already overwhelming me. I shrieked aloud, I wanted to call out, 'Let him go, you brutes!' but my voice died within me, and my cries would have been useless. When you had been thoroughly thrashed: 'How can it be,' I asked myself, 'that agreeable Candide and wise Pangloss have come to Lisbon, one to receive a hundred whiplashes, the other to be hanged by order of My Lord the Inquisitor, whose mistress I am? Pangloss must have deceived me cruelly when he told me that all is for the best in this world.'

—Frantic, exhausted, half out of my senses, and ready to die of weakness, I felt as if my mind were choked with the massacre of my father, my mother, my brother, with the arrogance of that ugly Bulgar soldier, with the knife slash he inflicted on me, my slavery, my cookery, my Bulgar captain, my nasty Don Issachar, my abominable inquisitor, with the hanging of Doctor Pangloss, with that great plainsong *miserere* which they sang while they flogged you—and above all, my mind was full of the kiss which I gave you behind the screen, on the day I saw you for the last time. I praised God, who had brought you back to me after so many trials. I asked my old woman to look out for you, and to bring you here as soon as she could. She did just as I asked; I have had the indescribable joy of seeing you again, hearing you and talking with you once more. But you must be frightfully hungry; I am, myself; let us begin with a dinner.

So then and there they sat down to table; and after dinner, they adjourned to that fine brocaded sofa, which has already been mentioned; and there they were when the eminent Don Issachar, one of the masters of the house, appeared. It was the day of the Sabbath; he was arriving to assert his rights and express his tender passion.

CHAPTER 9
What Happened to Cunégonde, Candide, the Grand Inquisitor, and a Jew

This Issachar was the most choleric Hebrew seen in Israel since the Babylonian captivity.

—What's this, says he, you bitch of a Christian, you're not satisfied with the Grand Inquisitor? Do I have to share you with this rascal, too?

So saying, he drew a long dagger, with which he always went

armed, and, supposing his opponent defenceless, flung himself on Candide. But our good Westphalian had received from the old woman, along with his suit of clothes, a fine sword. Out it came, and though his manners were of the gentlest, in short order he laid the Israelite stiff and cold on the floor, at the feet of the lovely Cunégonde.

—Holy Virgin! she cried. What will become of me now? A man killed in my house! If the police find out, we're done for.

—If Pangloss had not been hanged, said Candide, he would give us good advice in this hour of need, for he was a great philosopher. Lacking him, let's ask the old woman.

She was a sensible body, and was just starting to give her opinion of the situation, when another little door opened. It was just one o'clock in the morning, Sunday morning. This day belonged to the inquisitor. In he came, and found the whipped Candide with a sword in his hand, a corpse at his feet, Cunégonde in terror, and an old woman giving them both good advice.

Here now is what passed through Candide's mind in this instant of time; this is how he reasoned: —If this holy man calls for help, he will certainly have me burned, and perhaps Cunégonde as well; he has already had me whipped without mercy; he is my rival; I have already killed once; why hesitate?

It was a quick, clear chain of reasoning; without giving the inquisitor time to recover from his surprise, he ran him through, and laid him beside the jew.

—Here you've done it again, said Cunégonde; there's no hope for us now. We'll be excommunicated, our last hour has come. How is it that you, who were born so gentle, could kill in two minutes a jew and a prelate?

—My dear girl, replied Candide, when a man is in love, jealous, and just whipped by the Inquisition, he is no longer himself.

The old woman now spoke up and said:—There are three Andalusian steeds in the stable, with their saddles and bridles; our brave Candide must get them ready: my lady has some gold coin and diamonds; let's take to horse at once, though I can only ride on one buttock; we will go to Cadiz. The weather is as fine as can be, and it is pleasant to travel in the cool of the evening.

Promptly, Candide saddled the three horses. Cunégonde, the old woman, and he covered thirty miles without a stop. While they were fleeing, the Holy Brotherhood[7] came to investigate the house; they buried the inquisitor in a fine church, and threw Issachar on the dunghill.

Candide, Cunégonde, and the old woman were already in the lit-

7. A semireligious order with police powers, very active in eighteenth-century Spain.

tle town of Avacena, in the middle of the Sierra Morena; and there, as they sat in a country inn, they had this conversation.

CHAPTER 10

In Deep Distress, Candide, Cunégonde, and the Old Woman Reach Cadiz; They Put to Sea

—Who then could have robbed me of my gold and diamonds? said Cunégonde, in tears. How shall we live? what shall we do? where shall I find other inquisitors and jews to give me some more?

—Ah, said the old woman, I strongly suspect that reverend Franciscan friar who shared the inn with us yesterday at Badajoz. God save me from judging him unfairly! But he came into our room twice, and he left long before us.

—Alas, said Candide, the good Pangloss often proved to me that the fruits of the earth are a common heritage of all, to which each man has equal right. On these principles, the Franciscan should at least have left us enough to finish our journey. You have nothing at all, my dear Cunégonde?

—Not a maravedi, said she.

—What to do? said Candide.

—We'll sell one of the horses, said the old woman; I'll ride on the croup behind my mistress, though only on one buttock, and so we will get to Cadiz.

There was in the same inn a Benedictine prior; he bought the horse cheap. Candide, Cunégonde, and the old woman passed through Lucena, Chillas, and Lebrixa, and finally reached Cadiz. There a fleet was being fitted out and an army assembled, to reason with the Jesuit fathers in Paraguay, who were accused of fomenting among their flock a revolt against the kings of Spain and Portugal near the town of St. Sacrement.[8] Candide, having served in the Bulgar army, performed the Bulgar manual of arms before the general of the little army with such grace, swiftness, dexterity, fire, and agility, that they gave him a company of infantry to command. So here he is, a captain; and off he sails with Miss Cunégonde, the old woman, two valets, and the two Andalusian steeds which had belonged to My Lord the Grand Inquisitor of Portugal.

Throughout the crossing, they spent a great deal of time reasoning about the philosophy of poor Pangloss.

—We are destined, in the end, for another universe, said Candide; no doubt that is the one where everything is well. For in

8. Actually, Colonia del Sacramento. Voltaire took great interest in the Jesuit role in Paraguay, which he has much oversimplified and largely misrepresented here in the interests of his satire. In 1750 they did, however, offer armed resistance to an agreement made between Spain and Portugal. They were subdued and expelled in 1769.

this one, it must be admitted, there is some reason to grieve over our physical and moral state.

—I love you with all my heart, said Cunégonde; but my soul is still harrowed by thoughts of what I have seen and suffered.

—All will be well, replied Candide; the sea of this new world is already better than those of Europe, calmer and with steadier winds. Surely it is the New World which is the best of all possible worlds.

—God grant it, said Cunégonde; but I have been so horribly unhappy in the world so far, that my heart is almost dead to hope.

—You pity yourselves, the old woman told them; but you have had no such misfortunes as mine.

Cunégonde nearly broke out laughing; she found the old woman comic in pretending to be more unhappy than she.

—Ah, you poor old thing, said she, unless you've been raped by two Bulgars, been stabbed twice in the belly, seen two of your castles destroyed, witnessed the murder of two of your mothers and two of your fathers, and watched two of your lovers being whipped in an auto-da-fé, I do not see how you can have had it worse than me. Besides, I was born a baroness, with seventy-two quarterings, and I have worked in a scullery.

—My lady, replied the old woman, you do not know my birth and rank; and if I showed you my rear end, you would not talk as you do, you might even speak with less assurance.

These words inspired great curiosity in Candide and Cunégonde, which the old woman satisfied with this story.

CHAPTER 11
The Old Woman's Story

—My eyes were not always bloodshot and red-rimmed, my nose did not always touch my chin, and I was not born a servant. I am in fact the daughter of Pope Urban the Tenth and the Princess of Palestrina.[9] Till the age of fourteen, I lived in a palace so splendid that all the castles of all your German barons would not have served it as a stable; a single one of my dresses was worth more than all the assembled magnificence of Westphalia. I grew in beauty, in charm, in talent, surrounded by pleasures, dignities, and glowing visions of the future. Already I was inspiring the young men to love; my breast was formed—and what a breast! white, firm, with the shape of the Venus de Medici; and what eyes! what lashes, what black brows! What fire flashed from my glances and outshone the glitter

9. Voltaire left behind a comment on this passage, a note first published in 1829: "Note the extreme discretion of the author; hitherto there has never been a pope named Urban X; he avoided attributing a bastard to a known pope. What circumspection! what an exquisite conscience!"

of the stars, as the local poets used to tell me! The women who helped me dress and undress fell into ecstasies, whether they looked at me from in front or behind; and all the men wanted to be in their place.

—I was engaged to the ruling prince of Massa-Carrara; and what a prince he was! as handsome as I, softness and charm compounded, brilliantly witty, and madly in love with me. I loved him in return as one loves for the first time, with a devotion approaching idolatry. The wedding preparations had been made, with a splendor and magnificence never heard of before; nothing but celebrations, masks, and comic operas, uninterruptedly; and all Italy composed in my honor sonnets of which not one was even passable. I had almost attained the very peak of bliss, when an old marquise who had been the mistress of my prince invited him to her house for a cup of chocolate. He died in less than two hours, amid horrifying convulsions. But that was only a trifle. My mother, in complete despair (though less afflicted than I), wished to escape for a while the oppressive atmosphere of grief. She owned a handsome property near Gaeta.[1] We embarked on a papal galley gilded like the altar of St. Peter's in Rome. Suddenly a pirate ship from Salé swept down and boarded us. Our soldiers defended themselves as papal troops usually do; falling on their knees and throwing down their arms, they begged of the corsair absolution *in articulo mortis*.[2]

—They were promptly stripped as naked as monkeys, and so was my mother, and so were our maids of honor, and so was I too. It's a very remarkable thing, the energy these gentlemen put into stripping people. But what surprised me even more was that they stuck their fingers in a place where we women usually admit only a syringe. This ceremony seemed a bit odd to me, as foreign usages always do when one hasn't traveled. They only wanted to see if we didn't have some diamonds hidden there; and I soon learned that it's a custom of long standing among the genteel folk who swarm the seas. I learned that my lords the very religious knights of Malta never overlook this ceremony when they capture Turks, whether male or female; it's one of those international laws which have never been questioned.

—I won't try to explain how painful it is for a young princess to be carried off into slavery in Morocco with her mother. You can imagine everything we had to suffer on the pirate ship. My mother was still very beautiful; our maids of honor, our mere chambermaids, were more charming than anything one could find in all Africa. As for myself, I was ravishing, I was loveliness and grace su-

---

1. About halfway between Rome and Naples.
2. Literally, when at the point of death.

Absolution from a corsair in the act of murdering one is of very dubious validity.

preme, and I was a virgin. I did not remain so for long; the flower which had been kept for the handsome prince of Massa-Carrara was plucked by the corsair captain; he was an abominable negro, who thought he was doing me a great favor. My Lady the Princess of Palestrina and I must have been strong indeed to bear what we did during our journey to Morocco. But on with my story; these are such common matters that they are not worth describing.

—Morocco was knee deep in blood when we arrived. Of the fifty sons of the emperor Muley-Ismael,[3] each had his faction, which produced in effect fifty civil wars, of blacks against blacks, of blacks against browns, halfbreeds against halfbreeds; throughout the length and breadth of the empire, nothing but one continual carnage.

—Scarcely had we stepped ashore, when some negroes of a faction hostile to my captor arrived to take charge of his plunder. After the diamonds and gold, we women were the most prized possessions. I was now witness of a struggle such as you never see in the temperate climate of Europe. Northern people don't have hot blood; they don't feel the absolute fury for women which is common in Africa. Europeans seem to have milk in their veins; it is vitriol or liquid fire which pulses through these people around Mount Atlas. The fight for possession of us raged with the fury of the lions, tigers, and poisonous vipers of that land. A Moor snatched my mother by the right arm, the first mate held her by the left; a Moorish soldier grabbed one leg, one of our pirates the other. In a moment's time almost all our girls were being dragged four different ways. My captain held me behind him while with his scimitar he killed everyone who braved his fury. At last I saw all our Italian women, including my mother, torn to pieces, cut to bits, murdered by the monsters who were fighting over them. My captive companions, their captors, soldiers, sailors, blacks, browns, whites, mulattoes, and at last my captain, all were killed, and I remained half dead on a mountain of corpses. Similar scenes were occurring, as is well known, for more than three hundred leagues around, without anyone skimping on the five prayers a day decreed by Mohammed.

—With great pain, I untangled myself from this vast heap of bleeding bodies, and dragged myself under a great orange tree by a neighboring brook, where I collapsed, from terror, exhaustion, horror, despair, and hunger. Shortly, my weary mind surrendered to a sleep which was more of a swoon than a rest. I was in this state of weakness and languor, between life and death, when I felt myself

---

3. Having reigned for more than fifty years, a potent and ruthless sultan of Morocco, he died in 1727 and left his kingdom in much the condition described.

touched by something which moved over my body. Opening my eyes, I saw a white man, rather attractive, who was groaning and saying under his breath: '*O che sciagura d'essere senza coglioni!*'[4]

CHAPTER 12

The Old Woman's Story Continued

—Amazed and delighted to hear my native tongue, and no less surprised by what this man was saying, I told him that there were worse evils than those he was complaining of. In a few words, I described to him the horrors I had undergone, and then fainted again. He carried me to a nearby house, put me to bed, gave me something to eat, served me, flattered me, comforted me, told me he had never seen anyone so lovely, and added that he had never before regretted so much the loss of what nobody could give him back.

'I was born at Naples, he told me, where they caponize two or three thousand children every year; some die of it, others acquire a voice more beautiful than any woman's, still others go on to become governors of kingdoms.[5] The operation was a great success with me, and I became court musician to the Princess of Palestrina . . .'

'Of my mother,' I exclaimed.

'Of your mother,' cried he, bursting into tears; 'then you must be the princess whom I raised till she was six, and who already gave promise of becoming as beautiful as you are now!'

'I am that very princess; my mother lies dead, not a hundred yards from here, buried under a pile of corpses.'

—I told him my adventures, he told me his: that he had been sent by a Christian power to the King of Morocco, to conclude a treaty granting him gunpowder, cannon, and ships with which to liquidate the traders of the other Christian powers.

'My mission is concluded,' said this honest eunuch; 'I shall take ship at Ceuta and bring you back to Italy. *Ma che sciagura d'essere senza coglioni!*'

—I thanked him with tears of gratitude, and instead of returning me to Italy, he took me to Algiers and sold me to the dey of that country. Hardly had the sale taken place, when that plague which has made the rounds of Africa, Asia, and Europe broke out in full fury at Algiers. You have seen earthquakes; but tell me, young lady, have you ever had the plague?

—Never, replied the baroness.

—If you had had it, said the old woman, you would agree that it is far worse than an earthquake. It is very frequent in Africa, and I

---

4. "Oh what a misfortune to have no testicles!"
5. The castrate Farinelli (1705–1782), originally a singer, came to exercise considerable political influence on the Kings of Spain, Philip V and Ferdinand VI.

had it. Imagine, if you will, the situation of a pope's daughter, fifteen years old, who in three months' time had experienced poverty, slavery, had been raped almost every day, had seen her mother quartered, had suffered from famine and war, and who now was dying of pestilence in Algiers. As a matter of fact, I did not die; but the eunuch and the dey and nearly the entire seraglio of Algiers perished.

—When the first horrors of this ghastly plague had passed, the slaves of the dey were sold. A merchant bought me and took me to Tunis; there he sold me to another merchant, who resold me at Tripoli; from Tripoli I was sold to Alexandria, from Alexandria resold to Smyrna, from Smyrna to Constantinople. I ended by belonging to an aga of janizaries, who was shortly ordered to defend Azov against the besieging Russians.[6]

—The aga, who was a gallant soldier, took his whole seraglio with him, and established us in a little fort amid the Maeotian marshes,[7] guarded by two black eunuchs and twenty soldiers. Our side killed a prodigious number of Russians, but they paid us back nicely. Azov was put to fire and sword without respect for age or sex; only our little fort continued to resist, and the enemy determined to starve us out. The twenty janizaries had sworn never to surrender. Reduced to the last extremities of hunger, they were forced to eat our two eunuchs, lest they violate their oaths. After several more days, they decided to eat the women too.

—We had an imam,[8] very pious and sympathetic, who delivered an excellent sermon, persuading them not to kill us altogether.

'Just cut off a single rumpsteak from each of these ladies,' he said, 'and you'll have a fine meal. Then if you should need another, you can come back in a few days and have as much again; heaven will bless your charitable action, and you will be saved.'

—His eloquence was splendid, and he persuaded them. We underwent this horrible operation. The imam treated us all with the ointment that they use on newly circumcised children. We were at the point of death.

—Scarcely had the janizaries finished the meal for which we furnished the materials, when the Russians appeared in flat-bottomed boats; not a janizary escaped. The Russians paid no attention to the state we were in; but there are French physicians everywhere, and one of them, who knew his trade, took care of us. He cured us, and I shall remember all my life that when my wounds were healed, he made me a proposition. For the rest, he counselled us simply to

---

6. Azov, near the mouth of the Don, was besieged by the Russians under Peter the Great in 1695–1696. The janizaries were an élite corps of the Ottoman armies.

7. The Roman name of the so-called Sea of Azov, a shallow swampy lake near the town.

8. In effect, a chaplain.

have patience, assuring us that the same thing had happened in several other sieges, and that it was according to the laws of war.

—As soon as my companions could walk, we were herded off to Moscow. In the division of booty, I fell to a boyar who made me work in his garden, and gave me twenty whiplashes a day; but when he was broken on the wheel after about two years, with thirty other boyars, over some little court intrigue,[9] I seized the occasion; I ran away; I crossed all Russia; I was for a long time a chambermaid in Riga, then at Rostock, Vismara, Leipzig, Cassel, Utrecht, Leyden, The Hague, Rotterdam; I grew old in misery and shame, having only half a backside and remembering always that I was the daughter of a Pope; a hundred times I wanted to kill myself, but always I loved life more. This ridiculous weakness is perhaps one of our worst instincts; is anything more stupid than choosing to carry a burden that really one wants to cast on the ground? to hold existence in horror, and yet to cling to it? to fondle the serpent which devours us till it has eaten out our heart?

—In the countries through which I have been forced to wander, in the taverns where I have had to work, I have seen a vast number of people who hated their existence; but I never saw more than a dozen who deliberately put an end to their own misery: three negroes, four Englishmen, four Genevans, and a German professor named Robeck.[1] My last post was as servant to the jew Don Issachar; he attached me to your service, my lovely one; and I attached myself to your destiny, till I have become more concerned with your fate than with my own. I would not even have mentioned my own misfortunes, if you had not irked me a bit, and if it weren't the custom, on shipboard, to pass the time with stories. In a word, my lady, I have had some experience of the world, I know it; why not try this diversion? Ask every passenger on this ship to tell you his story, and if you find a single one who has not often cursed the day of his birth, who has not often told himself that he is the most miserable of men, then you may throw me overboard head first.

9. Voltaire had in mind an ineffectual conspiracy against Peter the Great known as the "revolt of the strelitz" or musketeers, which took place in 1698. Though easily put down, it provoked from the emperor a massive and atrocious program of reprisals.

1. Johann Robeck (1672–1739) published a treatise advocating suicide and showed his conviction by drowning himself. But he waited till he was 67 before putting his theory to the test. For a larger view of the issue, see L. G. Crocker, "The Discussion of Suicide in the 18th Century," *Journal of the History of Ideas*, XIII, 47–72 (1952).

How Candide Was Forced to Leave the Lovely
Cunégonde and the Old Woman

Having heard out the old woman's story, the lovely Cunégonde paid her the respects which were appropriate to a person of her rank and merit. She took up the wager as well, and got all the passengers, one after another, to tell her their adventures. She and Candide had to agree that the old woman had been right.

—It's certainly too bad, said Candide, that the wise Pangloss was hanged, contrary to the custom of autos-da-fé; he would have admirable things to say of the physical evil and moral evil which cover land and sea, and I might feel within me the impulse to dare to raise several polite objections.

As the passengers recited their stories, the boat made steady progress, and presently landed at Buenos Aires. Cunégonde, Captain Candide, and the old woman went to call on the governor, Don Fernando d'Ibaraa y Figueroa y Mascarenes y Lampourdos y Souza. This nobleman had the pride appropriate to a man with so many names. He addressed everyone with the most aristocratic disdain, pointing his nose so loftily, raising his voice so mercilessly, lording it so splendidly, and assuming so arrogant a pose, that everyone who met him wanted to kick him. He loved women to the point of fury; and Cunégonde seemed to him the most beautiful creature he had ever seen. The first thing he did was to ask directly if she were the captain's wife. His manner of asking this question disturbed Candide; he did not dare say she was his wife, because in fact she was not; he did not dare say she was his sister, because she wasn't that either; and though this polite lie was once common enough among the ancients,[2] and sometimes serves moderns very well, he was too pure of heart to tell a lie.

—Miss Cunégonde, said he, is betrothed to me, and we humbly beg your excellency to perform the ceremony for us.

Don Fernando d'Ibaraa y Figueroa y Mascarenes y Lampourdos y Souza twirled his moustache, smiled sardonically, and ordered Captain Candide to go drill his company. Candide obeyed. Left alone with My Lady Cunégonde, the governor declared his passion, and protested that he would marry her tomorrow, in church or in any other manner, as it pleased her charming self. Cunégonde asked for a quarter-hour to collect herself, consult the old woman, and make up her mind.

The old woman said to Cunégonde: —My lady, you have

2. Voltaire has in mind Abraham's adventures with Sarah (Genesis xii) and Isaac's with Rebecca (Genesis xxvi).

seventy-two quarterings and not one penny; if you wish, you may be the wife of the greatest lord in South America, who has a really handsome moustache; are you going to insist on your absolute fidelity? You have already been raped by the Bulgars; a jew and an inquisitor have enjoyed your favors; miseries entitle one to privileges. I assure you that in your position I would make no scruple of marrying My Lord the Governor, and making the fortune of Captain Candide.

While the old woman was talking with all the prudence of age and experience, there came into the harbor a small ship bearing an alcalde and some alguazils.[3] This is what had happened.

As the old woman had very shrewdly guessed, it was a long-sleeved Franciscan who stole Cunégonde's gold and jewels in the town of Badajoz, when she and Candide were in flight. The monk tried to sell some of the gems to a jeweler, who recognized them as belonging to the Grand Inquisitor. Before he was hanged, the Franciscan confessed that he had stolen them, indicating who his victims were and where they were going. The flight of Cunégonde and Candide was already known. They were traced to Cadiz, and a vessel was hastily dispatched in pursuit of them. This vessel was now in the port of Buenos Aires. The rumor spread that an alcalde was aboard, in pursuit of the murderers of My Lord the Grand Inquisitor. The shrewd old woman saw at once what was to be done.

—You cannot escape, she told Cunégonde, and you have nothing to fear. You are not the one who killed my lord, and, besides, the governor, who is in love with you, won't let you be mistreated. Sit tight.

And then she ran straight to Candide: —Get out of town, she said, or you'll be burned within the hour.

There was not a moment to lose; but how to leave Cunégonde, and where to go?

CHAPTER 14

How Candide and Cacambo Were Received by the Jesuits of Paraguay

Candide had brought from Cadiz a valet of the type one often finds in the provinces of Spain and in the colonies. He was one quarter Spanish, son of a halfbreed in the Tucuman[4]; he had been choirboy, sacristan, sailor, monk, merchant, soldier, and lackey. His name was Cacambo, and he was very fond of his master because his

3. Police officers.
4. A city and province of Argentina, to the northwest of Buenos Aires, just at the juncture of the Andes and the Grand Chaco.

master was a very good man. In hot haste he saddled the two Andalusian steeds.

—Hurry, master, do as the old woman says; let's get going and leave this town without a backward look.

Candide wept: —O my beloved Cunégonde! must I leave you now, just when the governor is about to marry us! Cunégonde, brought from so far, what will ever become of you?

—She'll become what she can, said Cacambo; women can always find something to do with themselves; God sees to it; let's get going.

—Where are you taking me? where are we going? what will we do without Cunégonde? said Candide.

—By Saint James of Compostela, said Cacambo, you were going to make war against the Jesuits, now we'll go make war for them. I know the roads pretty well, I'll bring you to their country, they will be delighted to have a captain who knows the Bulgar drill; you'll make a prodigious fortune. If you don't get your rights in one world, you will find them in another. And isn't it pleasant to see new things and do new things?

—Then you've already been in Paraguay? said Candide.

—Indeed I have, replied Cacambo; I was cook in the College of the Assumption, and I know the government of Los Padres[5] as I know the streets of Cadiz. It's an admirable thing, this government. The kingdom is more than three hundred leagues across; it is divided into thirty provinces. Los Padres own everything in it, and the people nothing; it's a masterpiece of reason and justice. I myself know nothing so wonderful as Los Padres, who in this hemisphere make war on the kings of Spain and Portugal, but in Europe hear their confessions; who kill Spaniards here, and in Madrid send them to heaven; that really tickles me; let's get moving, you're going to be the happiest of men. Won't Los Padres be delighted when they learn they have a captain who knows the Bulgar drill!

As soon as they reached the first barricade, Cacambo told the frontier guard that a captain wished to speak with My Lord the Commander. A Paraguayan officer ran to inform headquarters by laying the news at the feet of the commander. Candide and Cacambo were first disarmed and deprived of their Andalusian horses. They were then placed between two files of soldiers; the commander was at the end, his three-cornered hat on his head, his cassock drawn up, a sword at his side, and a pike in his hand. He nods, and twenty-four soldiers surround the newcomers. A sergeant then informs them that they must wait, that the commander cannot talk to them, since the reverend father provincial has forbidden all

5. The Jesuit fathers. R. B. Cunningham-Grahame has written an account of the Jesuits in Paraguay 1607–1767, under the title *A Vanished Arcadia*.

Spaniards from speaking, except in his presence, and from remaining more than three hours in the country.[6]

—And where is the reverend father provincial? says Cacambo.

—He is reviewing his troops after having said mass, the sergeant replies, and you'll only be able to kiss his spurs in three hours.

—But, says Cacambo, my master the captain, who, like me, is dying from hunger, is not Spanish at all, he is German; can't we have some breakfast while waiting for his reverence?

The sergeant promptly went off to report this speech to the commander.

—God be praised, said this worthy; since he is German, I can talk to him; bring him into my bower.

Candide was immediately led into a leafy nook surrounded by a handsome colonnade of green and gold marble and trellises amid which sported parrots, birds of paradise,[7] humming birds, guinea fowl, and all the rarest species of birds. An excellent breakfast was prepared in golden vessels; and while the Paraguayans ate corn out of wooden bowls in the open fields under the glare of the sun, the reverend father commander entered into his bower.

He was a very handsome young man, with an open face, rather blonde in coloring, with ruddy complexion, arched eyebrows, liquid eyes, pink ears, bright red lips, and an air of pride, but a pride somehow different from that of a Spaniard or a Jesuit. Their confiscated weapons were restored to Candide and Cacambo, as well as their Andalusian horses; Cacambo fed them oats alongside the bower, always keeping an eye on them for fear of an ambush.

First Candide kissed the hem of the commander's cassock, then they sat down at the table.

—So you are German? said the Jesuit, speaking in that language.

—Yes, your reverence, said Candide.

As they spoke these words, both men looked at one another with great surprise, and another emotion which they could not control.

—From what part of Germany do you come? said the Jesuit.

—From the nasty province of Westphalia, said Candide; I was born in the castle of Thunder-Ten-Tronckh.

—Merciful heavens! cries the commander. Is it possible?

—What a miracle! exclaims Candide.

6. In fact, the Jesuits, who had organized their Indian parishes into villages under a system of tribal communism, did their best to discourage contact with the outside world.
7. In this passage and several later ones, Voltaire uses in conjunction two words, both of which mean humming bird. The French system of classifying humming birds, based on the work of the celebrated Buffon, distinguishes *oiseaux-mouches* with straight bills from *colibris* with curved bills. This distinction is wholly fallacious. Humming birds have all manner of shaped bills, and the division of species must be made on other grounds entirely. At the expense of ornithological accuracy, I have therefore introduced birds of paradise to get the requisite sense of glitter and sheen.

—Can it be you? asks the commander.

—It's impossible, says Candide.

They both fall back in their chairs, they embrace they shed streams of tears.

—What, can it be you, reverend father! you, the brother of the lovely Cunégonde! you, who were killed by the Bulgars! you, the son of My Lord the Baron! you, a Jesuit in Paraguay! It's a mad world, indeed it is. Oh, Pangloss! Pangloss! how happy you would be, if you hadn't been hanged.

The commander dismissed his negro slaves and the Paraguayans who served his drink in crystal goblets. He thanked God and Saint Ignatius a thousand times, he clasped Candide in his arms, their faces were bathed in tears.

—You would be even more astonished, even more delighted, even more beside yourself, said Candide, if I told you that My Lady Cunégonde, your sister, who you thought was disemboweled, is enjoying good health.

—Where?

—Not far from here, in the house of the governor of Buenos Aires; and to think that I came to make war on you!

Each word they spoke in this long conversation added another miracle. Their souls danced on their tongues, hung eagerly at their ears, glittered in their eyes. As they were Germans, they sat a long time at table, waiting for the reverend father provincial; and the commander spoke in these terms to his dear Candide.

CHAPTER 15
How Candide Killed the Brother of His Dear Cunégonde

—All my life long I shall remember the horrible day when I saw my father and mother murdered and my sister raped. When the Bulgars left, that adorable sister of mine was nowhere to be found; so they loaded a cart with my mother, my father, myself, two serving girls, and three little murdered boys, to carry us all off for burial in a Jesuit chapel some two leagues from our ancestral castle. A Jesuit sprinkled us with holy water; it was horribly salty, and a few drops got into my eyes; the father noticed that my lid made a little tremor; putting his hand on my heart, he felt it beat; I was rescued, and at the end of three weeks was as good as new. You know, my dear Candide, that I was a very pretty boy; I became even more so; the reverend father Croust,[8] superior of the abbey, conceived a most tender friendship for me; he accepted me as a novice, and shortly after, I was sent to Rome. The Father General had need of

8. It is the name of a Jesuit rector at Colmar with whom Voltaire had quarreled in 1754.

a resupply of young German Jesuits. The rulers of Paraguay accept as few Spanish Jesuits as they can; they prefer foreigners, whom they think they can control better. I was judged fit, by the Father General, to labor in this vineyard. So we set off, a Pole, a Tyrolean, and myself. Upon our arrival, I was honored with the posts of sub-deacon and lieutenant; today I am a colonel and a priest. We are giving a vigorous reception to the King of Spain's men; I assure you they will be excommunicated as well as trounced on the battlefield. Providence has sent you to help us. But is it really true that my dear sister, Cunégonde, is in the neighborhood, with the governor of Buenos Aires?

Candide reassured him with a solemn oath that nothing could be more true. Their tears began to flow again.

The baron could not weary of embracing Candide; he called him his brother, his savior.

—Ah, my dear Candide, said he, maybe together we will be able to enter the town as conquerors, and be united with my sister Cunégonde.

—That is all I desire, said Candide; I was expecting to marry her, and I still hope to.

—You insolent dog, replied the baron, you would have the effrontery to marry my sister, who has seventy-two quarterings! It's a piece of presumption for you even to mention such a crazy project in my presence.

Candide, terrified by this speech, answered: —Most reverend father, all the quarterings in the world don't affect this case; I have rescued your sister out of the arms of a jew and an inquisitor; she has many obligations to me, she wants to marry me. Master Pangloss always taught me that men are equal; and I shall certainly marry her.

—We'll see about that, you scoundrel, said the Jesuit baron of Thunder-Ten-Tronckh; and so saying, he gave him a blow across the face with the flat of his sword. Candide immediately drew his own sword and thrust it up to the hilt in the baron's belly; but as he drew it forth all dripping, he began to weep.

—Alas, dear God! said he, I have killed my old master, my friend, my brother-in-law; I am the best man in the world, and here are three men I've killed already, and two of the three were priests.

Cacambo, who was standing guard at the entry of the bower, came running.

—We can do nothing but sell our lives dearly, said his master; someone will certainly come; we must die fighting.

Cacambo, who had been in similar scrapes before, did not lose his head; he took the Jesuit's cassock, which the commander had been wearing, and put it on Candide; he stuck the dead man's

square hat on Candide's head, and forced him onto horseback.
Everything was done in the wink of an eye.

—Let's ride, master; everyone will take you for a Jesuit on his
way to deliver orders; and we will have passed the frontier before
anyone can come after us.

Even as he was pronouncing these words, he charged off, crying
in Spanish: —Way, make way for the reverend father colonel!

CHAPTER 16

What Happened to the Two Travelers with Two Girls, Two Monkeys, and the Savages Named Biglugs

Candide and his valet were over the frontier before anyone in the
camp knew of the death of the German Jesuit. Foresighted
Cacambo had taken care to fill his satchel with bread, chocolate,
ham, fruit, and several bottles of wine. They pushed their Andalusian horses forward into unknown country, where there were no
roads. Finally a broad prairie divided by several streams opened before them. Our two travelers turned their horses loose to graze;
Cacambo suggested that they eat too, and promptly set the example. But Candide said: —How can you expect me to eat ham when
I have killed the son of My Lord the Baron, and am now condemned never to see the lovely Cunégonde for the rest of my life?
Why should I drag out my miserable days, since I must exist far
from her in in the depths of despair and remorse? And what will
the *Journal de Trévoux* say of all this?[9]

Though he talked this way, he did not neglect the food. Night
fell. The two wanderers heard a few weak cries which seemed to be
voiced by women. They could not tell whether the cries expressed
grief or joy; but they leaped at once to their feet, with that uneasy
suspicion which one always feels in an unknown country. The out-
cry arose from two girls, completely naked, who were running
swiftly along the edge of the meadow, pursued by two monkeys who
snapped at their buttocks. Candide was moved to pity; he had
learned marksmanship with the Bulgars, and could have knocked a
nut off a bush without touching the leaves. He raised his Spanish
rifle, fired twice, and killed the two monkeys.

—God be praised, my dear Cacambo! I've saved these two poor
creatures from great danger. Though I committed a sin in killing an
inquisitor and a Jesuit, I've redeemed myself by saving the lives of
two girls. Perhaps they are two ladies of rank, and this good deed
may gain us special advantages in the country.

He had more to say, but his mouth shut suddenly when he

9. A journal published by the Jesuit order, founded in 1701 and consistently
hostile to Voltaire.

saw the girls embracing the monkeys tenderly, weeping over their bodies, and filling the air with lamentations.

—I wasn't looking for quite so much generosity of spirit, said he to Cacambo; the latter replied: —You've really fixed things this time, master; you've killed the two lovers of these young ladies.

—Their lovers! Impossible! You must be joking, Cacambo; how can I believe you?

—My dear master, Cacambo replied, you're always astonished by everything. Why do you think it so strange that in some countries monkeys succeed in obtaining the good graces of women? They are one quarter human, just as I am one quarter Spanish.

—Alas, Candide replied, I do remember now hearing Master Pangloss say that such things used to happen, and that from these mixtures there arose pans, fauns, and satyrs, and that these creatures had appeared to various grand figures of antiquity; but I took all that for fables.

—You should be convinced now, said Cacambo; it's true, and you see how people make mistakes who haven't received a measure of education. But what I fear is that these girls may get us into real trouble.

These sensible reflections led Candide to leave the field and to hide in a wood. There he dined with Cacambo; and there both of them, having duly cursed the inquisitor of Portugal, the governor of Buenos Aires, and the baron, went to sleep on a bed of moss. When they woke up, they found themselves unable to move; the reason was that during the night the Biglugs,[1] natives of the country, to whom the girls had complained of them, had tied them down with cords of bark. They were surrounded by fifty naked Biglugs, armed with arrows, clubs, and stone axes. Some were boiling a caldron of water, others were preparing spits, and all cried out: —It's a Jesuit, a Jesuit! We'll be revenged and have a good meal; let's eat some Jesuit, eat some Jesuit!

—I told you, my dear master, said Cacambo sadly, I said those two girls would play us a dirty trick.

Candide, noting the caldron and spits, cried out: —We are surely going to be roasted or boiled. Ah, what would Master Pangloss say if he could see these men in a state of nature? All is for the best, I agree; but I must say it seems hard to have lost Miss Cunégonde and to be stuck on a spit by the Biglugs.

Cacambo did not lose his head.

—Don't give up hope, said he to the disconsolate Candide; I

---

1. Voltaire's name is "Oreillons" from Spanish "Orejones," a name mentioned in Garcilaso de Vega's *Historia General del Perú* (1609), on which Voltaire drew for many of the details in his picture of South America. See Richard A. Brooks, "Voltaire and Garcilaso de Vega" in *Studies in Voltaire and the 18th Century*, XXX, 189-204.

understand a little of the jargon these people speak, and I'm going to talk to them.

—Don't forget to remind them, said Candide, of the frightful inhumanity of eating their fellow men, and that Christian ethics forbid it.

—Gentlemen, said Cacambo, you have a mind to eat a Jesuit today? An excellent idea; nothing is more proper than to treat one's enemies so. Indeed, the law of nature teaches us to kill our neighbor, and that's how men behave the whole world over. Though we Europeans don't exercise our right to eat our neighbors, the reason is simply that we find it easy to get a good meal elsewhere; but you don't have our resources, and we certainly agree that it's better to eat your enemies than to let the crows and vultures have the fruit of your victory. But, gentlemen, you wouldn't want to eat your friends. You think you will be spitting a Jesuit, and it's your defender, the enemy of your enemies, whom you will be roasting. For my part, I was born in your country; the gentleman whom you see is my master, and far from being a Jesuit, he has just killed a Jesuit, the robe he is wearing was stripped from him; that's why you have taken a dislike to him. To prove that I am telling the truth, take his robe and bring it to the nearest frontier of the kingdom of Los Padres; find out for yourselves if my master didn't kill a Jesuit officer. It won't take long; if you find that I have lied, you can still eat us. But if I've told the truth, you know too well the principles of public justice, customs, and laws, not to spare our lives.

The Biglugs found this discourse perfectly reasonable; they appointed chiefs to go posthaste and find out the truth; the two messengers performed their task like men of sense, and quickly returned bringing good news. The Biglugs untied their two prisoners, treated them with great politeness, offered them girls, gave them refreshments, and led them back to the border of their state, crying joyously: —He isn't a Jesuit, he isn't a Jesuit!

Candide could not weary of exclaiming over his preservation.

—What a people! he said. What men! what customs! If I had not had the good luck to run a sword through the body of Miss Cunégonde's brother, I would have been eaten on the spot! But, after all, it seems that uncorrupted nature is good, since these folk, instead of eating me, showed me a thousand kindnesses as soon as they knew I was not a Jesuit.

CHAPTER 17

Arrival of Candide and His Servant at the Country of Eldorado,[2] and What They Saw There

When they were out of the land of the Biglugs, Cacambo said to Candide: —You see that this hemisphere is no better than the other; take my advice, and let's get back to Europe as soon as possible.

—How to get back, asked Candide, and where to go? If I go to my own land, the Bulgars and Abares are murdering everyone in sight; if I go to Portugal, they'll burn me alive; if we stay here, we risk being skewered any day. But how can I ever leave that part of the world where Miss Cunégonde lives?

—Let's go toward Cayenne, said Cacambo, we shall find some Frenchmen there, for they go all over the world; they can help us; perhaps God will take pity on us.

To get to Cayenne was not easy; they knew more or less which way to go, but mountains, rivers, cliffs, robbers, and savages obstructed the way everywhere. Their horses died of weariness; their food was eaten; they subsisted for one whole month on wild fruits, and at last they found themselves by a little river fringed with coconut trees, which gave them both life and hope.

Cacambo, who was as full of good advice as the old woman, said to Candide: —We can go no further, we've walked ourselves out; I see an abandoned canoe on the bank, let's fill it with coconuts, get into the boat, and float with the current; a river always leads to some inhabited spot or other. If we don't find anything pleasant, at least we may find something new.

—Let's go, said Candide, and let Providence be our guide.

They floated some leagues between banks sometimes flowery, sometimes sandy, now steep, now level. The river widened steadily; finally it disappeared into a chasm of frightful rocks that rose high into the heavens.[3] The two travelers had the audacity to float with the current into this chasm. The river, narrowly confined, drove them onward with horrible speed and a fearful roar. After twenty-four hours, they saw daylight once more; but their canoe was smashed on the snags. They had to drag themselves from rock to rock for an entire league; at last they emerged to an immense horizon, ringed with remote mountains. The countryside was tended for pleasure as well as profit; everywhere the useful was joined to the agreeable. The roads were covered, or rather decorated, with ele-

---

2. The myth of this land of gold somewhere in Central or South America had been widespread since the sixteenth century.

3. This journey down an underground river is probably adapted from a similar episode in the story of Sinbad the Sailor.

gantly shaped carriages made of a glittering material, carrying men and women of singular beauty, and drawn by great red sheep which were faster than the finest horses of Andalusia, Tetuan, and Mequinez.

—Here now, said Candide, is a country that's better than Westphalia.

Along with Cacambo, he climbed out of the river at the first village he could see. Some children of the town, dressed in rags of gold brocade, were playing quoits at the village gate; our two men from the other world paused to watch them; their quoits were rather large, yellow, red, and green, and they glittered with a singular luster. On a whim, the travelers picked up several; they were of gold, emeralds, and rubies, and the least of them would have been the greatest ornament of the Great Mogul's throne.

—Surely, said Cacambo, these quoit players are the children of the king of the country.

The village schoolmaster appeared at that moment, to call them back to school.

—And there, said Candide, is the tutor of the royal household.

The little rascals quickly gave up their game, leaving on the ground their quoits and playthings. Candide picked them up, ran to the schoolmaster, and presented them to him humbly, giving him to understand by sign language that their royal highnesses had forgotten their gold and jewels. With a smile, the schoolmaster tossed them to the ground, glanced quickly but with great surprise at Candide's face, and went his way.

The travelers did not fail to pick up the gold, rubies, and emeralds.

—Where in the world are we? cried Candide. The children of this land must be well trained, since they are taught contempt for gold and jewels.

Cacambo was as much surprised as Candide. At last they came to the finest house of the village; it was built like a European palace. A crowd of people surrounded the door, and even more were in the entry; delightful music was heard, and a delicious aroma of cooking filled the air. Cacambo went up to the door, listened, and reported that they were talking Peruvian; that was his native language, for every reader must know that Cacambo was born in Tucuman, in a village where they talk that language exclusively.

—I'll act as interpreter, he told Candide; it's an hotel, let's go in.

Promptly two boys and two girls of the staff, dressed in cloth of gold, and wearing ribbons in their hair, invited them to sit at the host's table. The meal consisted of four soups, each one garnished with a brace of parakeets, a boiled condor which weighed two hundred pounds, two roast monkeys of an excellent flavor, three hundred birds of paradise in one dish and six hundred humming birds in another, exquisite stews, delicious pastries, the whole thing served up in plates of what looked like rock crystal. The boys and girls of the staff poured them various beverages made from sugar cane.

The diners were for the most part merchants and travelers, all extremely polite, who questioned Cacambo with the most discreet circumspection, and answered his questions very directly.

When the meal was over, Cacambo as well as Candide supposed he could settle his bill handsomely by tossing onto the table two of those big pieces of gold which they had picked up; but the host and hostess burst out laughing, and for a long time nearly split their sides. Finally they subsided.

—Gentlemen, said the host, we see clearly that you're foreigners; we don't meet many of you here. Please excuse our laughing when you offered us in payment a couple of pebbles from the roadside. No doubt you don't have any of our local currency, but you don't need it to eat here. All the hotels established for the promotion of commerce are maintained by the state. You have had meager entertainment here, for we are only a poor town; but everywhere else you will be given the sort of welcome you deserve.

Cacambo translated for Candide all the host's explanations, and Candide listened to them with the same admiration and astonishment that his friend Cacambo showed in reporting them.

—What is this country, then, said they to one another, unknown to the rest of the world, and where nature itself is so different from our own? This probably is the country where everything is for the best; for it's absolutely necessary that such a country should exist somewhere. And whatever Master Pangloss said of the matter, I have often had occasion to notice that things went badly in Westphalia.

CHAPTER 18

What They Saw in the Land of Eldorado

Cacambo revealed his curiosity to the host, and the host told him: —I am an ignorant man and content to remain so; but we have here an old man, retired from the court, who is the most knowing person in the kingdom, and the most talkative.

Thereupon he brought Cacambo to the old man's house. Candide now played second fiddle, and acted as servant to his own valet. They entered an austere little house, for the door was merely of silver and the paneling of the rooms was only gold, though so tastefully wrought that the finest paneling would not surpass it. If the truth must be told, the lobby was only decorated with rubies and emeralds; but the patterns in which they were arranged atoned for the extreme simplicity.

The old man received the two strangers on a sofa stuffed with bird-of-paradise feathers, and offered them several drinks in diamond carafes; then he satisfied their curiosity in these terms.

—I am a hundred and seventy-two years old, and I heard from my late father, who was liveryman to the king, about the astonishing revolutions in Peru which he had seen. Our land here was formerly part of the kingdom of the Incas, who rashly left it in order to conquer another part of the world, and who were ultimately destroyed by the Spaniards. The wisest princes of their house were those who had never left their native valley; they decreed, with the consent of the nation, that henceforth no inhabitant of our little kingdom should ever leave it; and this rule is what has preserved our innocence and our happiness. The Spaniards heard vague rumors about this land, they called it El Dorado; and an English knight named Raleigh[4] even came somewhere close to it about a hundred years ago; but as we are surrounded by unscalable mountains and precipices, we have managed so far to remain hidden from the rapacity of the European nations, who have an inconceivable rage for the pebbles and mud of our land, and who, in order to get some, would butcher us all to the last man.

The conversation was a long one; it turned on the form of the government, the national customs, on women, public shows, the arts. At last Candide, whose taste always ran to metaphysics, told Cacambo to ask if the country had any religion.

The old man grew a bit red.

—How's that? he said. Can you have any doubt of it? Do you suppose we are altogether thankless scoundrels?

Cacambo asked meekly what was the religion of Eldorado. The old man flushed again.

—Can there be two religions? he asked. I suppose our religion is the same as everyone's, we worship God from morning to evening.

—Then you worship a single deity? said Cacambo, who acted throughout as interpreter of the questions of Candide.

—It's obvious, said the old man, that there aren't two or three or four of them. I must say the people of your world ask very remarkable questions.

Candide could not weary of putting questions to this good old man; he wanted to know how the people of Eldorado prayed to God.

—We don't pray to him at all, said the good and respectable

4. *The Discovery of Guiana,* published in 1595, described Sir Walter Raleigh's infatuation with the myth of Eldorado and served to spread the story still further.

sage; we have nothing to ask him for, since everything we need has already been granted; we thank God continually.

Candide was interested in seeing the priests; he had Cacambo ask where they were. The old gentleman smiled.

—My friends, said he, we are all priests; the king and all the heads of household sing formal psalms of thanksgiving every morning, and five or six thousand voices accompany them.

—What! you have no monks to teach, argue, govern, intrigue, and burn at the stake everyone who disagrees with them?

—We should have to be mad, said the old man; here we are all of the same mind, and we don't understand what you're up to with your monks.

Candide was overjoyed at all these speeches, and said to himself: —This is very different from Westphalia and the castle of My Lord the Baron; if our friend Pangloss had seen Eldorado, he wouldn't have called the castle of Thunder-Ten-Tronckh the finest thing on earth; to know the world one must travel.

After this long conversation, the old gentleman ordered a carriage with six sheep made ready, and gave the two travelers twelve of his servants for their journey to the court.

—Excuse me, said he, if old age deprives me of the honor of accompanying you. The king will receive you after a style which will not altogether displease you, and you will doubtless make allowance for the customs of the country if there are any you do not like.

Candide and Cacambo climbed into the coach; the six sheep flew like the wind, and in less than four hours they reached the king's palace at the edge of the capital. The entryway was two hundred and twenty feet high and a hundred wide; it is impossible to describe all the materials of which it was made. But you can imagine how much finer it was than those pebbles and sand which we call gold and jewels.

Twenty beautiful girls of the guard detail welcomed Candide and Cacambo as they stepped from the carriage, took them to the baths, and dressed them in robes woven of humming-bird feathers; then the high officials of the crown, both male and female, led them to the royal chamber between two long lines, each of a thousand musicians, as is customary. As they approached the throne room, Cacambo asked an officer what was the proper method of greeting his majesty: if one fell to one's knees or on one's belly; if one put one's hands on one's head or on one's rear; if one licked up the dust of the earth—in a word, what was the proper form?[5]

—The ceremony, said the officer, is to embrace the king and kiss him on both cheeks.

5. Candide's questions are probably derived from those of Gulliver on a similar occasion; see *Gulliver's Travels*, Book IV.

Candide and Cacambo fell on the neck of his majesty, who received them with all the dignity imaginable, and asked them politely to dine.

In the interim, they were taken about to see the city, the public buildings rising to the clouds, the public markets and arcades, the fountains of pure water and of rose water, those of sugar cane liquors which flowed perpetually in the great plazas paved with a sort of stone which gave off odors of gillyflower and rose petals. Candide asked to see the supreme court and the hall of parliament; they told him there was no such thing, that lawsuits were unknown. He asked if there were prisons, and was told there were not. What surprised him more, and gave him most pleasure, was the palace of sciences, in which he saw a gallery two thousand paces long, entirely filled with mathematical and physical instruments.

Having passed the whole afternoon seeing only a thousandth part of the city, they returned to the king's palace. Candide sat down to dinner with his majesty, his own valet Cacambo, and several ladies. Never was better food served, and never did a host preside more jovially than his majesty. Cacambo explained the king's witty sayings to Candide, and even when translated they still seemed witty. Of all the things which astonished Candide, this was not, in his eyes, the least astonishing.

They passed a month in this refuge. Candide never tired of saying to Cacambo: —It's true, my friend, I'll say it again, the castle where I was born does not compare with the land where we now are; but Miss Cunégonde is not here, and you doubtless have a mistress somewhere in Europe. If we stay here, we shall be just like everybody else, whereas if we go back to our own world, taking with us just a dozen sheep loaded with Eldorado pebbles, we shall be richer than all the kings put together, we shall have no more inquisitors to fear, and we shall easily be able to retake Miss Cunégonde.

This harangue pleased Cacambo; wandering is such pleasure, it gives a man such prestige at home to be able to talk of what he has seen abroad, that the two happy men resolved to be so no longer, but to take their leave of his majesty.

—You are making a foolish mistake, the king told them; I know very well that my kingdom is nothing much; but when you are pretty comfortable somewhere, you had better stay there. Of course I have no right to keep strangers against their will, that sort of tyranny is not in keeping with our laws or our customs; all men are free; depart when you will, but the way out is very difficult. You cannot possibly go up the river by which you miraculously came; it runs too swiftly through its underground caves. The mountains which surround my land are ten thousand feet high, and steep as walls; each one is more than ten leagues across; the only way down is over precipices. But since you really must go, I shall order my engineers to make a machine which can carry you conveniently. When we take you over the mountains, nobody will be able to go with you, for my subjects have sworn never to leave their refuge, and they are too sensible to break their vows. Other than that, ask of me what you please.

—We only request of your majesty, Cacambo said, a few sheep loaded with provisions, some pebbles, and some of the mud of your country.

The king laughed.

—I simply can't understand, said he, the passion you Europeans have for our yellow mud; but take all you want, and much good may it do you.

He promptly gave orders to his technicians to make a machine for lifting these two extraordinary men out of his kingdom. Three thousand good physicists worked at the problem; the machine was ready in two weeks' time, and cost no more than twenty million pounds sterling, in the money of the country. Cacambo and Candide were placed in the machine; there were two great sheep, saddled and bridled to serve them as steeds when they had cleared the mountains, twenty pack sheep with provisions, thirty which carried presents consisting of the rarities of the country, and fifty loaded with gold, jewels, and diamonds. The king bade tender farewell to the two vagabonds.

It made a fine spectacle, their departure, and the ingenious way in which they were hoisted with their sheep up to the top of the mountains. The technicians bade them good-bye after bringing them to safety, and Candide had now no other desire and no other object than to go and present his sheep to Miss Cunégonde.

—We have, said he, enough to pay off the governor of Buenos Aires—if, indeed, a price can be placed on Miss Cunégonde. Let us go to Cayenne, take ship there, and then see what kingdom we can find to buy up.

CHAPTER 19

*What Happened to Them at Surinam, and
How Candide Got to Know Martin*

The first day was pleasant enough for our travelers. They were encouraged by the idea of possessing more treasures than Asia, Europe, and Africa could bring together. Candide, in transports, carved the name of Cunégonde on the trees. On the second day two of their sheep bogged down in a swamp and were lost with their loads; two other sheep died of fatigue a few days later; seven or eight others starved to death in a desert; still others fell, a little after, from precipices. Finally, after a hundred days' march, they had only two sheep left. Candide told Cacambo: —My friend, you see how the riches of this world are fleeting; the only solid things are virtue and the joy of seeing Miss Cunégonde again.

—I agree, said Cacambo, but we still have two sheep, laden with more treasure than the king of Spain will ever have; and I see in the distance a town which I suspect is Surinam; it belongs to the Dutch. We are at the end of our trials and on the threshold of our happiness.

As they drew near the town, they discovered a negro stretched on the ground with only half his clothes left, that is, a pair of blue drawers; the poor fellow was also missing his left leg and his right hand.

—Good Lord, said Candide in Dutch, what are you doing in that horrible condition, my friend?

—I am waiting for my master, Mr. Vanderdendur,[6] the famous merchant, answered the negro.

—Is Mr. Vanderdendur, Candide asked, the man who treated you this way?

—Yes, sir, said the negro, that's how things are around here. Twice a year we get a pair of linen drawers to wear. If we catch a finger in the sugar mill where we work, they cut off our hand; if we try to run away, they cut off our leg: I have undergone both these experiences. This is the price of the sugar you eat in Europe. And yet, when my mother sold me for ten Patagonian crowns on the coast of Guinea, she said to me: 'My dear child, bless our witch doctors, reverence them always, they will make your life happy; you have the honor of being a slave to our white masters, and in this way you are making the fortune of your father and mother.' Alas! I don't know if I made their fortunes, but they certainly did not make mine. The dogs, monkeys, and parrots are a thousand times less unhappy than we are. The Dutch witch doctors who converted me tell me every Sunday that we are all sons of Adam, black and white alike. I am no genealogist; but if these preachers are right, we must all be remote cousins; and you must admit no one could treat his own flesh and blood in a more horrible fashion.

—Oh Pangloss! cried Candide, you had no notion of these abominations! I'm through, I must give up your optimism after all.

—What's optimism? said Cacambo.

—Alas, said Candide, it is a mania for saying things are well

6. A name perhaps intended to suggest VanDuren, a Dutch bookseller with whom Voltaire had quarreled. In particular, the incident of gradually raising one's price recalls VanDuren, to whom Voltaire had successively offered 1,000, 1,500, 2,000, and 3,000 florins for the return of the manuscript of Frederick the Great's *Anti-Machiavel*.

when one is in hell.

And he shed bitter tears as he looked at his negro, and he was still weeping as he entered Surinam.

The first thing they asked was if there was not some vessel in port which could be sent to Buenos Aires. The man they asked was a Spanish merchant who undertook to make an honest bargain with them. They arranged to meet in a cafe; Candide and the faithful Cacambo, with their two sheep, went there to meet with him.

Candide, who always said exactly what was in his heart, told the Spaniard of his adventures, and confessed that he wanted to recapture Miss Cunégonde.

—I shall take good care *not* to send you to Buenos Aires, said the merchant; I should be hanged, and so would you. The lovely Cunégonde is his lordship's favorite mistress.

This was a thunderstroke for Candide; he wept for a long time; finally he drew Cacambo aside.

—Here, my friend, said he, is what you must do. Each one of us has in his pockets five or six millions' worth of diamonds; you are cleverer than I; go get Miss Cunégonde in Buenos Aires. If the governor makes a fuss, give him a million; if that doesn't convince him, give him two millions; you never killed an inquisitor, nobody will suspect you. I'll fit out another boat and go wait for you in Venice. That is a free country, where one need have no fear either of Bulgars or Abares or jews or inquisitors.

Cacambo approved of this wise decision. He was in despair at leaving a good master who had become a bosom friend; but the pleasure of serving him overcame the grief of leaving him. They embraced, and shed a few tears; Candide urged him not to forget the good old woman. Cacambo departed that very same day; he was a very good fellow, that Cacambo.

Candide remained for some time in Surinam, waiting for another merchant to take him to Italy, along with the two sheep which were left him. He hired servants and bought everything necessary for the long voyage; finally Mr. Vanderdendur, master of a big ship, came calling.

—How much will you charge, Candide asked this man, to take me to Venice—myself, my servants, my luggage, and those two sheep over there?

The merchant set a price of ten thousand piastres; Candide did not blink an eye.

—Oh ho, said the prudent Vanderdendur to himself, this stranger pays out ten thousand piastres at once, he must be pretty well fixed.

Then, returning a moment later, he made known that he could not set sail under twenty thousand.

—All right, you shall have them, said Candide.

—Whew, said the merchant softly to himself, this man gives twenty thousand piastres as easily as ten.

He came back again to say he could not go to Venice for less than thirty thousand piastres.

—All right, thirty then, said Candide.

—Ah ha, said the Dutch merchant, again speaking to himself; so thirty thousand piastres mean nothing to this man; no doubt the two sheep are loaded with immense treasures; let's say no more; we'll pick up the thirty thousand piastres first, and then we'll see.

Candide sold two little diamonds, the least of which was worth more than all the money demanded by the merchant. He paid him in advance. The two sheep were taken aboard. Candide followed in a little boat, to board the vessel at its anchorage. The merchant bides his time, sets sail, and makes his escape with a favoring wind. Candide, aghast and stupefied, soon loses him from view.

—Alas, he cries, now there is a trick worthy of the old world!

He returns to shore sunk in misery; for he had lost riches enough to make the fortunes of twenty monarchs.

Now he rushes to the house of the Dutch magistrate, and, being a bit disturbed, he knocks loudly at the door; goes in, tells the story of what happened, and shouts a bit louder than is customary. The judge begins by fining him ten thousand piastres for making such a racket; then he listens patiently to the story, promises to look into the matter as soon as the merchant comes back, and charges another ten thousand piastres as the costs of the hearing.

This legal proceeding completed the despair of Candide. In fact he had experienced miseries a thousand times more painful, but the coldness of the judge, and that of the merchant who had robbed him, roused his bile and plunged him into a black melancholy. The malice of men rose up before his spirit in all its ugliness, and his mind dwelt only on gloomy thoughts. Finally, when a French vessel was ready to leave for Bordeaux, since he had no more diamond-laden sheep to transport, he took a cabin at a fair price, and made it known in the town that he would pay passage and keep, plus two thousand piastres, to any honest man who wanted to make the journey with him, on condition that this man must be the most disgusted with his own condition and the most unhappy man in the province.

This drew such a crowd of applicants as a fleet could not have held. Candide wanted to choose among the leading candidates, so he picked out about twenty who seemed companionable enough, and of whom each pretended to be more miserable than all the others. He brought them together at his inn and gave them a dinner, on condition that each would swear to tell truthfully his entire history. He would select as his companion the most truly miserable and rightly discontented man, and among the others he would distribute various gifts.

The meeting lasted till four in the morning. Candide, as he listened to all the stories, remembered what the old woman had told him on the trip to Buenos Aires, and of the wager she had made, that there was nobody on the boat who had not undergone great misfortunes. At every story that was told him, he thought of Pangloss.

—That Pangloss, he said, would be hard put to prove his system. I wish he was here. Certainly if everything goes well, it is in Eldorado and not in the rest of the world.

At last he decided in favor of a poor scholar who had worked ten years for the booksellers of Amsterdam. He decided that there was no trade in the world with which one should be more disgusted.

This scholar, who was in fact a good man, had been robbed by his wife, beaten by his son, and deserted by his daughter, who had got herself abducted by a Portuguese. He had just been fired from the little job on which he existed; and the preachers of Surinam were persecuting him because they took him for a Socinian.[7] The others, it is true, were at least as unhappy as he, but Candide hoped the scholar would prove more amusing on the voyage. All his rivals declared that Candide was doing them a great injustice, but he pacified them with a hundred piastres apiece.

CHAPTER 20

What Happened to Candide and Martin at Sea

The old scholar, whose name was Martin, now set sail with Candide for Bordeaux. Both men had seen and suffered much; and even if the vessel had been sailing from Surinam to Japan via the Cape of Good Hope, they would have been able to keep themselves amused with instances of moral evil and physical evil during the entire trip.

However, Candide had one great advantage over Martin, that he still hoped to see Miss Cunégonde again, and Martin had nothing to hope for; besides, he had gold and diamonds, and though he had lost a hundred big red sheep loaded with the greatest treasures of the earth, though he had always at his heart a memory of the Dutch merchant's villainy, yet, when he thought of the wealth that remained in his hands, and when he talked of Cunégonde, especially just after a good dinner, he still inclined to the system of Pangloss.

7. A follower of Faustus and Laelius Socinus, sixteenth-century Polish theologians, who proposed a form of "rational" Christianity which exalted the rational conscience and minimized such mysteries as the trinity. The Socinians, by a special irony, were vigorous optimists.

—But what about you, Monsieur Martin, he asked the scholar, what do you think of all that? What is your idea of moral evil and physical evil?

—Sir, answered Martin, those priests accused me of being a Socinian, but the truth is that I am a Manichee.[8]

—You're joking, said Candide; there aren't any more Manichees in the world.

—There's me, said Martin; I don't know what to do about it, but I can't think otherwise.

—You must be possessed of the devil, said Candide.

—He's mixed up with so many things of this world, said Martin, that he may be in me as well as elsewhere; but I assure you, as I survey this globe, or globule, I think that God has abandoned it to some evil spirit—all of it except Eldorado. I have scarcely seen one town which did not wish to destroy its neighboring town, no family which did not wish to exterminate some other family. Everywhere the weak loathe the powerful, before whom they cringe, and the powerful treat them like brute cattle, to be sold for their meat and fleece. A million regimented assassins roam Europe from one end to the other, plying the trades of murder and robbery in an organized way for a living, because there is no more honest form of work for them; and in the cities which seem to enjoy peace and where the arts are flourishing, men are devoured by more envy, cares, and anxieties than a whole town experiences when it's under siege. Private griefs are worse even than public trials. In a word, I have seen so much and suffered so much, that I am a Manichee.

—Still there is some good, said Candide.

—That may be, said Martin, but I don't know it.

In the middle of this discussion, the rumble of cannon was heard. From minute to minute the noise grew louder. Everyone reached for his spyglass. At a distance of some three miles they saw two vessels fighting; the wind brought both of them so close to the French vessel that they had a pleasantly comfortable seat to watch the fight. Presently one of the vessels caught the other with a broadside so low and so square as to send it to the bottom. Candide and Martin saw clearly a hundred men on the deck of the sinking ship; they all raised their hands to heaven, uttering fearful shrieks; and in a moment everything was swallowed up.

—Well, said Martin, that is how men treat one another.

8. Mani, a Persian mage and philosopher of the third century A.D., taught (probably under the influence of traditions stemming from Zoroaster and the worshippers of the sun god Mithra) that the earth is a field of dispute between two almost equal powers, one of light and one of darkness, both of which must be propitiated. Saint Augustine was much exercised by the heresy, to which he was at one time himself addicted, and Voltaire came to some knowledge of it through the encyclopedic learning of the seventeenth century scholar Pierre Bayle.

—It is true, said Candide, there's something devilish in this business.

As they chatted, he noticed something of a striking red color floating near the sunken vessel. They sent out a boat to investigate; it was one of his sheep. Candide was more joyful to recover this one sheep than he had been afflicted to lose a hundred of them, all loaded with big Eldorado diamonds.

The French captain soon learned that the captain of the victorious vessel was Spanish and that of the sunken vessel was a Dutch pirate. It was the same man who had robbed Candide. The enormous riches which this rascal had stolen were sunk beside him in the sea, and nothing was saved but a single sheep.

—You see, said Candide to Martin, crime is punished sometimes; this scoundrel of a Dutch merchant has met the fate he deserved.

—Yes, said Martin; but did the passengers aboard his ship have to perish too? God punished the scoundrel, and the devil drowned the others.

Meanwhile the French and Spanish vessels continued on their journey, and Candide continued his talks with Martin. They disputed for fifteen days in a row, and at the end of that time were just as much in agreement as at the beginning. But at least they were talking, they exchanged their ideas, they consoled one another. Candide caressed his sheep.

—Since I have found you again, said he, I may well rediscover Miss Cunégonde.

CHAPTER 21
Candide and Martin Approach the Coast of France: They Reason Together

At last the coast of France came in view.

—Have you ever been in France, Monsieur Martin? asked Candide.

—Yes, said Martin, I have visited several provinces. There are some where half the inhabitants are crazy, others where they are too sly, still others where they are quite gentle and stupid, some where they venture on wit; in all of them the principal occupation is lovemaking, the second is slander, and the third stupid talk.

—But, Monsieur Martin, were you ever in Paris?

—Yes, I've been in Paris; it contains specimens of all these types; it is a chaos, a mob, in which everyone is seeking pleasure and where hardly anyone finds it, at least from what I have seen. I did not live there for long; as I arrived, I was robbed of everything I possessed by thieves at the fair of St. Germain; I myself was taken for a thief, and spent eight days in jail, after which I took a proofreader's job to earn enough money to return on foot to Holland. I knew the writing gang, the intriguing gang, the gang with fits and convulsions.[9] They say there are some very civilized people in that town; I'd like to think so.

—I myself have no desire to visit France, said Candide; you no doubt realize that when one has spent a month in Eldorado, there is nothing else on earth one wants to see, except Miss Cunégonde. I am going to wait for her at Venice; we will cross France simply to get to Italy; wouldn't you like to come with me?

—Gladly, said Martin; they say Venice is good only for the Venetian nobles, but that on the other hand they treat foreigners very well when they have plenty of money. I don't have any; you do, so I'll follow you anywhere.

—By the way, said Candide, do you believe the earth was originally all ocean, as they assure us in that big book belonging to the ship's captain?[1]

—I don't believe that stuff, said Martin, nor any of the dreams which people have been peddling for some time now.

—But why, then, was this world formed at all? asked Candide.

—To drive us mad, answered Martin.

—Aren't you astonished, Candide went on, at the love which those two girls showed for the monkeys in the land of the Biglugs that I told you about?

—Not at all, said Martin, I see nothing strange in these sentiments; I have seen so many extraordinary things that nothing seems extraordinary any more.

—Do you believe, asked Candide, that men have always massacred one another as they do today? That they have always been liars, traitors, ingrates, thieves, weaklings, sneaks, cowards, backbiters, gluttons, drunkards, misers, climbers, killers, calumniators, sensualists, fanatics, hypocrites, and fools?

—Do you believe, said Martin, that hawks have always eaten pigeons when they could get them?

—Of course, said Candide.

—Well, said Martin, if hawks have always had the same character, why do you suppose that men have changed?

—Oh, said Candide, there's a great deal of difference, because freedom of the will . . .

As they were disputing in this manner, they reached Bordeaux.

9. The Jansenists, a sect of strict Catholics, became notorious for spiritual ecstasies. Their public displays reached a height during the 1720's, and Voltaire described them in *Le Siécle de Louis XIV* (chap. 37), as well as in the article on "Convulsions" in the *Philosophical Dictionary*.
1. The Bible. Voltaire is straining at a dark passage in Genesis 1.

CHAPTER 22

What Happened in France to Candide and Martin

Candide paused in Bordeaux only long enough to sell a couple of Dorado pebbles and to fit himself out with a fine two-seater carriage, for he could no longer do without his philosopher Martin; only he was very unhappy to part with his sheep, which he left to the academy of science in Bordeaux. They proposed, as the theme of that year's prize contest, the discovery of why the wool of the sheep was red; and the prize was awarded to a northern scholar who demonstrated[2] by A plus B minus C divided by Z that the sheep ought to be red and die of sheep rot.

But all the travelers with whom Candide talked in the roadside inns told him: —We are going to Paris.

This general consensus finally inspired in him too a desire to see the capital; it was not much out of his road to Venice.

He entered through the Faubourg Saint-Marceau,[3] and thought he was in the meanest village of Westphalia.

Scarcely was Candide in his hotel, when he came down with a mild illness caused by exhaustion. As he was wearing an enormous diamond ring, and people had noticed among his luggage a tremendously heavy safe, he soon found at his bedside two doctors whom he had not called, several intimate friends who never left him alone, and two pious ladies who helped to warm his broth. Martin said: —I remember that I too was ill on my first trip to Paris; I was very poor; and as I had neither friends, pious ladies, nor doctors, I got well.

However, as a result of medicines and bleedings, Candide's illness became serious. A resident of the neighborhood came to ask him politely to fill out a ticket, to be delivered to the porter of the other world.[4] Candide wanted nothing to do with it. The pious ladies assured him it was a new fashion; Candide replied that he wasn't a man of fashion. Martin wanted to throw the resident out the window. The cleric swore that without the ticket they wouldn't bury Candide. Martin swore that he would bury the cleric if he continued to be a nuisance. The quarrel grew heated; Martin took him by the shoulders and threw him bodily out the door; all of which caused a great scandal, from which developed a legal case.

2. The satire is pointed at Maupertuis Le Lapon, philosopher and mathematician, whom Voltaire had accused of trying to adduce mathematical proofs of the existence of God and whose algebraic formulae were easily ridiculed. 3. A district on the left bank, notably grubby in the eighteenth century. " 'As I entered [Paris] through the Faubourg Saint-Marceau, I saw nothing but dirty stinking little streets, ugly black houses, a general air of squalor and poverty, beggars, carters, menders of clothes, sellers of herb-drinks and old hats,' J.-J. Rousseau, *Confessions*, Book IV." 4. In the middle of the eighteenth century, it became customary to require persons who were grievously ill to sign *billets de confession*, without which they could not be given absolution, admitted to the last sacraments, or buried in consecrated ground.

Candide got better; and during his convalescence he had very good company in to dine. They played cards for money; and Candide was quite surprised that none of the aces were ever dealt to him, and Martin was not surprised at all.

Among those who did the honors of the town for Candide there was a little abbé from Perigord, one of those busy fellows, always bright, always useful, assured, obsequious, and obliging, who waylay passing strangers, tell them the scandal of the town, and offer them pleasures at any price they want to pay. This fellow first took Candide and Martin to the theatre. A new tragedy was being played. Candide found himself seated next to a group of wits. That did not keep him from shedding a few tears in the course of some perfectly played scenes. One of the commentators beside him remarked during the intermission: —You are quite mistaken to weep, this actress is very bad indeed; the actor who plays with her is even worse; and the play is even worse than the actors in it. The author knows not a word of Arabic, though the action takes place in Arabia; and besides, he is a man who doesn't believe in innate ideas.[5] Tomorrow I will show you twenty pamphlets written against him.[6]

—Tell me, sir, said Candide to the abbé, how many plays are there for performance in France?

—Five or six thousand, replied the other.

—That's a lot, said Candide; how many of them are any good?

—Fifteen or sixteen, was the answer.

—That's a lot, said Martin.

Candide was very pleased with an actress who took the part of Queen Elizabeth in a rather dull tragedy[7] that still gets played from time to time.

—I like this actress very much, he said to Martin, she bears a slight resemblance to Miss Cunégonde; I should like to meet her.

The abbé from Perigord offered to introduce him. Candide, raised in Germany, asked what was the protocol, how one behaved in France with queens of England.

—You must distinguish, said the abbé; in the provinces, you take them to an inn; at Paris they are respected while still attractive, and thrown on the dunghill when they are dead.[8]

—Queens on the dunghill! said Candide.

—Yes indeed, said Martin, the abbé is right; I was in Paris when

5. Descartes proposed certain ideas as innate, Voltaire followed Locke in categorically denying innate ideas. The point is simply that in faction fights all the issues get muddled together.
6. Here begins a long passage interpolated by Voltaire in 1761; it ends on p. 54.
7. *Le Comte d'Essex* by Thomas Corneille.
8. Voltaire engaged in a long and vigorous campaign against the rule that actors and actresses could not be buried in consecrated ground. The superstition probably arose from a feeling that by assuming false identities they denied their own souls.

Miss Monime herself[9] passed, as they say, from this life to the other; she was refused what these folk call 'the honors of burial,' that is, the right to rot with all the beggars of the district in a dirty cemetery; she was buried all alone by her troupe at the corner of the Rue de Bourgogne; this must have been very disagreeable to her, for she had a noble character.

—That was extremely rude, said Candide.

—What do you expect? said Martin; that is how these folk are. Imagine all the contradictions, all the incompatibilities you can, and you will see them in the government, the courts, the churches, and the plays of this crazy nation.

—Is it true that they are always laughing in Paris? asked Candide.

—Yes, said the abbé, but with a kind of rage too; when people complain of things, they do so amid explosions of laughter; they even laugh as they perform the most detestable actions.

—Who was that fat swine, said Candide, who spoke so nastily about the play over which I was weeping, and the actors who gave me so much pleasure?

—He is a living illness, answered the abbé, who makes a business of slandering all the plays and books; he hates the successful ones, as eunuchs hate successful lovers; he's one of those literary snakes who live on filth and venom; he's a folliculator . . .

—What's this word *folliculator*? asked Candide.

—It's a folio filler, said the abbé, a Fréron.[1]

It was after this fashion that Candide, Martin, and the abbé from Perigord chatted on the stairway as they watched the crowd leaving the theatre.

—Although I'm in a great hurry to see Miss Cunégonde again, said Candide, I would very much like to dine with Miss Clairon,[2] for she seemed to me admirable.

The abbé was not the man to approach Miss Clairon, who saw only good company.

—She has an engagement tonight, he said; but I shall have the honor of introducing you to a lady of quality, and there you will get to know Paris as if you had lived here four years.

Candide, who was curious by nature, allowed himself to be brought to the lady's house, in the depths of the Faubourg St.-

9. Adrienne Lecouvreur (1690–1730), so called because she made her debut as Monime in Racine's *Mithridate*. Voltaire had assisted at her secret midnight funeral and wrote an indignant poem about it.
1. A successful and popular journalist, who had attacked several of Voltaire's plays, including *Tancrède*. Voltaire had a fine story that the devil attended the first night of *Tancrède* disguised as Fréron: when a lady in the balcony wept at the play's pathos, her tear dropped on the devil's nose; he thought it was holy water and shook it off—psha! psha! G. Desnoiresterres, *Voltaire et Jean-Jacques Rousseau*, pp. 3–4.
2. Actually Claire Leris (1723–1803). She had played the lead role in *Tancrède* and was for many years a leading figure on the Paris stage.

Honoré; they were playing faro[3]; twelve melancholy punters held in their hands a little sheaf of cards, blank summaries of their bad luck. Silence reigned supreme, the punters were pallid, the banker uneasy; and the lady of the house, seated beside the pitiless banker, watched with the eyes of a lynx for the various illegal redoublings and bets at long odds which the players tried to signal by folding the corners of their cards; she had them unfolded with a determination which was severe but polite, and concealed her anger lest she lose her customers. The lady caused herself to be known as the Marquise of Parolignac.[4] Her daughter, fifteen years old, sat among the punters and tipped off her mother with a wink to the sharp practices of these unhappy players when they tried to recoup their losses. The abbé from Perigord, Candide, and Martin came in; nobody arose or greeted them or looked at them; all were lost in the study of their cards.

—My Lady the Baroness of Thunder-Ten-Tronckh was more civil, thought Candide.

However, the abbé whispered in the ear of the marquise, who, half rising, honored Candide with a gracious smile and Martin with a truly noble nod; she gave a seat and dealt a hand of cards to Candide, who lost fifty thousand francs in two turns; after which they had a very merry supper. Everyone was amazed that Candide was not upset over his losses; the lackeys, talking together in their usual lackey language, said: —He must be some English milord.

The supper was like most Parisian suppers: first silence, then an indistinguishable rush of words; then jokes, mostly insipid, false news, bad logic, a little politics, a great deal of malice. They even talked of new books.

—Have you seen the new novel by Dr. Gauchat, the theologian?[5] asked the abbé from Perigord.

—Oh yes, answered one of the guests; but I couldn't finish it. We have a horde of impudent scribblers nowadays, but all of them put together don't match the impudence of this Gauchat, this doctor of theology. I have been so struck by the enormous number of detestable books which are swamping us that I have taken up punting at faro.

—And the *Collected Essays* of Archdeacon T——[6] asked the abbé, what do you think of them?

3. A game of cards, about which it is necessary to know only that a number of punters play against a banker or dealer. The pack is dealt out two cards at a time, and each player may bet on any card as much as he pleases. The sharp practices of the punters consist essentially of tricks for increasing their winnings without corresponding risks.
4. A *paroli* is an illegal redoubling of one's bet; her name therefore implies a title grounded in cardsharping.
5. He had written against Voltaire, and Voltaire suspected him (wrongly) of having committed a novel, *L'Oracle des nouveaux philosophes.*
6. His name was Trublet, and he had said, among other disagreeable things, that Voltaire's epic poem, the *Henriade*, made him yawn and that Voltaire's genius was "the perfection of mediocrity."

—Ah, said Madame de Parolignac, what a frightful bore he is! He takes such pains to tell you what everyone knows; he discourses so learnedly on matters which aren't worth a casual remark! He plunders, and not even wittily, the wit of other people! He spoils what he plunders, he's disgusting! But he'll never disgust me again; a couple of pages of the archdeacon have been enough for me.

There was at table a man of learning and taste, who supported the marquise on this point. They talked next of tragedies; the lady asked why there were tragedies which played well enough but which were wholly unreadable. The man of taste explained very clearly how a play could have a certain interest and yet little merit otherwise; he showed succinctly that it was not enough to conduct a couple of intrigues, such as one can find in any novel, and which never fail to excite the spectator's interest; but that one must be new without being grotesque, frequently touch the sublime but never depart from the natural; that one must know the human heart and give it words; that one must be a great poet without allowing any character in the play to sound like a poet; and that one must know the language perfectly, speak it purely, and maintain a continual harmony without ever sacrificing sense to mere sound.

—Whoever, he added, does not observe all these rules may write one or two tragedies which succeed in the theatre, but he will never be ranked among the good writers; there are very few good tragedies; some are idylls in well-written, well-rhymed dialogue, others are political arguments which put the audience to sleep, or revolting pomposities; still others are the fantasies of enthusiasts, barbarous in style, incoherent in logic, full of long speeches to the gods because the author does not know how to address men, full of false maxims and emphatic commonplaces.

Candide listened attentively to this speech and conceived a high opinion of the speaker; and as the marquise had placed him by her side, he turned to ask her who was this man who spoke so well.

—He is a scholar, said the lady, who never plays cards and whom the abbé sometimes brings to my house for supper; he knows all about tragedies and books, and has himself written a tragedy that was hissed from the stage and a book, the only copy of which ever seen outside his publisher's office was dedicated to me.

—What a great man, said Candide, he's Pangloss all over.

Then, turning to him, he said: —Sir, you doubtless think everything is for the best in the physical as well as the moral universe, and that nothing could be otherwise than as it is?

—Not at all, sir, replied the scholar, I believe nothing of the sort. I find that everything goes wrong in our world; that nobody knows his place in society or his duty, what he's doing or what he ought to be doing, and that outside of mealtimes, which are cheerful and congenial enough, all the rest of the day is spent in useless quarrels, as of Jansenists against Molinists,[7] parliament-men against church-men, literary men against literary men, courtiers against courtiers, financiers against the plebs, wives against husbands, relatives against relatives—it's one unending warfare.

Candide answered: —I have seen worse; but a wise man, who has since had the misfortune to be hanged, taught me that everything was marvelously well arranged. Troubles are just the shadows in a beautiful picture.

—Your hanged philosopher was joking, said Martin; the shadows are horrible ugly blots.

—It is human beings who make the blots, said Candide, and they can't do otherwise.

—Then it isn't their fault, said Martin.

Most of the faro players, who understood this sort of talk not at all, kept on drinking; Martin disputed with the scholar, and Candide told part of his story to the lady of the house.

After supper, the marquise brought Candide into her room and sat him down on a divan.

—Well, she said to him, are you still madly in love with Miss Cunégonde of Thunder-Ten-Tronckh?

—Yes, ma'am, replied Candide. The marquise turned upon him a tender smile.

—You answer like a young man of Westphalia, said she; a Frenchman would have told me: 'It is true that I have been in love with Miss Cunégonde; but since seeing you, madame, I fear that I love her no longer.'

—Alas, ma'am, said Candide, I will answer any way you want.

—Your passion for her, said the marquise, began when you picked up her handkerchief; I prefer that you should pick up my garter.

—Gladly, said Candide, and picked it up.

—But I also want you to put it back on, said the lady; and Candide put it on again.

—Look you now, said the lady, you are a foreigner; my Paris lovers I sometimes cause to languish for two weeks or so, but to you I surrender the very first night, because we must render the honors of the country to a young man from Westphalia.

The beauty, who had seen two enormous diamonds on the two hands of her young friend, praised them so sincerely that from the fingers of Candide they passed over to the fingers of the marquise.

As he returned home with his Perigord abbé, Candide felt

---

7. The Jansenists (from Corneille Jansen, 1585–1638) were a relatively strict party of religious reform; the Molinists (from Luis Molina) were the party of the Jesuits. Their central issue of controversy was the relative importance of divine grace and human will to the salvation of man.

some remorse at having been unfaithful to Miss Cunégonde; the abbé sympathized with his grief; he had only a small share in the fifty thousand francs which Candide lost at cards, and in the proceeds of the two diamonds which had been half-given, half-extorted. His scheme was to profit, as much as he could, from the advantage of knowing Candide. He spoke at length of Cunégonde, and Candide told him that he would beg forgiveness for his beloved for his infidelity when he met her at Venice.

The Perigordian overflowed with politeness and unction, taking a tender interest in everything Candide said, everything he did, and everything he wanted to do.[8]

—Well, sir, said he, so you have an assignation at Venice?

—Yes indeed, sir, I do, said Candide; it is absolutely imperative that I go there to find Miss Cunégonde.

And then, carried away by the pleasure of talking about his love, he recounted, as he often did, a part of his adventures with that illustrious lady of Westphalia.

—I suppose, said the abbé, that Miss Cunégonde has a fine wit and writes charming letters.

—I never received a single letter from her, said Candide; for, as you can imagine, after being driven out of the castle for love of her, I couldn't write; shortly I learned that she was dead; then I rediscovered her; then I lost her again, and I have now sent, to a place more than twentyfive hundred leagues from here, a special agent whose return I am expecting.

The abbé listened carefully, and looked a bit dreamy. He soon took his leave of the two strangers, after embracing them tenderly. Next day Candide, when he woke up, received a letter, to the following effect:

—Dear sir, my very dear lover, I have been lying sick in this town for a week, I have just learned that you are here. I would fly to your arms if I could move. I heard that you had passed through Bordeaux; that was where I left the faithful Cacambo and the old woman, who are soon to follow me here. The governor of Buenos Aires took everything, but left me your heart. Come; your presence will either return me to life or cause me to die of joy.

---

8. Here ends the long passage interpolated by Voltaire in 1761, which began on p. 49. In the original version the transition was managed as follows. After the "commentator's" speech, ending: —Tomorrow I will show you twenty pamphlets written against him.

—Sir, said the abbé from Perigord, do you notice that young person over there with the attractive face and the delicate figure? She would only cost you ten thousand francs a month, and for fifty thousand crowns of diamonds . . .

—I could spare her only a day or or two, replied Candide, because I have an urgent appointment at Venice.

Next night after supper, the sly Perigordian overflowed with politeness and assiduity.

—Well, sir, said he, so you have an assignation at Venice?

This charming letter, coming so unexpectedly, filled Candide with inexpressible delight, while the illness of his dear Cunégonde covered him with grief. Torn between these two feelings, he took gold and diamonds, and had himself brought, with Martin, to the hotel where Miss Cunégonde was lodging. Trembling with emotion, he enters the room; his heart thumps, his voice breaks. He tries to open the curtains of the bed, he asks to have some lights.

—Absolutely forbidden, says the serving girl; light will be the death of her.

And abruptly she pulls shut the curtain.

—My dear Cunégonde, says Candide in tears, how are you feeling? If you can't see me, won't you at least speak to me?

—She can't talk, says the servant.

But then she draws forth from the bed a plump hand, over which Candide weeps a long time, and which he fills with diamonds, meanwhile leaving a bag of gold on the chair.

Amid his transports, there arrives a bailiff followed by the abbé from Perigord and a strong-arm squad.

—These here are the suspicious foreigners? says the officer; and he has them seized and orders his bullies to drag them off to jail.

—They don't treat visitors like this in Eldorado, says Candide.

—I am more a Manichee than ever, says Martin.

—But, please sir, where are you taking us? says Candide.

—To the lowest hole in the dungeons, says the bailiff.

Martin, having regained his self-possession, decided that the lady who pretended to be Cunégonde was a cheat, the abbé from Perigord was another cheat who had imposed on Candide's innocence, and the bailiff still another cheat, of whom it would be easy to get rid.

Rather than submit to the forms of justice, Candide, enlightened by Martin's advice and eager for his own part to see the real Cunégonde again, offered the bailiff three little diamonds worth about three thousand pistoles apiece.

—Ah, my dear sir! cried the man with the ivory staff, even if you have committed every crime imaginable, you are the most honest man in the world. Three diamonds! each one worth three thousand pistoles! My dear sir! I would gladly die for you, rather than take you to jail. All foreigners get arrested here; but let me manage it; I have a brother at Dieppe in Normandy; I'll take you to him; and if you have a bit of a diamond to give him, he'll take care of you, just like me.

—And why do they arrest all foreigners? asked Candide.

The abbé from Perigord spoke up and said: —It's because a beggar from Atrebatum[9] listened to some stupidities; that made him commit a parricide, not like the one of May, 1610, but like the one of December, 1594, much on the order of several other crimes committed in other years and other months by other beggars who had listened to stupidities.

The bailiff then explained what it was all about.[1]

—Foh! what beasts! cried Candide. What! monstrous behavior of this sort from a people who sing and dance? As soon as I can, let me get out of this country, where the monkeys provoke the tigers. In my own country I've lived with bears; only in Eldorado are there proper men. In the name of God, sir bailiff, get me to Venice where I can wait for Miss Cunégonde.

—I can only get you to Lower Normandy, said the guardsman.

He had the irons removed at once, said there had been a mistake, dismissed his gang, and took Candide and Martin to Dieppe, where he left them with his brother. There was a little Dutch ship at anchor. The Norman, changed by three more diamonds into the most helpful of men, put Candide and his people aboard the vessel, which was bound for Portsmouth in England. It wasn't on the way to Venice, but Candide felt like a man just let out of hell; and he hoped to get back on the road to Venice at the first possible occasion.

CHAPTER 23

Candide and Martin Pass the Shores of England; What They See There

—Ah, Pangloss! Pangloss! Ah, Martin! Martin! Ah, my darling Cunégonde! What is this world of ours? sighed Candide on the Dutch vessel.

—Something crazy, something abominable, Martin replied.

—You have been in England; are people as crazy there as in France?

—It's a different sort of crazy, said Martin. You know that these two nations have been at war over a few acres of snow near Canada, and that they are spending on this fine struggle more than Canada itself is worth.[2] As for telling you if there are more people

9. The Latin name for the district of Artois, from which came Robert-François Damiens, who tried to stab Louis XV in 1757. The assassination failed, like that of Châtel, who tried to kill Henri Quatre in 1594, but unlike that of Ravaillac, who succeeded in killing him in 1610.
1. The point, in fact, is not too clear since arresting foreigners is an indirect way at best to guard against home-grown fanatics, and the position of the abbé from Perigord in the whole transaction remains confused. Has he called in the officer just to get rid of Candide? If so, why is he sardonic about the very suspicions he is trying to foster? Candide's reaction is to the notion that Frenchmen should be capable of political assassination at all; it seems excessive.
2. The wars of the French and English over Canada dragged intermittently through the eighteenth century till the

in one country or the other who need a strait jacket, that is a judgment too fine for my understanding; I know only that the people we are going to visit are eaten up with melancholy.

As they chatted thus, the vessel touched at Portsmouth. A multitude of people covered the shore, watching closely a rather bulky man who was kneeling, his eyes blindfolded, on the deck of a man-of-war. Four soldiers, stationed directly in front of this man, fired three bullets apiece into his brain, as peaceably as you would want; and the whole assemblage went home, in great satisfaction.[3]

—What's all this about? asked Candide. What devil is everywhere at work?

He asked who was that big man who had just been killed with so much ceremony.

—It was an admiral, they told him.

—And why kill this admiral?

—The reason, they told him, is that he didn't kill enough people; he gave battle to a French admiral, and it was found that he didn't get close enough to him.

—But, said Candide, the French admiral was just as far from the English admiral as the English admiral was from the French admiral.

—That's perfectly true, came the answer; but in this country it is useful from time to time to kill one admiral in order to encourage the others.

Candide was so stunned and shocked at what he saw and heard, that he would not even set foot ashore; he arranged with the Dutch merchant (without even caring if he was robbed, as at Surinam) to be taken forthwith to Venice.

The merchant was ready in two days; they coasted along France, they passed within sight of Lisbon, and Candide quivered. They entered the straits, crossed the Mediterranean, and finally landed at Venice.

—God be praised, said Candide, embracing Martin; here I shall recover the lovely Cunégonde. I trust Cacambo as I would myself. All is well, all goes well, all goes as well as possible.

CHAPTER 24
About Paquette and Brother Giroflée

As soon as he was in Venice, he had a search made for Cacambo in all the inns, all the cafés, all the stews—and found no trace of

peace of Paris sealed England's conquest (1763). Voltaire thought the French should concentrate on developing Louisiana where the Jesuit influence was less marked.
3. Candide has witnessed the execution of Admiral John Byng, defeated off Minorca by the French fleet under Galisonnière and executed by firing squad on March 14, 1757. Voltaire had intervened to avert the execution.

him. Every day he sent to investigate the vessels and coastal traders; no news of Cacambo.

—How's this? said he to Martin. I have had time to go from Surinam to Bordeaux, from Bordeaux to Paris, from Paris to Dieppe, from Dieppe to Portsmouth, to skirt Portugal and Spain, cross the Mediterranean, and spend several months at Venice—and the lovely Cunégonde has not come yet! In her place, I have met only that impersonator and that abbé from Perigord. Cunégonde is dead, without a doubt; and nothing remains for me too but death. Oh, it would have been better to stay in the earthly paradise of Eldorado than to return to this accursed Europe. How right you are, my dear Martin; all is but illusion and disaster.

He fell into a black melancholy, and refused to attend the fashionable operas or take part in the other diversions of the carnival season; not a single lady tempted him in the slightest. Martin told him: —You're a real simpleton if you think a half-breed valet with five or six millions in his pockets will go to the end of the world to get your mistress and bring her to Venice for you. If he finds her, he'll take her for himself; if he doesn't, he'll take another. I advise you to forget about your servant Cacambo and your mistress Cunégonde.

Martin was not very comforting. Candide's melancholy increased, and Martin never wearied of showing him that there is little virtue and little happiness on this earth, except perhaps in Eldorado, where nobody can go.

While they were discussing this important matter and still waiting for Cunégonde, Candide noticed in St. Mark's Square a young Theatine [4] monk who had given his arm to a girl. The Theatine seemed fresh, plump, and flourishing; his eyes were bright, his manner cocky, his glance brilliant, his step proud. The girl was very pretty, and singing aloud; she glanced lovingly at her Theatine, and from time to time pinched his plump cheeks.

—At least you must admit, said Candide to Martin, that these people are happy. Until now I have not found in the whole inhabited earth, except Eldorado, anything but miserable people. But this girl and this monk, I'd be willing to bet, are very happy creatures.

—I'll bet they aren't, said Martin.

—We have only to ask them to dinner, said Candide, and we'll find out if I'm wrong.

Promptly he approached them, made his compliments, and invited them to his inn for a meal of macaroni, Lombardy partridges, and caviar, washed down with wine from Montepulciano, Cyprus,

---

4. A Catholic order founded in 1524 by Cardinal Cajetan and G. P. Caraffa, later Pope Paul IV.

and Samos, and some Lacrima Christi. The girl blushed but the Theatine accepted gladly, and the girl followed him, watching Candide with an expression of surprise and confusion, darkened by several tears. Scarcely had she entered the room when she said to Candide: —What, can it be that Master Candide no longer knows Paquette?

At these words Candide, who had not yet looked carefully at her because he was preoccupied with Cunégonde, said to her: —Ah, my poor child! so you are the one who put Doctor Pangloss in the fine fix where I last saw him.

—Alas, sir, I was the one, said Paquette; I see you know all about it. I heard of the horrible misfortunes which befell the whole household of My Lady the Baroness and the lovely Cunégonde. I swear to you that my own fate has been just as unhappy. I was perfectly innocent when you knew me. A Franciscan, who was my confessor, easily seduced me. The consequences were frightful; shortly after My Lord the Baron had driven you out with great kicks on the backside, I too was forced to leave the castle. If a famous doctor had not taken pity on me, I would have died. Out of gratitude, I became for some time the mistress of this doctor. His wife, who was jealous to the point of frenzy, beat me mercilessly every day; she was a gorgon. The doctor was the ugliest of men, and I the most miserable creature on earth, being continually beaten for a man I did not love. You will understand, sir, how dangerous it is for a nagging woman to be married to a doctor. This man, enraged by his wife's ways, one day gave her as a cold cure a medicine so potent that in two hours' time she died amid horrible convulsions. Her relatives brought suit against the bereaved husband; he fled the country, and I was put in prison. My innocence would never have saved me if I had not been rather pretty. The judge set me free on condition that he should become the doctor's successor. I was shortly replaced in this post by another girl, dismissed without any payment, and obliged to continue this abominable trade which you men find so pleasant and which for us is nothing but a bottomless pit of misery. I went to ply the trade in Venice. Ah, my dear sir, if you could imagine what it is like to have to caress indiscriminately an old merchant, a lawyer, a monk, a gondolier, an abbé; to be subjected to every sort of insult and outrage; to be reduced, time and again, to borrowing a skirt in order to go have it lifted by some disgusting man; to be robbed by this fellow of what one has gained from that; to be shaken down by the police, and to have before one only the prospect of a hideous old age, a hospital, and a dunghill, you will conclude that I am one of the most miserable creatures in the world.

Thus Paquette poured forth her heart to the good Candide in a hotel room, while Martin sat listening nearby. At last he said to Candide: —You see, I've already won half my bet.

Brother Giroflée[5] had remained in the dining room, and was having a drink before dinner.

—But how's this? said Candide to Paquette. You looked so happy, so joyous, when I met you; you were singing, you caressed the Theatine with such a natural air of delight; you seemed to me just as happy as you now say you are miserable.

—Ah, sir, replied Paquette, that's another one of the miseries of this business; yesterday I was robbed and beaten by an officer, and today I have to seem in good humor in order to please a monk.

Candide wanted no more; he conceded that Martin was right. They sat down to table with Paquette and the Theatine; the meal was amusing enough, and when it was over, the company spoke out among themselves with some frankness.

—Father, said Candide to the monk, you seem to me a man whom all the world might envy; the flower of health glows in your cheek, your features radiate pleasure; you have a pretty girl for your diversion, and you seem very happy with your life as a Theatine.

—Upon my word, sir, said Brother Giroflée, I wish that all the Theatines were at the bottom of the sea. A hundred times I have been tempted to set fire to my convent, and go turn Turk. My parents forced me, when I was fifteen years old, to put on this detestable robe, so they could leave more money to a cursed older brother of mine, may God confound him! Jealousy, faction, and fury spring up, by natural law, within the walls of convents. It is true, I have preached a few bad sermons which earned me a little money, half of which the prior stole from me; the remainder serves to keep me in girls. But when I have to go back to the monastery at night, I'm ready to smash my head against the walls of my cell; and all my fellow monks are in the same fix.

Martin turned to Candide and said with his customary coolness: —Well, haven't I won the whole bet?

Candide gave two thousand piastres to Paquette and a thousand to Brother Giroflée.

—I assure you, said he, that with that they will be happy.

—I don't believe so, said Martin; your piastres may make them even more unhappy than they were before.

—That may be, said Candide; but one thing comforts me, I note that people often turn up whom one never expected to see again; it may well be that, having rediscovered my red sheep and Paquette, I will also rediscover Cunégonde.

5. His name means "gillyflower," and Paquette means "daisy." They are lilies of the field who spin not, neither do they reap.

—I hope, said Martin, that she will some day make you happy; but I very much doubt it.

—You're a hard man, said Candide.

—I've lived, said Martin.

—But look at these gondoliers, said Candide; aren't they always singing?

—You don't see them at home, said Martin, with their wives and squalling children. The doge has his troubles, the gondoliers theirs. It's true that on the whole one is better off as a gondolier than as a doge; but the difference is so slight, I don't suppose it's worth the trouble of discussing.

—There's a lot of talk here, said Candide, of this Senator Pococurante,[6] who has a fine palace on the Brenta and is hospitable to foreigners. They say he is a man who has never known a moment's grief.

—I'd like to see such a rare specimen, said Martin.

Candide promptly sent to Lord Pococurante, asking permission to call on him tomorrow.

CHAPTER 25
Visit to Lord Pococurante, Venetian Nobleman

Candide and Martin took a gondola on the Brenta, and soon reached the palace of the noble Pococurante. The gardens were large and filled with beautiful marble statues; the palace was handsomely designed. The master of the house, sixty years old and very rich, received his two inquisitive visitors perfectly politely, but with very little warmth; Candide was disconcerted and Martin not at all displeased.

First two pretty and neatly dressed girls served chocolate, which they whipped to a froth. Candide could not forbear praising their beauty, their grace, their skill.

—They are pretty good creatures, said Pococurante; I sometimes have them into my bed, for I'm tired of the ladies of the town, with their stupid tricks, quarrels, jealousies, fits of ill humor and petty pride, and all the sonnets one has to make or order for them; but, after all, these two girls are starting to bore me too.

After lunch, Candide strolled through a long gallery, and was amazed at the beauty of the pictures. He asked who was the painter of the two finest.

—They are by Raphael, said the senator; I bought them for a lot of money, out of vanity, some years ago; people say they're the finest in Italy, but they don't please me at all; the colors have all turned brown, the figures aren't well modeled and don't stand out

6. His name means "small care."

enough, the draperies bear no resemblance to real cloth. In a word, whatever people may say, I don't find in them a real imitation of nature. I like a picture only when I can see in it a touch of nature itself, and there are none of this sort. I have many paintings, but I no longer look at them.

As they waited for dinner, Pococurante ordered a concerto performed. Candide found the music delightful.

—That noise? said Pococurante. It may amuse you for half an hour, but if it goes on any longer, it tires everybody though no one dares to admit it. Music today is only the art of performing difficult pieces, and what is merely difficult cannot please for long. Perhaps I should prefer the opera, if they had not found ways to make it revolting and monstrous. Anyone who likes bad tragedies set to music is welcome to them; in these performances the scenes serve only to introduce, inappropriately, two or three ridiculous songs designed to show off the actress's sound box. Anyone who wants to, or who can, is welcome to swoon with pleasure at the sight of a castrate wriggling through the role of Caesar or Cato, and strutting awkwardly about the stage. For my part, I have long since given up these paltry trifles which are called the glory of modern Italy, and for which monarchs pay such ruinous prices.

Candide argued a bit, but timidly; Martin was entirely of a mind with the senator.

They sat down to dinner, and after an excellent meal adjourned to the library. Candide, seeing a copy of Homer [7] in a splendid binding, complimented the noble lord on his good taste.

—That is an author, said he, who was the special delight of great Pangloss, the best philosopher in all Germany.

—He's no special delight of mine, said Pococurante coldly. I was once made to believe that I took pleasure in reading him; but that constant recital of fights which are all alike, those gods who are always interfering but never decisively, that Helen who is the cause of the war and then scarcely takes any part in the story, that Troy which is always under siege and never taken—all that bores me to tears. I have sometimes asked scholars if reading it bored them as much as it bores me; everyone who answered frankly told me the book dropped from his hands like lead, but that they had to have it in their libraries as a monument of antiquity, like those old rusty coins which can't be used in real trade.

—Your Excellence doesn't hold the same opinion of Virgil? said Candide.

7. Since the mid-sixteenth century, when Julius Caesar Scaliger established the dogma, it had been customary to prefer Virgil to Homer. Voltaire's youthful judgments, as delivered in the *Essai sur la poésie épique* (1728), are here summarized with minor revisions—upward for Ariosto, downward for Milton.

—I concede, said Pococurante, that the second, fourth, and sixth books of his *Aeneid* are fine; but as for his pious Aeneas, and strong Cloanthes, and faithful Achates, and little Ascanius, and that imbecile King Latinus, and middle-class Amata, and insipid Lavinia, I don't suppose there was ever anything so cold and unpleasant. I prefer Tasso and those sleepwalkers' stories of Ariosto.

—Dare I ask, sir, said Candide, if you don't get great enjoyment from reading Horace?

—There are some maxims there, said Pococurante, from which a man of the world can profit, and which, because they are formed into vigorous couplets, are more easily remembered; but I care very little for his trip to Brindisi, his description of a bad dinner, or his account of a quibblers' squabble between some fellow Pupilus, whose words he says *were full of pus*, and another whose words *were full of vinegar*.[8] I feel nothing but extreme disgust at his verses against old women and witches; and I can't see what's so great in his telling his friend Maecenas that if he is raised by him to the ranks of lyric poets, he will strike the stars with his lofty forehead. Fools admire everything in a well-known author. I read only for my own pleasure; I like only what is in my style.

Candide, who had been trained never to judge for himself, was much astonished by what he heard; and Martin found Pococurante's way of thinking quite rational.

—Oh, here is a copy of Cicero, said Candide. Now this great man I suppose you're never tired of reading.

—I never read him at all, replied the Venetian. What do I care whether he pleaded for Rabirius or Cluentius? As a judge, I have my hands full of lawsuits. I might like his philosophical works better, but when I saw that he had doubts about everything, I concluded that I knew as much as he did, and that I needed no help to be ignorant.

—Ah, here are eighty volumes of collected papers from a scientific academy, cried Martin; maybe there is something good in them.

—There would be indeed, said Pococurante, if one of these silly authors had merely discovered a new way of making pins; but in all those volumes there is nothing but empty systems, not a single useful discovery.

—What a lot of stage plays I see over there, said Candide, some in Italian, some in Spanish and French.

—Yes, said the senator, three thousand of them, and not three dozen good ones. As for those collections of sermons, which all to-

---

8. The reference is to Horace, *Satires* I. vii; Pococurante, with gentlemanly negligence, has corrupted Rupilius to Pupilus. Horace's poems against witches are *Epodes* V, VIII, XII; the one about striking the stars with his lofty forehead is *Odes* I.i.

gether are not worth a page of Seneca, and all these heavy volumes of theology, you may be sure I never open them, nor does anybody else.

Martin noticed some shelves full of English books.

—I suppose, said he, that a republican must delight in most of these books written in the land of liberty.

—Yes, replied Pococurante, it's a fine thing to write as you think; it is mankind's privilege. In all our Italy, people write only what they do not think; men who inhabit the land of the Caesars and Antonines dare not have an idea without the permission of a Dominican. I would rejoice in the freedom that breathes through English genius, if partisan passions did not corrupt all that is good in that precious freedom.

Candide, noting a Milton, asked if he did not consider this author a great man.

—Who? said Pococurante. That barbarian who made a long commentary on the first chapter of Genesis in ten books of crabbed verse? That clumsy imitator of the Greeks, who disfigures creation itself, and while Moses represents the eternal being as creating the world with a word, has the messiah take a big compass out of a heavenly cupboard in order to design his work? You expect me to admire the man who spoiled Tasso's hell and devil? who disguises Lucifer now as a toad, now as a pigmy? who makes him rehash the same arguments a hundred times over? who makes him argue theology? and who, taking seriously Ariosto's comic story of the invention of firearms, has the devils shooting off cannon in heaven? Neither I nor anyone else in Italy has been able to enjoy these gloomy extravagances. The marriage of Sin and Death, and the monster that Sin gives birth to, will nauseate any man whose taste is at all refined; and his long description of a hospital is good only for a gravedigger. This obscure, extravagant, and disgusting poem was despised at its birth; I treat it today as it was treated in its own country by its contemporaries. Anyhow, I say what I think, and care very little whether other people agree with me.

Candide was a little cast down by this speech; he respected Homer, and had a little affection for Milton.

—Alas, he said under his breath to Martin, I'm afraid this man will have a supreme contempt for our German poets.

—No harm in that, said Martin.

—Oh what a superior man, said Candide, still speaking softly, what a great genius this Pococurante must be! Nothing can please him.

Having thus looked over all the books, they went down into the garden. Candide praised its many beauties.

—I know nothing in such bad taste, said the master of the house;

we have nothing but trifles here; tomorrow I am going to have one set out on a nobler design.

When the two visitors had taken leave of his excellency: —Well now, said Candide to Martin, you must agree that this was the happiest of all men, for he is superior to everything he possesses.

—Don't you see, said Martin, that he is disgusted with everything he possesses? Plato said, a long time ago, that the best stomachs are not those which refuse all food.

—But, said Candide, isn't there pleasure in criticizing everything, in seeing faults where other people think they see beauties?

—That is to say, Martin replied, that there's pleasure in having no pleasure?

—Oh well, said Candide, then I am the only happy man . . . or will be, when I see Miss Cunégonde again.

—It's always a good thing to have hope, said Martin.

But the days and the weeks slipped past; Cacambo did not come back, and Candide was so buried in his grief, that he did not even notice that Paquette and Brother Giroflée had neglected to come and thank him.

CHAPTER 26

About a Supper that Candide and Martin Had with Six Strangers, and Who They Were

One evening when Candide, accompanied by Martin, was about to sit down for dinner with the strangers staying in his hotel, a man with a soot-colored face came up behind him, took him by the arm, and said: —Be ready to leave with us, don't miss out.

He turned and saw Cacambo. Only the sight of Cunégonde could have astonished and pleased him more. He nearly went mad with joy. He embraced his dear friend.

—Cunégonde is here, no doubt? Where is she? Bring me to her, let me die of joy in her presence.

—Cunégonde is not here at all, said Cacambo, she is at Constantinople.

—Good Heavens, at Constantinople! but if she were in China, I must fly there, let's go.

—We will leave after supper, said Cacambo; I can tell you no more; I am a slave, my owner is looking for me, I must go wait on him at table; mum's the word; eat your supper and be prepared.

Candide, torn between joy and grief, delighted to have seen his faithful agent again, astonished to find him a slave, full of the idea of recovering his mistress, his heart in a turmoil, his mind in a whirl, sat down to eat with Martin, who was watching all these events coolly, and with six strangers who had come to pass the carnival season at Venice.

Cacambo, who was pouring wine for one of the strangers, leaned respectfully over his master at the end of the meal, and said to him: —Sire, Your Majesty may leave when he pleases, the vessel is ready.

Having said these words, he exited. The diners looked at one another in silent amazement, when another servant, approaching his master, said to him: —Sire, Your Majesty's litter is at Padua, and the bark awaits you.

The master nodded, and the servant vanished. All the diners looked at one another again, and the general amazement redoubled. A third servant, approaching a third stranger, said to him: —Sire, take my word for it, Your Majesty must stay here no longer; I shall get everything ready.

Then he too disappeared.

Candide and Martin had no doubt, now, that it was a carnival masquerade. A fourth servant spoke to a fourth master: —Your majesty will leave when he pleases—and went out like the others. A fifth followed suit. But the sixth servant spoke differently to the sixth stranger, who sat next to Candide. He said: —My word, sire, they'll give no more credit to Your Majesty, nor to me either; we could very well spend the night in the lockup, you and I. I've got to look out for myself, so good-bye to you.

When all the servants had left, the six strangers, Candide, and Martin remained under a pall of silence. Finally Candide broke it.

—Gentlemen, said he, here's a funny kind of joke. Why are you all royalty? I assure you that Martin and I aren't.

Cacambo's master spoke up gravely then, and said in Italian: —This is no joke, my name is Achmet the Third.[9] I was grand sultan for several years; then, as I had dethroned my brother, my nephew dethroned me. My viziers had their throats cut; I was allowed to end my days in the old seraglio. My nephew, the Grand Sultan Mahmoud, sometimes lets me travel for my health; and I have come to spend the carnival season at Venice.

A young man who sat next to Achmet spoke after him, and said: —My name is Ivan; I was once emperor of all the Russias.[1] I was dethroned while still in my cradle; my father and mother were locked up, and I was raised in prison; I sometimes have permission to travel, though always under guard, and I have come to spend the carnival season at Venice.

The third said: —I am Charles Edward, king of England[2]; my

9. His dates are 1673–1736; he was deposed in 1730.

1. Ivan VI reigned from his birth in 1740 till 1756, then was confined in the Schlusselberg, and executed in 1764.

2. This is the Young Pretender (1720–1788), known to his supporters as Bonnie Prince Charlie. The defeat so theatrically described took place at Culloden, April 16, 1746.

father yielded me his rights to the kingdom, and I fought to uphold them; but they tore out the hearts of eight hundred of my partisans, and flung them in their faces. I have been in prison; now I am going to Rome, to visit the king, my father, dethroned like me and my grandfather; and I have come to pass the carnival season at Venice.

The fourth king then spoke up, and said: —I am a king of the Poles[3]; the luck of war has deprived me of my hereditary estates; my father suffered the same losses; I submit to Providence like Sultan Achmet, Emperor Ivan, and King Charles Edward, to whom I hope heaven grants long lives; and I have come to pass the carnival season at Venice.

The fifth said: —I too am a king of the Poles[4]; I lost my kingdom twice, but Providence gave me another state, in which I have been able to do more good than all the Sarmatian kings ever managed to do on the banks of the Vistula. I too have submitted to Providence, and I have come to pass the carnival season at Venice.

It remained for the sixth monarch to speak.

—Gentlemen, said he, I am no such great lord as you, but I have in fact been a king like any other. I am Theodore; I was elected king of Corsica.[5] People used to call me *Your Majesty*, and now they barely call me *Sir*; I used to coin currency, and now I don't have a cent; I used to have two secretaries of state, and now I scarcely have a valet; I have sat on a throne, and for a long time in London I was in jail, on the straw; and I may well be treated the same way here, though I have come, like your majesties, to pass the carnival season at Venice.

The five other kings listened to his story with noble compassion. Each one of them gave twenty sequins to King Theodore, so that he might buy a suit and some shirts; Candide gave him a diamond worth two thousand sequins.

—Who in the world, said the five kings, is this private citizen who is in a position to give a hundred times as much as any of us, and who actually gives it?[6]

3. Augustus III (1696–1763), Elector of Saxony and King of Poland, dethroned by Frederick the Great in 1756.

4. Stanislas Leczinski (1677–1766), father-in-law of Louis XV, who abdicated the throne of Poland in 1736, was made Duke of Lorraine and in that capacity befriended Voltaire.

5. Theodore von Neuhof (1690–1756), an authentic Westphalian, an adventurer and a soldier of fortune, who in 1736 was (for about eight months) the elected king of Corsica. He spent time in an Amsterdam as well as a London debtor's prison.

6. A late correction of Voltaire's makes this passage read: —Who is this man who is in a position to give a hundred times as much as any of us, and who actually gives it? Are you a king too, sir?

—No, gentlemen, and I have no desire to be.

But this reading, though Voltaire's on good authority, produces a conflict with Candide's previous remark: —Why are you all royalty? I assure you that Martin and I aren't.

Thus, it has seemed better for literary reasons to follow an earlier reading. Voltaire was very conscious of his situation as a man richer than many princes; in 1758 he had money

Just as they were rising from dinner, there arrived at the same establishment four most serene highnesses, who had also lost their kingdoms through the luck of war, and who came to spend the rest of the carnival season at Venice. But Candide never bothered even to look at these newcomers because he was only concerned to go find his dear Cunégonde at Constantinople.

CHAPTER 27

Candide's Trip to Constantinople

Faithful Cacambo had already arranged with the Turkish captain who was returning Sultan Achmet to Constantinople to make room for Candide and Martin on board. Both men boarded ship after prostrating themselves before his miserable highness. On the way, Candide said to Martin: —Six dethroned kings that we had dinner with! and yet among those six there was one on whom I had to bestow charity! Perhaps there are other princes even more unfortunate. I myself have only lost a hundred sheep, and now I am flying to the arms of Cunégonde. My dear Martin, once again Pangloss is proved right, all is for the best.

—I hope so, said Martin.

—But, said Candide, that was a most unlikely experience we had at Venice. Nobody ever saw, or heard tell of, six dethroned kings eating together at an inn.

—It is no more extraordinary, said Martin, than most of the things that have happened to us. Kings are frequently dethroned; and as for the honor we had from dining with them, that's a trifle which doesn't deserve our notice.[7]

Scarcely was Candide on board than he fell on the neck of his former servant, his friend Cacambo.

—Well! said he, what is Cunégonde doing? Is she still a marvel of beauty? Does she still love me? How is her health? No doubt you have bought her a palace at Constantinople.

—My dear master, answered Cacambo, Cunégonde is washing dishes on the shores of the Propontis, in the house of a prince who has very few dishes to wash; she is a slave in the house of a onetime king named Ragotski,[8] to whom the Great Turk allows three crowns a day in his exile; but, what is worse than all this, she has lost all her beauty and become horribly ugly.

on loan to no fewer than three highnesses, Charles Eugene, Duke of Wurtemburg; Charles Theodore, Elector Palatine; and the Duke of Saxe-Gotha.
7. Another late change adds the following question: —What does it matter whom you dine with as long as you fare well at table?
I have omitted it, again on literary grounds (the observation is too heavy and commonplace), despite its superior claim to a position in the text.
8. Francis Leopold Rakoczy (1676–1735) who was briefly king of Transylvania in the early eighteenth century. After 1720 he was interned in Turkey.

—Ah, beautiful or ugly, said Candide, I am an honest man, and my duty is to love her forever. But how can she be reduced to this wretched state with the five or six millions that you had?

—All right, said Cacambo, didn't I have to give two millions to Señor don Fernando d'Ibaraa y Figueroa y Mascarenes y Lampourdos y Souza, governor of Buenos Aires, for his permission to carry off Miss Cunégonde? And didn't a pirate cleverly strip us of the rest? And didn't this pirate carry us off to Cape Matapan, to Melos, Nicaria, Samos, Petra, to the Dardanelles, Marmora, Scutari? Cunégonde and the old woman are working for the prince I told you about, and I am the slave of the dethroned sultan.

—What a lot of fearful calamities linked one to the other, said Candide. But after all, I still have a few diamonds, I shall easily deliver Cunégonde. What a pity that she's become so ugly!

Then, turning toward Martin, he asked: —Who in your opinion is more to be pitied, the Emperor Achmet, the Emperor Ivan, King Charles Edward, or myself?

—I have no idea, said Martin; I would have to enter your hearts in order to tell.

—Ah, said Candide, if Pangloss were here, he would know and he would tell us.

—I can't imagine, said Martin, what scales your Pangloss would use to weigh out the miseries of men and value their griefs. All I will venture is that the earth holds millions of men who deserve our pity a hundred times more than King Charles Edward, Emperor Ivan, or Sultan Achmet.

—You may well be right, said Candide.

In a few days they arrived at the Black Sea canal. Candide began by repurchasing Cacambo at an exorbitant price; then, without losing an instant, he flung himself and his companions into a galley to go search out Cunégonde on the shores of Propontis, however ugly she might be.

There were in the chain gang two convicts who bent clumsily to the oar, and on whose bare shoulders the Levantine[9] captain delivered from time to time a few lashes with a bullwhip. Candide naturally noticed them more than the other galley slaves, and out of pity came closer to them. Certain features of their disfigured faces seemed to him to bear a slight resemblance to Pangloss and to that wretched Jesuit, that baron, that brother of Miss Cunégonde. The notion stirred and saddened him. He looked at them more closely.

—To tell you the truth, he said to Cacambo, if I hadn't seen Master Pangloss hanged, and if I hadn't been so miserable as to murder the baron, I should think they were rowing in this very galley.

9. From the eastern Mediterranean.

At the names of 'baron' and 'Pangloss' the two convicts gave a great cry, sat still on their bench, and dropped their oars. The Levantine captain came running, and the bullwhip lashes redoubled.

—Stop, stop, captain, cried Candide. I'll give you as much money as you want.

—What, can it be Candide? cried one of the convicts.

—What, can it be Candide? cried the other.

—Is this a dream? said Candide. Am I awake or asleep? Am I in this galley? Is that My Lord the Baron, whom I killed? Is that Master Pangloss, whom I saw hanged?

—It is indeed, they replied.

—What, is that the great philosopher? said Martin.

—Now, sir, Mr. Levantine Captain, said Candide, how much money do you want for the ransom of My Lord Thunder-Ten-Tronckh, one of the first barons of the empire, and Master Pangloss, the deepest metaphysician in all Germany?

—Dog of a Christian, replied the Levantine captain, since these two dogs of Christian convicts are barons and metaphysicians, which is no doubt a great honor in their country, you will give me fifty thousand sequins for them.

—You shall have them, sir, take me back to Constantinople and you shall be paid on the spot. Or no, take me to Miss Cunégonde.

The Levantine captain, at Candide's first word, had turned his bow toward the town, and he had them rowed there as swiftly as a bird cleaves the air.

A hundred times Candide embraced the baron and Pangloss.

—And how does it happen I didn't kill you, my dear baron? and my dear Pangloss, how can you be alive after being hanged? and why are you both rowing in the galleys of Turkey?

—Is it really true that my dear sister is in this country? asked the baron.

—Yes, answered Cacambo.

—And do I really see again my dear Candide? cried Pangloss.

Candide introduced Martin and Cacambo. They all embraced; they all talked at once. The galley flew, already they were back in port. A jew was called, and Candide sold him for fifty thousand sequins a diamond worth a hundred thousand, while he protested by Abraham that he could not possibly give more for it. Candide immediately ransomed the baron and Pangloss. The latter threw himself at the feet of his liberator, and bathed them with tears; the former thanked him with a nod, and promised to repay this bit of money at the first opportunity.

—But is it really possible that my sister is in Turkey? said he.

—Nothing is more possible, replied Cacambo, since she is a dish-washer in the house of a prince of Transylvania.

At once two more jews were called; Candide sold some more diamonds; and they all departed in another galley to the rescue of Cunégonde.

CHAPTER 28

What Happened to Candide, Cunégonde, Pangloss,
Martin, &c.

—Let me beg your pardon once more, said Candide to the baron, pardon me, reverend father, for having run you through the body with my sword.

—Don't mention it, replied the baron. I was a little too hasty myself, I confess it; but since you want to know the misfortune which brought me to the galleys, I'll tell you. After being cured of my wound by the brother who was apothecary to the college, I was attacked and abducted by a Spanish raiding party; they jailed me in Buenos Aires at the time when my sister had just left. I asked to be sent to Rome, to the father general. Instead, I was named to serve as almoner in Constantinople, under the French ambassador. I had not been a week on this job when I chanced one evening on a very handsome young ichoglan.[1] The evening was hot; the young man wanted to take a swim; I seized the occasion, and went with him. I did not know that it is a capital offense for a Christian to be found naked with a young Moslem. A cadi sentenced me to receive a hundred blows with a cane on the soles of my feet, and then to be sent to the galleys. I don't suppose there was ever such a horrible miscarriage of justice. But I would like to know why my sister is in the kitchen of a Transylvanian king exiled among Turks.

—But how about you, my dear Pangloss, said Candide; how is it possible that we have met again?

—It is true, said Pangloss, that you saw me hanged; in the normal course of things, I should have been burned, but you recall that a cloudburst occurred just as they were about to roast me. So much rain fell that they despaired of lighting the fire; thus I was hanged, for lack of anything better to do with me. A surgeon bought my body, carried me off to his house, and dissected me. First he made a cross-shaped incision in me, from the navel to the clavicle. No one could have been worse hanged than I was. In fact, the executioner of the high ceremonials of the Holy Inquisition, who was a subdeacon, burned people marvelously well, but he was not in the way of hanging them. The rope was wet, and tightened badly; it caught on a knot; in short, I was still breathing. The cross-

1. A page to the sultan.

shaped incision made me scream so loudly that the surgeon fell over backwards; he thought he was dissecting the devil, fled in an agony of fear, and fell downstairs in his flight. His wife ran in, at the noise, from a nearby room; she found me stretched out on the table with my cross-shaped incision, was even more frightened than her husband, fled, and fell over him. When they had recovered a little, I heard her say to him: 'My dear, what were you thinking of, trying to dissect a heretic? Don't you know those people are always possessed of the devil? I'm going to get the priest and have him exorcised.' At these words, I shuddered, and collected my last remaining energies to cry: 'Have mercy on me!' At last the Portuguese barber[2] took courage; he sewed me up again; his wife even nursed me; in two weeks I was up and about. The barber found me a job and made me lackey to a Knight of Malta who was going to Venice; and when this master could no longer pay me, I took service under a Venetian merchant, whom I followed to Constantinople.

—One day it occurred to me to enter a mosque; no one was there but an old imam and a very attractive young worshipper who was saying her prayers. Her bosom was completely bare; and between her two breasts she had a lovely bouquet of tulips, roses, anemones, buttercups, hyacinths, and primroses. She dropped her bouquet, I picked it up, and returned it to her with the most respectful attentions. I was so long getting it back in place that the imam grew angry, and, seeing that I was a Christian, he called the guard. They took me before the cadi, who sentenced me to receive a hundred blows with a cane on the soles of my feet, and then to be sent to the galleys. I was chained to the same galley and precisely the same bench as My Lord the Baron. There were in this galley four young fellows from Marseilles, five Neapolitan priests, and two Corfu monks, who assured us that these things happen every day. My Lord the Baron asserted that he had suffered a greater injustice than I; I, on the other hand, proposed that it was much more permissible to replace a bouquet in a bosom than to be found naked with an ichoglan. We were arguing the point continually, and getting twenty lashes a day with the bullwhip, when the chain of events within this universe brought you to our galley, and you ransomed us.

—Well, my dear Pangloss, Candide said to him, now that you have been hanged, dissected, beaten to a pulp, and sentenced to the galleys, do you still think everything is for the best in this world?

—I am still of my first opinion, replied Pangloss; for after all I am a philosopher, and it would not be right for me to recant since Leibniz could not possibly be wrong, and besides pre-established harmony is the finest notion in the world, like the plenum and subtle matter.[3]

2. The two callings of barber and surgeon, since they both involved sharp instruments, were interchangeable in the early days of medicine.

CHAPTER 29
How Candide Found Cunégonde and the Old Woman Again

While Candide, the baron, Pangloss, Martin, and Cacambo were telling one another their stories, while they were disputing over the contingent or non-contingent events of this universe, while they were arguing over effects and causes, over moral evil and physical evil, over liberty and necessity, and over the consolations available to one in a Turkish galley, they arrived at the shores of Propontis and the house of the prince of Transylvania. The first sight to meet their eyes was Cunégonde and the old woman, who were hanging out towels on lines to dry.

The baron paled at what he saw. The tender lover Candide, seeing his lovely Cunégonde with her skin weathered, her eyes bloodshot, her breasts fallen, her cheeks seamed, her arms red and scaly, recoiled three steps in horror, and then advanced only out of politeness. She embraced Candide and her brother; everyone embraced the old woman; Candide ransomed them both.

There was a little farm in the neighborhood; the old woman suggested that Candide occupy it until some better fate should befall the group. Cunégonde did not know she was ugly, no one had told her; she reminded Candide of his promises in so firm a tone that the good Candide did not dare to refuse her. So he went to tell the baron that he was going to marry his sister.

—Never will I endure, said the baron, such baseness on her part, such insolence on yours; this shame at least I will not put up with; why, my sister's children would not be able to enter the Chapters in Germany.[4] No, my sister will never marry anyone but a baron of the empire.

Cunégonde threw herself at his feet, and bathed them with her tears; he was inflexible.

—You absolute idiot, Candide told him, I rescued you from the galleys, I paid your ransom, I paid your sister's; she was washing dishes, she is ugly, I am good enough to make her my wife, and you still presume to oppose it! If I followed my impulses, I would kill you all over again.

—You may kill me again, said the baron, but you will not marry my sister while I am alive.

3. Rigorous determinism requires that there be no empty spaces in the universe, so wherever it seems empty, one posits the existence of the "plenum." "Subtle matter" describes the soul, the mind, and all spiritual agencies—which can, therefore, be supposed subject to the influence and control of the great world machine, which is, of course, visibly material. Both are concepts needed to round out the system of optimistic determinism.

4. Knightly assemblies.

CHAPTER 30
Conclusion

At heart, Candide had no real wish to marry Cunégonde; but the baron's extreme impertinence decided him in favor of the marriage, and Cunégonde was so eager for it that he could not back out. He consulted Pangloss, Martin, and the faithful Cacambo. Pangloss drew up a fine treatise, in which he proved that the baron had no right over his sister and that she could, according to all the laws of the empire, marry Candide morganatically.[5] Martin said they should throw the baron into the sea. Cacambo thought they should send him back to the Levantine captain to finish his time in the galleys, and then send him to the father general in Rome by the first vessel. This seemed the best idea; the old woman approved, and nothing was said to his sister; the plan was executed, at modest expense, and they had the double pleasure of snaring a Jesuit and punishing the pride of a German baron.

It is quite natural to suppose that after so many misfortunes, Candide, married to his mistress, and living with the philosopher Pangloss, the philosopher Martin, the prudent Cacambo, and the old woman—having, besides, brought back so many diamonds from the land of the ancient Incas—must have led the most agreeable life in the world. But he was so cheated by the jews[6] that nothing was left but his little farm; his wife, growing every day more ugly, became sour-tempered and insupportable; the old woman was ailing and even more ill-humored than Cunégonde. Cacambo, who worked in the garden and went into Constantinople to sell vegetables, was worn out with toil, and cursed his fate. Pangloss was in despair at being unable to shine in some German university. As for Martin, he was firmly persuaded that things are just as bad wherever you are; he endured in patience. Candide, Martin, and Pangloss sometimes argued over metaphysics and morals. Before the windows of the farmhouse they often watched the passage of boats bearing effendis, pashas, and cadis into exile on Lemnos, Mytilene, and Erzeroum; they saw other cadis, other pashas, other effendis coming, to take the place of the exiles and to be exiled in their turn. They saw various heads, neatly impaled, to be set up at the Sublime Porte.[7] These sights gave fresh impetus to their discussions; and

5. A morganatic marriage confers no rights on the partner of lower rank or on the offspring. Pangloss always uses more language than anyone else to achieve fewer results.
6. Voltaire's anti-Semitism, derived from various unhappy experiences with Jewish financiers, is not the most at-tractive aspect of his personality.
7. The gate of the sultan's palace is often used by extension to describe his government as a whole. But it was in fact a real gate where the heads of traitors and public enemies were gruesomely exposed.

when they were not arguing, the boredom was so fierce that one day the old woman ventured to say: —I should like to know which is worse, being raped a hundred times by negro pirates, having a buttock cut off, running the gauntlet in the Bulgar army, being flogged and hanged in an auto-da-fé, being dissected and rowing in the galleys—experiencing, in a word, all the miseries through which we have passed—or else just sitting here and doing nothing?

—It's a hard question, said Candide.

These words gave rise to new reflections, and Martin in particular concluded that man was bound to live either in convulsions of misery or in the lethargy of boredom. Candide did not agree, but expressed no positive opinion. Pangloss asserted that he had always suffered horribly; but having once declared that everything was marvelously well, he continued to repeat the opinion and didn't believe a word of it.

One thing served to confirm Martin in his detestable opinions, to make Candide hesitate more than ever, and to embarrass Pangloss. It was the arrival one day at their farm of Paquette and Brother Giroflée, who were in the last stages of misery. They had quickly run through their three thousand piastres, had split up, made up, quarreled, been jailed, escaped, and finally Brother Giroflée had turned Turk. Paquette continued to ply her trade everywhere, and no longer made any money at it.

—I told you, said Martin to Candide, that your gifts would soon be squandered and would only render them more unhappy. You have spent millions of piastres, you and Cacambo, and you are no more happy than Brother Giroflée and Paquette.

—Ah ha, said Pangloss to Paquette, so destiny has brought you back in our midst, my poor girl! Do you realize you cost me the end of my nose, one eye, and an ear? And look at you now! eh! what a world it is, after all!

This new adventure caused them to philosophize more than ever.

There was in the neighborhood a very famous dervish, who was said to be the best philosopher in Turkey; they went to ask his advice. Pangloss was spokesman, and he said: —Master, we have come to ask you to tell us why such a strange animal as man was created.

—What are you getting into? answered the dervish. Is it any of your business?

—But, reverend father, said Candide, there's a horrible lot of evil on the face of the earth.

—What does it matter, said the dervish, whether there's good or evil? When his highness sends a ship to Egypt, does he worry whether the mice on board are comfortable or not?

—What shall we do then? asked Pangloss.

—Hold your tongue, said the dervish.

—I had hoped, said Pangloss, to reason a while with you concerning effects and causes, the best of possible worlds, the origin of evil, the nature of the soul, and pre-established harmony.

At these words, the dervish slammed the door in their faces.

During this interview, word was spreading that at Constantinople they had just strangled two viziers of the divan,[8] as well as the mufti, and impaled several of their friends. This catastrophe made a great and general sensation for several hours. Pangloss, Candide, and Martin, as they returned to their little farm, passed a good old man who was enjoying the cool of the day at his doorstep under a grove of orange trees. Pangloss, who was as inquisitive as he was explanatory, asked the name of the mufti who had been strangled.

—I know nothing of it, said the good man, and I have never cared to know the name of a single mufti or vizier. I am completely ignorant of the episode you are discussing. I presume that in general those who meddle in public business sometimes perish miserably, and that they deserve their fate; but I never listen to the news from Constantinople; I am satisfied with sending the fruits of my garden to be sold there.

Having spoken these words, he asked the strangers into his house; his two daughters and two sons offered them various sherbets which they had made themselves, Turkish cream flavored with candied citron, orange, lemon, lime, pineapple, pistachio, and mocha coffee uncontaminated by the inferior coffee of Batavia and the East Indies. After which the two daughters of this good Moslem perfumed the beards of Candide, Pangloss, and Martin.

—You must possess, Candide said to the Turk, an enormous and splendid property?

I have only twenty acres, replied the Turk; I cultivate them with my children, and the work keeps us from three great evils, boredom, vice, and poverty.

Candide, as he walked back to his farm, meditated deeply over the words of the Turk. He said to Pangloss and Martin: —This good old man seems to have found himself a fate preferable to that of the six kings with whom we had the honor of dining.

—Great place, said Pangloss, is very perilous in the judgment of all the philosophers; for, after all, Eglon, king of the Moabites, was murdered by Ehud; Absalom was hung up by the hair and pierced with three darts; King Nadab, son of Jeroboam, was killed by Baasha; King Elah by Zimri; Ahaziah by Jehu; Athaliah by Jehoiada; and Kings Jehoiakim, Jeconiah, and Zedekiah were enslaved. You know how death came to Croesus, Astyages, Darius, Dionysius of Syracuse, Pyrrhus, Perseus, Hannibal, Jugurtha, Ariovistus, Caesar, Pompey, Nero, Otho, Vitellius, Domitian, Rich-

8. Intimate advisers of the sultan.

ard II of England, Edward II, Henry VI, Richard III, Mary Stuart, Charles I, the three Henrys of France, and the Emperor Henry IV? You know . . .

—I know also, said Candide, that we must cultivate our garden.

—You are perfectly right, said Pangloss; for when man was put into the garden of Eden, he was put there *ut operaretur eum*, so that he should work it; this proves that man was not born to take his ease.

—Let's work without speculating, said Martin; it's the only way of rendering life bearable.

The whole little group entered into this laudable scheme; each one began to exercise his talents. The little plot yielded fine crops. Cunégonde was, to tell the truth, remarkably ugly; but she became an excellent pastry cook. Paquette took up embroidery; the old woman did the laundry. Everyone, down even to Brother Giroflée, did something useful; he became a very adequate carpenter, and even an honest man; and Pangloss sometimes used to say to Candide: —All events are linked together in the best of possible worlds; for, after all, if you had not been driven from a fine castle by being kicked in the backside for love of Miss Cunégonde, if you hadn't been sent before the Inquisition, if you hadn't traveled across America on foot, if you hadn't given a good sword thrust to the baron, if you hadn't lost all your sheep from the good land of Eldorado, you wouldn't be sitting here eating candied citron and pistachios.

—That is very well put, said Candide, but we must cultivate our garden.

Backgrounds

Candide is at the same time a novel of abstract ideas with long, complex histories and a highly personal book, into which Voltaire poured an immense amount of himself—his experiences, his enmities, his learning, his desires, his anguish. Two sorts of preliminary background material are therefore pretty much indispensable: one a background of intellectual history, the other a background of personal history. The following section contains materials toward the construction of these two backgrounds.

Summary: The Intellectual Backgrounds

There is no ultimate answer to the question why an omniscient, omnipotent, benevolent God made a world with a great deal of evil in it; but, like most insoluble questions, this one has proved hard for mankind to set aside. It was present to man's consciousness long before the eighteenth century, and before the Christian religion itself—an essential part of which is a story designed to answer this very question. The stories of the fall of Satan and of the linked, analogous fall of man, growing as they do out of the daily perception of evil in the world, are narratives framed to provide an answer to the query, How did things get this way? But when we phrase the question logically instead of historically, even these answers become subject to question. How did God, omnipotent, omniscient, and good, shape man in such a way that he would fall—without Himself incurring responsibility for that fall? If He had the making of all things, including Satan, and knew when He framed him that immense evil would result—how can He be absolved of the charge of deliberate malice toward His creatures? These are challenges which have confronted every thoughtful Christian believer since the faith began.

The orthodox answer is to assert freedom of the will in God's creatures, to say that He made them (Satan and Adam alike) sufficient to stand but free to fall; therefore the fall is the fault of the creatures and not of the Creator. But a belief in original sin, if it is not to be totally despairing, requires a complementary belief in vicarious atonement (i.e., that Christ's death on the cross atoned at least partially for Adam's fall); it also implies a belief in the existence of a Christian church and the value of its sacraments, a belief in the Last Judgment, and in reward or punishment in an afterlife. A classic expression of this view is Milton's *Paradise Lost*; it is perfectly congruent (so far as these general outlines are concerned) with that found in Saint Augustine's *City of God*.

But in the late seventeenth and early eighteenth centuries another doctrine began to be heard. By analogy with previous heresies, it was sometimes known as "Pelagianism" or "Socinianism"; more often it was called "deism," "rational Christianity," or "natural religion"; it had close affinities with "philosophical optimism" and "systematic idealism." Though differently colored in each of these manifestations, the new assumption which underlay all of them consisted essentially of a tendency to deny or minimize the fall of man. Theologically it tended to resemble modern Unitarianism; but its social application (like that of many other skeptical movements)

81

was strongly conservative. One reason why it is hard to define is its transitional, provisional nature; its exponents were often trying to justify social attitudes like submission and benevolence without recourse to the theological sanctions which had been traditional. They aimed at a secular, social ethic which could be defended "by reason," i.e., without appeal to supernatural revelation, and which would therefore be universal and secure. The consequences for traditional theology were so revolutionary that it is not altogether easy to see why the new tone in philosophy won acceptance as placidly as it did. For if the entire human race did not fall with Adam, then it did not have to be redeemed by Christ, does not have to belong to the true church wherever that may be found, does not have to partake of supernatural faith, will not be judged after death and given up to salvation or damnation. Perhaps the new mood in philosophy drew tacit support from the great achievements in psychology and physics of John Locke and Isaac Newton. Having explained so much in the universe on the basis of the three laws of motion and the rational understanding of material evidence, men felt more ready to dispense with theological hypotheses. Partly too, no doubt, the way had been cleared for optimism by the great war of sects which accompanied the Puritan revolution. With fifty squabbling sects, all believing in the Bible, all interpreting it differently, and all denouncing one another as heretical, a civilized man could be excused for doubting if any of them knew a safe way to salvation—and if nobody knew, why bother? All parties to the English revolutions of 1640 and 1688 emerged from them relatively disillusioned with, and skeptical of, the social influence of the clergy —doubtful of their social wisdom, contemptuous of their social power. Under the circumstances, the separation of ethics from its previous reliance on theology seems to have appeared a thoroughly prudent and conservative step.

Whatever the reasons, one finds in eighteenth-century Europe increasing readiness to doubt man's fallen condition and to question the absolute need of supernatural revelation or inspired faith. In a familiar metaphor, God is a remote clock-maker, an artisan or an artist; the natural universe is his masterpiece; and man best fulfills the divine purpose by accepting gratefully, unquestioningly, whatever role has been assigned to him in its operation. He must not set himself up as private judge of the social forms, must not become so inflamed with the private spirit of religious enthusiasm (the pursuit of individual salvation, in other words) that he questions or rebels against the rational arrangements of society. He should submit to the rules of social convenience, even—*especially*—if they inconvenience him, in the full assurance that he is thereby fulfilling the larger will of God as well as that of man. For no religious duties are demanded of him as indispensably necessary to salvation which are incompatible with common sense and the general reason.

Inevitably, this new philosophy of social optimism and rational religion raised afresh the old question of evil. If the universe, or society, was a divinely planned unity, with an overriding welfare of its own to which individual men must conform and submit, one had to be sure it was not malfunctioning. But everyday experience showed that it did malfunction, regularly, horribly—in wars and diseases and natural catastrophes and the daily terrible toll of pointless misery and injustice. What then to do, what to think? It is this central question with which *Candide* (and in fact much of Voltaire's intellectual life) was concerned. Almost all the classic positions in the immemorial debate over the origins of evil are represented in *Candide*—represented, if not endorsed. For the better understanding of the book and its counterpointed ideas there follows a list, in rough chronological order, of these classic positions and their exponents:

1. THE MANICHEES were a sect of heretic Christians, of Near-Eastern origin, with deep pre-Christian roots. They limited the omnipotence of God by proclaiming that He ruled only half the universe. He ruled it, of course, for good, but He was incapable of controlling the operations of the Devil, who ruled, with absolute authority and for his own dark ends, the other half. The Manichees thus disposed of the origin of evil by saying that it had no origin, it had always been there in the original constitution of the universe; and they impugned one of the Christian God's most cherished attributes, his omnipotence. They flourished from the third to the fifth centuries A.D.; their reappearance in modern controversy was largely due to Pierre Bayle—see 4 below.

2. SAINT AUGUSTINE, whose *City of God* was completed in 426, is included here as a representative of orthodox Catholic Christianity; it was his view that God originally created the universe entirely good, but that owing to an original spontaneous act of Satan's will evil entered the world. God can, and someday will destroy Satan and evil altogether; meanwhile, however, man with the aid of Christ and His church is to struggle in dubious battle with the forces of darkness and to earn, as a result of his good or evil service, salvation or damnation.

3. BLAISE PASCAL, whose *Pensées* were first published in mutilated form in 1670, eight years after his death, saw the presence of evil in the world as evidence of man's radically flawed nature. Being so faulty, so limited, and so corrupt, man is unable to perceive God's justice in the world, but instead thinks it injustice and evil. Therefore he must believe in an afterlife, where justice will be done and the nature of God's earthly justice will at last be under-

stood. The very desperation of man's condition on earth constitutes a motive for him to believe in a better sphere and the possibility of a clearer vision elsewhere.

4. PIERRE BAYLE in his *Dictionnaire historique et critique* (1697) undertook to argue for religious toleration by showing that theologians had been largely unable to agree among themselves on any single version of the truth. Among the great religious questions which he described as unsolved was that of the origin of evil; having shown how most of the proposed solutions impugned either God's goodness, His intelligence, or His power, he concluded that the question was insoluble, and that the Manichees, who in effect begged it, had come closest to a solution. Bayle was one of the first modern authors to revive Manicheism from its resting-place among the forgotten heresies.

5. GOTTFRIED WILHELM VON LEIBNIZ published his *Théodicée* in 1710; he described the world as organized, according to a pre-established harmonious plan, in a series of ascending "monads" or indivisible unities, of which the highest was God. This system, having been created by the loftiest and most benevolent of minds, must be, taken as a whole, the best of all possible systems; within it, all events are linked by a chain of cause and effect, and what looks to our limited view like evil and injustice will, when the web of cause and effect is unravelled, be found to cause greater compensating goods. CHRISTIAN WOLFF (1679–1754) was Leibniz's most energetic and vociferous disciple; if he added nothing to the structure of the system, he did much to render it popularly accessible.

6. ANTHONY ASHLEY COOPER, THIRD EARL OF SHAFTESBURY, whose works were collected in three volumes under the unpromising title *Characteristics of Men, Manners, Opinions, and Societies* (1711), discounted all metaphysics and supernatural dogmas, but disliked also a certain cold, selfish pursuit of interest which he thought was inculcated by Thomas Hobbes and Locke. Instead, he tried to elaborate a system of virtue founded on natural principles and dedicated to benevolence. Suspicious of religious enthusiasm and enthusiasts, he invoked an earnest but somewhat vague optimism regarding the power of man to derive a "moral sense" from his natural instincts. Since Shaftesbury saw human nature as naturally good and naturally attuned to God, it followed that for him the world is "governed, ordered, or regulated for the best by a designing principle or mind necessarily good and permanent."

7. BERNARD MANDEVILLE published in 1704 and 1715 a *Fable of the Bees* in rough, witty doggerel verse; the second edition added a prose commentary which directly attacked Shaftesbury's doctrine of the "moral sense," arguing instead that man is inherently vicious and selfish, and that most virtues are simply well-disguised and

publicly-approved vices. We note with edification that as soon as morality is rooted in the ways of the world, clever rascals like Mandeville become better casuists than men of high-minded good will like Shaftesbury.

8. HENRY ST. JOHN VISCOUNT BOLINGBROKE was an English grandee and statesman who during the 1720's, after his return from exile in France, began to philosophize in the vein of a Shaftesbury somewhat toughened by reading Mandeville. His own work is languid and textureless, and he is best known for his influence on Pope's *Essay on Man*, much of which was written in consultation with him. Too skeptical to build a "system," he thought sensible men could reach all the truth they needed by studying natural religion without the help of the clergy. They would thus arrive at the religious view which all sensible men share (total skepticism) and which they are too sensible ever to admit.

9. ALEXANDER POPE, in his poem *Essay on Man* (1733–34), emphasized the duty of man to "submit" because "whatever is is right" and everything which seems like "partial evil" is really "universal good." In Pope's poem the principle that nature must contain a plenum, or full range of creatures from the lowest to the highest, no longer serves merely to justify the existence of creatures with various imperfections; it bears witness to God's surpassing excellence, which could only have been manifested in the full diapason of the creatures. But for man as he finds himself the lesson of submission is explicit; he cannot ask (judging matters according to his lowly "scale of sense") for greater powers or more commodity, lest he disturb the order of the universe and cast doubt on the workings of Providence. The disasters which occasionally afflict him are caused by general laws, beneficent in their overall character, at whose working in specific instances he must not repine. In asking that things be differently and more conveniently arranged, man reveals himself a creature of madness, pride, and impiety; for, given his necessary degrees of blindness and weakness, things in general are quite as good as they can be.

10. JEAN-JACQUES ROUSSEAU addressed his "Letter on Providence" to Voltaire (August 18, 1756) in response to Voltaire's poem on the Lisbon earthquake. Rousseau argued that God was not to blame for natural disasters like the earthquake, or for the presence of evil in the world. Man has brought many misfortunes on himself by crowding into cities when he should have been living naturally and safely in the country. Indeed, says Rousseau, there may have been individuals in Lisbon to whom sudden death was a blessing in disguise. In any event, Providence works, not for the benefit of this or that individual, but through general laws to which we must reverentially submit.

11. The Marquis de Sade comes too late, historically, to influence Voltaire (most of his work was published in the 1790's), but he supplies one clear terminus of the argument over evil. He accepts the two fundamental dogmas of the age, that evil exists in the world and that God is all-powerful, but he draws the unwelcome conclusion which everyone had been trying to dodge: *therefore* God is malignant and brutish, and the way for man to serve Him is to imitate Him by being as natural, as cruel, and as vicious as possible. With a single stroke of thought, de Sade escaped all the tensions of two incompatible beliefs. It would be interesting to compare him with William Blake, who also, and at the same time, but to very different effect, stood the eighteenth-century world on its head by asserting that Satanic energy was good and divine conformity evil.

VOLTAIRE

Well, Everything Is Well†

I beg of you, gentlemen, explain for me this phrase, *all is well*, I don't understand it.

Does it mean, *everything is arranged, everything is ordered*, according to the laws of moving bodies? I understand, I agree.

Or do you mean by it that everyone is well off, that he has the means of living well, that nobody suffers? You know how false that is.

Is it your idea that the lamentable calamities which afflict the earth are good, in relation to God, and please him? I don't believe this horrible idea, nor do you.

So please, explain this phrase *all is well*. Plato the philosopher deigned to allow God the freedom of creating five worlds, for the reason, as he said, that there are only five regular bodies in geometry: the tetrahedron, cube, hexahedron, dodecahedron, and icosahedron. But why restrict divine power in this way? Why not allow him the sphere, which is even more regular, and even the cone, the pyramid with various faces, the cylinder, and so on?

God chose, according to Plato, the best of possible worlds. This concept has been embraced by various Christian philosophers, though it seems repugnant to the doctrine of original sin; for our globe, after that transgression, is no longer the best of globes; it was

† Voltaire's essay appeared under the title "Bien, Tout est Bien" as an entry in the *Dictionnaire Philosophique* (1764). This large collection of Voltaire's miscellaneous thoughts had been many years in the gathering; it contained mostly articles of religious or philosophical interest, with of course a strong leaning toward skeptical rationalism. Translation by Robert M. Adams.

before, and could be again, but now plenty of people think it the worst of worlds instead of the best.

Leibnitz, in his *Theodicy*, took the part of Plato. Many a reader has complained of being able to understand one no more than the other. For our part, having read both of them more than once, we avow our ignorance, according to our custom; and since the Evangelist has revealed nothing to us on this score, we remain without regret in our shadows.

Leibnitz, who speaks of everything, has spoken of original sin as well; and as every man with a system gets into his scheme everything that contradicts it, he imagined that man's disobedience to God, and the shocking evils which ensued, were integral parts of the best of worlds, necessary ingredients of the highest possible felicity. *Calla calla señor don Carlos; todo che se haze es por su ben.*[1]

What! to be driven out of a delightful garden where one could have lived forever if one hadn't eaten an apple! What! to give birth in anguish to miserable and sinful children, who will suffer everything themselves and make everyone else suffer! What! to experience every sickness, feel every grief, die in anguish, and then in recompense to be roasted for eternity! This fate is really the best thing possible? It's not too good for us; and how can it be good for God?

Leibnitz sensed there was nothing to be said in reply; and so he made big fat books in which he confused himself.

A denial that evil exists: it can be made in jest, by a Lucullus in good health, who is eating a fine dinner with his friends and his mistress in the hall of Apollo; but let him stick his head out the window, he'll see miserable people; let him catch a fever, he'll be miserable himself.

I don't like to quote;—it's a prickly job at best, for one leaves out

---

1. The first eight paragraphs of the article as printed in the text were compressed in a later edition into the following passages:

"It made a great noise in the schools and even among thinking people, when Leibnitz, paraphrasing Plato, constructed his edifice of the best of all possible worlds and imagined that everything was for the best. He asserted, in the north of Germany, that God could make only a single world. Plato had allowed Him at least the liberty of making five, because there are only five solid regular bodies: tetrahedron, or pyramid with three faces and an equal base: cube, hexahedron, dodecahedron, and icosahedron. But as our world isn't in the shape of any one of the five bodies of Plato, one ought to allow God a sixth way of building it.

"Let's leave the divine Plato there. Leibnitz, who was certainly a better geometrician and a more profound metaphysician, did the human race this service, of letting us see that we should be very contented, and that God could not do any more for us; that he had necessarily chosen, among all the possible options, the best one conceivable.

"'What happens to original sin?' they asked him. 'Let it look after itself,' said Leibnitz and his friends; but in public he wrote that original sin necessarily entered into the best of possible worlds."

The earlier version is reprinted in the text because it makes livelier reading. The quotation in Spanish means "Peace, peace, señor don Carlos; everything which is being done is for your good"; it no doubt comes from one of a dozen or so dramas inspired by the insanity and death of unhappy Don Carlos, prince of Asturias and son of Philip II (1545–1568).

what precedes and follows one's chosen passage, and thus lies exposed to a thousand complaints. But I must cite Lactantius, father of the church, who in Chapter XIII of his treatise *On the Wrath of God* makes Epicurus talk in this fashion:[2]

> Either God wants to remove evil from the world and cannot; or he can and does not want to; or he cannot and does not want to, either one; or else, finally, he wants to and can. If he wants to and cannot, that is impotence, which is contrary to the nature of God; if he can and does not want to, that is malice, which is equally contrary to his nature; if he neither wants to nor can, that is malice and impotence at the same time; if he wants to and can (and this is the only one of the alternatives that is consistent with all the attributes of God), then where does all the evil of the world come from?

The argument is pressing; and Lactantius gets out of it very awkwardly, by saying that God wishes the evil but that he has given us the wisdom to acquire good. The answer, it must be confessed, is less potent than the objection, for it supposes that God could give wisdom only by producing evil; and thus, what a pleasant wisdom we have!

The origin of evil has always been a pit of which nobody could see the bottom. This is what reduced so many philosophers and legislators to positing two principles, one good and the other bad. Typhon was the bad principle for the Egyptians; Arimane for the Persians.[3] As is known, the Manichees adopted this theology; but as they never had conversations with either the good principle or the bad, one needn't take it on their word.

Among the absurdities with which the world is choked, and which one can include among our evils, it is not a trifling achievement to have predicated a pair of all-powerful beings fighting over which of the two should put most of himself into the world, and making a treaty like Molière's two doctors: let me have the emetic, and you can have the bleeding-cup.

After the Platonists, Basilides[4] pretended in the first centuries of the church that God had allotted the making of our world to his latest angels and that they, not being very skilful, made things as we see them. This theological fable crumbles to dust before the terrible objection that it is not in the nature of an omnipotent, omniscient

2. Epicurus is the Greek philosopher who placed the true end of life in pleasure; Lactantius, a Church father known as "the Christian Cicero," wrote his treatise *On the Wrath of God* in the early fourth century. Voltaire's skepticism was more erudite than the faith of most true believers.
3. Typhon, a mythical monstrous deity usually represented as a crocodile, was held responsible for the death and dismemberment of his brother the good Osiris; Arimane was the principle of darkness in the Zoroastrian philosophy, who opposes Mazda or Ormuzd, the god of light.
4. Basilides was a subtle Alexandrian Christian of the second century, and a celebrated gnostic.

Deity to have a world built by architects who don't know their trade.

Simon,[5] who felt the force of this objection, tried to forestall it by saying that the angel who supervised the workshop is damned for botching his work; but burning that angel does us no good.

The Greek story about Pandora meets the objection no better. The box in which all the evils are hidden, and at the bottom of which rests hope, is a charming allegory; but this Pandora was made by Vulcan only to be revenged on Prometheus, who had formed a man from clay.

The Indians have not succeeded either. God, having created man, gave him a drug to keep him healthy forever; the man loaded the drug on his donkey, the donkey got thirsty, the serpent told him of a spring, and while he was drinking, the serpent took the drug for himself.

The Syrians imagined that when man and woman were created in the fourth heaven, they decided to eat a cake instead of the ambrosia which was their natural diet. The ambrosia they could exhale through their pores; but after eating the cake, they had to go to the toilet. Man and woman together asked an angel where were the facilities.—Look ye, says the angel, see that little planet down there, no bigger than a minute, some sixty million leagues from here? That's the privy for the whole universe; now get there right away.— So they went, and were left there; and that's why, ever since, our world has been what it is.

Of course you can ask the Syrians why God let man eat the cake and allowed such a swarm of evils to follow from his doing so.

I pass quickly from this fourth heaven to Lord Bolingbroke, to keep from being bored. This man, who no doubt had a great genius, gave the celebrated Pope his idea for "all is well," which can be found word for word in the posthumous works of Lord Bolingbroke, and which Lord Shaftesbury had formerly inserted in his *Characteristics*. Read in Shaftesbury the chapter on the Moralists, and you will find these words:

> Much is alleged in answer to show why Nature errs, and how she came thus impotent and erring from an unerring hand. But I deny she errs. . . . 'Tis from this order of inferior and superior things that we admire the world's beauty, founded thus on contrarieties, whilst from such various and disagreeing principles a universal concord is established. . . . The vegetables by their death sustain the animals, and animal bodies dissolved enrich the earth, and raise again the vegetable world. . . . The central powers, which hold the lasting orbs in their just poise and movement, must not be controlled to save a fleeting form, and rescue

5. Voltaire's knowledge of that shadowy figure Simon the Samaritan probably came from Irenaeus' treatise *Against the Heretics*, I, 23.

from the precipice a puny animal, whose brittle frame, however protected, must of itself soon dissolve.

Bolingbroke, Shaftesbury, and Pope, who gave their ideas a shape, resolve the question no better than their predecessors; their *all is well* means nothing but that all is directed by unchangeable law. Who doesn't know that? You teach us nothing when you tell us, what every little child knows, that flies are born to be eaten by spiders, spiders by swallows, swallows by shrikes, shrikes by eagles, eagles to be killed by men, men to kill one another, and to be eaten by worms and then by devils—at least a thousand of them for every one who meets another fate.

There, now, is an order, neat and regular, among the animals of every species; there is order everywhere. When a stone forms in my bladder, it's an admirable mechanism; various chalky deposits assemble in my blood, pass through my kidneys, descend the urethra, and deposit themselves in my bladder, assembling there in an excellent demonstration of Newtonian attraction. The pebble forms, grows, I suffer pains a thousand times worse than death, through the most elegant arrangement in the world. A surgeon, having perfected the art invented by Tubal Cain, comes to stick a sliver of sharp steel through my perinaeum; he grasps the stone in his pincers, it breaks under the pressure by a necessary mechanism, and by the same necessity I die in horrible torments. *All this is well*, it is all the evident consequence of unalterable physical principles, I agree; and I knew it just as well as you did.

If we were insentient beings, there would be nothing to say to this physics. But that's not the question; we ask you if there are not sensible evils, and if there are, where they come from. Pope says in his Fourth Epistle, *There are no evils; if there are private evils, they compose the universal good.*[6]

This implies a remarkable definition of *private*, including the stone, the gout, all the crimes, all the sufferings of mankind, death, and damnation.

The fall of man is the plaster we put on all these individual maladies of soul and body which make up the *general health*. Shaftesbury and Bolingbroke dared to attack original sin directly; Pope doesn't talk about it; but it is clear that their system undermines the very foundations of the Christian religion, and explains nothing at all.

Yet this system has since won the approval of several theologians

---

6. The passage Voltaire paraphrases partially and inaccurately must be this one:
"What makes all physical or moral ill?/ There deviates nature, and here wanders will./ God sends not ill; if rightly understood,/ Or partial ill is universal good,/ Or change admits, or nature lets it fall,/ Short, and but rare, till man improved it all." (*Essay on Man*, IV. 111–16).

who cheerfully accept contradictions; and in fact one shouldn't grudge anyone the consolation of accounting as he can for the flood of evils that overwhelm us. It's only fair to let men who are desperately sick eat whatever they want. Some have gone so far as to pretend that the system is consoling. God, says Pope,

> sees with equal eye, as God of all,
> A hero perish, or a sparrow fall;
> Atoms or systems into ruins hurled,
> And now a bubble burst, and now a world.
> *Essay on Man*, I, 87–90

Here, I confess, is a pleasant consolation; don't you find great comfort in Lord Shaftesbury's remark that God isn't going to disturb his eternal laws for a miserable little animal like man? But you must grant this miserable little animal the right to exclaim humbly and to seek, as he exclaims, why these eternal laws are not made for the well-being of each individual.

This system of *all is well* represents the author of all nature as a potent, malicious king, who never worries if his designs mean death for four or five hundred thousand of his subjects, and poverty and tears for the rest, as long as they gratify him.

Far from consoling, the *best of all possible worlds* doctrine is a doctrine of despair for those who embrace it. The question of good and evil remains an insoluble chaos for those who seek in good faith for an answer; it's a joke only for those who debate over it, they are slave-laborers who play with their chains. As for thoughtless people, they are like fish carried from a river to a tank; they don't suspect that they are there only to be eaten next Friday. Just so, we too know nothing at all, by our unaided powers, of the causes of our destiny.

Let us put, at the end of almost all these chapters of metaphysics, the two letters that Roman judges used when they couldn't understand a case: NL, *non liquet*, it's not clear. Let us above all impose silence on the rascals who, even as they are overwhelmed, like the rest of us, by the sheer weight of human calamity, add to it the furious rage of calumny. Let us confound their execrable impostures by appealing to faith and Providence.

Some logicians have pretended that it isn't in the nature of the Being of all beings that things should be other than they are. It's an audacious assertion; I don't know enough even to dare examine it.

GUSTAVE LANSON

Voltaire at *Les Délices* and at Ferney†

Philosophers have to have two or three underground burrows to escape from the dogs that chase them.

Tavernier . . . , asked by Louis XIV why he had chosen a home in Switzerland, answered as you know: *Sire, I very much wanted to have something which belonged just to me.*[1]

—XXIX, 198.

It was with much these feelings that Voltaire, escaped fom Berlin and thoroughly scarmentado,[2] leased at Monrion, on the slope between Lausanne and the lake, a winter-house well protected from the cold north wind. And for the summers, he acquired, at a price of 87,000 francs, a property near Geneva, at Saint-Jean, which he named *Les Délices;* from it, he could see at a glance "Geneva, the lake, the Rhône, another river [the Arve], some fields, and the Alps."[3] A little later, as Monrion had neither garden nor adequate heating, he rented at Lausanne, for nine years, a large and comfortable house, with fifteen front windows looking out over the lake and the Alps of Savoy.

A delightful sense of ease and well-being pervaded his spirit. He looked with charmed eyes on the elegant yet grandiose landscape of lake and mountains; before the beauty of the Alpine countryside he recalled, with unaccustomed enthusiasm, the heroic stories of Swiss liberty. He was exalted nearly to lyricism.

But he did not fall to dreaming. Action caught him up, as soon as he felt himself safe. He built, planted, and gardened at *Les Délices.* He had his six mares serviced—vainly, alas—by a too-elderly Danish stallion. He gave dinners to all the most distinguished company of the district; he received all the notable travelers

† From Gustave Lanson, *Voltaire* (Paris: Hachette, 1906), pp. 133–46. Reprinted by permission of John Wiley & Sons, Inc. Translation by Robert M. Adams. Lanson's note gives the following references:
Longchamp et Wagnière, *Mémoires sur Voltaire et ses ouvrages*, 1825, 2 vols.; Desnoiresterres, V–VIII; Perey et Maugras, *Voltaire aux Délices et à Ferney*, 1885; Maugras, *Voltaire et Jean-Jacques Rousseau*, 1886; L. Foisset, *Voltaire et le Président de Brosses*, 1858; H. Tronchin, *Le Conseiller François Tronchin et ses amis*, 1895; E. Asse, *Lettres de Mmes. de Graffigny, d'Epinay, Suard*, etc. (sur leur séjour auprés de Voltaire), 1878; *Zeitschrift für franz. Spr. und Litt.* (Stengel, "Lettres de Voltaire et de Mme. de Gallatin au Landgrave de Hesse-Cassel"), 1887, vol. VII; *Revue de Paris*, 1905 (H. Jullemier).

1. XXXIX, 198; Best. 6519. [All references are to the Moland edition (Garnier, 1877–85); all cross-references to the Besterman edition are by the editor.]
2. From the hero of Voltaire's novel of the same name; embittered and disillusioned, Scarmentado settles down, is married, cuckolded, and happy. Used in the sense here of "back from one's travels and rather disillusioned by them" [*Editor*].
3. XXXVIII, 390; Best. 5640.

who came through Lausanne and Geneva—Palissot, Lekain, Mmes. d'Epinay and du Bocage, the English philosopher Gibbon, the Italian Jesuit Bettinelli. He took great pains to disavow *La Pucelle*,[4] overwhelmed his secretary Collini with dictation and copying chores, reworked his *Essai sur les moeurs*, wrote a Chinese tragedy,[5] disputed with Providence and Leibnitz over the Lisbon disaster, deplored the war which broke out in 1756, made up with the king of Prussia while still keeping one fang bared for him, tried to take a hand in peace negotiations, wrote to England on behalf of Admiral Byng, took service with the *Encyclopédie*, exchanged insults with Grasset, squabbled with Haller,[6] went to visit the Elector Palatine, bemoaned the Margrave of Bayreuth, prodded d'Alembert into writing for the *Encyclopedia* an article on "Geneva" full of praise for reasonable Christianity, the pure deism of the modern Calvinists, and then urged him to refuse the Genevan pastors the retraction which, for political or pious reasons they demanded.

The storm which blew up over the article on "Geneva" gave him pause for reflection. Gradually he came to sense the incompatibilities of temper and outlook between himself and the Genevans.[7] The Magnificent Council forbade the citizens and merchants to take part in, or even attend, theatrical performances at Voltaire's residences; Voltaire himself was told not to sponsor a playhouse within the borders of the Christian republic. He evaded the ruling by "playing the actor" in his house at Lausanne, or at Monrepos, estate of the Marquis of Gentil. But at Lausanne still other points of Calvinist zeal disturbed him.

He returned then to French soil. He bought, in the district of Gex a half-hour from Geneva, the estate of Fernex (he always wrote it Ferney, as it is pronounced); and he rented for life, from the Président de Brosses, the estate of Tournay. This time he was safe on all sides, with his forefeet, as he said, at Lausanne and Geneva, and his back feet at Ferney and Tournay. He could erect his stages at Ferney, and especially at Tournay, in his lobby, defying the Magnificent Council, the Consistory, and all the preachers; and if the sky looked dark over Paris or Versailles, a short ride on horseback would put him over the border, thumbing his nose at the ministry, the Parlement, and the church. Only once, in 1766, after the

4. Published in 1755, this poem was Voltaire's most disastrous failure to estimate public taste; it is a bawdy, mock-heroic poem about Joan of Arc [*Editor*].
5. *L'Orphelin de la Chine* (1755) [*Editor*].
6. François Grasset was an irresponsible bookseller and printer, who put out an inopportune collection of Voltaire's polemics; Albert von Haller, a botanist and philosopher of some distinction, was understood to have supported Grasset against Voltaire's demands for drastic punishment [*Editor*].
7. Geneva had received, under John Calvin in the sixteenth century, the tone of austere sobriety and prudence which it still, in part, retains. By the eighteenth century most of the persecuting and some of the censorious tendencies of the city had melted away, but the Consistory of preachers and the Magnificent Council of city fathers kept an eye out for evidences of flagrant scandal—in close proximity to which they usually discovered M. de Voltaire [*Editor*].

death of the Chevalier de la Barre,[8] was he seriously scared, and indulged the momentary fantasy of going off to found a colony of philosophers, a "truth factory," with a printing press in the country of Cleves which belonged to the king of Prussia.

After 1760, he resided ordinarily at Ferney, where he had built up a splendid establishment. His fortune was immense and steadily increasing. He had investments in trade, in banks,[9] at Cadiz, Leipzig, and Amsterdam. But he generally placed his liquid capital in annuities, at such profitable rates as would make his old age comfortable and keep his "complexion clear."[1] Among his debtors were noblemen of France and princes of Germany, marshal Richelieu, the Elector Palatine, and the Duke of Wurtenburg; though often careless about their payments, they were men who wound up paying in the end, with whom one lost no more than one would with Jews and bankers, and who atoned for the lateness of their payments with publicity and protection. Voltaire's bookkeeper told Collé in 1768 that his employer had 80,000 francs in annuities, 40,000 francs in income from real estate, and 60,000 francs in portfolio investments. In 1775 an authentic summary mentions 177,000 francs of income, over and above 235,000 of liquid assets.

Expenses at Ferney were enormous. The manor built by Voltaire was small but elegant. The staff was considerable; over and above the regular residents, on days when a play was produced, supper was served to sixty or eighty special guests. In 1768, after an energetic reform of his household, Voltaire established the budget for Ferney at 4,000 francs a year, for the support of a dozen horses and sixteen persons.

Habitual guests at Ferney were fat Mme. Denis,[2] who spent her time arguing and making up with her uncle,[3] the faithful secretary Wagnière, who succeeded Collini, and to whom were added, in 1763, the copyist Simon Bigex, and Father Adam, a Jesuit whom Voltaire picked up to play chess with. From 1760 to 1763, it was the great granddaughter of Pierre Corneille, little dark Marie, ugly but with big beautiful black eyes, whom he raised and supplied with a dowry;[4] later, Mlle. de Varicourt, "beautiful and good,"[5] to whom he gave no dowry because the Marquis de Villette, who married her, was rich and needed no more money.

---

8. A young man of Abbéville, the Chevalier de la Barre was accused with four others of mutilating a crucifix. He was convicted, tortured, and executed July 1, 1766; a copy of the *Philosophical Dictionary* was found in his library and burnt with his corpse [*Editor*].

9. XXXVIII, 189; Best. 5071.

1. *Memoirs of Collini*.

2. Asse, *Lettres de Mme. de Graffigny*, etc., p. 263.

3. XXXVIII, 186–87; Best. 5067.

4. Fréron, with his usual gift for malignant insinuation, spread dark rumors about the fate of Mlle. Corneille; but in fact she was the idol of the household at Ferney, and the patriarch himself took time out from his furious schedule of work to correct her themes [*Editor*].

5. Voltaire's nickname for her was "Belle et Bonne" [*Editor*].

Always some visitor was in residence at Ferney, for weeks or months; it might be the other niece, Mme. de Fontaine, with the Marquis de Florian, her second husband, and pretty little "Florianet." Or it was was cousin Daumart, musketeer to the king, or supple Ximenès, or little LaHarpe and his wife, or poor Durey de Morsan, after his ruin.[6] It might be the Duc de Villars, passionately devoted to the tragic stage.[7] A crowd of Genevans made themselves at home with Voltaire, coming and going continually between town and Ferney; they were like members of his family, rather than friends. All the Tronchins, the household of Rilliet, the two Cramers, Mme. Gallatin, Huber the clever snipper of sihouettes which sometimes infuriated the patriarch; and let's not forget "Monsieur the fornicator" Covelle.[8]

And what visitors, of every class, of every nation! Voltaire was a European curiosity, whom one simply had to see. Ferney was the spot to which free spirits and sensitive hearts made pilgrimage. Through its doors filed D'Alembert, Turgot, the Abbé Morellet, the royal musician and *valet de chambre* Laborde, the Chevalier de Boufflers, Chabanon, Grétry, the Englishmen Sherlock and Moore, the prince of Brunswick, the Margrave of Hesse, Mme. Suard, the Marquis de Villette—and so many more, one would never finish naming them.[9] It was a declaration of principles and a personal affront when the Count of Falkenstein, one day to be [the Holy Roman Emperor] Joseph II, chose *not* to go out of his way to visit Ferney.

Some of the visitors have left their impressions. They allow us to see this lean old skeleton with the sparkling eyes, wrapped in his blue dressing-gown, or else, on special days, in his full dress suit of reddish-brown velvet, with a huge wig, and lace at the wrists falling to his fingertips; cleanly, erect, dry, quick, abstemious, taking only a few cups of coffee with cream; always perishing of some ailment,

6. Durey de Morsan was a ne'er-do-well of good family, whom Voltaire salvaged from the scrap heap and housed for a while; LaHarpe was the critic and poet, who could get along with no one else, but knew Voltaire as "papa grand homme"; while the Marquis of Ximenès, though he had stolen a MS from Voltaire and been driven from the house for it, re-established himself with a set of satiric letters on the *New Heloïse*. Does not this little group of damaged derelicts remind one of Candide's collection? [*Editor*].

7. Unimportant son of a famous father, the duc de Villars was not even a good actor; Voltaire once said drily he played an impassioned rôle "like a duke and a peer of the realm" [*Editor*].

8. Something of a simpleton, Covelle was summoned before the ecclesiastical court at Geneva on charges of fornication, and condemned to beg pardon on his knees. He admitted the fact but refused to perform the public act of contrition; and for his successful act of defiance (in which he was abetted by Voltaire), he became as it were a household pet at Ferney under the title of "M. le fornicateur." All the servants announced him in this sonorous way, to whatever company; and Voltaire wrote a mock-heroic poem about his story, *The Civil Wars at Geneva* [*Editor*].

9. For all these characters and their relations with Voltaire, see Gustave Desnoiresterres, *Voltaire et la Société au XVIIIe Siècle*, in eight volumes [*Editor*].

always taking medicine, working in bed part of every day and receiving visitors there; very much the lord of the manor, conscious of his rights and his honors, a landowner to the bottom of his soul, proud of his buildings, his plantings, his herds, his church, eager to close a deal for the sale of watches or silk stockings made in his factories; lordly and gracious with the friends and vassals who celebrated his birthdays with triumphal arches, fireworks, and adulatory verses; always wild for the theater, for poetry, and for wit, a delightful talker with the gift of charming gaiety; but capricious, fantastic, irritable, a despot; generous to all who cajoled him, stingy or tricky with anyone to whom he took a dislike; peddling a hunting knife at an outrageous price, or going to law with the Président de Brosses over a few sticks of wood, which he was enraged to have to pay for; a haggler and petty bargainer, greedy and intriguing, in all affairs involving Geneva; and mad to make fun of everyone, always being bitten and biting back, dragging after him a whole swarm of enemies to whom he added at his pleasure, Fréron, La Beaumelle, Chaumeix, the Pompignans, Nonnotte, Patouillet, Larcher, Cogé;[1] never at rest, always wanting to have the last blow, whether with words or deeds, a diabolical torturer of unhappy Jean-Jacques[2] whom he would cheerfully receive in his house, blackening at every opportunity the name of the great Montesquieu,[3] whom he had defended during his lifetime, an unwearied prober after the weak spots of those he detested and sometimes of those he did not detest; not always malicious against those whom he withered under his deadly sarcasms, often reconciled by an advance or a bit of fair dealing, and so making up with Trublet, with Buffon; without rancor, even against the friends or disciples who betrayed him, who robbed him, so long as they did not brag of it; at war with the parish priest and the bishop, and highly amused to talk them into giving him absolution unintentionally;[4] not a mean man at heart, nor a stingy one; indulgent, liberal, generous to his nieces and Marie Corneille; and hospitable, rescuing, protecting, and encouraging I know not

1. Fréron we have seen before, an implacable, malicious, and skilful publicist, who never missed a chance to wound or insult Voltaire. LaBeaumelle had criticized "The Century of Louis XIV," Larcher "The Philosophy of History." Patouillet wrote as an avowed polemicist for the Society of Jesus; the Pompignans, Jean-Jacques a nobleman and Jean-Georges a bishop, were ardent supporters of the church and enemies of the philosophers. Chaumeix, Nonnotte, and Cogé were miscellaneous volunteer enemies of Voltaire. M. Charles Nisard has described, in a well-populated volume, *Les Ennemis de Voltaire* (Paris, 1853) [*Editor*].

2. Jean-Jacques Rousseau.

3. Distinguished eighteenth-century philosopher, author of the *Lettres Persanes* and *Esprit des Lois*.

4. Banned from the sacraments by the bishop of Annecy for a burlesque sermon on theft delivered from the pulpit of "his" church (it bore the inscription *Deo Erexit Voltaire*, Voltaire Built it for God), Voltaire took cruel revenge. He feigned mortal illness, and by a series of bluffs, threats, bribes, pretences, and bullyings, extorted from the parish priest an absolution for his sins to which he was not entitled and in which he did not believe. This whole game against the clergy was played in a spirit of malicious irreverence deeply humiliating to the churchmen involved [*Editor*].

how many people; reconciling Champfleur the younger with his father, paying for the journey of a little Pichon or the marriage of a
pregnant daughter in the same way as he conducted the campaign
for Calas[5] or the war against Fréron; a Paris street urchin, a brat
spoiled to the absolute limit, all self-esteem and nerves, and never,
in his follies, doing anyone else as much harm as he did himself.[6]

From his little kingdom at Ferney he exchanges truths and claw-
scratches with Frederick, whom he knows down to the ground, and
who knows him; he trades philosophy and compliments with the
Empress Catherine,[7] who perhaps pulls the wool over his eyes a bit
in the matter of Poland. He flirts with all sorts of kings and princes.
He engages in political dalliance with the court of France; he flat-
ters and teases the Pompadour[8] during her lifetime, without sus-
pecting the incurable wound he inflicted with a passing phrase in the
dedication of *Tancrède*. He draws what he can from his old and
uncertain friend, Marshal Richelieu, as also from the passing parade
of ministers; he repays them lavishly in adulation: Babet the flower-
girl—that is, Cardinal Bernis—the Duc de Choiseul, the Duc
D'Aiguillon, Maupeou, and finally Turgot, the real minister after his
heart, and the only one for whom his compliments were never in-
sincere.[9] Of all of them he asked not only protection, favors for himself, for Ferney, and for the philosophers; he wanted reforms, encouraged them, and supported them whenever they were attempted.

That is the spectacle which, from *Les Délices* and Ferney, for
twenty-three years, Voltaire displayed to a Europe alternately en-
thusiastic and scandalized, but always amused. For twenty-three
years he succeeded in this miracle, of being the news of the day, of
providing the last word, comic or serious but always unexpected,
which filled the public ear. His Easter duties and his indigestions,
Tancrède or *La Pucelle*, the adoption of Marie Corneille, a letter to
the king of Prussia, the dismissal or return of Mme. Denis, a generous effort in behalf of Calas or LaBarre, a salvo of malicious jokes

5. Jean Calas, a Protestant merchant
of Toulouse, was hideously tortured
and executed in 1762 for a crime he
did not commit; religious prejudice
was largely responsible. Voltaire undertook to rehabilitate his good name, and
in 1765, after a vigorous and skilful
campaign in which many people were
involved, the sentence was revoked
[*Editor*].
6. See *Lettres de Mme. de Graffigny*,
pp. 247–483, and Bibliothèque Natio-
nale manuscript 12 285, the notebook
of Voltaire, especially p. 21.
7. Empress Catherine II (the Great)
of Russia was a German adventuress
who, after many lofty philosophic pro-
fessions of liberalism, ruthlessly par-
titioned Poland with the help of
Frederick (also the Great) in 1772.

8. Madame de Pompadour was the
mistress of Louis XV, but also the
most influential and best informed of
his ministers. Voltaire had said "If
some censorious person disapproves of
the homage I render you, he must have
been born with a hard, ungrateful
heart." Some poison-pen letter writer
at court told Mme. de Pompadour that
the mere supposition implied disrespect,
and she believed it [*Editor*].
9. Of these various ministers of Louis
XV, the duc de Choiseul and Turgot
were the most consistently sympathetic
to the party of the philosophers. Cardinal Bernis was known as "Babet la
Bouquetière" because of some dainty
verses he had indiscreetly made in his
youth [*Editor*].

on LaBeaumelle or Jean-Jacques, all the flowers of good sense and humanity, all the stenches of filth and impiety—he was capable of all this; and of this amazing mixture he emitted something every day, and never the same thing two days in a row. For twenty-three years, Voltaire's was the noisiest toy trumpet in Europe.

No doubt noise was agreeable to him and popular applause necessary. He never worried if there was a little contempt in the laughter of the gallery; he had never donned the stiff armor of moralism, the shell of dignity which makes the vainest and most ambitious of men preserve the postures of decorum. Having the glories of wit and beneficence, he did not disdain those won by contortions and grimaces. But in all his harlequinades he had his idea, which never quitted him any more than his self-esteem. He wanted to improve the social order. After 1755, and above all from 1760 to his death, one may say he never wrote a single page which did not criticize an abuse or propose a reform, which is not an appeal to the government or the public against one and for the other. At eighty years of age, he was as violent in his feelings as at sixty. One must be blind with prejudice not to sense the profound and disinterested conviction which lies behind his principal attitudes.

He had returned from Germany at the moment when the enlightened nation, despairing at last of the king and the court, was becoming impatient before the problem of social evil; when the war-machine of the *Encyclopédie*,[1] around which free thought organized itself into a party, was just being mounted; when, alongside the old religious factions (Jansenists and defenders of the bull *Unigenitus*)[2] groups of men were forming with the intention of expanding enlightenment and contributing to the general welfare—philosophers, economists, *patriots*; when all the individual voices of reason and liberty were certain of rousing widespread echoes in every state and province; when men who had the gift of expression felt themselves more and more lifted to the forefront by it, drawn by the crowd which was ready to hear them.

The forces of conservatism were powerful; more than the court, irregular and erratic, the Sorbonne and the Parlement of Paris opposed to "reason" a resistance of which the principal episodes were the condemnation of the thesis of the Abbé of Prades (1752), the condemnation of *L'Esprit des Lois* (1758), the condemnation of

1. The immense project of writing a new encyclopedia of human knowledge, which originated with a cartel of Paris booksellers, brought together all the liveliest pens in France, and provided a rallying-point for the party of the *philosophes*. But if it was actually a war-machine (the phrase was originated by Desnoiresterres), the *Encyclopédie* was such a cumbersome, many-handed, ill-directed machine that a full and adequate history of its operation has yet to be written. Voltaire's relations with the apparatus have been studied by Raymond Naves, *Voltaire et l'Encyclopédie* (Paris, 1938) [*Editor*].

2. Clement XI promulgated this bull on September 8, 1713; it declared heretical more than a hundred doctrines [*Editor*].

Emile (1762), the suppression and suspension of the *Encyclopédie* (1752 and 1758), and the censure of *Bélisaire* (1767).[3]

Voltaire threw himself furiously into the fight. He is "the man who laughs at all the trifling stupidities and tries to correct those which are cruel."[4] Disillusioned himself, he wanted to disillusion other people; and he boiled with impatience at the idea that progress might well take two or three hundred years to achieve.[5] He fought, by no means heroically, but stubbornly, seeking to obtain the maximum results with the minimum risk. He knew the terrain as well as the enemy, and showed himself a wonderful tactician.

He knew that neither immunity nor tacit permission was to be expected. Underground printing, in France or abroad, and above all in Geneva, saved him the bother of dealing with censors, but it brought close to him all the dangers of smuggling and dealing fraudulently in forbidden merchandise. Serious punishments were decreed for authors, booksellers, and traffickers in forbidden books. The latter were almost the only ones ever caught, and for these poor devils it was chains, the galleys, and the branding-iron. The writer who got himself caught might be let off with a humiliating retraction; but it would have been imprudent to count on this resource.

Voltaire took cover. His position on the border, supplemented by anonymity, pseudonyms, and categorical denials of authorship, kept him safe. Formal justice paused before denials which never deceived the public and often amused it.

To block the men of ill-will and prevent the *lettres de cachet*[6] which were always possible, to ensure a free circulation for his pamphlets, he cultivated friendships at court—Bernis and Choiseul, Richelieu, Villars, and LaVallière—and made use of them to cool off the zeal of their subordinates. He scarcely needed Malesherbes, director of the Louvre library and the censorship; but he tried to stand well with police lieutenants, postal inspectors, district supervisors, and undersecretaries. The postal official Damilaville, first secretary of the twentieth precinct, maintained for some years a correspondence with Ferney as one of the curiosities of the postal service. Finally, Voltaire had as accomplices the entire public, all travelers returning from abroad, the ambassadors and their staffs, the officers of the army, who arrived at Paris with suitcases full of Voltaire's "scandal-sheets"[7] even before "the man named Huguet and the

3. In all these controversies the party of repression was the Church, particularly the Jesuit wing of it, acting against the "philosophes" and their friends. For a compact history of these events, see Léon Cahen, *Les querelles religieuses et parlementaires sous Louis XV* (Paris, 1913) [*Editor*].
4. XLIII, 104; Best. 10830.
5. XXV, 344, 318; XXVI, 95.
6. *Lettres de cachet* could be obtained

from the king, upon presentation to him of a grievance or an alleged grievance; the recipient was ordered forthwith to jail, house arrest, or exile. No process of law protected the victim [*Editor*].
7. Gustave Lanson, "Quelques Documents Inédits" in *Annales de la Société Jean-Jacques Rousseau, I* (Genève, 1905), 129.

woman known as Léger"[8] had received their supply for clandestine distribution.

As long as he had the public on his side, he was sure to get around all the spiritual and temporal powers. And this public, he knew how to get hold of it; a public intelligent and fickle, inquisitive and sophisticated, whom one trifle would displease and another trifle amuse, a public with a narrow and delicate taste, with a short attention-span, which one must constantly catch and intrigue. Every single day for twenty-three years he served up to it the sauce of wit, satire, jokes, and smut with which it was necessary to season his ideas.

Above all, he wrote clear, short, and quick. No more big works. Little twelve-page tracts, leaflets a couple of pages long. "Twenty volumes in folio," he said, thinking of the *Encyclopédie*," will never make a revolution; it's the little pocket-volumes at thirty cents apiece that have to be watched. If the New Testament had cost 4,200 sesterces, the Christian religion would never have taken root."[9] These "little pot-pies," these portable scandal-sheets, easy to read, and continuously exciting, came out of the factory at Ferney for twenty-three years; they emerged in all forms, on all subjects, in verse, in prose, dictionaries, stories, tragedies, diatribes, extracts on history, literature, metaphysics, religion, the sciences, politics, legislation, Moses, snails, Shakespeare, and notes written by a gentleman. In reality, dearly as he prized the arts of literature and poetry, they became nothing more for him than a means to an end. Tragedies and verses served to hasten the spread of his ideas.

He repeated himself, he went over the same ground again and again. He was aware of it, and started the same old ideas on still another round. For he knew that ideas enter the public mind only by dint of repetition. But the seasoning must be varied, to prevent disgust; and at that art he was a past master.

He has all the qualities, with many of the faults, of the journalist, above all the gift of the immediate, and the penetrating voice which carries and fixes our attention through the noisy confusion of life. But it is not enough to say Voltaire is a journalist; all by himself he is a journal, a great journal. He does the whole thing himself, the serious articles, the spot-reporting, the gossip column, the funny-papers, the crossword puzzles. He is a journal, but also a review, an encyclopedia; all the jobs of popularization, propaganda, polemic, and information fall together in his hands. This quick old man is a a whole press, a complete popular library.

Finally, by means of his innumerable letters, which reached peo-

8. Huguet and Léger, denominated in contemporary police papers as suspected distributors of subversive books, were respectively a bookseller living in the Temple and the wife of a bookbinder living in the Rue Chartière [*Editor*].
9. XXXXIII, 520; Best. 12362.

ple of every rank and every nation—the king of Prussia, the Empress Catherine, German princes, Russian or Italian gentlemen, English thinkers, ministers, courtiers, provincials, judges, comedians, abbés, men of letters, administrators, merchants, lawyers, women of the world—by these thousands of letters, of which there is not so to speak one which does not contain a compliment to the addressee's self-esteem, a joke for his amusement, and a thought for him to mull over, Voltaire interested I know not how many individuals in the success of his propaganda. He made them carriers, voluntary and uncontrollable, of his ideas. He strengthened, he doubled, by means of his correspondence, the effect of his pamphlets.

ANDRÉ MORIZE

[The "Moment" of *Candide* and the Ideas of Voltaire]†

Here is Voltaire, on his return from England, once more in contact with the libertine, intelligent, and pleasure-loving society of Paris; next he is seen in his studious retreat at Cirey, in quarters where he enjoys the comforts for which he has paid: lacquers and porcelains, and gilt-ware of Germain; a well-stocked medicine-chest; friendship, and love. Life is good to him, and very sweet; his epicureanism is that of a refined follower of Saint-Evremond, who has been introduced at Ninon's, and at the Temple.[1] Like the gentle Bernier,[2] he inclines to the view that "abstinence from pleasures may well be a sin," and holds that, despite the theologians who denounce and the moralists who declaim, one must accept the progress which has placed commerce, the arts, and industry in the service of man's needs and pleasures. "Oh the good time, this age of iron!"[3] Letters, bits of verse, epistles, and madrigals all breathe this light optimism, compounded of carelessness, gaiety, and the joy of life. It is the age of *Le Mondain, The Man of the World.*[4]

It is also the period of scientific studies and of "Newtonianism."

† From the "Introduction" to Professor Morize's critical edition of *Candide* (Paris: Hachette, 1913, reissued 1931, 1957). Reprinted by permission of the Société des Textes Français Modernes. Translation by Robert M. Adams.
1. Saint-Evremond (1610–1703) was a disciple of Gassendi the epicurean, a wit, a rake, and a freethinker. Voltaire had been introduced to Ninon de Lenclos (famous for her practical epicureanism) when he was eleven and she

eighty-five; he had also been invited, as a youthful prodigy, to gay banquets at the old Temple de Paris [*Editor*].
2. François Bernier (1625–1688), philosopher, doctor, and traveler; an early disciple of Gassendi and exponent of neo-epicureanism [*Editor*].
3. *Le Mondain*, line 21 [*Editor*].
4. Cf. G. Lanson, *Voltaire* (Hachette, 1906) Chapters I–II; A. Morize, *L'Apologie du Luxe au XVIIIe siècle: Le Mondain et ses sources* (1909).

Voltaire rereads Pope, writes the *Discours en Vers sur l'Homme* and *Eléments de la Philosophie de Newton*. From both directions he absorbs the idea of the admirable arrangement of the universe, the great chain of things and beings. Thus, reinforcing the "practical" and realistic optimism of *Le Mondain*, there is this other optimism, scientifically grounded and English in its origins. The rather slack affirmations of the *Traité de Métaphysique* (1734) limit without negating it. There is evil in the world, and Leibnitz is wrong not to recognize it; but there is also good. One can always hope for realistic improvement; on any terms, life is possible and acceptable; evil is a necessary part of the general mechanism, and must be seen as such, without bitterness or revolt. Voltaire at this moment is not far from believing in freedom of the will. No doubt, in the *Eléments*, the objections "terrify" him, and he knows that one can only reply to them with "a vague eloquence"; still, he cannot make up his mind to give up freedom of the will, and clings, at least, to the word *liberty*.[5]

But years pass, and with their passing come experience, reflection, a sharper critical mind, a less vital flow of the life force. Voltaire reaches the age of fifty. The deals and tricks of power, the pain of exile and persecution, the loss of a philosophic mistress and the end of his happy life at Cirey—all these things embitter and sadden him, troubling his thoughts. He no longer inhabits the "earthly paradise" of Cirey; that is the most brutal blow of life at its most malign. Objections arise, press forward, thrust themselves upon him. Freedom of the will? Insoluble problem, where the wisest of men "are like Milton's devil, scrambling through chaos."[6] One minute more, one step further, and Voltaire, renouncing his dreams, will give himself over to radical negations. "I had a great desire to think we are free; I did all I could to believe it. Experience and reason convinced me that we are machines, made to run for a certain time, as it pleases God."[7] Besides, this is the period in which, as we have seen, his final rejection of metaphysics takes form: "What is the soul? I know nothing of it . . . Vanity of vanities, and metaphysical vanity!"[8] But he no longer adds, nowadays: "It is a strange madness, that of some gentry who absolutely prefer that we should be miserable!" There is evil on the earth, evil both physical and moral, and one must be resigned to it: "Everything is dangerous here on earth, and everything is necessary."[9] Jesrad, the Leibnitzian angel, teaches Zadig the necessity of evil and the need for resignation. "But what's this, said Zadig, it's necessary

5. See G. Lanson, *Voltaire*, pp. 66–67, and G. Pellissier, *Voltaire philosophe*, p. 56 *seq*.
6. Letter to Helvétius c. January 20, 1738; Best. 1368.

7. XXXVI, 565; Best. 3349.
8. XXXVI, 65 to S'Gravesende (1 August, 1741); Best. 2359.
9. *Zadig*, "L'Hermite."

then that there should be crimes and miseries? and that the miseries
fall on good people?. . . . There is no evil, Jesrad replied, from
which a good does not spring. . . . But, said Zadig, if there were only
good and no evil?"[1] The optimism of 1736 is singularly wise and
placid. God, says a poem to Frederick,

> Has two great barrels, whence both ill and good
> Fall like eternal rain, a ceaseless flood,
> On many varied worlds, and on each beast. . . .[2]

To deny evil is a puerility. But then must one turn to a pessimistic
view of the universe? It would be blind folly and ingratitude, and in
an important page, dated 1752, Voltaire fixes his attitude upon the
question. Maupertuis had picked up the old argument of the corruption of the age; look, he had said, and you will find everywhere
lies, murders, and thefts, everywhere vice will be found more common than virtue. Voltaire answered him, and one sees here that the
reflections of the last fifteen years have not made him renounce his
faith in the general welfare and in progress. No doubt, there is evil;
but, strike a fair balance, and the right conclusion will be apparent:
"This ancient, threadbare objection does not have as much force as
various people have thought. It is very untrue that men are more
frequently robbed and murdered than left in free possession of their
property and their lives. Visit a thousand villages, you will not find
ten murders and ten thefts in a century. In London, Rome, Constantinople, and Paris, there are no more than ten murders a year.
There are years when none occur at all. After the great plagues,
wars are the worst killers; but out of the hundred thousand inhabitants of Europe, over a century war causes the death of no more
than a thirtieth part of the males, who are replaced each year by a
new generation. When one examines these commonplaces carefully,
one sees that in fact *there is much more good than evil on the
earth.* One sees clearly enough that these reproaches which are continually addressed to Providence come only from the secret delight
men have in complaining, and that they are much more impressed
with the evils from which they suffer than with the advantages they
enjoy. History, which is full of tragic events, generally does a great
deal to spread the idea that there is incomparably more evil than
good; but people don't reflect that history is merely the representa-
tion of great events, the quarrels of kings and nations. It takes no
account of the ordinary condition of men. *This ordinary condition
is one of quiet and security in society.* There is no city in the world
which has not existed in tranquillity twenty times longer than it has
spent undergoing seditions. *This ancient, wornout question of
moral and physical evil should only be revived when one has some-*

---

1. *Ibid.*   2. **X**, 361, "To the King of Prussia"
                                    (1751).

thing new to say of it."[3] Comes the catastrophe at Lisbon, and on that day there will be "something new"; on that day too Voltaire will speak up, and using this revived text will pronounce his sermon.

But one must not exaggerate the influence of the Lisbon disaster on the evolution of Voltaire's ideas; it was an occasion, a "topic," it was not the crisis, the upheaval, the conversion. For, from around 1752 until the *Poème* of 1756, one notices a deep and silent transformation, a slow but decisive turn toward pessimism. I even think there would be no paradox in maintaining that Voltaire's pessimism is more discouraged, more despondent, before than after 1756, and that in the conclusion of *Candide* there is more energy and hope than in various letters of 1754.

Around him, Voltaire sees the suffering and injustice caused by fate and by men. "It's one of nature's prodigalities; she is extravagant with evils; a swarm of them appear from the tiniest seed."[4] Or again, all life is badly planned; "destiny plays with poor human beings as with tennis balls"[5] and "amid these stormy days which we call our life,"[6] "miseries pour down on every side."[7] Here he is, "nearly of the same opinion as those who think an evil genie bundled this nether world together."[8] Everywhere, human stupidity and heavenly cruelty: "How stupid and petty this mid-eighteenth-century is!"[9] During the whole year of 1754 this pessimistic note grows stronger and darker. "I see hardly anything agreeable; let us endure life, Madame; once upon a time we enjoyed it," says he, with a melancholy reflection on the time when he was writing apologies for luxury. The trouble is that "all the illusions fly away, as soon as one has lived a while. . . . Destiny derides us and carries us off. Let's live as much as we can and as best we can. Let's try . . . . Let's try. . . . What a word! Nothing depends on us; we are clocks, machines."[1] Pessimism and fatalism go together: "big news is usually bad";[2] on all sides he sees nothing but disasters in the world,[3] he "finds both hemispheres the height of the ridiculous,"[4] and judges, like the Manichee Martin, that "the devil is mixed up in all societies, from kings to philosophers."[5] Destiny controls everything, we are nothing but puppets[6]—as will be the heroes of *Candide*, philosophers, kings, slaves, travelers, monks, whores. And isn't this the very tone of the conclusion to *Candide*, appearing in a letter to an unknown correspondent and written before the news from Lisbon: "Destiny plays with men, who are noth-

3. XXII, 536, "Extract from the *Bibliothèque raisonnée*" (July 1752).
4. XXXVIII, 36; Best. 4670.
5. XXXVIII, 115; Best. 4845.
6. XXXVIII, 119; Best. 4855; also pp. 133, 184; Best. 4898 and 5061.
7. XXXVIII, 133; Best. 4898.
8. XXXVIII, 149; Best. 4950.

9. XXXVIII, 158; Best. 4987.
1. XXXVIII, 233; Best. 5209.
2. XXXVIII, 222; Best. 5176.
3. XXXVIII, 263; Best. 5282.
4. XXXVIII, 273; Best. 5303.
5. XXXVIII, 301; Best. 5380.
6. XXXVIII, 361; Best. 5559.

ing but moving atoms pushed hither and thither according to the general law of motion, which scatters them under the great shock of the world's events, a law they can neither foresee nor prevent nor understand. . . . I wish for you, Madame, happiness, if there is such a thing, or at least tranquility, insipid as it is."[7]

It is possible to see some of the sources of this pessimism: the Providence which Voltaire will no longer admit of in his metaphysics he now wishes to exclude from history. He has cast a sweeping glance over the annals of humanity, the "thoughts and customs" of nations, and has found there neither consolation for the present nor hope for the future. Out of all his researches for the *Essai sur les mœurs*, that profound plunge into the past of races, nations, religions, and systems, he has derived only disgust and skepticism. "It is a vast picture doing little honor to the human race,"[8] a portrait of the horrors of ten centuries,[9] it is atrocities and stupidities.[1] Nobody knows the degree to which the human race is dumb and mean,[2] and he thinks he has not succeeded in showing "the learned sufficiently silly, the statesmen sufficiently mean, or nature sufficiently crazy."[3] The *Essai sur les mœurs* will be "the madhouses of the universe," and as for the universe itself, it is only "a vast scene of brigandage, given over to the laws of accident." [4]

This impression is exactly the one which emerges from *Candide*, and to tell the truth it does not appear that the Lisbon earthquake was needed to set the tone, the intention, the emotional pitch of the novel. In fact, for the inspiration of the whole, as well as of the details, it is less close to the *Poème sur Lisbonne* than to the *Essai sur les mœurs*; and the catastrophe of November 1st, far from being the "sufficient reason" of the work, is really only an episode in its growth.[5]

The disaster is merely, for Voltaire, an additional bit of evidence in his developing argument against the idea of Providence; there is nothing in his philosophical development at this point which resembles an about-face; but for the public, for the facile people "who dance and who sing," Lisbon was an admirable preparative for hearing those melancholy truths to which Voltaire was already attuned. The "all's well" optimism, the idea of pre-established harmony, the

7. XXXVIII, 494; Best. 5775.
8. XXXVIII, 502; Best. 5908.
9. XXXIX, 161; Best. 6433.
1. XXXIX, 189; Best. 6497.
2. XXXIX, 217; Best. 6577.
3. XXXIX, 207; Best. 6560.
4. XIII, 140, *Essai sur les mœurs*.
5. Let us note, besides, that independently of the Lisbon disaster, earthquakes in general are a traditional objection. Voltaire found some in Pope: "But errs not Nature from this gracious end,/ From burning suns when livid deaths descend,/ When earthquakes swallow, or when tempests sweep,/ Towns to one grave, whole nations to the deep?" (*Essay on Man*, I, 141–44); "Shall burning Aetna, if a sage requires,/ Forget to thunder, and recall her fires?/ On air or sea new motions be imprest,/ Oh blameless Bethel! to relieve thy breast?/ When the loose mountain trembles from on high,/ Shall gravitation cease, if you go by?" (*Essay on Man*, IV, 123–28). It is the logic of Pangloss at Lisbon.

great chain of being, the perfection of the organized universe, all take on a new meaning, a tragic irony; from the first day, the first allusion, Voltaire has his line of argument: "People will be hard put to explain how the laws of motion bring about such frightful disasters in the best of all possible worlds; a hundred thousand ants, our neighbors, wiped out at one stroke in this single ant-hill, and half of them perishing no doubt in indescribable agonies amid ruins from which they could not be dragged; families ruined at the ends of Europe, the fortunes of a hundred traders of your country buried in the ruins of Lisbon—what a terrible gamble is the game of human life!"[6] ". . . If Pope had been at Lisbon, would he have dared to say, *All is well?*[7] ". . . This *All is well* of Mathew Garo and Pope is a bit crazy."[8] ". . . There is a terrible argument against optimism."[9] ". . . Are you aware that on the 21st of December there was a new earthquake at Lisbon, which caused the death of seventy-eight persons? Some optimism, all that!"[1] Such is the tone of more than twenty letters: no astonishment, as before an unexpected event which overthrows acquired notions and adopted opinions; at this moment, Voltaire could not be less of an optimist suddenly stripped of his creed; he is a pessimist who has been vindicated.

On December 16, 1755, the *Poème sur le Désastre de Lisbonne* was printed; in March, Voltaire issued a larger edition, with "handsome notes, of great interest to the curious,"[2] and the "sermon" was distributed, meeting with resounding success. Its conclusions are simple and its philosophy not very deep; the catastrophe raises directly the question of good and evil. What must one think of it? admit two principles? believe that everything is well? The philosophers offer *a priori* solutions, metaphysical and absolute. The optimism of Pope and Leibnitz is nothing but a discouraging fatalism; physical and moral reality give it the lie direct. To go about telling the victims of Lisbon, as Pangloss will do, that everything is well and conforms to the universal reason, is to make a mockery of them, and to show oneself incapable of human pity. Evil exists, and a just God exists, and yet we must reconcile these two contradictory principles. "Why then do we suffer under a just master?"[3] What to think? Revolt, bluster, abase oneself without understanding, persist in affirmations which one cannot believe? No, but let the metaphysicians talk, keep one's eyes open to evil, and *hope*; only thus are life and thought possible. There is evil everywhere in the universe at present, but perhaps, with the passage of time, the domain of evil

6. XXXVIII, 511; Best. 5933.
7. XXXVIII, 512; Best. 5939.
8. XXXVIII, 513; Best. 5942. Mathew Garo is a simpleton in La Fontaine who is always wrong; the Fable of the Acorn and the Pumpkin shows how he learns that everything is in its right place, and pumpkins shouldn't grow on oak trees (IX, 4) [*Editor*].
9. XXXVIII, 513; Best. 5941.
1. XXXVIII, 513; Best. 6031.
2. XXXIX, 30; Best. 6159.
3. *Poème sur le Désastre de Lisbonne*, line 78.

will be somewhat abridged. *Everything is well right now,* that is the dream, the illusion, the fraud; *things will be better, things may be well enough tomorrow,* that is a healthy and revivifying hope.[4]

Such is the conclusion of the poem, and the affirmation without discouragement, at which Voltaire paused when the Lisbon disaster led him to give full expression to the pessimistic thoughts which had been occupying him for the last five or six years. Such too will be the tone of *Candide*'s conclusion; if we must "cultivate our garden," it is because all is not lost, we can still hope for a harvest.[5]

---

4. See IX, 465 and 468 (Preface to the *Poème*): "The author is not at war with the illustrious Pope, whom he has always admired and loved; he thinks like him on almost all points; but, struck with the miseries of mankind, he has risen up against the abuses inflicted on that ancient axiom, *all is well.* He adopts this melancholy and still more ancient slogan, *that there is evil on the face of the earth;* and he declares that the saying *all is well,* taken in an absolute sense and without hope for future improvement, is nothing less than an insult to the miseries of our life." See also lines 218–219 of the poem itself: " 'One day things may be well,'—so all profess;/ But that they're well right now—is foolishness."
5. Did the intervention of J.-J. Rousseau have an influence on the genesis of *Candide?*—Let us first set forth the facts. Voltaire wrote the *Poème sur le Désastre de Lisbonne* and asked Thieriot to "be so good as to send copies to Messrs. d'Alembert, Diderot, and Rousseau" (XXXIX, 51; Best. 6203). Thieriot did so: "I sent the three copies of your fine sermon to the three doctors, Diderot, d'Alembert, and Rousseau. It was M. Duclos himself who asked me particularly to send it to Rousseau, so that he might by good fortune get a look at it while there (*Review of Literary History,* 1908, p. 41; Best. 6244). Thus it was Voltaire himself who sent Jean-Jacques the *Poème,* contrary to what Maugras has said (*Voltaire and Jean-Jacques Rousseau,* pp. 45–55). Jean-Jacques replied to the gift on August 18th, 1756 with his long *Letter on Providence* (Best. 6289), and awaited the response of Voltaire; he had sent the letter through Doctor Tronchin, who was the more gratified to perform this service because the doctrine of the *Poème* had shocked him, and he had begged Voltaire to burn it (see Henry Tronchin, "Rousseau et le Docteur Tronchin" in *Annales de J.-J. Rousseau,* I [Genève, 1905], pp. 29–30, also Rousseau, *Correspondance,* ed. Dufour, II, 324–25). "I hope," he wrote to Rousseau, "that he will read your fine letter carefully. If it produces no effect, the reason will

be that at sixty it is hard to be cured of ailments which began at eighteen" (Streckeisen-Moultou, *J.-J. Rousseau His Friends and Enemies* [Paris, 1865] I, 324). In fact, Voltaire did not answer, he hedged and evaded; his niece was sick, so was he, overwhelmed with work, he would answer, but later, when he had more time. . . . Jean-Jacques accepted or pretended to accept the excuse, and declared himself "charmed with the answer of M. de Voltaire" (H. Tronchin, *loc. cit.*); later, he began to suspect evasions and deceits, and declared that the real answer to his letter, the attack he was expecting, came in *Candide* (see *Confessions,* IX, in *Œuvres,* ed. Hachette, VIII, 308). "Since then, Voltaire has published this reply, which he had promised me but never sent. It is no other than the novel *Candide,* of which I cannot speak since I have not read it." See also the letter of March 14, 1764 to the Prince of Wurtemburg: "You are surprised that my *Letter on Providence* did not prevent the genesis of *Candide.* On the contrary, it was the letter which caused it to be born; *Candide* is an answer to it" (*Œuvres,* XI, 123).

Nothing supports this statement, and there seems no reason to give the *Letter on Providence* a privileged position. To be sure, though it cannot have made Voltaire reflect, it may have irked him. With a cleverness just the least bit tricky, Rousseau drew a contrast between Voltaire, happy, rejoicing in all the pleasures of the world and the spirit, yet pessimistic—and Jean-Jacques, "poor, unhappy, and adoring the divine goodness." This irritation shows through the casual and impertinent note of September 12, in which Voltaire dodged the problem of an answer. We must look at the whole situation: between the *Poème* and *Candide* a thousand things accumulate and combine to prepare for the sudden birth of the terrible novel—personal experiences, readings, conversations, reflections, rancors, bad news from the four corners of the globe. All these things aggravate the pessimism of Voltaire; and at the same time, he is settling into new quarters, among the tulips, arbors, and gardens, the

From one work to the other stretches an unbroken train of thought. The metaphysical questions to which Voltaire returned[6] with skepticism while he was writing the *Poème sur Lisbonne*—liberty, future contingencies, the great chain of linked destinies, the origin of evil—find their echo in the *Dialogue entre un Bramin et un Jésuite*[7] and the *Dialogue entre Lucrèce et Posidone*.[8] In pronouncing his "lamentations" and preaching his "sermon," Voltaire was serious and grave; now he is amusing himself, and we watch the sharpening of that special irony which derives its point from the technical terms of philosophy, and which will be the mode of *Candide*:

"—I shall always think the horrible action of Ravaillac[9] one of those future contingencies which might very well not have happened, for in fact. . . .

—Eh, what's going to become of future contingencies? said the Jesuit.

—They'll become what they can, said the Brahmin."

Then, month after month, as bad news continues to engulf Voltaire—news of the war, of business losses, of his friends— he repeats: "Optimism and *all's well* are getting some rude shocks in Sweden."[1] ". . . Here's twenty thousand men dead already in this quarrel, in which not a one of them had any real interest. That's another one of the charms of this best of possible worlds. What miseries, what horrors!"[2] ". . . Ah, this best of all possible worlds, isn't it also the craziest?"[3] He measures the distance which separates his present temper from the joyous philosophy of former years. "After having spoken at sufficient length about the pleasures of the world, I have begun to hymn its griefs; without being wise, I have done like Solomon, I have seen that nearly everything is vanity and affliction, and that there is certainly evil on the face of the earth."[4] This correspondence of 1756–1759 should be read in its

happy landscape of *Les Délices* and Ferney. In this period of preparation, the business of Rousseau's letter is an incident to be noted, and nothing more.
6. The same preoccupation recurs in a fragment which Voltaire in 1756 added at the end of the 22nd *Lettre philosophique*: "The basis for Pope's *Essay on Man* is found, complete, in the *Characteristics* of Lord Shaftesbury, and I don't know why Pope gives the credit exclusively to M. de Bolingbroke, without saying a word of the celebrated Shaftesbury, pupil of Locke. . . . As everything pertaining to metaphysics has already been thought in every age and among every nation which cultivates its brains, this system has much in common with that of Leibnitz, who pretends that of all the possible worlds God has chosen the best, and that in

this "best" it is necessary that the irregularities of the world and the idiocies of its inhabitants should find a place. It resembles also that idea of Plato's that in the infinite chain of being, our earth, our body, and our soul are all necessary links. . . ." *Lettres Philosophiques*, ed. G. Lanson (Paris, 1909) II, 139; compare *Candide*, Chapter III.
7. XXIV, 53 *seq.* (1756).
8. XXIV, 57 *seq.* (1756).
9. Ravaillac assassinated Henri IV in 1610 [*Editor*].
1. XXXIX, 101; Best. 6292.
2. XXXIX, 121; Best. 6333.
3. XXXIX, 128; Best. 6360.
4. XXXIX, 41. Compare the *Poème sur Lisbonne* (IX, 748): "I once was heard, in less despairing measures,/ To sing the joyous laws of dulcet pleas-

entirety; from day to day, Voltaire has the feeling—almost obsessive, it would seem—that everything around him is going badly, that things are topsy-turvy, that madness looms, that across Paris, Europe, and the entire world a fierce wind of criminal insanity is blowing. The war drags on and spreads out, Byng is executed, the king's life attempted; parliament men gobble up churchmen and are excommunicated by them; Fréron raves on, and Frederick betrays. "I know only that Englishmen have heads of oak and hearts of stone, that Germany will be reduced to a shambles, that Paris is wretched, that money is scarce, and life is no bed of roses."⁵ At Paris, he reports, "people are absolutely insane";⁶ nothing, he thinks, could be "more insane and more atrocious than our ridiculous age."⁷ A subtlety here, to be underlined: Voltaire talks less and less of tragedy, more and more of the ridiculous; the universe is less sombre than insane, and human existence, taken as a whole, less melancholy than naïvely comic. Life is an immense stage play which has to "be seen from a good box seat, where we are very much at our ease."⁸ And this, then, is the hour no longer of philosophical meditations and metaphysical discussions, but of stinging sarcasms and short bursts of laughter, in which irony mingles with skepticism—the hour of *Candide*.⁹

ures./ New times, new ways; old age has made me see/ And share the griefs of weak humanity./ Lost in the gloomy night, by stars unlit,/ All I can do is suffer and submit."
5. XXXIX, 188; Best. 6494.
6. XXXIX, 170; Best. 6449.
7. XXXIX, 189; Best. 6497.
8. XXXIX, 202; Best. 6529.
9. One could multiply texts to infinity. See for example (XXXVIII, 556; Best. 6066) the letter of February 28, 1756 to Elie Bertrand: "The question centers, then, precisely on this axiom, or rather on this joke, *All is well, all is as it should be, and the present general happiness results from the present evils of each creature.* Now this is completely ridiculous. . . . Men of all ages and all religions have felt so sharply the misery of human nature, that they have all declared the work of God has been changed. Egyptians, Greeks, Persians, Romans, all have imagined something close to the fall of man. It must be confessed that Pope's poem destroys that truth, and my little work leads us back to it; *for if all is well, there is no fallen nature.* On the other hand, if evil is abroad in the world, that evil points to a past act of corruption, and a reparation to come, etc. *Optimism is despair;* it is a cruel philosophy under a consoling name." Or again: "*All's well* seems very silly to me, when there is evil on the face of the earth—and the ocean too" (XXXVIII, 543; Best.

6110). ". . . Things are happening at this moment which seem to us very shocking, very sad; but read the history of other centuries, and you will find things still worse. Every age has had its public miseries" (XXXIX, 151; Best. 6416). ". . . Today's horrors don't leave one time enough to read about yesterday's" (XXXIX, 173; Best. 6456). ". . . This world is one great shipwreck; every man for himself" (XXXIX, 210; Best. 6565). ". . . The best of possible worlds has been pretty ugly for two years now; but really, it has been that way for even longer. This new earthquake does not approach those of other centuries; but no doubt in time we shall equal all the miseries and horrors of the most heroic ages. . . . We can't yet say *All is well,* but things are not bad, and in time optimism will be demonstrated" (XXXIX, 224; Best. 6600). ". . . Physical evil and moral evil are flooding the earth" (XXXIX, 281; Best. 6724). ". . . You [he is addressing the Croats, both irregular infantry and cavalry] seek to make this world the most abominable of all possible ones, and she [the Duchess of Saxe-Gotha] would like to make it the best. She is a little distressed by the system of Leibnitz; she doesn't know what to do in the face of so much physical and moral evil, to establish optimism in your minds; but it is you who are the cause of her troubles, you accursed cav-

Once more, we must take care; the glance which Voltaire sends forth over public events and the world is no doubt cynical, cruel, and pessimistic. All goes ill in a universe of incoherence, malice, and folly. But in the life of Ferney, which is both busy and quiet, in this monastic cell where thirty people sit down to dinner, where the respectful or amused pilgrims file past from every corner of Europe where people read and think, and out of which, without too much danger, there can flow a stream of the most audacious pamphlets—in this happy seat, things don't go too badly. There are gardens, tulips, and rabbits who scratch their long ears with their paws; there is a good fat niece who lives in high style in an opulent apartment; there is the comedy at the gates of Geneva, there is a distinguished doctor, there are faithful correspondents. In point of fact, one is no more than a walking skeleton, but to take this skeleton about one has a fine carriage, and to nourish it, twenty-pound trout: all this makes up a life which one would be ungrateful to despise, and while Voltaire discovers everywhere physical evil and moral evil, he mingles in his sarcasms and derisions something like a secret remorse at being so comfortable himself. "When I deplored in verse the miseries of my fellowmen," he wrote, shortly after the *Poème sur Lisbonne*, "it was out of simple generosity, for, the feeble state of my health apart, I am so happy that I am ashamed of it."[1] The world is in shambles, blood flows, Jesuits and Molinists rage, innocents are slaughtered and dupes exploited; but there are in the world delicious asylums, where life remains possible, joyous, and sweet: let us cultivate our garden.

For this subtlety is in the conclusion of *Candide*. A work of desolation and depression? Not at all, but a work of clear vision and pessimism without despair. Voltaire does not choose to make his last word one of derision and discouragement; and so the book does not decline at all into a "What's the use?" of nihilism without hope. It ends with a word in behalf of work and effort. Metaphysics is a snare and a delusion, action is good and fruitful. Candide, having seen so much, cannot believe that all is over; but, mellowed by his experience of universal evil, he now counts only on himself to create a tolerable existence. "Work keeps at a distance three great evils: boredom, vice, and need." "I have read a great deal," said Voltaire, "and I have discovered nothing but doubts, lies and fanat-

alrymen; it is through your doing that evil is on the face of the earth; you are the offspring of the dark, the evil principle" (XXXIX, 347; Best. 6855). ". . . We will see how this bloody tragedy, so vital and complex, turns out. Happy the man who watches with untroubled eyes all these great doings in the best of all possible worlds" (XXXIX, 355; Best. 6866).

1. XXXIX, 47; Best. 6199. Similarly, XXXIX, 41; Best. 6180: "For my part, if I dared, I should be thoroughly content with my lot." And on a playing card he scribbled for Tronchin: "My dear friend, this little corner of earth is the best of all possible worlds" (H. Tronchin, *Counsellor Tronchin* [Paris, 1895] p. 150).

icism; I am just about as wise, in what really concerns our existence, as I was in the cradle. What I like best is to plant, sow, build, and above all to be free."[2]

A. O. LOVEJOY

The Principle of Plenitude and Eighteenth-Century Optimism†

The common thesis of eighteenth-century optimists was, as is notorious, the proposition that this is the best of possible worlds; and this fact, together with the connotation which the term "optimism" has come to assume in popular usage, has given rise to the belief that the adherents of this doctrine must have been exuberantly cheerful persons, fatuously blind to the realities of human experience and of human nature, or insensible to all the pain and frustration and conflict which are manifest through the entire range of sentient life. Yet there was in fact nothing in the optimist's creed which logically required him either to blink or to belittle the facts which we ordinarily call evil. So far from asserting the unreality of evils, the philosophical optimist in the eighteenth century was chiefly occupied in demonstrating their necessity. To assert that this is the best of possible worlds implies nothing as to the absolute goodness of this world; it implies only that any other world which is metaphysically capable of existence would be worse. The reasoning of the optimist was directed less to showing how much of what men commonly reckon good there is in the world of reality than to showing how little of it there is in the world of possibility—in that eternal logical order which contains the Ideas of all things possible and compossible, which the mind of God was conceived to have contemplated "before the creation," and by the necessities of which, ineluctable even by Omnipotence, his creative power was restricted.

At bottom, indeed, optimism had much in common with that Manichaean dualism, against Bayle's defence of which so many of the theodicies were directed. Optimism too, as Leibniz acknowledged, had its two antagonistic "principles." The rôle of the "evil principle" was simply assigned to the divine reason, which imposed singular impediments upon the benevolent intentions of the divine will. The very ills which Bayle had argued must be attributed to the

2. XL, 11; Best. 7322.
†From *The Great Chain of Being* (Cambridge, Mass., 1936), pp. 208–226 (Chapter VII). Copyright 1936 by the President and Fellows of Harvard College, and 1964. Reprinted by permission of the publishers, Harvard University Press. The present editor has translated quotations originally in French.

interference of a species of extraneous Anti-God, for whose existence and hostility to the good no rational explanation could be
given, were by the optimist attributed to a necessity inhering
in the nature of things; and it was questionable whether this was
not the less cheerful view of the two. For it was possible to hope
that in the fullness of time the Devil might be put under foot, and
believers in revealed religion were assured that he would be; but
logical necessities are eternal, and the evils which arise from them
must therefore be perpetual. Thus eighteenth-century optimism not
only had affinities with the dualism to which it was supposed to be
antithetic, but the arguments of its advocates at times sounded
strangely like those of the pessimist—a type by no means unknown
in the period.[1] The moral was different, but the view of the concrete facts of experience was sometimes very much the same; since
it was the optimist's contention that evil—and a great deal of it—is
involved in the general constitution of things, he found it to his
purpose to dilate, on occasion, upon the magnitude of the sum of
evil and upon the depth and breadth of its penetration into life. It
is thus, for example, that Soame Jenyns, in one of the typical theodicies of the middle of the century, seeks to persuade us of the
admirable rationality of the cosmic plan:

> I am persuaded that there is something in the abstract nature
> of pain conducive to pleasure; that the sufferings of individuals
> are absolutely necessary to universal happiness. . . . Scarce one
> instance, I believe, can be produced of the acquisition of pleasure
> or convenience by any creatures, which is not purchased by the
> previous or consequential sufferings of themselves or others. Over
> what mountains of slain is every mighty empire rolled up to the
> summit of prosperity and luxury, and what new scenes of desola-
> tion attend its fall? To what infinite toil of men, and other ani-
> mals, is every flourishing city indebted for all the conveniences
> and enjoyments of life, and what vice and misery do those very
> equipments introduce? . . . The pleasures annexed to the pres-
> ervation of ourselves are both preceded and followed by number-
> less sufferings; preceded by massacres and tortures of various
> animals preparatory to a feast, and followed by as many diseases
> lying wait in every dish to pour forth vengeance on their de-
> stroyers.[2]

1. See, for an example, the writer's paper "Rousseau's Pessimist," *Mod. Lang.
Notes*, XXXVIII (1923), 449; and for
an earlier one, Prior's *Solomon* (1718),
a poetical elaboration of the thesis that
"the pleasures of life do not compen-
sate our miseries; age steals upon us
unawares; and death, as the only cure
of our ills, ought to be expected, not
feared."
2. *A Free Inquiry into the Nature and*

Origin of Evil (1757), 60–62. Jenyns
for the most part merely puts into
clear and concise form the arguments
of King, Leibniz, and Pope; but he differs from these in unequivocally and
emphatically rejecting the freedomist
solution of the problem of moral evil.
His book had a considerable vogue,
went into numerous editions, and was
translated into French.

This gloomy rhetoric was perfectly consistent in principle with optimism, and it manifested at least one natural tendency of the champions of that doctrine; for the more numerous and monstrous the evils to be explained, the greater was the triumph when the author of a theodicy explained them.

The argument, indeed, in some of its more naïve expressions tends to beget in the reader a certain pity for an embarrassed Creator, infinitely well-meaning, but tragically hampered by "necessities in the nature of things" in his efforts to make a good world. What could be more pathetic than the position in which—as Soame Jenyns authoritatively informs us—Omnipotence found itself when contemplating the creation of mankind?

> Our difficulties arise from our forgetting how many difficulties Omnipotence has to contend with: in the present instance it is obliged either to afflict innocence or be the cause of wickedness; it has plainly no other option.[3]

In short the writings of the optimists afforded abundant ground for Voltaire's exclamation:

> You cry "All is well" in a tearful voice!

Voltaire's chief complaint of these philosophers in the *Poem on the Lisbon Disaster* was not, as has often been supposed, that they were too indecently cheerful, that their view of the reality of evil was superficial; his complaint was that they were too depressing, that they made the actual evils we experience appear yet worse by representing them as inevitable and inherent in the permanent structure of the universe.

> Enough! you need no more display to me
> The changeless laws of cruel necessity!

An evil unexplained seemed to Voltaire more endurable than the same evil explained, when the explanation consisted in showing that from all eternity the avoidance of just that evil had been, and through all eternity the avoidance of others like it would be, logically inconceivable.[4] In this his own feeling, and his assumption about the psychology of the emotions in other men, were precisely

3. *Ibid.*, 104, where the curious reader may, if he will, find why this option was "necessary," and how "Infinite Wisdom" made the best of it.

4. Voltaire, however, is arguing in the poem against two distinct and essentially opposed types of theodicy: the philosophical and necessitarian type, which endeavored to explain such a thing as the Lisbon earthquake as "l'effet des éternelles lois/ Qui d'un Dieu libre et bon nécessitent le choix" [out of eternal laws it rose,/ Which even on heaven's freedom may impose], and the theological and indeterminist type, which saw in such catastrophes special interpositions of deity in punishment of men's free choice of moral evil. The reasonings aimed at these two opposite objectives Voltaire confusingly runs togther.

opposite to Spinoza's, who believed that everything becomes endurable to us when we once see clearly that it never could have been otherwise: *quatenus mens res omnes ut necessárias intelligit, eatenus minus ab affectibus patitur.*[5] [So far as the mind understands all things as necessary, so much the less is it subjected to them emotionally.] Though most of the optimistic writers of the eighteenth century were less thorough-going or less frank in their cosmical determinism that Spinoza, such philosophic consolation as they offered was at bottom the same as his. It was an essentially intellectual consolation; the mood that it was usually designed to produce was that of reasoned acquiescence in the inevitable, based upon a conviction that its inevitableness was absolute and due to no arbitrary caprice; or, at a higher pitch, a devout willingness to be damned—that is, to be as much damned as one was—for the better demonstration of the reasonableness of the general scheme of things. Whether confronted with physical or with moral evils, wrote Pope, "to reason well is to submit"; and again:

> Know thy own point; this kind, this due degree,
> Of blindness, weakness, Heaven bestows on thee.
> Submit!

It is, of course, true that the optimistic writers were eager to show that good comes out of evil; but what it was indispensable for them to establish was that it could come in no other way. It is true, also, that they were wont, when they reached the height of their argument, to discourse with eloquence on the perfection of the Universal System as a whole; but that perfection in no way implied either the happiness or the excellence of the finite parts of the system. On the contrary, the fundamental and characteristic premise of the usual proof of optimism was the proposition that the perfection of the whole depends upon, indeed consists in, the existence of every possible degree of imperfection in the parts. Voltaire, once more, summarized the argument not altogether unjustly when he wrote:

> 'mid this sad anarchy, you will compose
> A general happiness from private woes.

The essence of the optimist's enterprise was to find the evidence of the "goodness" of the universe not in the paucity but rather in the multiplicity of what to the unphilosophic mind appeared to be evils.

All this can best be shown by an analysis of the argument in its logical sequence, as it is set forth in the earliest and, perhaps, when both its direct and indirect influence are considered, the most influential, of eighteenth-century theodicies—the *De origine mali* (1702) of William King, then Bishop of Derry, afterwards Arch-

5. *Ethics,* V, Prop. 6.

bishop of Dublin. The original Latin work does not appear to have had wide currency; but in 1731 an English version appeared,[6] with copious additions, partly extracts from King's posthumous papers, partly original notes "tending to vindicate the author's principles against the objections of Bayle, Leibnitz, the author of a philosophical Inquiry concerning Human Liberty, and others," by the translator, Edmund Law, subsequently Bishop of Carlisle. The translation went through five editions during Law's lifetime;[7] and it seems to have been much read and discussed. Law was a figure of importance in his day, being the spokesman of "the most latitudinarian position" in the Anglican theology of the time; and his academic dignities as Master of Peterhouse and Knightbridge Professor of Moral Philosophy at Cambridge in the 1750's and 60's doubtless increased the range of his influence.[8] There can hardly be much doubt that it was largely from the original work of King that Pope derived, directly or through Bolingbroke, the conceptions which, rearranged with curious incoherency, served for his vindication of optimism in the First Epistle of the *Essay on Man*;[9] for it is unlikely that Pope derived them from their fountain-head, the *Enneads of* Plotinus.

It can by no means be said that King begins his reflection on the subject by putting on rose-tinted spectacles. He recognizes from the outset all the facts which seem most incompatible with an optimis-

6. *An Essay on the Origin of Evil by Dr. William King, translated from the Latin with Notes and a Dissertation concerning the Principle and Criterion of Virtue and the Origin of the Passions; By Edmund Law, M.A., Fellow of Christ College in Cambridge.* I quote from the second edition (London, 1732) here referred to as "Essay."
7. The dates are 1731, 1732, 1739, 1758, 1781.
8. Stephen, *English Thought in the 18th Century*, II, 121.
9. Bolingbroke in the *Fragments* quotes King frequently and with respect. I can see no sufficient reason for doubting that in the *Fragments* as printed we have, as Bolingbroke asserted, in a somewhat expanded form "the notes which were communicated to Mr. Pope in scraps, as they were written," and utilized by the latter in writing the *Essay on Man;* the numerous and exact verbal parallels between passages in the *Fragments* and the *Essay* are not susceptible of any other probable explanation (see Bolingbroke's *Works*, 1809 edition, VII, 278, and VIII, 356). Law wrote in the preface to the 1781 edition of the *Essay on the Origin of Evil:* "I had the satisfaction of seeing that those very principles which had been maintained by Archbishop King were adopted by Mr. Pope in the *Essay on*

Man." When this was challenged by a brother-bishop, Pope's truculent theological champion Warburton, Law replied by referring to the testimony of Lord Bathurst, "who saw the very same system in Lord Bolingbroke's own hand, lying before Mr. Pope while he composed his *Essay*"; and added: "The point may also be cleared effectually whenever any reader shall think it worth his while to compare the two pieces together, and observe how exactly they tally with one another" (*op. cit.,* p. xvii). Such a comparison seems to me to give reason to believe that Pope made use of King's work directly, as well as of Bolingbroke's adaptation of a part of it. Since it was in 1730 that Pope and Bolingbroke were "deep in metaphysics," and since by 1731 the first three Epistles seem to have been completed (cf. Courthope, V, 242), it must have been from the Latin original, not Law's translation, that the poet and his philosophic mentor drew. Thus essentially the same theodicy appeared almost simultaneously in Law's English prose rendering and in Pope's verse. On the relation of King's work to Haller's *Ueber den Ursprung des Uebels* (1734) cf. L. M. Price in *Publications of the Modern Language Association of America*, XLI (1926), 945–948.

tic view: the "perpetual war between the elements, between animals, between men"; "the errors, miseries and vices" which are "the constant companions of human life from its infancy"; the prosperity of the wicked and the suffering of the righteous. There are "troops of miseries marching through human life." And King is innocent of the amazing superficiality of Milton's theodicy; while he, too, assumes the freedom of the will, he sees clearly that this assumption can touch only a fraction of the problem. Not all evils are "external, or acquired by our choice"; many of them proceed from the constitution of Nature itself.[1] The dualistic doctrine of Bayle, while it, too, has the advantage of "acquitting God of all manner of blame," is philosophically an "absurd hypothesis." King, in short, is to attribute evil, not—at least not primarily nor chiefly—either to the mysterious perversity of man's will or to the machinations of the Devil; he is to show its necessity from a consideration of the nature of deity itself. His undertaking is nothing less than that of facing all the evils of existence and showing them to be "not only consistent with infinite wisdom, goodness and power, but necessarily resulting from them."[2]

The traditional division of evils into three classes—evils of limitation or imperfection, "natural" evils, and moral evils—provides the general scheme of the argument, which is, in brief, that there could not conceivably have been any creation at all without the first sort of evil; and that all of the second sort, at least, follow with strict logical necessity from the first. Even Omnipotence could not create its own double; if any beings other than God were to exist they must in the nature of the case be differentiated from him through the "evil of defect"—and, as is assumed, be differentiated from one another by the diversity of their defects. Evil, in short, is primarily privation; and privation is involved in the very concept of all beings except one. This Law puts in the terms of Aristotelian and Scholastic philosophy in his summary of King's "scheme":

> All creatures are necessarily imperfect, and at infinite distance from the perfection of the Deity, and if a negative principle were admitted, such as the Privation of the Peripatetics, it might be said that every created being consists of existence and non-existence; for it is nothing in respect both of those perfections which it wants; and of those which others have. And this . . . mixture of non-entity in the constitution of created beings is the necessary principle of all natural evils, and of a possibility of moral ones.[3]

1. *Essay*, I, 208.
2. *Ibid.*, 109–113.
3. *Ibid.*, xix. This argument remained as the usual starting point of a numerous series of subsequent theodicies, some of which have a place in literature: e.g., Victor Hugo still thought it needful to devote a number of lines to the exposition of it in *Les Contemplations* ("Ce que dit la Bouche d'Ombre," 1905 ed., 417 ff.).

In other words, in King's own phrase, "a creature is descended from God, a most perfect Father; but from Nothing as its mother, which is Imperfection." And the virtually dualistic character of this conception is shown by the fact that the inferior parent, in spite of the purely negative rôle which appeared to be implied by her name, was conceived to be responsible for many seemingly highly positive peculiarities of the offspring. This, however, was felt to be an unobjectionable dualism, partly because the second or evil principle was *called* "Nothing," and partly because its existence as a factor in the world, and the effects of it, could be regarded as logically necessary and not as a mysterious accident.

But the significant issue did not lie in this simple, almost tautological piece of reasoning. Doubtless, if the Absolute Being was not to remain forever in the solitude of his own perfection, the prime evil of limitation or imperfection must characterize whatever other beings he brought forth. But that evil was not thereby justified unless it were shown, or assumed, that the creation of such other, necessarily defective beings is itself a good. This crucial Plotinian assumption King unhesitatingly makes, as well as a further assumption which seems far from self-evident. Even if it were granted that it is good that *some* beings other than God, some finite and imperfect natures, should exist, would it not (some might ask) have been less irrational that only the highest grade of imperfection should be generated—as had, indeed, been originally the case, according to an account of the creation supported by a considerable weight of authority in the theological tradition of Christianity and comparatively recently revived by Milton?[4] If God could be supposed to need company—which it seemed philosophically a paradox and was theologically a heresy to admit—should it not at least have been good company, a *civitas dei* composed wholly of pure spirits? King saw no way of achieving a satisfactory theodicy unless this latter question were answered (again with the support of many ancient and medieval writers) in the negative. It was requisite to show that not only imperfection in general, but every one of the observable concrete imperfections of the actual world, ought to have been created; and this could not be shown unless it were laid down as a premise that it is inherently and absolutely good that *every* kind of thing (however far down in the scale of possibles) should actually be, so far as its existence is logically conceivable, i.e., involves no contradiction.

This proposition then—expressed in theological terminology—was the essential thesis in the argument for optimism propounded by

4. See the patristic authorities cited by Sumner in his translation of Milton's *Christian Doctrine*, 187, n. 4. The view adopted by Milton, however, was of dubious orthodoxy. It had been rejected by Thomas Aquinas, *Summa Theologica*, I, q. 61, a.3; and by Dante, *Paradiso*, XXIX, 37.

King and Law. There is inherent in the divine essence, as an element in God's perfection, a special attribute of "goodness," which makes it necessary that all other and less excellent essences down to the very lowest—so far as they are severally and jointly possible—shall have actual existence after their kind.

> God might, indeed, have refrained from creating, and continued alone, self-sufficient and perfect to all eternity; but his infinite Goodness would by no means allow it; this obliged him to produce external things; which things, since they could not possibly be perfect, the Divine Goodness preferred imperfect ones to none at all. Imperfection, then, arose from the infinity of Divine Goodness.[5]

And, thus committed by his own nature to the impartation of actual being to some imperfect essences, God could not refuse the boon of existence to any:

> If you say, God might have omitted the more imperfect beings, I grant it, and if that had been best, he would undoubtedly have done it. But it is the part of infinite Goodness to choose the very best; from thence it proceeds, therefore, that the more imperfect beings have existence; for it was agreeable to that, not to omit the very least good that could be produced. Finite goodness might possibly have been exhausted in creating the greater beings, but infinite extends to all. . . . There must then be many, perhaps infinite, degrees of perfection in the divine works. . . . It was better not to give some so great a degree of happiness as their natures might receive, than that a whole species of being should be wanting to the world.[6]

Not only must all possible species enjoy existence, but, adds King's editor, "from the observation that there is no manner of chasm or void, no link deficient in this great Chain of Being, and the reason of it, it will appear extremely probable also that every distinct order, every class or species, is as full as the nature of it would permit, or [Law devoutly but, upon his own principles, tautologically adds] as God saw proper."

The foundation, then, of the usual eighteenth-century argument for optimism was the principle of plenitude. * * *

The theodicy of Leibniz was in most essentials the same as that of his English precursor;[7] and in summarizing with approval the

---

5. King, *op. cit.*, I, 116 f. For the same conception of the Scale of Being and its necessary completeness in a well-ordered universe, cf. Bolingbroke, *Fragments* (*Works*, 1809, VIII, 173, 183, 186, 192, 218 f., 232, 363, 364–365). 6. *Op. cit.*, 137 f., 129–131 f., 156. Both King and Law fell into curious waverings, and in the end into self-contradiction, when the question was raised whether the number of degrees in the scale of being is actually infinite. Into this it is unnecessary to enter here. 7. There is no question of any influence of King upon Leibniz or of Leibniz upon King. Though the *Théodicée* was not published until 1710, eight years after the *De origine mali*, the greater part of it was written between 1697 and the beginning of 1705; and the

main argument of the archbishop's *bel ouvrage, plein de savoir et d' élégance* [handsome work, full of erudition and elegance], Leibniz significantly accentuated the theological paradox contained in it:

> Why, someone asks, did not God refrain from creating things altogether? The author well replies that the abundance of God's goodness is the reason. He wished to communicate himself, even at the expense of that delicacy which our imaginations ascribe to him, when we assume that imperfections shock him. Thus he preferred that the imperfect should exist, rather than nothing.[8]

In this emphasis upon the implication that the Creator of the actual world cannot be supposed to be a "delicate" or squeamish God, caring only for perfection—and that, in fact, he would, if more nicely selective in his act of creation, have thereby shown himself the less divine—the consequence latent from the first in the principle of plenitude is put with unusual vividness and candor; and in general, the German philosopher, in developing the theory of value thus implicit in optimism, is franker, more ardent, and more cheerful than the Anglican theologian. Some analogies in human life to the standards of valuation which the optimists had applied in explaining the supposed purpose of the deity in the creation are not obscurely suggested by Leibniz.

> Wisdom requires variety (*la sagesse doit varier*). To multiply exclusively the same thing, however noble it be, would be a superfluity; it would be a kind of poverty. To have a thousand well-bound copies of Vergil in your library; to sing only airs from the opera of Cadmus and Hermione; to break all your porcelain in order to have only golden cups; to have all your buttons made of diamonds; to eat only partridges and to drink only the wine of Hungary or of Shiraz—could any one call this reasonable?[9]

Something very similar to this had, in point of fact, been regarded as the essence of reasonableness both by neo-classical aesthetic theorists and by a multitude of influential moralists. It would scarcely have seemed evident to the former that two copies of Vergil are of less value than one copy *plus* a copy of the worst epic ever written—still less that a reading of the first followed by a reading of the second is preferable to two readings of Vergil. And the apparent object of the endeavor of most ethical teaching had been to produce a close approach to uniformity in human character and behavior,

ideas it contains had long been familiar to Leibniz. Cf. Gerhardt's preface to Leibniz's *Philosophische Schriften*, VI, 3–10.

8. "Remarques sur le livre sur l'origine du mal publié depuis peu en Angleterre," appended to the *Théodicée, Philosophische Schriften*, VI, 400 ff. Leibniz observes that he is in agreement with King "only in respect to half of the subject"; the disagreement relates chiefly to King's chapter on liberty and necessity, which (quite inconsistently with the implications of his argument for optimism) asserts that God exercised a *liberum arbitrium indifferentiae* in creating the world.

9. *Théodicée*, § 124.

and in men's political and social institutions. The desire for variety —or for change, the temporal form of it—had rather commonly been conceived to be a non-rational, indeed a pathological, idio-syncrasy of human creatures. But Leibniz not only gave it a sort of cosmic dignity by attributing it to God himself, but also represented it as the very summit of rationality.

The ethically significant consequence which is most plainly drawn from this by Leibniz is that neither what is commonly called moral goodness, nor pleasure, is the most important thing in the world. Both hedonism, in short, and an abstract moralism (such, for example, as Kant and Fichte were afterwards to express) were equally contrary to the value-theory implicit in the principle of plenitude. Virtue and happiness both, of course, have their place in the scale of values; but if it were the highest place, it is inconceiv-able that God would have made the kind of world he has made.

> The moral or physical good or evil of rational creatures does not infinitely transcend the good or evil which is purely meta-physical, that is to say, the good which consists in the perfection of the other creatures. . . . No substance is either absolutely precious or absolutely contemptible in the sight of God. It is certain that God attaches more importance to a man than to a lion, but I do not know that we can be sure that he prefers one man to the entire species of lions.[1]

To this thesis Leibniz reverts again and again in the *Théodicée:*

> [It is] a false maxim that the happiness of rational creatures is the sole purpose of God. If that had been so, there would, perhaps, have been neither sin nor unhappiness, not even as con-comitants. God would have chosen a set of possibles from which all evils were excluded. But he would in that case have fallen short of what is due to the universe, that is, what is due to him-self. . . . It is true that one can imagine possible worlds without sin and without suffering, just as one can invent romances about Utopias or about the Sévarambes; but these worlds would be much inferior to ours. I cannot show this in detail; you must infer it, as I do, *ab effectu,* since this world, as it is, is the world God chose. . . . Virtue is the noblest quality of created things, but it is not the only good quality of creatures. There is an in-finite variety of others that attract the inclination of God; it is from all these inclinations taken together that the greatest pos-sible sum of good results; and there would be less good than there is if there were nothing but virtue, if only rational creatures existed. . . . Midas was less rich when he possessed only gold.[2]

1. *Ibid.,* § 118; cf. the remark of Thomas Aquinas about the value of two angels as compared with that of one angel and one stone. Kant was still enunciating the same principle, varying only the illustration, in 1755: lice "may in our eyes be as worthless as you like, nevertheless it is of more consequence to Nature to conserve this species as a whole than to conserve a small number of members of a superior species" (*All-gemeine Naturgeschichte,* 127).

2. *Théodicée,* §§ 120, 10, 124; cf. also § 213.

Leibniz adds the trite aesthetic argument for the indispensability of contrasts in the production of beauty in a work of art, and, indeed, in the mere physical pleasure of the gustatory sense:

> Sweet things become insipid if we eat nothing else; sharp, tart and even bitter things must be combined with them so as to stimulate the taste. He who has not tasted bitter things does not deserve sweet, and, indeed, will not appreciate them.

Thus these subtle philosophers and grave divines, and the poets like Pope and Haller who popularized their reasonings, rested their assertion of the goodness of the universe ultimately upon the same ground as Stevenson's child in the nursery:

> The world is so full of a number of things.

This did not, it is true, necessarily make them "as happy as kings." That was a matter of individual temperament; and in point of fact most of them had not the child's robust delight in the sheer diversity and multiplicity of things. They were often men whose natural taste or training would have inclined them rather to prefer a somewhat thin, simple, and exclusive universe. The philosophers of optimism were not, in short, as a rule of a Romantic disposition; and what they were desirous of proving was that reality is rational through and through, that every fact of existence, however unpleasant, is grounded in some reason as clear and evident as an axiom of mathematics. But in the exigencies of their argument to this ambitious conclusion, they found themselves constrained to attribute to the Divine Reason a conception of the good extremely different from that which had been most current among men, and frequently among philosophers; and they were thus led, often against their original temper and intention, to impress upon the minds of their generation a revolutionary and paradoxical theory of the criterion of all value, which may be summed up in the words of a highly Romantic and optimistic lover of paradox in our own day:

> One thing alone is needful: Everything.
> The rest is vanity of vanities.

* * *

Criticism

Formal critical appreciation of *Candide* as a work of literary art does not have a very long history. For its own age it was too light and unpretentious a book, too "easy" to need any sort of formal study. The usual eighteenth- or nineteenth-century discussion touches on the pace and rhythm of its prose, the gaiety of its ridicule—and then gets on to the more satisfying question of its morality or immorality. But recently the book has come to seem less simple than it once did—perhaps because Voltaire's irony, for all its swiftness and levity, appears to have a destructive power which is hard to limit. Hence the opening up of some interesting questions about how the book should be read—on which the following pages present a scattering of views.

In order to render more accessible the discussions, it seems useful to prefix a technical definition, as well as a brief list of Voltaire's major works, other than *Candide,* to which the various essayists refer. A *conte,* therefore, is in set, formal terms, an account of an anecdote or adventure, marvellous or otherwise, told for purposes of amusement. A *conte* can be what we in English would call a short story, but it can also be a very short parable, a fable, or a novelette (like *Candide*). As they grow longer, more substantial in their social renderings, and more serious in their moral tonality, *contes* tend to be called *nouvelles,* as *nouvelles,* by heightening these qualities still further, turn into *romans. Contes* are the slightest, lightest, and least pretentious of prose narratives.

THE CONTES OF VOLTAIRE,
AND OTHER WRITINGS

A complete listing of Voltaire's publications constitutes in itself a volume of several hundred pages. The present short list aims merely to name those of his works which are most often mentioned in connection with *Candide*, to translate the title where possible, indicate the genre and date, and with respect to a few of the most important, to give summary indication of the contents.

Aventure Indienne ("An Indian Adventure"), 1766, conte.
Babouc (see *Le Monde comme il va*).
Cosi-Sancta, 1784, conte.
Le Crocheteur borgne ("The One-Eyed Porter"), 1774, conte.
Les Deux Consolés ("The Two Who Were Comforted"), 1756, conte.

Dialogue entre un Bramin et un Jésuite ("Dialogue Between a Brahmin and a Jesuit"), 1756, philosophical dialogue.
Dialogue entre Lucrèce et Posidone ("Dialogue Between Lucretius and Posidonius"), 1756, philosophical dialogue.
Dictionnaire Philosophique ("Philosophical Dictionary"), 1764. The many short articles and satiric definitions of this one-man encyclopedia give it stature as one of Voltaire's most implacable and weighty assaults on "l'infâme."
Discours en Vers sur l'Homme ("Discourses on Man"), 1738, poem. Inspired by Pope's "Essay on Man," these six discourses try similarly to sum up an attitude toward human life.
Eléments de la Philosophie de Newton ("Elements of Newton's Philosophy"), 1738, prose exposition.

Epître à Uranie ("Epistle to Urania"), 1722, poem.
Essai sur les mœurs ("Essay on Customs," also sometimes known as the "Universal History"), 1756, an essay in history, folklore, and comparative anthropology. The omnivorous reading which Voltaire did for this immense survey of human behavior-patterns is particularly reflected in the cosmopolitan perspectives of *Candide*.
Fragments sur l'Inde ("Fragments on India"), 1773, polemic on aspects of British rule.
La Henriade—originally *La Ligue ou Henri le Grand* ("The Henriad") published 1723 under one title and 1728 under the other, an epic poem on Henry IV.
Histoire d'un bon Bramin ("The Story of a Good Brahmin"), 1761, conte.

L'Histoire de Jenni ("Jenny's Story"), 1775, conte.
Histoire des voyages de Scarmentado ("The Travels of Scarmentado"), 1756, conte. A rascal from Crete, Scarmentado gyrates rapidly through the world, from one scrape to another, finally returns home, and settles into complacent domesticity.

Homélies prononcées à Londres en 1765 ("Homilies delivered in London in 1765"), 1767, lay sermons, on atheism, superstition, and the Old and New Testaments. They were not, of course, delivered at London.

L'Homme aux quarante écus ("The Man with Forty Pounds a Year"), 1768, conte. A sensible, simple, middle-of-the-road fellow, the man with forty pounds a year wanders about, discussing with various frauds he meets such disagreeable eventualities as taxation, syphilis, and war. He has read *Candide*, cites it frequently, and finds it a useful guide to things as they are.

Il faut prendre un parti ("One Must Take Sides"), 1772, polemic.

L'Ingénu ou le Huron ("Simplicity"), 1767, conte. A man brought up among the Mohawk Indians returns to France and finds he is the son of a French couple; his simplicity suffers all sorts of checks and frustrations in adapting to the sophistications and corruptions of French society.

Jeannot et Colin ("Johnny and Colin"), 1764, conte. A morality on social arrogance.

Lettres d'Amabed ("Letters from Amabed"), 1769, conte. An innocent Brahmin wanders into Europe and describes its peculiar institutions.

Lettres Philosophiques ("Philosophic Letters"), 1733–34, essays largely descriptive of English culture and thought.

Memnon, 1749, conte. (Not to be confused with *Zadig*, which originally appeared under this title.)

Micromégas, 1752, conte. An inhabitant of Sirius, who is immense, and his friend from Saturn, who, though still immense by human standards, is a dwarf compared to the Sirian, go adventuring through the universe.

Le Mondain ("The Worldly Man"), 1736?, poem. A defence of luxury.

Le Monde comme il va ("The World As It Is"), 1748, conte.

Les Oreilles du Comte de Chesterfield ("Lord Chesterfield's Ears"), 1775, conte. Chesterfield was deaf; but his ears have almost nothing at all to do with this discussion of whether and in what sense man is a machine.

L'Orphelin de la Chine ("The Chinese Orphan"), 1755, tragedy.

Le Pauvre Diable ("The Poor Devil"), 1758, verse satire.

Poème sur le Désastre de Lisbonne ("Poem on Lisbon"), 1756, philosophical poem.

Précis de l'Ecclésiaste ("Ecclesiastes Abridged"), 1759, verse translation.

La Princesse de Babylone ("The Princess of Babylon"), 1768, conte. Amazan, in love with Formosanta, Princess of Babylon, travels round the world in search of her—meanwhile furnishing Voltaire with opportunities for witty comment and satire.

La Pucelle ("The Maid"), 1755, mock-heroic poem, in more than dubious taste, on Joan of Arc.

Questions sur L'Encyclopédie ("Questions on the Encyclopedia"), 1770–1772, commentary and criticism in nine volumes.

Le Siècle de Louis XIV ("The Century of Louis XIV"), 1751, history—

social, intellectual, and cultural, as well as diplomatic and military.

Tancrède, 1760, tragedy. Love and misunderstanding in XI-century Sicily, with a noble corsair for a hero, a noble young lady for *ingenue*, and a ridiculous plot.

Le Taureau blanc ("The White Bull"), 1774, conte.

Traité de métaphysique ("Treatise on Metaphysics"), 1734, philosophy.

Zadig ou la destinée, 1747, conte. Persecuted by persistent ill fortune, Zadig after many trials, and with the help of illumination from an angel named Jesrad, finally wins the hand of Queen Astarte.

Zaïre, 1732, tragedy.

GEORGES ASCOLI

[Voltaire: The Storyteller's Art] †

We should have only an incomplete notion of the skills which
Voltaire brought to his propaganda, and should deprive ourselves of
a royal bounty, if we did not linger for a few minutes over the
stories in prose which even today constitute, no doubt, the most
exquisite and living part of Voltaire's entire work. These stories,
composed in short chapters which constitute as it were so many
scenes of a comedy, these stories laced with satire and moral reflections, written in the most nervous and racy language, make manifest the full spectrum of Voltaire's special gifts. The special talent
of Voltaire for the short story made itself felt early in his career;
several such swift, sardonic sketches are found as early as the *Philosophic Letters*. Let us note for example the tale of how George Fox
founded the sect of the Quakers:

> A man named George Fox, from the county of Leicester, son
> of a silk-worker, took it upon himself to preach as a true apostle
> (so he pretended), that is, without knowing how to read or write;
> he was a young man of twenty-five years, impeccably behaved
> and divinely mad. He dressed in leather from head to foot, and
> went from town to town crying out against war and the clergy.
> So long as he preached only against the military, he had nothing
> to fear, but he attacked the churchmen, so he soon found him-
> self in prison. They brought him to Darby, to appear before the
> justice of the peace. Fox appeared before the justice with his
> leather cap on his head. A sergeant cuffed him and said: —You
> beggarly fellow, don't you know enough to take off your hat be-
> fore His Honor? Fox turned the other cheek and begged the ser-
> geant to give him another cuff, for the love of God. The justice
> of Darby asked him to take an oath before giving evidence: —My
> friend, said he, you should know that I never take the name of
> the Lord in vain. The judge, seeing that this fellow addressed
> him familiarly, had him sent to the Darby Insane Asylum for a
> whipping. George Fox went to the madhouse, praising God all
> the while, and underwent the full sentence of the judge. The
> whippers were surprised when he begged them for a couple of
> extra lashes, for the good of his soul. But they hastened to oblige;
> Fox had his double dose, thanked them heartily, and began to
> preach to them. First they laughed, then they listened; and as
> enthusiasm is a disease which spreads by contagion, several were
> converted, and the whippers became his first disciples.[1]

† From "Voltaire" in the *Revue des
cours et conférences*, XXVI, 619–626.
Translated by Robert M. Adams.

1. *Philosophic Letters*, ed. Lanson, I,
32–33.

Is there any need to cite also the famous story of the misdeeds of the east wind, in the *Letter to M. . . .* , written about the same time, but which Voltaire did not himself put into his book?[2]

It was during his stay at Court, in order to please the worldly (for he sensed quickly that one overcomes them only by amusing them), that Voltaire composed his first stories. They were, first, in 1747, *Le Monde comme il va; Le Crocheteur borgne; Cosi-Sancta; Aventure Indienne;* and *Zadig*, the first which was really worked out, for which Voltaire wrote new chapters on several occasions—a masterpiece. While at Frederick's court, Voltaire composed *Micromégas*, a proper philosophic novel (1752); then, after his return to France, *Les Deux Consolés, Les Voyages de, Scarmentado* (1756); *Histoire d'un bon Bramin;* and finally *Candide*, the model of the form (1759). Till the end of his life, Voltaire was continually returning to this form, so well suited to his talents. *Jeannot et Colin* dates from 1764; *L'Ingénu ou le Huron* from 1767; *l'Homme aux quarante écus* and *La Princesse de Babylone* from 1768; the *Lettres d'Amabed* from 1769; *Le Taureau blanc* from 1773; and *l'Histoire de Jenni* and *Les Oreilles du Comte de Chesterfield* from 1775. As in his dramas, Voltaire had a tendency toward the end of his life to leave more and more space in his novels for the discussion of ideas and for propaganda, at the expense of imagination, the picturesque and the artistic—though these were never altogether absent. But from his very first attempts a philosophic purpose was evident, though the contrary has been pretended by certain grave critics who evidently find it hard to believe that one can think and jest at the same time.

There are several essential ideas, of unequal value, to which Voltaire is continually returning in his stories. They are human mutability and human fragility, above all in women; hatred of war, which finds expression in *Le Monde comme il va, Micromégas* (Chapter VII), and *Candide* (Chapter II); and the relativity of things—*Micromégas* insists on this idea, pre-eminently philosophical, that the human world is infinitely small within the universe. On the other hand, the variety of opinions and beliefs reveals itself in the joining, within a single story, of the most diverse civilizations, or in the contrast between a civilized and a savage country (*L'Ingénu*). Finally, we are shown in every story the emptiness of virtue as defined by men, and their tendency to prefer secret vice over blunt virtue (*Cosi-Sancta* and *Zadig* in the matter of jealousy). That a strict virtue often causes great evils is the moral taught by Cosi-Sancta, who "because she was too good caused her lover's death and her husband's death-sentence; and because she yielded a little, preserved her brother, her son, and her husband for future life." Such

2. *Ibid.*, II, 261–63.

too is the evidence of beautiful Almona, who sacrifices her modesty to save Zadig, and of Mlle. de Saint-Yves, "who perishes of her virtue." The moral problem is always before Voltaire, who shows himself convinced that in human affairs vices and virtues are closely linked. If nothing is good, everything is at least passable; that is the lesson of *Le Monde comme il va* or *Le Crocheteur borgne*, happy because he has lost the eye "that sees the bad side of things." *Zadig* shows that all things are ruled by chance; fine behavior has wretched consequences, but the wise man will not be discouraged, for after the injustices and evils which are inevitable, the time of happiness will come, also inevitably, and without any better reason than its predecessors. Soon Voltaire's vision darkens; *Le bon Bramin* demonstrates that it is impossible for an intelligent man to be happy, and *Candide* runs off an impressive list of all the evils from which man suffers—physical, moral, and social calamities. Against the facile, feeble optimism of the official philosophers Voltaire can hardly find sarcasms enough. Yet even then he does not want man to lose courage, for as soon as one forswears vain talk, happiness shows signs of appearing in simplicity (*Jeannot et Colin*) or in work. That is the conclusion of *Candide*: "Let's work without rationalizing, it's the only way to make life bearable."

Alongside these important lessons, we find in the stories allusions to lesser problems; sometimes Voltaire criticizes the corruption of contemporary customs, sometimes he lashes out at social abuses. He attacks the venality of law courts and their excessive charges, the grasping tax-collectors, the literary tastes of the age, the degeneracy of the stage, the absurd sermons in fashion, the fads and follies of literary people. He attacks all those prejudices of the aristocracy, the religious orders, and the intellectuals, which spoil men's lives. And he demonstrates, on the other hand, the utility of commerce and luxury, a utility far greater than the inevitable evils which they also nourish. Finally, these works present to us a sardonic and lively commentary on all those contemporary events which had struck Voltaire's notice and influenced the formation of his ideas, such as the Lisbon earthquake and the execution of Admiral Byng; they are enriched by his studies (those made for the *Essai sur les mœurs*, for example); and they talk to us on every occasion of those men whom the author had known and loathed, sometimes under their real names (Rollin, Fréron, Larcher), sometimes under the disguise of transparent anagrams (Linro = Rollin; Yebor = Boyer; Orcan = Rohan).

To get these elements into the work, any means will serve. Voltaire makes little use of the fairy story which had recently been popular, but which he considered a bit old hat; on occasion he mocks its conventions (end of *Le Crocheteur borgne*). Nor is he any better pleased with the novel of passion; he much prefers the story of a light, libertine adventure which he can tell in a tone of banter; he jests over the tears, swoons, and tender sentiments of which the abbé Prévost was so fond. What he likes best of all are Oriental tales which lend themselves to marvelous and colorful events and which carry us into lands where wisdom seems to spring from the earth itself. These are travel-tales which allow one to paint various scenes and to fill one's pages with many different manners and moral ideas. Zadig travels through the Orient, Scarmentado and Candide across the face of the whole globe. All these stories have very modest plots, and often a completely exterior *leit-motiv* redeems the unity of the whole: now it is the thought of a beloved woman whom the hero has lost and is seeking (*Zadig* and *Candide*); in *Zadig*, too, it is the dream of happiness, a dream forever being deceived but forever renewed; while in *Candide* it is Pangloss' obstinate reaffirming of his doctrine every time it seems irresistibly overcome by the facts. The whole story constitutes a trim, attractive tale, original even when Voltaire makes use of outside sources; for the story-teller, no less than the poet, sometimes needs exterior props to support his imagination. But it is a sign of his power, and an augury of his work's longevity, that he uses his models very freely, surpassing them and often casting them altogether into the shade.

His characters, sketched in a few sharp lines, are instinct with truth, and unforgettable. Here, in brief and alive, is an entire family portrait:

> The Baron was one of the most mighty lords of Westphalia, for his castle had a door and windows. His great hall was even hung with a tapestry. The dogs of his courtyard made up a hunting pack on occasion, with the stableboys as huntsmen; the village priest was his grand almoner. They all called him "My Lord," and laughed at his stories.
>
> The Baroness, who weighed in the neighborhood of three hundred and fifty pounds, was greatly respected for that reason, and did the honors of the house with a dignity which rendered her even more imposing. Her daughter, Cunégonde, aged seventeen, was a ruddy-cheeked girl, fresh, plump, and desirable. The Baron's son seemed in every way worthy of his father. The tutor Pangloss was the oracle of the household, and little Candide listened to his lectures with all the good faith of his age and character.[3]

Sometimes portraiture is carried farther, and the character represents, all by himself, a social condition, an ambience, a nation. In *La Princesse de Babylone* such a figure is Lord What-then, the Eng-

3. *Candide,* Chapter I.

lishman; while in *Zadig* the hero is a type of the Oriental, with all
the Oriental's wisdom, his taste for the marvelous and the opulent,
his violence, and his supreme disdain for women. The backgrounds
are sketched in a few lines, sober and precise; and against this
décor, which nowhere seems laid on, the simple, subtle narrative
runs its course with an air of elegant detachment. Anyone who
wants to savor its quality should simply compare the delicious chapter of the Nose in *Zadig* with the Chinese story which, along with
The Matron of Ephesus, served as a model.[4] There are no long
speeches in Voltaire, there is more wit, the formulas are swift yet
reticent, there is more psychological realism and more malice, more
delicate and more expressive gestures; it is a tidier art, with more
elegance and less cynicism. The story-teller delights us, and affirms
his own control over the story. And we must admire too the ease
with which Voltaire makes vivid in concrete details the idea which
he wants to define and retains, even in the midst of a philosophic
argument, the pleasures of the picturesque. So, too, when his giants
of Sirius and Saturn are walking about the earth, they are not mere
animated ideas:[5]

> So there they are, back where they started, having seen that
> sea, almost imperceptible to them, which we call the *Mediter-*
> *ranean*, and that other little inlet which, under the name of the
> *Great Ocean*, surrounds our mole-burrow. The dwarf had barely
> got his knees wet, and the other had scarcely moistened his heel.
> They did everything they could in the way of walking about and
> looking high and low to see if this globe was inhabited or not.
> They got down on their knees, they lay flat, they poked every-
> where; but their eyes and their hands being all out of proportion
> to the tiny creatures which crawl about here, they could have no
> sensation whatever that we and our kind, the other inhabitants of
> this globe, have the honor of existing on it.

The reproach may be raised that Voltaire sometimes amused
himself with stories of somewhat bawdy characters; this or that
chapter of *L'Ingénu* or *Candide* will seem racy and a bit loose. But
in all justice we must recall that, in an age when the most refined
spirits took pleasure in loose talk, Voltaire mostly contented
himself with piquant hints which are redeemed by his light
touch and exquisite form. There is not a single word which could
shock the most delicate ears in the story, so gay and exact and
deftly balanced, of how Candide and Cunégonde fell in love.[6] And

4. *The Matron from the land of Soung,*
which was in Volume III of Father du
Halde's great collection, *A Description
of China,* was reprinted several times
in the nineteenth century. It is to be
found in Durand, *Satires of Petronius,*
newly translated (1803) and in Abel

Rémusat, *Chinese Stories,* Volume III
(1827).
5. *Micromégas,* Chapter IV. The Sa-
turnian, though a giant in our eyes, is
only a dwarf alongside the man from
Sirius.
6. *Candide,* Chapter I, toward the end.

can anything finer and more delicate be imaged than the chapter in which Zadig dissuades a young Arabian widow from burning herself alive on her husband's funeral-pyre?

> He had himself introduced to her, and after preparing the way by praising her beauty and telling her what a shame it was that so much loveliness should perish in the flames, he heaped even more praises on her for her constancy and her courage. —You loved your husband prodigiously, then? he asked her. —Who, me? Not a bit of it, replied the Arabian lady. He was a brute, a jealous brute, an insufferable man; but all the same, I am determined to throw myself on the funeral-pyre. —I see, said Zadig, then there must be some really delicious pleasure in the experience of being burned alive? —Ah, at the very thought of it Nature stands appalled, said the lady; nonetheless, I must. I am a religious woman, I would lose all my reputation for piety and everyone would make fun of me, if I didn't burn myself alive. Zadig pointed out to her that she was burning herself to please other people, and out of vanity; then he talked to her at length in a manner calculated to revive her love of life and even inspire in her a certain kindness for the one who was talking to her. —What would you do, said he, if you did not think yourself bound to burn yourself alive? —Ah, said the lady, in that case I think I would ask you to marry me.
>
> Zadig was too full of the idea of Astarte to take this declaration very seriously, but he went at once to the tribal chiefs, told them what had happened, and advised them to pass a law forbidding any widow to burn herself alive unless she had first had an intimate conversation, for at least an hour, with a young man. Since that time, no woman has burned herself alive in Arabia. . . .[7]

The qualities of the story-teller make themselves felt beyond the limits of the formal stories. In many Voltairean jokes and games of wit, one finds the same merits of picturesque vivacity in the narration and the same smooth style which yields to every twist and turn of the thought. Take for example this shrewd, sharp story, with its play on sounds, its repetition of key words and phrases, its picturesque qualities, and its sharp, malicious phrasing which tacks every point firmly in place:

> It was the twelfth of October, 1759, when Brother Berthier went, for his sins, from Paris to Versailles with Brother Coutu, his usual travelling companion. Berthier had put in the carriage several copies of the *Journal de Trévoux* which he was to present to his patrons and protectors, as for example to the chambermaid of my lady the head nurse, to a scullery boy, to one of the king's apothecary's apprentices, and to several other gentlemen who are making a career of their talents. On the road, Berthier began to feel nauseated; his head grew heavy, he yawned frequently.

7. *Zadig*, Chapter XI.

—What it is I don't know, says he to Coutu, but I never yawned so much in my life. —Reverend father, says Brother Coutu, it's nothing but a turnabout. —What's that? What do you mean with your turnabout? says Brother Berthier. —I mean, says Brother Coutu, that I'm yawning too, and I don't know why, for I haven't read anything all day and you haven't said anything to me since we've been on the road. As he said these words, Brother Coutu yawned more than ever. Berthier replied with a set of yawns which went on and on. The coachman looked back and, seeing them yawning away, began to yawn too. All the passersby were afflicted; in all the houses by the roadside people began to yawn; so powerfully does the mere presence of a learned man sometimes work to influence people.

Meanwhile a little cold sweat came over Berthier. —What it is I don't know, says he, but I'm frozen. —I believe it, says his companion. —What's that? What do you mean by that? says Berthier. —I mean, says Coutu, that I'm frozen too. —I'm getting sleepy, says Berthier. —I'm not surprised, says the other. —Eh, how's that? says Berthier. —Because I'm getting sleepy too, says the companion. So there they are, the two of them, wholly overcome by a soporific and lethargic condition, and in this state they draw up before the gate at Versailles. The coachman, opening the door, tried to wake them from their deep sleep; he made no headway, and called for help. Finally the companion, who was more vigorous than Berthier, gave a few signs of life; but Berthier was out cold! Several doctors of the court, on their way back from dinner, passed by the coach and were asked to cast an eye on the invalid. One of them, after taking his pulse, walked off, saying he no longer practiced medicine since he was at court. Another, having looked him over more carefully, declared that the whole trouble arose from the gall bladder, which had always been too full; still a third was confident that the ailment had its center in the brain, which had always been too empty.

While they were disputing, the patient took a turn for the worse, a series of convulsions threatened the end, and already the three fingers with which one holds a pen were starting to mortify, when the chief doctor, who had studied his Mead and Boerhaave and who knew more than the others, opened Berthier's mouth with a tongue-depressor, and having duly considered the stench which exhaled, announced that the man had been poisoned.

At this word, everyone exclaimed. —Yes, gentlemen, continued the doctor, he has been poisoned; you need only touch his skin to see that the vapors of a cold poison have invaded his pores; and I maintain this poison must be worse than a mixture of hemlock, black hellebore, opium, nightshade, and belladonna. Coachman, are you sure you didn't have in your carriage some package for our apothecary? —No, sir, replied the coachman; here is the only parcel I put in, at the request of the reverend father himself. Then he dug in the trunk and drew forth two dozen copies of the *Journal de Trévoux*.—Well, said the great doctor, was I wrong?[8]

When he recounts an historical episode, at this period, Voltaire arranges it with the same aritistic skill. The bare anecdote furnished by the annalists is tranformed in his mind by the demands of his imagination and his passions; it becomes symbolic, tendentious, and before long there remains almost nothing of the original story. Thus, wishing to deride religious enthusiasm, he makes allusion to an event which occurred in London at the beginning of the century, and in which the chief actors had been some refugees from the Cévennes overcome with prophetic delirium. They had announced that on a certain day fixed in advance they would raise from the dead one of their friends who had died some time before; and this promise stirred the public to a pitch of excitement. The English government, respecting all manifestations of piety, did not wish to bar entry into the cemetery to the enthusiasts; but it did take measures so that there should be neither scandal nor public turmoil. At the last minute the enthusiasts themselves declined a test, failure in which would have damaged their cause. But this sensible, pitiful conclusion is not at all to Voltaire's taste, and he tells the story in his own way:

> Crowds formed behind the barricades; soldiers were placed to keep the living in order and the dead from desecration; the magistrates took their places, and the clerk of court wrote everything down in the public registers—for when new miracles occur, one cannot be too careful to have a record of them. A body was dug up at the direction of the Saint; he prayed, he fell to his knees, he contorted himself most piously, and all his companions did likewise. In vain; the corpse gave no sign of life, and they put it back into its hole.[9]

Nothing could be more lively, more witty, or more instructive than this story; what a pity that things didn't actually happen that way! But also, how can we fail to recognize the dangers which threaten this admirably endowed spirit? In a story made to give pleasure, every artistic arrangement which can contribute to our diversion is no doubt permitted; but can a narrator indulge in the same freedoms when he is describing an historic event? Too often Voltaire, delighted with his own artistic flair, and driven by his passions, gives us amusing stories, the veracity of which is highly suspect. Let us take them for what they are, not giving too much historical credit to the anecdotes in his pamphlets but tasting freely of the delights of well-told stories.

8. *Story of the confession, death, and ghostly reappearance of the Jesuit Berthier* (1759). [This brilliantly told story may have been suggested by some of Jonathan Swift's pamphlets on the Circumcision and Illness and Death of Edmund Curll. R. M. A.]

9. *Dictionnaire Philosophique*, "Fanaticism," Section V.

RENÉ POMEAU

[Providence, Pessimism, and Absurdity]†

If *Candide* opposed optimism only with arguments, it would not be the masterpiece of Voltaire. *Candide* demolishes Leibnitzian optimism with the obsessive power of a style. Optimism and pessimism are experienced, not so much as ideas, but as contrasted modes of existence. As a writer of temperament, Voltaire expresses the one and the other by means of a rhythm. The conventional disdain for his work in verse has prevented people from noting the original use which he makes of the ten-syllable line. Voltaire had an ear; the decasyllabic meter scans the dry destiny of *Le Pauvre Diable*[1] as well as the bawdy exploits of *La Pucelle*. This verse, which has, not amplitude, but swift movement, is the quickest in French metrics; it is the meter of Voltaire. Sharp and quick, it follows the pace of Voltaire's life. It is significant that *Le Mondain* and the *Anti-Mondain*[2] are both written in ten-syllable verses. The same rhythm, which skips from point to point, serves at one point to express vital energy and at another point the slackening of a relaxed existence. Voltaire fails altogether when in the *Précis de l'Ecclésiaste*[3] he tries to draw out a mood of melancholy languor by means of the alexandrine. Not that the *Précis* does not contain some successes:

> I sought that bliss which vanished from my care
> In cedarn castles, by a hundred wells,
> I sought it in my sirens' vocal spells,

But the quatrain limps heavily through its last line:

> It was no longer in me, anywhere.

Voltaire was not incapable of feeling pre-romantic melancholy. He knew how to describe, if only briefly, "the pleasure of tears"; and he chose, in answer to Mme. de Pompadour's request, precisely this book of *Ecclesiastes*, because he recognized its poetry. But he could not support for long the tone of elegiac sentimentality. That is why the *Précis* combines quatrains of alexandrines with quatrains of trimeter; a mixture which, far from attaining rhythmic alternation,

---

† From *La Religion de Voltaire* (Paris: Nizit, 1956), pp. 303–308. Reprinted by permission of the publisher, Librairie A. G. Nizet. Translation by Robert M. Adams.
1. *Le Pauvre diable* (*Œuvres*, ed. Moland, X, 99) is a satire on Fréron written in 1760; *La Pucelle* (IX, 25) is Voltaire's bawdy mock-epic on Joan of Arc (1755) [*Editor*].
2. *Le Mondain* (X, 83) was a poem of Voltaire's in praise of luxury (1736).
3. In the *Précis de l'Ecclésiaste* (IX, 485), Voltaire undertook to reduce the Book of Ecclesiastes to salon dimensions for the benefit of Mme. de Pompadour. A delightfully eighteenth-century undertaking! [*Editor*].

achieves nothing but dissonance. The true tone of Voltairean pessimism is very different; the feeling of discontinuity which lends its special resonance to the alacrity of a very active character finds its natural expression in the decasyllable, and it asserts itself particularly in the free rhythms of Voltaire's prose.

Nowhere, surely, more than in *Candide*, does it appear that Voltaire's style is a style of life. For ten years, Voltaire had been building toward the perfect success of 1759. Through those sketches for *Candide* which are known as *Babouc*, *Memnon*, *Zadig*, and *Scarmentado*, his optimism-pessimism sought its finished expression. Voltaire-Candide discovers it after ten years of wandering have made him acquainted with the bad and the good side of human existence. The moral of *Candide* is born out of its style; it is the art of extracting happiness from the desolate hopping-about of the human insect.

Candide upsets the world, not only of Leibnitz, but of all dogmatists about Providence. *Candide* is an anti-Bossuet,[4] as surely as the *Essai sur les mœurs*. Whether one looks at the universe as existing in space or time, the conclusion must be the same. Candide, Cunégonde, the old woman, Cacambo, and Martin struggle to escape as best they can from chaos; no one can believe that this swamp was specifically arranged for his greatest good. Candide is the standard hero of the eighteenth century. He runs his course through the great world like Gil Blas, like Figaro, like Jacques the fatalist and his master.[5] Like them, he reasons about men, reasons on the bizarre connection of events. He discovers this desolating truth of modern man, that the human being has been placed, no one knows why, in a universe which does not fit his measure. A universe specially conceived so that man could inhabit it would be Pangloss's "best of possible worlds," if it existed. This "best of worlds" is logical, and its coherence permits logical deductions *a priori*: "for thus" . . . "it has been shown." . . . Derisive emphases, in view of the sleazy texture of the real world. The vain construction of a metaphysician who has eyes in order not to see, the snug world of providential harmony bursts like a bubble the minute it comes into contact with the real one. Again the question rises: is the philosophy of *Candide* a philosophy of the "absurd"? Certainly not. Candide is not, any more than Jacques or Figaro, a hero tragically abandoned in a wrong world. Whatever surprises existence may hold for them,

4. Jacques Bossuet (1627–1704) was a controversialist and divine of great energy and learning, as well as strong authoritarian convictions; most of his work was aimed at justifying the king, the church, and Christ, in that order [*Editor*].
5. Gil Blas (hero of a romance by LeSage), Figaro (Beaumarchais' barber of Seville), and Jacques the fatalist (who gives his name to a novel by Diderot) are all picaresque heroes of the eighteenth century, amiable rogues who look at life with sardonic humor from the underside [*Editor*].

these wanderers are not "outsiders." In the port of Lisbon, the boat swamps and sinks, but Candide and Pangloss find just in time a plank which bears them to shore. Amid the worst disasters, Candide's universe always furnishes a lifesaving plank. Nobody dies in that world. In *Candide*, the chief scene of an absurd world is missing— the scene of death and burial, that ultimate effort of human pomp to cover over the gulf of the absurd. *Candide's* world is one in which people live. Voltaire's swiftness makes perfectly plain, in this work, its ambiguity. The quick and feeble career of the little troop ends in a garden which is the best of possible paradises, granted the instability of things and men.

Candide traces the arc of the Voltairean parabola. Alain saw in it "a kind of Biblical grandeur."[6] Voltaire, who was a great Bible-reader, sought consciously for this resonance. Little Candide is first placed in a Westphalian Eden. Pangloss is right. The castle of My Lord the Baron is indeed the best of possible castles. Reality corresponds marvelously with *a priori* reasonings; everything is for the best, since Miss Cunégonde is lovely and Candide sees her every day. But here is the catastrophe which destroys the paradox of a childish love-affair. Candide and Cunégonde taste, behind a screen, of the forbidden fruit. Up rises the Baron, and projects the sinner forth into outer darkness:

> Candide, ejected from the earthly paradise, wandered for a long time without knowing where he was going, weeping, raising his eyes to heaven, and gazing back frequently on the most beautiful of castles which contained the most beautiful of Baron's daughters. He slept without eating, in a furrow of a plowed field, while the snow drifted over him.

And shortly the lost paradise will fall to dust. A vestige of childish Eden still survives, however; Pangloss is the jolly good-fellow of children's stories, simple and pure like them; Pangloss, a caricature without any malice, a grotesque innocent whom one loves sincerely. His childish pedantic soul will recommend him for a place in Candide's garden. The story conducts the hero on his travels from one "paradise" to another through this "vale of tears." But halfway through, Candide stops in the paradise of Eldorado, and here he is tempted to end his journey. Physical abundance, here, supports a life of calm content. Opportunity responds precisely to desire; the natives are all wise and virtuous. Alas! the dream of the discoverers of America is only a dream. Eldorado, surrounded by impossible mountains, is as if it never existed, a Utopian country peopled by Utopian men. For man as he really is, there is only one garden, one paradise: Candide's. After their vari-

6. Alain, *Propos sur la religion*, p. 207.

ous escapes, the adventurers of the story live there for a while without knowing what it is. The teaching is clear; all men are already in
the only paradise possible. It is up to them to recognize it. The
great force of this wisdom is that it addresses itself to everyday humanity. The workers on the little farm possess no unusual measure
of beauty, wisdom, or virtue. Candide sets to work a wife who has
become "really ugly," a pimping monk, an ancient bawd, and a
whore. . . . Out of their motion he derives joyous activity. He frees
them from the "convulsions of distress" and saves them from the
"lethargy of boredom," by the simplest of prescriptions. In order to
discover it, one needs only a little good sense; in order to practice it,
one need only set to work with gaiety. Good humor prevents problems of social adjustment from arising. No direction, no subordina-
tion in the "little society." Voltaire, a man who found it easy to
live, supposed that work organizes itself spontaneously, whereas, on
the estate of M. de Wolmar, unsociable Rousseau had supposed
himself obliged to invent an extremely complicated code for com-
munal living. "Our whole duty and our highest duty on this
earth is to cultivate it."[7] This moral of Candide's rests on a philosophy, ultimately optimistic, which supposes that the earth is cultiva-
ble. Candide, Pangloss, and Martin have consulted "a very famous
dervish who passed for the best philosopher in Turkey." A brusk
fellow, this dervish; he does not have much to say, but the little he
says is Voltaire's solution to the problem of evil:

> When his highness sends a vessel to Egypt, does he worry
> whether the mice on board are comfortable or not?

"We are the mice" in the building of the "divine architect"; so
Voltaire was writing, as early as 1736.[8] And the sixth of the Discours sur l'Homme relegated to its assigned corner each living creature, mankind included.[9] The metaphysical conclusion of Candide
picks up a constant theme of Voltaire's:

> The number of sufferers is infinite; nature derides individuals.
> Provided the great machine of the universe continues to func-
> tion, the mites which live in it are of no great importance.[1]

Human beings enjoy no privileges in the creation. Man is even an
outlaw on an earth which was not specially designed for him. We
find here a profoundly anti-Christian philosophy, which refuses to
admit that God takes any interest in man. Voltaire, and particularly in this tale of Candide, is moving in the same direction as the
whole of Western civilization since the Renaissance, toward the

7. XL, 80; Best. 7547. Cf. Candide,
ed. Morize, p. 224.
8. XXXIV, 108; Best. 1094. Quoted
by Morize, p. 220.

9. The last of the six Discours sur
l'Homme (1738) [Editor].
1. XXXIX, 108.

separation of God from man. And *Candide* makes clear again that
this movement releases human activity. The mice in the hold pay
little attention to "His Highness," who is indifferent to them.
There is no chapel in Candide's garden, for the central affair of life
is no longer man's relation to God, but man's relation to the world.
Work replaces prayer. The philosophy of *Candide* is of a piece with
that of *Le Siècle de Louis XIV* and that of the *Encyclopédie*.

And yet God, though remote, is not wholly eliminated. "His
Highness" remains the captain of the vessel. From the limited point
of view of the men-mice, the world is chaotic, because it was not
arranged for the mice in the hold. But it was arranged; the divine
structure has a builder, in whom one can trust, and this Voltairean
universe will never be the world of the absurd. As was made plain in
the conclusion of the *Poème sur Lisbonne*, the divine plan author-
izes hope; it is by virtue of "His Highness's" wisdom that the mice
are allowed to vegetate more or less tolerably in the hold of the
vessel. Ultimately, *Candide* denies, not Providence, but Providen-
tialism. Noses were not made to carry spectacles, nor Lisbon harbor
so that Jacques the Anabaptist could be drowned in it. Voltaire
derides the pretension of Pangloss to discover the thread which binds
every event to an intention of the Supreme Being. He reveals the
sophistry of false Leibnitzian legalisms: "If you had not been driven
out of the castle with great kicks in the behind . . . you wouldn't
be sitting here eating candied citron and pistachios." But he does
not deny the existence of a real law, almost as unknowable to man
in its details as the intentions of "His Highness" are to the mice.

And finally it must be said that not all of Voltaire is in *Candide*.
We have seen him elsewhere building up between God and man
the relation of adoration. God then is not so distant; and so it
comes that confidence in the divine goodness, another Voltairean
theme, humanizes slightly the supreme being. The conclusion of
Candide departs even more from the strict determinism of the 1752
Dialogue entre un Bramin et un Jésuite and from the Malebranch-
ist[2] themes of the second *Dialogue entre Lucrèce et Posidone*.
These texts, which assert that the heavy hand of a divine legislator
lies on every event and every thought, occur at the low point of the
pessimist curve. But *Candide* puts a period to one depressive phase
in Voltaire's life. The master of Ferney no longer finds that "this
vale of tears" is all that melancholy; "I complain all the time, as
usual; but at bottom, I'm very comfortable."[3] *Candide* is a spark
from the pugnacity which will presently be exercising itself on
"l'infâme."

2. Malebranche (1638–1715) had argued that God works through such
general laws that evil creeps into the
world through their particular application [*Editor*].
3. XL, 156; Best. 7719.

I. O. WADE

[Voltaire and *Candide*]†

The *Journal encyclopédique*[1] was far from favorable in its review of *Candide*. Indeed, it was so severe that Voltaire felt constrained to take its editors to task for what he deemed their ineptitude. Their article, however, certainly merits attention, since it contains the type of ambiguous evaluation characteristic of all criticism of *Candide* down to the present day:

> How to pass judgment on this novel? Those who have been amused by it will be furious at a serious criticism, those who have read it with a critical eye will consider our lenity a crime. The partisans of Leibnitz, far from considering it a refutation of optimism, will consider it a joke from one end to the other, a joke which may be good for a laugh but proves nothing; the opponents of Leibnitz will maintain that the refutation is complete, because Leibnitz's system, being nothing but a fable, can only be attacked effectively by another fable. Those who seek in fiction only a portrayal of the manners and customs of the age will find its touches too licentious and too monotonous. In short, it is a freak of wit which, in order to please a wide public, needs a bit of decency and some more circumspection. We wish the author had spoken more respectfully concerning religion and the clergy, and that he had not made use of the miserable story of Paraguay, which as it appears here contributes nothing new or amusing. . . .

Thus the author of the article assumed that if the conte were intended to refute Leibnitz, its success would be doubtful, and even if it were effective as a refutation, it could not be considered a work of art because of its indecencies and exaggerations. In general, the *Journal*'s criticism gives the impression that *Candide* can neither be taken seriously nor dismissed lightly.

Voltaire found present in his period this same peculiar ambiguity noted by the *Journal encyclopédique* in its review. At the time he was writing the conte, he commented again and again that Paris "qui chante et qui danse" had abandoned its frivolous air for the serious air of the English. Instead of being "singes" [monkeys] performing "singeries," [monkey-business] which was perfectly normal and natural, Parisians had become "ours," [bears] debating and prattling about serious things. One gathers from his comment that he deplored the change, and in fact he does so in his *Correspond-*

† From I. O. Wade, *Voltaire and Candide* (Princeton University Press, 1959), pp. 311–322. Copyright 1959; reprinted by permission of the publisher.

Quotations from the French have been translated by the present editor.
1. March 15, 1759, p. 103.

ance, but in Chapter xxii of the novel itself, he condemns Paris "qui chante et qui danse," Paris of the "singeries." His attitude toward this situation is not the important thing, however; the author's attitude never is, in a work of art. What is really significant is that the conte has absorbed the ambiguity of its time and of its author. *Candide* is the product of those "qui dansent et qui chantent," the "singes" and their "singeries," but also of the "ours" who take themselves seriously. And it is difficult to know which is the real, authentic *Candide*.

Grimm's review in the *Correspondance littéraire*, less favorable still, did precisely what the author of the *Journal encyclopédique* article deemed impossible. Renouncing any attempt to treat the work seriously, Grimm insisted that the only way to handle it was to take it lightly. After finding the second half superior to the first, after condemning the chapter on Paris, after denying the conte every serious literary and philosophical quality, he found only Voltaire's gaiety to praise:

> Gaiety is one of the rarest qualities to be found among wits. It is a long time since we read anything joyous in literature; M. de Voltaire has just delighted [but *égayer* has also the sense of "mock"] us with a little novel called *Candide, or optimism*, translated from the German of Dr. Ralph. There is no need to judge this performance by high standards; it would never stand up to serious criticism. There is in *Candide* neither arrangement nor plan nor wisdom nor any of those happy strokes which one sometimes finds in English novels of the same sort; instead, you will find in it plenty of things in bad taste, low touches, smut and filth deprived of that discreet veil which renders them supportable; but gaiety and facility never abandon M. de Voltaire, who banishes from his most frivolous as from his most carefully worked writings that air of pretension which spoils everything. The fine touches and gay sallies which he gives off at every moment make the reading of *Candide* a very amusing experience.

Thus *Candide* became for Grimm what Voltaire often called it: "une plaisanterie" [a jest].

Mme. de Staël, on the other hand, takes a position the very opposite of Grimm's. She admits willingly that the book abounds in laughter, but considers it in no way a "plaisanterie," for this laughter contains something inhumanly diabolical. She concedes that *Candide* basically was directed against Leibnitz, but stresses that it was directed against the fundamental propositions which preoccupy mankind, especially those philosophical opinions which enhance the spirit of man. Nothing could be more serious:

> Voltaire had so clear a sense of the influence which metaphysical systems exert on the direction of our thinking, that he

composed *Candide* to combat Leibnitz. He took a curious attitude of hostility toward final causes, optimism, free will, and in short against all these philosophic opinions which tend to raise the dignity of man; and he created *Candide*, that work of diabolic gaiety. For it seems to have been written by a creature of a nature wholly different from our own, indifferent to our lot, rejoicing in our sufferings, and laughing like a demon or an ape at the misery of this human race with which he has nothing in common.

While Grimm stresses the conte's gaiety, and Mme de Staël its seriousness, Linguet in his *Examen des ouvrages de M. de Voltaire* (Bruxelles, 1788) notes its dual character, that is to say, the glee with which Voltaire destroys the philosophy of optimism by graphically describing the tragic miseries of humanity:

> Candide offers us the saddest of themes disguised under the merriest of jokes, the joking being of that philosophical variety which is peculiar to M. de Voltaire, and which, I repeat, seems like the equipment of an excellent comedian. He makes the *all's well* system, upheld by so many philosophers, look completely ridiculous, and cracks a thousand jests even as he holds before our eyes at every instant the miseries of society and portrays them with a very energetic pencil (p. 170).

Without being too dogmatic, we can confidently assert that these four opinions, though based on the same fundamental abiguous assumptions, are widely divergent and represent the cardinal points of all *Candide* critics. There are those who, like the author of the *Journal encyclopédique*, feel that the work can be taken neither seriously nor lightly, those who maintain with Grimm that it must be treated only lightly, those who aver with Mme de Staël that it can be taken only seriously, and finally those who like Linguet, find that it must be taken seriously and lightly at the same time.

This double quality of gaiety and seriousness, so characteristic of Voltaire and of his time, is apparent at every turn throughout the conte, but it is not a simple matter to grasp the deep ambiguity of its personality. When the reader is ready to revolt in horror, a sudden reflection, a quick turn in events, an unexpected quip, or the mere insertion of a remark brings him back to normal. When he is inclined to levity, an incident, an observation, or an injustice brings him back to consider the deadly earnest attack which is being made on all aspects of life.

The difficulty in harmonizing these two attitudes in the reader's understanding has led to divers partial interpretations of *Candide*, practically all of them valid in their way but each woefully deficient in itself. If the book is to be taken lightly, how lightly? Can it be dismissed as the "crème fouettée de l'Europe," [whipped cream of

Europe] or is it a "bonne plaisanterie," with a "fonds le plus triste" [an undertone of sadness]? Does Candide, like Figaro, rail at everything to keep himself from weeping? Is it, as Montaigne once said of Rabelais, "simplement plaisant" [naïvely comic] on the surface, but "triste" underneath? There is a similar progression in the opposite attitude. How far does Voltaire go in his satire? Does he, for instance, merely castigate the social conditions of his time, as Boileau or Horace had done before him, or does he satirize the fundamental conditions of life, like a Homer or a Racine, or does he push his revolt to the point of satirizing the Creator of life? These are difficult, almost irreverent, questions. The answers must always be yes, although every yes is contradicted by another yes, or a yes and no by another yes and no. Far from being a structure of "clear and distinct ideas," *Candide* is confusion confounded. But it is the confusion of a universe clearly and distinctly controlled. Whatever happens may be terribly and devastatingly irrational, but once it has been sifted through Voltaire's intelligence, it has been ordered by the keenest sort of criticism into a created form which does not differ from the form of life itself. *Candide* embraces everything that has occurred in the life of Voltaire as well as everything that had occurred in the eighteenth century. It is astounding in its comprehensiveness, and quite as remarkable in other aspects: the rhythmical arrangement of the above-mentioned phenomena, the careful selection and presentation, the exact apportionment, and the very orderly expression.

That is the reason why every judgment of *Candide* is bound to be partial, one-sided, contradictory, and vague, just like every judgment we make of life or of our individual lives. Since every man is a "Démocrite" and a "Héraclite," he must be "Jean-qui-pleure" and "Jean-qui-rit."[2] But every man must be these two characters at the same time: he is neither optimist nor pessimist, rebellious nor submissive, free nor enslaved, formed nor unformed, real nor unreal. He must make a reality of these necessary contradictions.

The four opinions expressed above, while representing the four cardinal positions in *Candide* criticism, in no way exhaust the range of partial interpretations given the work. I pass over Voltaire's own sly remark that it was written to convert Socinians, as well as the superficial, but amusing, epigram current at the time of its appearance:

> Candide is a little crook,
> Shameless and weak in the head;

2. Title of a poem by Voltaire which concludes: "We're formed of clay divine, so much I know,/ And all, one day, will rise to heavenly glory;/ But here on earth we see a different story,/ Souls are machines, which fate bids stop or go./ Watch nature change her giddy mood;/ Although, like Heraclitus, he was sad,/ Let business suddenly be good,/ And man will, like Democritus, be glad" [*Editor*].

> You can tell by his sly look,
> He's kid brother to The Maid.[3]

> His old dad would give a pack
> Just to be young again:
> His youth will come back,
> He's writing like a young man.

> Life isn't great, take a look,
> He proves it six different ways,
> You'll even see in this book
> Things really stink, like he says.

Of more importance is the qualification printed in the *Nouvelles ecclésiastiques*:[4] "Bad novel, full of filth, perhaps the most impious and pernicious work ever to come from the pen of M. de Voltaire," or the opinion attributed the Patriarch [i.e., Voltaire himself] by the unknown author of the *Confession de Voltaire*:[5] "It follows from the reading of *Candide* that the earth is a sewer of horror and abominations [with a quotation from Job 10:22 'A land of misery and shadows, where is no order but eternal horror dwells']; more than one chapter of it was composed during attacks of migraine. . . ." or the more drastic qualification of Jules Janin in *Le dernier volume des Œuvres de Voltaire*.[6]

> The book was much read in high society, where it was not understood. People saw nothing but romantic adventures where Voltaire with fiendish logic had intended to ridicule God.

After so many categorical statements, made with appropriately French nuance, it may seem idle to seek a clearer view of *Candide's* reality. It is quite possible to agree that the work is a "vaurien" [nogood], or obscene, or perhaps the most impious ever written by Voltaire, or that its portrayal of the earth is abomination and horror incarnate. One might even go so far as to agree with Janin that "Voltaire avait voulu railler Dieu" [Voltaire intended to ridicule God]. But to understand that the work is at the same time a revolt and a submission, an attack and a defense, a joy and a suffering, a destruction and a creation requires more than ordinary insight, patience, and serenity. There is, indeed, the temptation to dismiss it as only one thing, as too simple, too superficial.

What is dangerous in *Candide* is not its simplicity, but its duplicity. *Candide* is always deceptively two. Its unremitting ambiguity leads inevitably to a puzzling clandestinity, and the reader, beset with difficulties in forming a well-considered opinion, settles for trite commonplaces. The work actually encourages him in this. Let us take as an example the oft-repeated remark that Voltaire at-

3. Voltaire's *La Pucelle.*
4. September 3, 1760, p. 158.

5. Geneva, 1762, p. 39.
6. Paris, 1861, p. 103.

tacked Leibnitz. Though true, this statement adds nothing to the comprehension of *Candide*'s reality.

It would be useful, nevertheless, to understand the relationship between *Candide* and Leibnitz. Undeniably, Voltaire satirized Leibnitzian terminology in his conte but ample testimony has been adduced to show that he never rejected Leibnitzianism: he rejected some things in it—the theory of monads, for example—but he readily accepted other ideas such as the principle of sufficient reason. We have already shown that he needed Leibnitz's principles, just as they were needed by the eighteenth century at large. It is a particularly carefree criticism that envisages the development of ideas as a matter of acceptance or rejection. Voltaire was certainly more realistic in his attitude. What he satirized was the terminology; not the philosophy, but what in that philosophy was now contributing to making life sterile. Moreover, at the moment he was writing *Candide*, he stated explicitly that people had ceased paying attention to what Leibnitz said. Soon after, when a new edition of Leibnitz's works was published, he complimented the editor. The truth of the matter is that Voltaire, like his time, had to integrate Descartes, Pascal, Leibnitz, Spinoza, Malebranche, Locke and Newton in order to create an Enlightenment philosophy. Leibnitz was as important to that philosophy as any of the others, and fully as useful. It is probable that in 1750 he had played his role and in that sense had ceased to claim people's attention. But even this assessment is subject to caution.

This dilemma has led certain critics to insist that what Voltaire is attacking is not a philosopher, but a philosophy. Ever since the article of March 15, 1759, in the *Journal encyclopédique*, some critics have insisted that Voltaire definitely aimed his attack not against Leibnitz or Pope, but against a system of philosophy to which Leibnitz, Pope, and many others had contributed and which we now call optimism. Since he himself entitled his work *Candide, ou l'optimisme*, it would be extremely difficult to deny that he directed his satire at this way of looking at life. To conclude, however, with Linguet, that "il tourne complètement en ridicule le système du tout est bien" [he makes the *all's well* system look completely ridiculous"], or, with Lanson, that "le but est de démolir l'optimisme" ["his aim is to demolish optimism"], is misplacing the emphasis. It would not take a very skillful lawyer to prove that Voltaire's treatment of optimism is quite as optimistic as the treatment of the optimists themselves, that he says no more for or against it than Leibnitz, Pope, King, and hundreds of others. Voltaire is assailing all feeling of complacency which nullifies and stultifies human effort in a universe requiring a maximum of human effort to realize itself—he is assailing, in a word, all restraints upon the creative spirit of man.

It must be admitted that his attitude toward optimism is difficult to trace because of the ambiguity of his position. He was congenitally opposed to any attitude which complacently asseverated that "tout est bien," mainly because such a belief limited human effort. But he was quite as opposed to any attitude which despairingly asserted that "tout est mal," chiefly because such a standpoint also limited human effort. But other considerations were important, too. Voltaire knew that "tout n'est pas bien" because there are numerous concrete cases of evil, and he knew also that "tout n'est pas mal" because there are many concrete cases of good. Throughout the conte, he draws a constant parallel between the wretchedness of others and his own happiness, and he continually wavers between the achievements of his time and its follies. He weighs facts as scrupulously as Montaigne weighed truth: the facts prove two things, two exasperatingly contradictory things. Cacambo's friendship and loyalty make him "un tres bon homme" [a very good man], while Vanderdendur's duplicity makes him "un homme très dur" [a very hard man], but both are realities, just as the "duretés" of the "homme noir" and the kindness of the "bon Jacques" are realities. There is thus in *Candide* a compensatory quality, common to all Voltaire's works and to the eighteenth century in general, that is, that good is counterbalanced by evil. This is no new attitude: it is evident throughout his works from the *Epître à Uranie* to *Candide*. *Le Monde comme il va*, *Micromégas*, *Zadig* hold steadily to this idea.

It is not the view, however, that is important, but the conclusion to be drawn from it. Should one conclude for optimism, or surrender to pessimism? Should one be content with weighing impassively this against that, refusing to take sides, enjoying fully his own happiness? This skeptical conclusion, characteristic of the Renaissance in general and of Montaigne in particular, did not find favor with Voltaire, although he, like most Frenchmen, was strongly attracted to it. The ambiguity of Candide's garden, and of its actual prototype at Les Délices and Ferney, was occasioned in fact by this skeptical conclusion. But Voltaire's skepticism, which is as positive as Montaigne's, is no proof against his cynicism. It was impossible to "jouir largement de son être" [enjoy freely his existence] in 1758 after the fiasco at Berlin, the Lisbon Earthquake, and the Seven Years War. It was possible, perhaps, to criticize, blame, satirize, laugh mockingly, always with indifference, in this completely mad world. Voltaire attempted to adopt this attitude also but found it quite unsatisfactory.

Candide is thus in its inner substance not *wholly* optimistic, or pessimistic, or skeptical, or cynical: it is *all* of these things at the same time. Since every created thing resembles its creator and the moment of its creation, it is precisely what Voltaire and his time were: optimistic, pessimistic, skeptical, and cynical, a veritable "moment de la crise" [moment of crisis]. Facts had produced ideas, it is true, but ideas had not yet produced ideals, and no one knew what *to do*.

There are, of course, several ways of meeting this situation. First, there is resignation: Christian or even philosophical resignation, both unacceptable to Voltaire. Having rejected Christianity, dogma and all, he could find no solace in an attitude leading to consequences that he could not accept, and having long since adopted libertine Epicureanism, he saw no sense in any form of stoicism, Christian or pagan.

Second, there is the way of attack, for if conditions are intolerable, they can be denounced. It is as easy to ridicule distasteful facts, offensive people, disagreeable incidents, and unfair judgments as to satirize an unacceptable view of the universe. Voltaire responded freely and fully to this temptation: the list of things and persons he assails is practically endless: kings, religious intolerance, the Inquisition; Fréron, Vanduren, Trublet; war, inequality, injustice; disease, earthquake, tidal waves; petty thievery, rape, social pride; Jesuits, Jansenists, slavery. In this mass and single attack there is a complete upheaval of the social order; in the political area we find deep criticism of monarchy, the policing of the state, the lack of freedom and equality before the law. In the realm of religion there are powerful accusations against persecution, intolerance, useless dogma, and hierarchical institution. In the moral order, dishonesty, shame, false pride, prostitution, rape, all the petty inhumanities of man against man are viciously assailed. In the natural order, disease, cataclysms, malformations are damned with an irreverence barely short of blasphemy. And yet, though *Candide* attacks, it does not ultimately destroy. The reason for this is very simple: life is full of miseries, but it also has its pleasures. It is perhaps true that few people would like to relive it, but also true that few voluntarily renounce it. Voltaire was certainly not one to abdicate.

Nevertheless, as the crisis developed, he was torn between cynical renunciation and the urge to create. He was completely aware that the forces restraining this urge were powerful enough to eliminate not only the desire but the person desiring. Experience had taught him the stupidities of man, the horrors of war, the power of kings, and the eccentricities of nature. Any one of these could easily suppress him and his urge to create. He was thus literally reduced to living by his wits, like J. F. Rameau and Figaro, and living by his wits meant very literally indeed the application of wit to all this stupid phenomenon. The world had become a paradox and Voltaire responded with a revolt.

It is imperative to understand the nature of this revolt, since the whole eighteenth century and subsequent centuries have derived from it. Voltaire's response was born of both anger and despair. He was "fâché" [angry] with kings, "fâché" with earthquakes, "fâché" with God. Agamemnon, the great Earthshaker and Zeus had "let him down," just as they had seemed to abandon Achilles in a far distant moment. The two urns which stand at the feet of Zeus poured forth both good and evil upon the old Patriarch and he, in his frustration, became deeply unhappy, the more so since events transcended all understanding by the human mind:

> Poor feeble reason, blind, misled, bemused,
> If with God's insights it be not suffused,
> Will ne'er conceive what power out of hell
> Mingled so much of ill with what is well.

Voltaire's attitude toward Providence must be considered very carefully if we are to grasp the meaning of *Candide*. It was perhaps well to ask ourselves what role Rousseau's letter played in the composition of the conte. While it is extremely unlikely that the *Lettre sur la Providence* provoked *Candide,* as Rousseau would have us believe, it is nevertheless true that Rousseau's defense of Providence touched Voltaire in his sensitive spot. The conclusion of *Zadig,* it will be recalled, had definitely been a defense of Providence, along more rational, Popian lines than Rousseau's later defense. The problem is therefore posed as to Voltaire's subsequent attitude.

If, to be specific, Voltaire felt that Pope's arguments no longer "justified the ways of God to man," and Leibnitz's were equally deficient, did he think that he had better ones, or that he could find better ones elsewhere? In other words, was his quarrel with the optimists whose arguments could not justify God's ways or with God whose way could not be rationally justified? And did he assail the philosophers with fiendish glee because he did not know how to attack Providence which was really responsible for evil? Why did he not heed Rousseau's letter as the Duke de Wurtemburg thought he should have done? Why was it rather an incitement to *Candide,* just as Rousseau thought? These are strange and almost irreverent questions, and totally unanswerable in any critical way, but necessary in divining Voltaire's state of mind. It is undoubtedly true that his act was not a critique but a revolt, a titanic revolt brought about by a breakdown in the power of critique. Having reached the place where understanding was irrational, Voltaire had no other resource than to attack overtly those who thought they understood, and who gave good rational reasons for their comprehension. Simply put, he could only attack the irrationality, the ambiguity of the universe by annihilating rationally all rationality. In that respect his wit is a spiritual, not a rational, instrument for assailing the ambiguity, the clandestinity of a universe which refuses to make itself known.

This state of things explains why one never knows in reading *Candide* whether to laugh with Voltaire or at him, whether to laugh with the philosophers or at them, whether indeed to laugh with or at Providence; whether, in fact, to laugh at all. In uncertainty and despair there is much ground for hesitation, uneasiness, bitterness, frustration. Taken seriously, the moment of *Candide* is a tragic affair. But should it be taken seriously? Mme d'Epinay in her characterization of Voltaire states that when he has become most serious he immediately starts making fun of himself and everybody else. This reaction seems to hold true for *Candide*. Certainly no one takes himself too seriously in *Candide*. When the moment of revolt becomes too intense, each person resorts to his wit to save the situation. Thus wit is not only a means of revolt, it is at the same time an instrument for the release of intolerable pressures and better still, it serves as a release for the inner forces of man; it is a force, too, a creative effort, an urge to be. Standing face to face with the power of annihilation, impotent to solve either the rationality or the irrationality of things, witness to an impossibly ludicrous cosmic tragedy, *Candide* proclaims loudly, not that

> The play is the tragedy Man
> And its hero, the Conqueror Worm

but that the play is puny, insignificant, unregenerate man, and its hero an unconquerable, defiant, eternal wit.

J. G. WEIGHTMAN

The Quality of *Candide*†

It may seem late in the day to ask how good a book *Candide* really is. Has the world not been long agreed that it is a masterpiece? It started triumphantly by being banned in Paris and Geneva, and has gone on selling ever since. It has provided France and the world with two or three proverbial expressions. Schopenhauer praised it in the most emphatic terms;[1] Flaubert said that it contained the quintessence of Voltaire's writings;[2] H. N. Brailsford

† From *Essays Presented to C. M. Girdlestone* (University of Durham, 1960) Pp. 335–347. Reprinted by permission of the Editors and J. G. Weightman. Quotations from the French have been translated by the present editor.
1. "I can see no other merit in Leibniz's *Theodicy* except that of having furnished the great Voltaire with the occasion of his immortal *Candide.*" Quoted in *La Table Ronde,* Feb., 1958, p. 111.
2. *Correspondance,* ed. Conard, II, p. 348.

declared that it "ranks in its own way with *Don Quixote* and *Faust*".[3] So alive is it, indeed, that it was recently turned into an American musical and has thus shared with *Manon Lescaut* and *Les Liaisons dangereuses* the honour of being relaunched in the twentieth century as a work with a universal appeal for mass audiences.

But, on second thoughts, this may appear a doubtful honour and make us wonder on what level of success *Candide* has been operating. *Manon Lescaut* and *Les Liaisons dangereuses* are perhaps compromising connections, since their moral and aesthetic acceptability has often been questioned by literary critics. And it is true that Voltaire himself is still often referred to as if he were, generally speaking, rather disreputable; irreverent, outmoded, a mere maker of debating points. Faguet's 'un chaos d'idées claires' [a chaos of clear ideas] is a Voltairean jibe that has been used, effectively, against Voltaire. Mr. Martin Turnell, a contemporary English critic with a stern approach to French Literature, refers briefly to 'the flashy vulgarity of *Candide*'.[4] Even those people who have a genuine interest in Voltaire often imply that we should not look for depths or complexities in him. Carl Becker, after doubting whether Voltaire really understood the brilliance of his own witticisms, suggests that his scepticism did not amount to much, and that *Candide* is not a central text:

> The cynicism of Voltaire was not bred in the bone . . . It was all on the surface, signifying nothing but the play of a supple and irrepressible mind, or the sharp impatience of an exasperated idealist. In spite of *Candide* and all the rest of it, Voltaire was an optimist, though not a naïve one.[5]

The late Professor Saurat, introducing a selection of Voltaire's tales, differs from Becker in crediting Voltaire with deep feeling. However, he then goes on to deny him depth of intelligence:

> The jesting of *Candide* is the mournful levity of a belief expiring in the face of the facts, but which nonetheless persists. He would have preferred Leibniz to be right; but his intelligence, though so quick, was not deep enough to let him see that Leibniz was right.[6]

Professor Saurat does not explain in what way Leibniz is in the right.

Already in 1913, in his critical edition of *Candide*, André Morize had emphasized that Voltaire did not appear to have a detailed knowledge of Leibniz's arguments:

3. *Candide and Other Tales*, Everyman's Library, 1937, p. xxiv.
4. *The Novel in France*, Hamish Hamilton, 1950, p. 189.
5. *The Heavenly City of the Eighteenth Century Philosophers*, Yale University Press, 1957 edition, pp. 36, 37.
6. *Le Taureau blanc*, etc., The Hyperion Press, 1945, p. 5.

Candide or Optimism is by no means the product of a metaphysician to whom Leibniz and the *Theodicy* were familiar.[7]

Richard Aldington, in his introduction to the Broadway Translation
of 1927, gives a summary of the philosophical controversy from
which *Candide* emerged, because—he says—the book 'is often represented as a merely amusing squib'. But his own conclusion seems
strangely self-contradictory:

> Its popularity is due to its amusing adventures, its clear rapid
> style, its concentrated wit, its vitality and alertness, and *to its
> triumphant disposal of facile optimism. Whether it really proves
> anything may admit of doubt* . . .[8]

Dr. W. H. Barber, who gives a beautifully clear and meticulous account of the shifts in Voltaire's position with regard to optimism,
makes a comment on *Candide* which might appear to reduce the
book to personal satire on minor Neo-Leibnizians:

> Voltaire is not concerned to refute a doctrine by careful argu-
> ment; his object is to ridicule a band of enthusiasts whose ideas
> he thinks absurd; and the immediate and lasting popularity of
> *Candide* is some measure of his success.[9]

A similar statement is made by Hugo Friedrich in a special number
of *La Table Ronde* devoted to Voltaire:

> At bottom it was not Leibnitz whom Voltaire attacked, but the
> cheap optimism fashionable in Paris salons, as seasoned with
> obscure German lucubrations. We must not read *Candide* as a
> novel with a thesis . . . we must let ourselves be amused by
> watching a free spirit playing with very grave questions for lack
> of power to resolve them.[1]

All these judgements must seem rather slighting to anyone who has
a high regard for *Candide*, because they suggest that the book is, in
fact, more of a squib than anything else. Consequently, there may
be a case for reopening the argument and trying to decide what exactly *Candide* achieves.

The first thing to establish, if possible, is that *Candide* is basically serious. Of course, Voltaire was never at any time fair-minded,
and there seems every reason to believe that he did not bother to
reread, or even read, Leibniz's *Théodicée* before writing his satire.
As both Morize and Barber point out, he mixes up the two main
forms of the theory of optimism: the belief that evil is an effect of
the human angle of vision, and the belief that evil is a necessary

7. Librairie E. Droz, p. xiii.
8. Routledge, p. 16. My [Weight-
man's] italics.
9. *Leibniz in France*, O.U.P., 1955, p.
232.
1. *La Table Ronde*, February 1958,
pp. 111–115.

part of creation. He makes no attempt to distinguish between the different degrees of sophistication represented by Leibniz, Pope and Wolff. Leibniz neither denied the existence of evil nor held the simple finalistic views which Voltaire attributes to Pangloss. Also, as Barber shows, Leibniz was an activist whose purpose was to encourage men to virtuous initiative within the all-embracing framework of God's will, and as such he was, in a sense, on Voltaire's side. If one wished to press the accusation of superficiality still further against Voltaire, one could recall that he himself began by being an optimist who declared in the *Traité de métaphysique* that moral evil was 'une chimère' ["a dream"] and the notion of evil a relative one:

> To be quite sure that a thing is evil one must see at the same time that something better is possible.[2]

The Angel Jesrad in *Zadig*, which comes before *Candide*, is on the whole Leibnizian in his statement that a world without evil would be another kind of world. So is the Quaker, Freind, in the very late conte, *L'Histoire de Jenni*. In other works of his later years—the *Homélies prononcées à Londres en 1765*, *Questions sur l'Encyclopédie*, *Il faut prendre un parti* and *Fragments historiques sur l'Inde*—Voltaire contradicts himself, saying in one place that God is obviously limited and repeating in another that evil exists only from the human point of view and must be unknown to God in His perfection.

Have we to conclude, then, that Voltaire had a shallow mind which casually adopted different sets of ideas at different times? Is *Candide* an irresponsible attack on beliefs that he was capable of putting forward as his own, when they happened to serve his purpose? Is he simply a jester who does not understand what the philosophers are about? I do not think so. The extraordinary resonance of *Candide* and the strange frenzy in which Voltaire seems to have lived during most of his life, and particularly during the latter half, point to a very different conclusion. Here was a man who, through his personal experience, his reading of history and his observation of contemporary events, gradually came to be obsessed with the scandal of the presence of evil in the universe. At the same time, with his clear and vigorous brain he could only suppose that God was an immeasurably greater Voltaire who had organized the universe on rational lines and was not, ultimately, responsible for evil. How could God have willed evil since Voltaire, like any decent person, found it intolerable? Yet evil existed, and God must be good. But how could a good God . . . etc. He never escaped from the dilemma, but tried out different verbal solutions at different stages

2. *Traité de métaphysique*, ed. H.T. Patterson, Manchester U.P., 1937, p. 16.

and was presumably never convinced by any of them. Through some psychological accident of which we shall no doubt always remain ignorant (perhaps he went through a phase like Shakespeare's tragic period), he produced *Candide* at a time when his awareness of evil was at its most violent and his vitality at its strongest. In this one book, the horror of evil and an instinctive zest for life are almost equally matched and it is the contrast between them, inside the paragraph and even inside the sentence, which produces the unique tragicomic vibration. The lesson of *Candide* is the permanent one that there is no verbal, that is intellectual, solution to the problem of evil, but that we go on living even so, and even when we think we have no faith.

If this interpretation is correct, two consequences follow. In the first place, Voltaire is not simply attacking Pope or Leibniz or the Neo-Leibnizians or J.-J. Rousseau; he is also attacking himself, because when he trusted to the philosophical use of language, he found himself arguing like them. He himself is Pangloss, just as he is Candide, Martin and Pococurante. The book is a transposition of his inner debate. And it is surely an underestimation of his wit to imply that his rapid jokes are not valid against the more elaborate explanations of evil. They are genuine caricatures. To the question: 'Why, if God is good (and we must suppose that He is), does evil exist?' there is no articulate answer which is not a juggling with words. Book VII of St. Augustine's *Confessions* is quite elaborate, but are its logical fallacies not obvious? Chapter VII of Book III of St. Thomas's *Summa Contra Gentiles* seems no less purely verbal. And when we open Leibniz to see how Voltaire misunderstood him, we find this sort of argument:

> For God sees from the beginning of time that there will be a certain Judas; and the notion or idea that God has of him contains this future free action. Only this question now remains, why this Judas, the traitor, who is only a possibility in the idea of God, exists in actuality. But to this question there can be no answer here below, except that in general one can say that since God found it proper that he should exist in spite of the sin He foresaw, it must be that this evil will be repaid with interest somewhere else in the universe, that God will derive a greater good from it, and in short it will be found that the sequence of events which includes the existence of this sinner is the most perfect of all those which were possible. But to explain in every instance the admirable economy of a particular choice, that cannot be done while we inhabit this transitory sphere; it suffices to know it without understanding it.[3]

3. *Discours de Métaphysique*, 30, in *Leibnizens Gesammelte Werke*, Hannover 1846.

156 · J. G. Weightman

The 'admirable economy' of a choice we know nothing about and only suppose to have existed is an excellent example of Panglossian applauding of the cosmos. Before Leibniz wrote the *Théodicée*, Bayle had said all there was to be said about this kind of circular argument in dealing with Lactantius, St. Basil and Maximus of Tyre,[4] and he was not adequately refuted by Leibniz. In particular intellectual gifts, Bayle and Voltaire may have been much inferior to Leibniz, but on this precise issue they saw more clearly the futility of verbalizations. As Barber says:

> Leibniz . . . never really abandons *a priori* argument. He bases his knowledge of God's nature on *a priori* rational considerations . . . and once God's infinite goodness and wisdom have thus been established, all else also follows deductively. Thus he never really meets Bayle on his own ground. To all Bayle's paradoxes he has at bottom only one reply, though his subtlety of argument sometimes conceals the fact; the world as it is is God's creation, therefore no better world is possible.[5]

In the second place, *Candide* is not in the last resort a message of hope, or at least not exactly in the way suggested by some critics who take a favourable view of it. Morize, Barber and René Pomeau, the author of *La Religion de Voltaire*, all seem to me to underestimate the virulence of the work. Morize writes:

> The world is in shambles, blood flows, Jesuits and Molinists rage, innocents are slaughtered and dupes exploited; but there are in the world delicious asylums, where life remains possible, joyous, and sweet: let us cultivate our garden.[6]

This suggests an ability to shut out the spectacle of the world which Voltaire never possessed, and does not correspond to the tone of dogged persistence in the final chapters of *Candide*. According to Barber:

> The practical philosophy to which Candide finally attains is the application to the limited field of personal activity of that *espérance* which Voltaire had offered to humanity on a transcendental level in the conclusion of the *Poème sur le désastre de Lisbonne*.
> In rejecting the doctrines of Pangloss and his like . . . he is seeking . . . a safe foundation in an insecure world for that profound belief in the value of activity which is characteristic of European man and was particularly strong in him.[7]

But does he find any such foundation? There is no evidence in *Candide*, and very little in his biography, that he had a profound belief in the value of activity. He believed in man's need for activity

4. See footnotes 2 and 4 page 88 above [*Editor*].
5. Op. cit., p. 88.
6. Op. cit., p. xlvii.
7. Op. cit., p. 233.

and he himself had a tremendous urge to be active, but these can be independent of any conviction of value. Would it not be more plausible to suppose that his feverish busyness was the only relief he could find for his acute awareness of evil? Pomeau speaks of the "epicurean motive for action which is the last word of the tale" and says that Voltaire "will make a philosophy of activity . . . A lesson revolutionary in its banality." No doubt, Voltaire borrowed the image of the garden from Epicurus, but he has no trace of Epicurean serenity or moderation. Actually, Pomeau is uncertain about the ultimate significance of the work. In *La Religion de Voltaire* (1956), he declares roundly:

> Is the philosophy of *Candide* a philosophy of the "absurd"? Certainly not. Candide is not, any more than Jacques or Figaro, a hero tragically abandoned in a wrong world. Whatever surprises existence may hold for them, these wanderers are not "outsiders" . . . Amid the worst disasters, Candide's universe always furnishes a lifesaving plank.[8]

However, in his critical edition of 1959, after making some excellent remarks about the poetic quality of *Candide*, he contradicts his earlier statement:

> Spontaneously, from the poetry of the unforeseen, there arises a philosophy of the absurd.[9]

Only one critic appears to have stressed unequivocally the strength of the dark side of Voltaire's temperament, which is so obvious in *Candide* and in the correspondence. This is André Delattre, in his stimulating little book, *Voltaire l'impétueux*, where we read:

> It is only when, in *Candide*, he accepts certain perspectives of Pascal's, it is only when he ceases to strain against a dark and healthy pessimism, and ceases to hold open the empty sack of his optimism, that he finally creates, after his sixtieth year, his real masterpiece.[1]

This is a good pointer to the quality of the work. *Candide* is not just a clever, unfair satire on optimism which concludes with the bracing recommendation that we should do what we can to improve matters in our immediate vicinity. It is a work in which an unappeasable sense of the mystery and horror of life is accompanied, at every step, by an instinctive animal resilience. Negative and positive are juxtaposed (as they are, indeed, in some religious temperaments) with no unsatisfactory ratiocinative bridge between them. Voltaire has a faith, but it is not a political faith nor an easily defined religious one. It is the sort of faith that keeps the severed frac-

8. Librairie Nizet, 1956, p. 305.   1. Mercure de France, 1947, p. 69.
9. Librairie Nizet, 1959, p. 70.

tions of a worm still wriggling, or produces laughter at a funeral. In this sense, Voltaire's humanism is a very basic and simple characteristic, exceptional only in that it has at its service extraordinary intelligence and wit.

I say 'at its service' advisedly, because *Candide* is not, in the first place, an intellectual work. Its driving force is an intellectual bewilderment, which is felt as a strong emotion. Pomeau makes the interesting suggestion that the chronological irregularity in the composition of the *contes* is proof of their springing from a level well below Voltaire's everactive, normal consciousness:

> The intermittent quality of the invention in the tales makes clear that here a deeper self is finding outlet, which does not get expressed every day.[2]

He also adduces evidence to show that *Candide,* instead of being a rapid improvisation as has often been thought, was probably written at intervals over a period of a year. He concludes that it shows signs of deliberate artistry:

> A work of spontaneous fantasy, no doubt, but in the course of working on it, retouchings and additions appear, which make plain a very conscious impulse toward artistic form.[3]

I think it is possible to accept the first suggestion, while remaining unconvinced by the second. The alterations and additions Pomeau mentions are comparatively slight, and although *Candide* may have been in the making for a year, it could still be a happy fluke in which the artistry is largely unconscious. Voltaire himself seems never to have realized that it was his masterpiece, and he probably devoted more deliberate attention to denying its authorship than he had to its composition. His still-born tragedies he composed with great care, passing them round amongst his friends for comment and improvement. His tales were rattled off much more spontaneously, and he does not appear to have understood how original and gifted he was in this *genre*. If he had, he would presumably have taken more pains with some of the others, which are all either imperfect or slight. It is impossible not to agree with Delattre on this score:

> As for the tales, apart from *Candide* which is in a class by itself, they are really thin, quite slender.[4]

There is no progression up to *Candide,* nor any sign of further development afterwards. Good *contes* and less good were written higgledy-piggledy. *Zadig,* which came twelve years before *Candide,*

2. Edition critique, p. 7.
3. Edition critique, p. 46.
4. Op. cit., p. 96.

and *L'Ingénu*, written eight years after, are probably the next best, but the first is uncertain in design and ends feebly, while the second begins in one tone and finishes rather abruptly in another, without the transition having been properly justified. Neither is firmly centered on a major theme. Other *contes*, such as *Le Monde comme il va* and *Micromégas*, which keep to one theme, repeat the same effect rather monotonously. It is very curious that, in *Zadig, Le Monde comme il va, Memnon* and *Scarmentado*, Voltaire should appear to be fumbling towards *Candide* and then, having produced his masterpiece, that he should go on to imperfect works such as *L'homme aux quarante écus* and *L'Histoire de Jenni*, which we would be tempted, on artistic grounds, to place before *Candide*, if we did not know their date of composition. *Candide* is the only *conte* which has an overall pattern, a major theme worked out with a variety of incidental effects, a full complement of significant characters and an almost constant felicity of style.

Some slight discrepancies show that Voltaire did not finish the work with absolute care. Pomeau mentions the abrupt change, between Chapters I and II, from a springlike atmosphere to a shower of snow. Voltaire could, no doubt, have replied that fine spring days are quite often followed by snowstorms. More definite slips are the attribution of young wives to old men in Chapter III, the use by the inhabitants of El Dorado of gold and precious stones for the adornment of their houses, while referring to these commodities as '*boue*' [mud] and '*cailloux*' [pebbles] and the implication in Chapter XX that Manicheism is a belief in the all-powerfulness of evil. But these flaws pass unnoticed in the general effectiveness of the work.

I think H. N. Brailsford is right in saying that *Candide* "ranks in its own way with *Don Quixote* and *Faust*," and the reason is that, like them, it is a parable of an aspect of the human plight. It is a pilgrim's progress, only this pilgrim can find no meaning in life nor establish any relationship with the transcendent. Candide has, of course, a clear literary ancestry; he is adapted from the hero of the picaresque novel of adventure, who could so easily represent the post-Renaissance displaced individual engaged on some more or less significant journey. More immediately, he is Voltaire himself, who was *déclassé* like the picaresque hero, had been beaten and snubbed, '*tremblait comme un philosophe*' ["trembled like a philosopher"] and had been frequently on the move. But he is also a symbol of the central part of the human soul which never loses its original innocence and, as Simone Weil says, always goes on expecting that good will be done to it rather than evil. And again, in spite of Pomeau's denial, he is *l'étranger* [the outsider], a fatherless bastard whose cosy sense of belonging to a coherent society and a comprehensible universe is a childhood illusion, soon to be shattered at the onset of puberty. Cunégonde is at first Eve who tempts him, with the result that he is driven out of the early paradise by the irate master of his little world. Then Cunégonde becomes the symbol of a lost happiness which will be recovered in the future, when the world falls again into some pattern reminiscent of the patriarchal social cell which preceded adulthood. But gradually it becomes clear that the world has no pattern, all human communities are in a state of perpetual flux and strife, and the best Candide can do is to reconstitute the battered Westphalian society of his childhood as a refugee colony on the borders of barbarism, with himself as its disillusioned head, in place of the self-confident Baron Thunder-Ten-Tronckh. Pangloss, the linguistic part of the brain, is still looking irrepressibly for explanations, but the numbed soul now knows that the quest is futile.

Just as the Candide/Cunégonde conjunction is far more significant than the parallel couples, Zadig/Astarte and Ingénu/St. Yves, so the structure of Candide is more complex and much better balanced than that of the other contes. It is not just one story, like the adventures of Zadig or the Ingénu; it is an interweaving of several different stories, which are linked and knotted and contrasted in an almost musical way. Dorothy M. McGhee, in her study, Voltairian Narrative Devices,[5] gives an interesting diagram showing that one method of analyzing Candide is to see it as a series of oscillations between Candide's "mental path of optimism" and the "level of reality" to which he is always being brought back by disaster. But there is much more to it than this. In addition to the up-and-down movement, there are complexities in the linear development. The stories of Candide, Cunégonde and La Vieille [the Old Woman] follow each other like three variations on the same theme, each slightly more preposterous than the previous one and with an increasing urbanity of tone as the events become more shocking. The pope's daughter, whose exquisite breeding has remained unaffected by the excision of a buttock, gives her account while the scene of action is shifting from Europe to America. In the New World, the same figure is repeated once more with a final flourish in the Jesuit's story, which leads into the El Dorado episode. This is an interlude of calm, coming in Chapter XVII, almost exactly in the middle of the book. Candide is now as far away as he ever will be from Europe and from the realities of ordinary life. Then, since the beatific vision can never be more than a fleeting experience, he begins on his long return journey, picking up the threads in the reverse order. The second half is, however, different

5. Menasha, Wisconsin, George Banta Publishing Co., 1933, p. 55.

from the first in two important respects. Candide is no longer an underdog; he has acquired money and he sees the world from a new angle. At the same time, he has lost his initial freshness; Martin has replaced the absent Pangloss and the accumulated experience of horror has added a permanent sob to the gaiety of the music. The hero has mastered life to some small extent, in that the terrible accidents no longer happen so often to him, but this is a hollow achievement since it leaves him freer to contemplate the sufferings of others. The second half of the book may seem weaker, artistically, precisely because Candide has become a spectator, but it is psychologically true in the sense that adulthood involves awareness of general evil.

Other aspects of the musical dance of the characters provide further refinements in the pattern. Each is killed once or more and bobs up again with heartening inconsequentiality. Voltaire expresses the strength of man's unconquerable soul by making Pangloss and the Baron, for instance, step out of the galley and begin at once behaving with characteristic foolishness, as if they had never been hanged, stabbed or beaten. He also balances the horror of evil by never leaving the hero in solitude for very long. Candide is always part of a group of two or more, and he is always assuming solidarity until it is proved illusory. A minority of human beings are, like himself, decent and well-meaning; the majority are selfish and stupid, but the implication is that all are involved in evil in more or less the same way. In this respect, Candide is both fiercely critical of human nature and curiously tolerant. The Grand Inquisitor, the brutal sailor and the *levanti patron* are carried along on the same inevitable melody as Maître Jacques or Martin. In this one work, especially, Voltaire strikes a note which is very much deeper than propaganda and which is perhaps, in the last analysis, not very far removed from inarticulate religious faith.

The parallel with music can be carried further. *Candide*, more clearly than the other *contes*, is written in such a way that the reader has to perform it mentally at a certain speed. As Pomeau says:

> That this style is not everyday prose, the loose style of the marketplace, is apparent in the first lines of the text.[6]

Voltaire is by no means the only eighteenth century author who can write *allegro vivace*. Lesage, in parts of *Gil Blas*, is almost his equal.[7] Voltaire has Lesage's main qualities: an overall rhythm, a euphemistically noble vocabulary and an ability always to imply more than is actually said. But he also has features not to be found

6. Edition critique, p. 55.
7. See the excellent *'récit de Lucinde'* (Livre V, Ch. I), which may have helped to suggest the stories of Cunégonde and La Vieille.

in Lesage or the other gay stylists of the century. He uses repetition
and recapitulation very effectively in Candide to produce a constant
impression (which at first sight would seem difficult to achieve in a
typically eighteenth century style) of the welter of chance events. It
is astonishing that so short a book should create such a vision of the
teeming multifariousness of incomprehensible Necessity. His ellipti-
cal expressions are more frequent and more startling than those to
be found in the prose of his contemporaries, and so he jerks the
reader again and again into awareness of a metaphysical perspec-
tive behind his apparently innocent recital of events. Each important character has his or her *motif* which sounds at appropriate intervals; less obvious, but no less telling, than Candide's simplicity or
Pangloss's silliness are Cunégonde's accommodating sensuality and
Cacambo's practical good sense. And the mixture of rapidity, irony,
allusion, ellipsis, merciless satire of human nature and affectionate
understanding of the human plight produces an unmistakable, singing, heartrending lilt, of which only Voltaire is capable in prose and
that only Mozart, perhaps, could have transferred to the stage. Admittedly, there are passages in *Candide* that might have been written by Lesage; for instance, parts of the Old Woman's account, in
Chapter XI, of her sufferings at the hands of the pirates:

> C'est une chose admirable que la diligence avec laquelle ces
> messieurs déshabillent le monde. Mais ce qui me surprit davan-
> tage, c'est qu'ils nous mirent à tous le doigt dans un endroit où
> nous autres femmes nous ne nous laissons mettre d'ordinaire que
> des canules. Cette cérémonie me paraissait bien étrange: voilà
> comme on juge de tout quand on n'est pas sorti de son pays.[8]

But in the more characteristic passages, Voltaire infuses feeling into
this bright, eighteenth century melody, without falling into the sog-
giness of *sensibilité*, the usual weakness of eighteenth century writers when they try to be serious. Chapter I, in its deceptive simplicity, is no doubt the most perfect example of his style and one of
the highest achievements in all French writing. However, practically
every chapter contains what can only be described as unique, ironical prose poetry.[9] I quote, at random, the description of the auto-
da-fe in Chapter VI:

8. For translation, see p. 20.
9. An exhaustive and useful analysis of Voltaire's irony has been made by Ruth C. Flowers in *Voltaire's Stylistic Transformation of Rabelaisian Satirical Devices*, The Catholic University of America Press, Washington, D.C., 1951. Dr. Flowers distinguishes (pp. 63 et seq.) eight varieties of 'Satirical Detail Elements' and nine varieties of 'Compound Satirical Devices' and con- cludes: 'Unquestionably, Voltaire is the greatest master of satire by "small art", a witty almost epigrammatic sat- ire, a satire whose ironical impact de- pends entirely and exclusively on little things, strategically placed'. It is ironical, however, that Dr. Flowers should not notice the emotion which governs the strategic placing of these little things. She says (p. 90) that Vol- taire's heart is 'coolly detached, super- ficially moved'.

. . . la mitre et le sanbenito de Candide étaient peints de flammes renversées et de diables qui n'avaient ni queues ni griffes: mais les diables de Pangloss portaient griffes et queues, et les flammes étaient droites. Ils marchèrent en procession ainsi vêtus, et entendirent un sermon très pathétique, suivi d'une belle musique en faux-bourdon. Candide fut fessé en cadence pendant qu'on chantait: le Biscayen et les deux hommes qui n'avaient point voulu manger de lard furent brûles, et Pangloss fut pendu, quoique ce ne soit pas la coutume. Le même jour la terre trembla de nouveau avec un fracas épouvantable.

Candide, épouvanté, interdit, éperdu, tout sanglant, tout palpitant, se disait à lui-même: "Si c'est ici le meilleur des mondes possibles, que sont donc les autres? Passe encore si je n'étais que fessé, je l'ai été chez les Bulgares; mais, ô mon cher Pangloss! le plus grand des philosophes, faut-il vous avoir vu pendre sans que je sache pourquoi! O! mon cher anabaptiste, le meilleur des hommes, faut-il que vous ayez été noyé dans le port! O! mademoiselle Cunégonde, la perle des filles, faut-il qu'on vous ait fendu le ventre!"

Il s'en retournait se soutenant à peine, prêché, fessé, absous et béni, lorsqu'une vieille l'aborda et lui dit: "Mon fils, prenez courage, suivez-moi."

Candide ne prit point courage, mais il suivit la vieille . . .[1]

It is one of the mysteries of literary composition that the *Poème sur le Désastre de Lisbonne* should be so flat and unpoetical, whereas Voltaire's treatment of the same theme in prose is at once rich, funny and deeply moving. Perhaps the explanation is to be sought in the fact that there is a philosophical ambiguity running through Candide, in addition to the contrast between vitality and awareness of evil. The *Poème* is a direct, but feeble, reproach to God, which ends with a still feebler hope that life will be better in the world to come than it is here. Voltaire was not, temperamentally, a God-defier. He invokes God convincingly only when it is a question of enlisting Him on the side of virtue, as in *Le Traité de la tolérance*. He was incapable of saying outright, with Baudelaire:

> For truly, Lord, this is the highest gage
> That we can offer of our dignity,
> This ardent sigh, which rolls from age to age,
> Dying on the shore of your eternity.

He can only criticize God freely when he does so, by implication, through human nature. It may be that the almost pathological violence of his onslaughts on the Church is to be accounted for, to some extent, by the transference of an unexpressed exasperation with the unknowable Creator onto a part of creation which is particularly irritating precisely through its claim to understand some-

1. For translation, see p. 12.

thing about the Creator. At any rate, it is remarkable that, in *Candide,* the distinction between evil which is an act of God (and therefore from the human point of view gratuitous) and evil which is an effect of human wickedness or stupidity, is not clearly maintained. It is made, in Chapter XX, when Candide and Martin are watching the shipwreck, but in the form of a joke against Candide. God's indifference to humanity is again stressed in Chapter XXX when the dervish slams his door in Pangloss's face, and this time the joke—admittedly a rather sour one—is on Pangloss. It seems almost as if Voltaire were unwilling to come out into the open and accuse God, so much so that, from one point of view, the El Dorado episode can be seen as a logical flaw. That happy country, where the inhabitants never quarrel and worship God without a church, does not provide a fair contrast with the ordinary world; how would the people of El Dorado retain their serenity if their capital were shattered by an earthquake? The only way to justify the El Dorado chapters is to suppose that they are really a conscious or unconscious criticism of God. They occur as a sunny interlude between two series of disasters to show how happy and pious we might have been, had God not given us our ungovernable natures and put us into a world containing inexplicable evil. And the book as a whole, although so critical of mankind, tends to show human nature as a blind and passionate force driving helplessly on against a background of mystery. In other words, Voltaire, like Diderot, had not made up his mind about free-will, because the determinism/ free-will dilemma is just another formulation of the God/no-God issue. The question is left open in Chapter XXI:

> —Croyez-vous, dit Martin, que les éperviers aient toujours mangé des pigeons quand ils en ont trouvé? —Oui, sans doute, dit Candide. —Eh bien! dit Martin, si les éperviers ont toujours eu le même caractère, pourquoi voulez-vous que les hommes aient changé le leur? —Oh! dit Candide, il y a bien de la différence, car le libre arbitre . . . En raisonnant ainsi, ils arrivèrent à Bordeaux.[2]

Yet the whole weight of Voltaire's emotion is obviously against accepting the parallel between men and animals. *Candide* throbs from end to end with a paradoxical quality which might be described as a despairing hope or a relentless charity, and which comes from seeing the worst steadily, without either capitulating to it or sentimentalizing its impact. Although, as Delattre says, no great writer wrote more often below his best than Voltaire did, in this short tale he managed to hold fundamental opposites in suspense and so produced, from the heart of a century that wished to deny evil, an allegorical prose poem about evil which is still perfectly apt, exactly two hundred years later.

2. For translation, see p. 47.

ROBERT M. ADAMS

Candide on Work and Candide as Outsider

I

> "He ground his teeth."
> —Flaubert

When writers make categorical affirmations about the Values in Life—and it has long been accepted as part of their function to do so—the options available to them are not really very many. They may believe in Love or Peace or Self-Fulfillment; they may recommend us to Devotion, Resignation, Wisdom, or Fun with Girls: not infrequently they choose to emphasize Hard Work.

Why not? The human animal is incurably lazy; and there is always a latent reservation, a tacit condition, in the advice. "Work" always carries with it the connotation of "honest labor"; that is, it is contrasted, not with honorable ease and repose, but with violence, cunning, or parasitism. Fortified with virtue from this context, "work" appears before us with shining face, and proposes its inherent honesty. Strictly speaking, it should get no such marks. Laborious devotion to a task may arise from avarice, fear, malice, lust, or some motive still less creditable than these. Not infrequently a murderer in the act is a surpassingly industrious fellow. But we close these excesses and oddities out of the picture because, when "work" is recommended as a value in life, the recommendation clearly concerns a process and not an end. An end more potent and limiting than work would become the recommendation itself if we tolerated it as a modifier. And this is a first important aspect of the "morality of work"—tacitly or explicitly, it puts the ultimate end of the work outside the question. It is a weak recommendation, and therefore supposes that the strong ones have been deliberately neglected or are understood. Being so weak positively, the recommendation to hard work is surpassingly strong and various of application, negatively. A man who endorses "hard work" may well be thinking of labor as contrasted with consumption; under these circumstances, abstinence, or at least moderation, is not far from his thoughts. On the other hand, he may be saying, "Work, don't fight," or "Work, don't think," or more generally, "Work, don't do any of the other things you might be doing, just work is enough." In fact, he need not have in mind any very positive ideas about work itself; precisely because it has no specific positive content, the recommendation to work is sometimes an invitation to quiescence.

"Work hard" may be simply a nice way of saying "Mind your own business," for it implies "Concentrate on your particular task"—politics, for instance, are not work. "Follow your specialty, and don't meddle with general ideas." Actually, the recommendation of hard work sometimes constitutes a denial of moral responsibility rather than a fulfillment of it. Keeping your nose to the grindstone may be a way of keeping your nose clean; it is sometimes the best way precisely because "hard work" is morally so unexceptionable.

In addition, there may be and often is an implication behind the injunction to "work hard" that work is somehow good for one's character, not because it accomplishes anything, but because it is calisthenic and vaguely disagreeable. Work is recommended as a tonic, a therapy; it stiffens the moral fiber. Or, lastly, to make an arbitrary end to this arbitrary enumeration, there is that amazing inversion perpetrated by Puritanism, according to which work is not work at all but passive obedience; having received a command from the Lord, the Puritan will work like a fiend to fulfill it, all the time protesting that his individual will counts for nothing, that he is merely the agent of a higher power.

This Puritan paradox on work, fascinating at any time, undergoes particularly complex modification during the eighteenth century. At that time specifically, because at that time the spirit of private inspiration and enthusiasm, which under the forms and in the name of religion blew up so furious a storm in the seventeenth century, was beginning to be tempered slowly and by an infinitely complex series of adaptations toward the uses and usages of a capitalist economy. Much has been written on this subject, unhappily not very much of it in the form of detailed studies. But I shall take it as a cliché of history, no less true for being trite, that ideals which were first formulated in terms of the Kingdom of God were adapted in the course of time to the service of a commercial and acquisitive society.

The strain of thought and feeling which was common to both the brave builders of the heavenly city and the more amply rewarded laborers in the earthly vineyards of capitalism may fairly be called the Puritan spirit. Its essence is a doctrine of work, a spirit of individual enterprise which makes it precisely man's spiritual duty to pursue with all the energy at his command his earthly calling. The puritan is an ascetic because sensual pleasure distracts from his calling; he is neither a recluse nor a contemplative because those characters are incompatible with activity in a calling; he is a revolutionary whenever fleshly authority threatens to interfere with his calling. Two sanctions bless his labor, one heavenly, the other earthly; and if he sometimes seems a little complacent, it is no doubt because having both God and Mammon in the same pocket must be a remarkably heady experience. But his complacency is only outward, for he is an insatiable enterpriser, and in the exercise of his calling, he knows no rest or limitations. Do we not see him, this busy, pragmatical fellow, as William Prynne, that brave, insufferable babbler against stage plays—as John Bunyan, the unsilenceable preaching tinker—as Ben Franklin, the projecting printer—as Daniel Defoe, the writing tradesman of genius? And, gathering all these figures into one spiritual quintessence, would we not get an image very close to Lemuel Gulliver and the snoopy, nameless, endlessly enterprising compiler of *A Tale of a Tub?*

As the great enemy of the Puritan spirit, Swift was forever caricaturing and deriding it. Here we need only remind the reader of the immense satiric energy which *A Tale of a Tub* puts into its assault on the "wind" of private inspiration, the "breath" of enthusiasm. Wind, or the private spirit which drives a man out of the conventional ways of life, is a vapor, a steam, a fume; puncture the container, physically or metaphorically, and it will escape, perhaps popping the container, but sparing the world many troubles. Bottled up, it will seek expression in an intellectual system, a military conquest, or (least harmfully) as out-and-out madness. So the trick is to let it out of afflicted man a little at a time. The title suggests that the book itself is intended to serve as a release-mechanism for the hysterical winds of private inspiration which, Swift supposes, are either tormenting or threatening his colicky readers. Menaced by the whale of madness, who might send their ship to the bottom, mariners throw out a tub to divert his attention. So the story, bubbling and cork-like, serves to divert the latent madness of reader and author. And this indeed is the real use which Swift, in the isolated and limited passages where he touches on the topic, finds for work. It is a safety valve, ridiculous enough in itself, probably useless as far as practical results are concerned; but valuable to prevent the overinflated human being from bursting out into a philosophical system or a military aggression. Madness will serve the same purpose just as well; and when Swift compares the madman, foaming in his cell and dabbling in his own filth, with a chemist making an experiment, one sees that all the trades and employments of life could be subjected to the same reductive comparison. Swift's praise of the useful and practical is just as astringent. The King of Brobdignag will think well of the man who can make two blades of grass grow where one grew before, not because anyone needs more grass, least of all the grower, but because the grower has humbled his individual reason before a social need. He is like Pococurante, who would think well of a man who invented a new way to make pins. The meanness of the achievement, in both instances, is evidence that a principle is involved, not a project.

Always, for Swift, the ideal of work is a negative ideal; the troubles it keeps you out of are more important than the rewards it earns you. In Franklin, on the other hand—but here we need merely quote at random from Poor Richard:

"Sloth, like Rust, consumes faster than Labor wears: the used key is always bright."

"Industry, Perseverance, and Frugality make Fortune yield."

"Hide not your Talents, they for Use were made; What's a Sun-Dial in the Shade?"

"Since thou art not sure of a Minute, throw not away an Hour."

"The sleeping Fox catches no Poultry. Up! Up!"

"God gives all things to Industry."

"Plough deep while Sluggards sleep, And you shall have Corn, to sell and to keep."

"The second Vice is lying, the first is running in debt."

"If you know how to spend less than you get, you have the Philosopher's Stone."

Here the emphasis is entirely on acquisition, on work as morally and practically rewarding. An occasional aphorism points out that if you keep busy, you will be less likely to get in trouble, but the overwhelming burden of the adages is that hard work, perseverance, and frugality will reward you psychologically as well as materially. Franklin sees work under the image of piling up benefits, Swift sees it predominantly under the image of a device to prevent disastrous accidents from happening.

And now, as between these two radically different alternatives, where does Voltaire stand? Remembering always that he is not in the same line of development as his English-speaking contemporaries, that his background is more Catholic and courtly than Protestant and bourgeois, reserving one's sense that he is in some ways more different from them both than they are from one another—it is hardly possible to doubt that, in his attitude to work, Voltaire stands closer to Swift than to Franklin. What will we accomplish by cultivating our gardens? The answer could not be clearer; we will accomplish nothing, we will avoid something. Three great evils, to be sure: boredom, vice, and want. But of these three enemies, one is not directly opposed in any way by work. There is no assurance whatever that a busy man will be less vicious than an idle one—certainly the fable of *Candide* has shown us nothing of the sort. The inhabitants of Eldorado, who do little work or none at all, are less vicious than the hardworking sailor who drowns Jacques the Anabaptist, than the Levant captain of the Turkish galley (who not only works hard himself, but is the cause of hard work in others), or than the Dutch merchant Vanderdendur—in all of whom a complete moral blindness is sensed, as a result of their addiction to commercial values which clearly include work. As for want, work undeniably preserves one from it (unless one is a slave, as almost all of Candide's little troop have been, at one time or another). But Candide is preserved from want not by work, but by his Eldorado diamonds. He is not suffering at all from want when the recommendation to cultivate his garden is made to him. We have never seen work do anyone any good in the book; it did not help Martin or Cacambo or the old woman, it made Cunégonde ugly, and it has made nobody rich except the old Turk, whose appearance is pretty much *ad hoc*. No, the real enemy against which work fights is boredom; that we have seen, that we can believe. And Voltaire himself understood and dreaded boredom; poverty he had never known and vice he would not have admitted, but boredom! "The further I go down life's path," he wrote, "the more I find work necessary. In the long run, it becomes the greatest of pleasures, and takes the place of all the illusions one has lost."[1] Or again: "I have always considered work as the greatest consolation for the evils inseparable from the human condition."[2] Poverty is not inseparable from the human condition, nor is vice, but boredom comes rather closer; it speaks more fully to Voltaire's condition, to Candide's, and to that of the human race.

As for the ideas that work improves the character, or leads man toward a better state or is good in itself, or finds a reward on high —one will look in vain for such ideas in *Candide*, or elsewhere in Voltaire. "Scientific and bourgeois" says André Maurois of the ending of *Candide*; he is echoing René Berthelot.[3] The judgment is wrong; not just exaggerated, but wrong, untrue to a careful reading of the text, flat wrong in both parts. There is nothing scientific about working to avoid boredom, vice, and want. There is nothing bourgeois either; the bourgeois may work, but he does so for wholly different reasons, and if he works for these reasons, there is nothing specifically bourgeois about his working. Voltaire does not believe in work as nutriment for the human creature, he believes in it as an anodyne; he does not believe it will make you any better, just that it may help you to support evils which are inevitable.

1. *Œuvres* (ed. Moland) XXXVII, 304; Best. 3958.
2. XXXVIII, 162; Best. 5009.
3. A. Maurois, *Voltaire*, tr. H. Miles (New York, 1932), p. 100.

II

In fact, *Candide* is the story of human solitude.
—FERDINANDO NERI, *Candide*[4]

But if we take most of the comfort out of Voltaire's "doctrine of work" as expressed in *Candide*, aren't we left with a pretty desolate document? Precisely. When we look at the book carefully, it hardly appears cruel or malicious, but it does show mankind subject to the working of inexorable, indifferent laws, against which there is no appeal at all. The desolation of the world within which the characters move is profound and horrible. Physical pain there is in plenty —the blind and wanton brutality of armies and galley-slave-drivers, and that magnificent fantasy of a plainsong *miserere*, to which Candide is flogged in cadence—as if humanity were completely dead, even to hatred, and the only thing left was this vast procession of robots which wails and whacks and pauses to serve refreshments to the ladies, as if operated by a clockwork. It is less the idea of a beating that makes us cringe here, than the absolute alienation of one suffering human mind in the midst of thousands. Like running the Bulgar gauntlet, flogging in an *auto-da-fé* is mechanical, mathematical, as regular as if controlled by a metronome. But these are merely external blows. What cuts deepest into Candide's ever-innocent heart is a stroke of mechanism which is not physical at all; it is the cold and calculating villainy of Vanderdendur, the cold, unruffled indifference of the magistrate. It is, Voltaire tells us, the "sang froid" with which these men commit their "méchancetés" that finally drives Candide to despair. They are villains, black villains, and they hardly even know it; the magistrate enforces his rules in perfect mathematical isolation from Candide's human situation. He is what someone has called a "moral idiot"; his organs of sympathy are as if seared with a hot iron, he can no more appreciate Candide's feelings than a blind man could see his anguished features.[5]

Work is no refuge against the chill wind of human indifference, except as it enables one to cultivate a counter-indifference. The coming together of the little troop of survivors on an alien shore under a hostile or at best indifferent sky, is a closing of the human circle indeed; but it is like a festival in a dungeon, a scarecrow's sabbath, at which there is nothing much but survival to celebrate. In effect, the machine of the world has succeeded in grinding down the characters till they too are nothing but mechanisms. The

4. *Rassegna*, XXV, 5, 337–342.
5. Other examples of moral idiocy in the book are the Protestant preacher of Chapter 3 and the indifference of Pangloss to Candide's anguish at the Lisbon earthquake (Chapter 5).

baron's automatic arrogance, Cunégonde's pathetic insistence that she is still lovely and Candide is still madly in love with her, the interminable empty clack of Pangloss, in all these details we are reminded of the dry husks of human beings. Their arguments are summarized now, instead of being given *in extenso;* for they have nothing new to say, and no longer believe most of what they are forced to repeat. While the dervish slams his door in Pangloss' face, Candide shrinks, like a neurotic mouse, from saying anything at all on any subject. He has not, in fact, been very successful at talking with people, and there is a kind of retrospective pathos to that moment, on the trip back to Europe, when he is for once able to open his heart to Martin. Even if it was only to compare misfortunes and to wrangle hopelessly over the meaning of them, they had their instant. "But at least they were talking, they exchanged their ideas, they consoled one another." But now even that gleam has faded, Martin is sour and laconic, and, in his exaggerated cynicism, more often wrong than right. Candide is alone at the end of the book, as he has been alone all along, enclosed in the prison of his slightly addled head as inexorably as Don Quixote.[6]

Candide really is a Quixote, slightly tinged with the spirit of Mary Baker Eddy; he rode forth, not to right wrongs, but to prove —a bolder venture by far—that there were never any wrongs to right. Like Quixote, he encountered in the first part of his adventures imaginary physical blows and real comic hostility on the part of the reader: "How can he be so crazy, so deluded? He must be knocked on his prat, so that truth may enter at that portal, if no other." But both heroes quickly graduate to more subtle encounters, in which they gain a measure of revenge on common sense. While Candide is rich with the money of Eldorado, it is as if myth were every instant getting some of its own back from practical reality.

6. Mr. William F. Bottiglia's painstaking and scholarly study of *Candide* (*Studies in Voltaire and the 18th Century,* Vols. 7 and 7A) takes a consistently hardheaded and literal view of Voltaire's *conte.* Eldorado is an ideal state, which Candide and Cacambo are too immature to appreciate, and the meaning of Candide's garden is happiness through cooperative labor—*Freude,* as it were, *durch Kraft.* There is no doubt that these points can be sustained by scrutinizing Chapter 18 and Chapter 30 separately; unexplainable contradiction does not even arise from putting them together, though the story then becomes a real strain to read. This is particularly so because Mr. Bottiglia, who has some excellent ideas on how to hear *Candide,* wants it read aloud by a single voice at a considerable clip (pp. 243 ff.). But what depresses one most is the idea that there should be, in this lean, swift, hard book, two suety passages of moral teaching, exempt from irony. It may be that Voltaire wrote the book that Mr. Bottiglia presents—if so, the less Voltaire he. This isn't just a gibe at Mr. Bottiglia's expense; his book is an admirable one, but its total effect—despite the author's obvious intentions—is to present a much more heavy-minded and musclebound Voltaire than we could have had for the same expenditure of energy. He gives us a bourgeois Voltaire, and makes us work hard for him. The limber, universal play of the glittering Voltairean irony seems to me the last thing we should sacrifice to an interpretation. Unfortunately, literary qualities of this order aren't subject to demonstration by a process of A plus B minus C divided by Z.

And our sympathies reverse too, for not only do Quixote and Candide play on our latent hatred of civilization by suffering from it out of all proportion to their harmless "provocations"; we come to see them as adventurers on whom our own entertainment depends. So it becomes important to us precisely that the bubble of madness which constitutes their genius *not* be broken; and we feel a secret exultation when some quirk of nature or the unnatural reinforces their mania just when it seemed doomed to fatal puncturing. Without losing our sense of the hero's absurdity, we acquire an equal sense of the absurdity of the institutions against which he is pitted. Real innocence, which has always something sacred as well as idiotic about it, is a mirror in which are reflected our own deep instabilities, including that deepest one between laughter and tears.

But Candide does not, like Quixote, transform the world; he never encounters his own myth, never meets with men who have been reading *Candide* and who will therefore humor him and his Sancho Panzas by creating a special world for them. The phrase "another world" and the emphatic expression "this world" (which implies the existence of another, or others) run through the book like a ground bass, but the other world never for an instant threatens to become palpable. It is an aching void, a hole where we used to have a tooth. Even this present world, as Voltaire represents it, is unlike Quixote's in being flat, not deep; it has none of those layered and delicate correspondences which produce—for example—such exquisite courtesies between the Duchess and Teresa Panza. The curiously damped and empty episode of the six kings illustrates this point. Candide has no real use for these unemployed gentry; they are curiosities at whom he stares, as at caged animals, and he draws from the dumb-show only an old medieval morality about the instability of earthly power. Quixote's dealing with the secular authorities, whether actual or imagined, is never so naked, he has things to say to them, and things to learn from them.

Thus Candide, when he settles down to cultivate his garden, is surrendering to the brute imbecility as well as to the wisdom of the world. His acceptance of the world and its ways is not simply an imaginative achievement, a wedding; it is also a funeral and the beginning of a wake. Something is dead, an illusion, an ambition, an attitude; it is the energy of delusion, by which Candide has existed in our minds. In token of the fact that a wholly reasonable being has no interest for us, as soon as he has resigned himself to a rational task, Candide's book comes to an end. His garden will be planted over the rotten corpse of his animating delusion, and there is nothing merry or hopeful about the change.

I said that Candide, without losing his own absurdity, made the institutions against which he bumped look absurd too. From one point of view he is a pariah, from the other a saint. But in neither capacity is he—till the end of the book—one of us. Mme. de Staël very rightly points to the tremendous gap, the immense ironic distance, between this pathetic innocent and the grinning, invulnerable Voltaire. But this distance does not make Voltaire a demon or a monkey. Faced with a choice between the two, a modern reader is likely to conclude that Candide, not Voltaire, belongs to a different species than our own. In contemporary terminology, Voltaire is continually asking his creation the always-cogent question, *Man, are you for real?* And of course Candide isn't. For he leaves us as he came to us, still bearing the white, insoluble questions of innocence in his hands—questions which, because they are insoluble, act as a ferocious solvent upon every human, historical institution to which they are applied. Being a bastard without family and an innocent without experience (that is, essential, absorbed experience), Candide exists only in an ethical dimension, outside history and time. Almost all the other characters age in the course of the book, and Pangloss is noticeably tattered by the end of it, but not Candide. He has never really been with us, and now he is going back where he came from, to some place outside Europe, outside history, outside people, to a cold and lonely garden where the vegetable he cultivates most assiduously will be his own indifference, his own self-sufficiency. He was, is, and always will be, an outsider; and of course we know that Voltaire, as the creature of that intimate, social, lighthearted, commonsense eighteenth century, could not possibly have had any sympathy for him. But he did. And maybe that is a reason why *Candide* has survived to be read, and read with vital interest, in a day when the notion of weeping for *Tancrède* or thrilling to the *Henriade* is more than a little comic.[7]

7. André Delattre emphasizes the extent to which *Candide* represents a turnabout in Voltaire's life and thought, *Voltaire L'Impétueux* (Paris, 1947), pp. 92 ff.

The Climate of
Controversy

Extended critiques of *Candide* do not start appearing till more than a century and a half after its publication; but Voltaire was a figure so central to French intellectual life and so deeply imbedded in it—he was such a fighter, and took memorable positions on so wide a range of topics—that his name, and that of his most famous story, crop up again and again in the great controversies of the nineteenth and twentieth centuries. For a Frenchman, one's opinion of Voltaire is like one's opinion of the Church or the Revolution or Napoleon—it is a key to one's whole historical and ethical outlook. Wherever a crucial issue of French civilization makes its appearance, there will also be found an epigram of Voltaire's, lucid, cocksure, infuriating, and unforgettable. Even when Voltaire is not himself the subject and center of a conversational storm, he is often brought in to illustrate an argument, deplore a tendency, or formulate an attitude. His vast and miscellaneous production lends itself to occasional use. People can discuss Voltaire without declining at once into literary shop-talk, can make use of his phrases for practical purposes without the uneasy sense of desecrating a literary masterpiece. Voltaire is wonderfully accessible to the popular mind.

Put to so many different purposes, seen from so many different points of view, he fractures remarkably. The cast of features which one man describes as the bestial rictus of a malicious satyr will seem to another the compassionate visage of a Saint of Humanity. But he becomes deeper and more complicated, too. In the course of this continuing controversial discussion of Voltaire, many of the most acute and penetrating observations upon his mind and character get made—as by-blows, many times, in the course of a larger controversy. Even when they are not explicitly controversial, little passing comments about Voltaire run like a murmuring undercurrent through French intellectual life of the nineteenth and twentieth centuries. In a phrase of a letter-writer or an observation of a journal-keeper, one will find commentary on Voltaire serving to define some purpose of the writer's, some aspect of contemporary literary endeavor. Properly speaking, this sort of incidental discussion is not literary criticism; but it may serve to represent a current of literary opinion within which Voltaire has never ceased vitally to exist, and which has defined a whole series of still-agitated questions about his nature and influence. All translations of the selections which follow have been made by the present editor.

VOLTAIRE'S FAITH

We begin with a letter by Voltaire himself on the subject of *Candide*. It pretends to be a response to a notice of *Candide* which had appeared in the *Journal encyclopédique* of March 15, 1759 (Professor Wade's essay reproduces that notice, cf. above p. 142). But though this letter of Voltaire's is dated April 1, 1759, it appeared only on July 15, 1762. The date of April 1 suggests that it is an April Fool's joke, a *poisson d'avril*; and in fact it is a piece of obvious hocus-pocus. But, as usual, Voltaire was doing something quite serious behind his foolery. A controversy had broken out in 1762 regarding the political role of the Jesuits; Voltaire's letter was designed to stir up hostility against them by bringing once again to public attention the fact that Jesuits had not always been docile servants of secular governments. In addition, its claim that *Candide* was written to convert the Socinians raises a real question about Voltaire's own creed.

VOLTAIRE: Letter on the Subject of Candide

Gentlemen,

You say, in the March issue of your journal,[1] that some sort of little novel called *Optimism* or *Candide* is attributed to a man known as Monsieur de V . . . I do not know what Monsieur V . . . you mean; but I can tell you that this book was written by my brother, Monsieur Demad, presently a Captain in the Brunswick regiment; and in the matter of the pretended kingdom of the Jesuits in Paraguay, which you call a wretched fable, I tell you in the face of all Europe that nothing is more certain. I served on one of the Spanish vessels sent to Buenos Aires in 1756 to restore reason to the nearby settlement of Saint Sacrament; I spent three months at Assumption; the Jesuits have to my knowledge twenty-nine provinces, which they call "Reductions," and they are absolute masters there, by virtue of eight crowns a head for each father of a family, which they pay to the Governor of Buenos Aires—and yet they only pay for a third of their districts. They will not allow any Spaniard to remain more than three days in their Reductions. They have never wanted their subjects to learn Spanish. They alone teach the Paraguayans the use of firearms; they alone lead them in the field. The Jesuit Thomas Verle, a native of Bavaria, was killed in the attack on the village of Saint Sacrament while mounting to the attack at the head of his Paraguayans in 1737—and not at all in 1735 as the Jesuit Charlevoix has reported; this author is as insipid as he is

1. N.B. This letter was lost in the post for a long time; as soon as it reached us, we began trying—unsuccessfully—to discover the existence of Monsieur Demad, Captain of the Brunswick Regiment [Note by the *Journal*].

ignorant. Everyone knows how they waged war on Don Antequera, and defied the orders of the Council in Madrid.

They are so powerful that in 1743 they obtained from Philip the Fifth a confirmation of their authority which no one has been able to shake. I know very well, gentlemen, that they have no such title as King, and therefore you may say it is a wretched fable to talk of the Kingdom of Paraguay. But even though the Dey of Algiers is not a King, he is none the less master of that country. I should not advise my brother the Captain to travel to Paraguay without being sure that he is stronger than the local authorities.

For the rest, gentlemen, I have the honor to inform you that my brother the Captain, who is the best-loved man in his regiment, is an excellent Christian; he amused himself by composing the novel *Candide* in his winter quarters, having chiefly in mind to convert the Socinians. These heretics are not satisfied with openly denying the Trinity and the doctrine of eternal punishment; they say that God necessarily made our world the best of all possible ones, and that everything is well. This idea is manifestly contrary to the doctrine of original sin. These innovators forget that the serpent, who was the subtlest beast of the field, tempted the woman created from Adam's rib; that Adam ate the forbidden fruit; that God cursed the land He had formerly blessed: *Cursed is the ground for thy sake: in the sweat of thy face shalt thou eat bread.* Can they be ignorant that all the church fathers without a single exception found the Christian religion on this curse pronounced by God himself, the effects of which we feel every day? The Socinians pretend to exalt providence, and they do not see that we are guilty, tormented beings, who must confess our faults and accept our punishment. Let these heretics take care not to show themselves near my brother the Captain; he'll let them know if everything is well.

I am, gentlemen, your very humble, very obedient servant,

Demad

At Zastrou, April first, 1759

P.S. My brother the Captain is the intimate friend of Mr. Ralph, well-known Professor in the Academy of Frankfort-on-Oder, who was of great help to him in writing this profound work of philosophy, and my brother was so modest as actually to call it a mere translation from an original by Mr. Ralph. Such modesty is rare among authors.

Voltaire's little joke that *Candide* was written to refute the "Socinians" is a proper bit of ironic duplicity. As the Socinians (Polish followers of Faustus and Laelius Socinus, sixteenth-century theologians) were convinced optimists, *Candide* could appropriately claim to refute that part of their

creed. But they were much better known for their denial of original sin—
that, not optimism, was what made them heretical—and Voltaire could
not very well refute that belief, because, as an active and prominent deist,
he shared it.[2] Or did he? A curious figure in *Candide* is that officer of the
Inquisition who peeps into the last half-page of Chapter 5, utters two
sentences which hang up Pangloss like a split fish, and then disappears
forever. His argument is that the "all's well" philosophy, by denying
original sin and the fall of man, removes all grounds for belief in supernatural reward or punishment; and by making God wholly and directly
responsible for the present wretched state of the world, it destroys the
possibility of human freedom.

Now these were arguments with which Voltaire was thoroughly familiar.
They had been used against him, several years before *Candide*, by an
orthodox critic named Bouillier, who had caught up some overoptimistic
statements to which Voltaire committed himself in the *Remarques sur
Pascal* (Article XVIII).[3] The heart of them is the reaffirmation of the
doctrines of fall and redemption. Voltaire evidently saw the strength of the
position as Bouillier used it against him, for he transferred the arguments
to his own armory, using them again and again—in the Preface to the *Poème
sur Lisbonne*, for example, and in a letter to Pastor Elie Bertrand dated
February 28, 1756. It is odd enough to see Voltaire, in his own person,
vindicating the supernatural dogmas of the Christian faith against un-
believing optimists; but even odder to see him, in his fiction, assigning to
an officer of the hated Inquisition an argument which he had made seriously in his own person. Perhaps Voltaire, like many later unbelievers, especially those with Jesuit training, continued to respect the logic of the church
in which he no longer believed. Or perhaps, like many good controversial-
ists, what he believed in at heart was neither one cause nor the other, but
sharp weapons skilfully wielded. It is the economy of the poursuivant's
style—the snip-snip of his logical scissors on the sleazy texture of Pangloss'
verbosity—that represents his triumph in Voltaire's eyes. In any event, one
could argue that the officer of the Inquisition is, metaphysically speaking,
a hero of the book; the point would be that, like the tough-minded dervish
of the last chapter, he has his philosophical legs under him.

Two other comments on Voltaire's religious views carry whatever sort
of authority one wants to attribute to them. William Blake, who was accustomed to talk at length with the souls of those dead and gone, reports
on a conversation he had with Voltaire in the other world, and André
Delattre undertakes to psychoanalyze him.

2. From an orthodox point of view,
Voltaire pluming himself on having
refuted the "Socinians" is like a police-
man posing as an enemy of crime because he has given a speeding ticket to
robbers on their way home from loot-
ing a bank. "Socinians" were especially
useful to Voltaire as a stalking-horse
because there weren't very many of
them, they were far away (the sect
had its roots in Poland), and nobody
was quite sure what they believed,
since one of their chief tenets was that
nobody was bound to believe anything
against his conscience.
3. Voltaire's "Anti-Pascal" was first
published in 1733 and variously modified thereafter; Bouillier's sharp attack
on his excessive optimism appeared
as an *Apologie de la Métaphysique*
(Amsterdam, 1753); the argument that
optimism is unchristian appears on
p. 83. See Lanson's edition of the
Remarques sur Pascal, II, 209.

WILLIAM BLAKE†

I have had much intercourse with Voltaire, and he said to me: "I blasphemed the Son of Man, and it shall be forgiven me; but they [presumably his enemies] blasphemed the Holy Ghost in me, and it shall not be forgiven them."

ANDRÉ DELATTRE‡

Let's try for a hypothesis which will explain adequately this religious or anti-religious (no matter which) obsession. The origin of the deepest emotion in his life can only be of an emotive order; it was for no purely intellectual reasons that he persecuted *l'infâme* with ever-growing enthusiasm for more than sixty years.

Voltaire, son of a bourgeois Jansenist, was situated from his birth in the opposition, and he would become a leader of it. Jansenists in France, like Puritans in England, were both a religious movement and the central political force of the rising bourgeoisie; both currents, being essentially united, made up between them a dynamism, perhaps the most powerful of the age. But between the Jansenist father with his austerities and the frivolous son, there was a clash, or could one perhaps say a traumatic breach with determining effects? We recall that Voltaire's mother died when he was seven years old. Then, the second son of M. Arouet was in further conflict with his elder brother Armand, a fanatical Jansenist who finally became a convulsionary.[1] This older brother was tough and made his sibling suffer * * * Later, Voltaire disputed with his brother over the affections of their sister's children * * * In the matter of religion, Voltaire himself flatly opposed his attitude to that of Armand Arouet * * *

So far we deal with matters of unquestioned fact. The hypothesis begins here: this hostility against father and older brother, could it have caused in Voltaire's sensibility a wound sufficient to determine his entire life? Is it possible that Voltaire was anti-lyric, anti-mystic ("the mystics," he said, "are the alchemists of religion"—*Works*, ed. Moland, XV, 73)—anti-dionysian in a word, as a reaction against Armand, that dionysian miracle-maker? * * * Let us embroider freely: through the mask of Pascal whom he attacks, he is striking at his Jansenist brother. His profound repulsion in his youth for this pious, hard, dry brother turned him toward the

---

† William Blake quoted by Henry Crabb Robinson, *Books and their Writers* (London, 1938), I, 333 (February 16, 1826).
‡ André Delattre, *Voltaire L'Impétueux*

(Paris, 1957), pp. 67–69.
1. M. Arouet was pleased with neither of his boys, and used to say he had two madmen (*fous*) for sons, one in verse and one in prose.

rational, the clearly defined things of this earth, the anti-supernatural; and it knotted up within him a whole creative, vital, poetic self to which, nonetheless, he struggled to give expression—vainly. Voltaire clings desperately [to the material] in order to keep himself from plunging into that mysticism toward which his powerful primitive impulses keep dragging him.

VOLTAIRE'S GREATNESS

Whether Voltaire was really a great man and, if so, what his greatness consisted in, were questions in which shifting political passions and shifting literary tastes played a major role. His voluminous production seemed to include no single outstanding book, no unquestioned masterpiece. Though they continued to hold the stage well into the nineteenth century, Voltaire's tragedies came under increasingly heavy fire as being pompous and dull. His poetry fell by the wayside even earlier, and his histories (with the possible exception of *Le Siècle de Louis XIV*) lost stature with the passage of time. At the same time his little short stories, farces, and entertainments—which were certainly not pompous but sometimes uncomfortably irreverent—came to the fore. Thus conservatives who despised Voltaire's principles but remained susceptible to his rhetoric were often found to rank him higher in the literary pantheon than those who admired his ideas but deplored his neo-classic taste.

JOSEPH DE MAISTRE†

* * * His much-vaunted wit is far from unblameable; the laugh it raises is never legitimate; it is a grimace. Have you never noticed that God's anathema was written on his face? After so many years, it's time to look and see. Go, look at his face, in the Hermitage; I never see it without rejoicing that it was not recorded for us by an artist of Greece, who would have spread over it the veil of ideal beauty. Here everything is natural. There is as much truth in this head as in a death-mask. Look at this low brow, to which shame will never bring a blush, these two cold craters where one still seems to see the last bubblings of luxury and hate. This mouth—I speak evil, perhaps, but it is not my fault—this horrible rictus, running from one ear to the other, these lips pinched tight by cruel malice, like a coiled spring ready to let fly some blasphemy or sarcasm. Don't talk to me of that man, I can't support the very idea of him. Ah! what harm he has done us! Like that insect, the bane of gardens, which seeks out and gnaws the roots of the most precious plants,

---

† Joseph de Maistre, *Les Soirées de Saint-Pétersbourg*, "Quatrième Entretien." *Loquitur* le conte.

Voltaire, with his needle-pointed style, stabs continually at the two roots of society, women and young people; he fills them full of his venoms, which he transmits thus from one generation to the next. It is in vain that his stupid admirers, trying to cover up his inexpressible crimes, deafen us by repeating the sonorous tirades in which he has spoken worthily of the most venerable topics. These selfblinded folk don't see that, in this way, they complete our condemnation of this guilty writer. If Fénelon, with the same pen which depicted the joys of Elysium, had written the book of *The Prince*, he would be a thousand times more vile, more guilty, than Machiavelli. The great crime of Voltaire is the abuse of his talent, the deliberate prostitution of a genius created to celebrate God and virtue. He could not plead, as so many others have done, youth, carelessness, the force of passion, or, in short, the melancholy weakness of our nature. Nothing absolves him; his corruption is of a sort which belongs to him alone; it is rooted in the deepest fibres of his heart, and fortified with all the energy of his understanding. Always akin to sacrilege, it defies God while destroying man. With unexampled fury, this insolent blasphemer rises to the height of declaring himself the personal enemy of the Savior of mankind; he dares, from the depths of his nothingness, to give Him a ridiculous name, and that marvellous law which the Man-God brought to earth he refers to as "*l'infâme*." Abandoned by God, who punishes by withdrawing, he knows no rein or check. Other cynics astonished the virtuous, Voltaire amazed the vicious. He plunges into filth, rolls in it, saturates himself; he yields his imagination to the enthusiasm of hell, which lends all its forces to drag him to the absolute limits of evil. He invents monsters, prodigies which cause one to blench. Paris crowned him, Sodom would have banished him. Shameless profaner of the universal tongue and its greatest names, the last of men after those who admire him! How can I tell you what I experience at the thought of him? When I see what he could have done and what he actually did, his inimitable talents inspire in me nothing more than a kind of sacred rage for which there is no name. Torn between admiration and horror, sometimes I think of raising a statue for him—by the hand of the common hangman.

VICTOR HUGO[†]

* * * I have pronounced the word "smile." Let me pause over it. In Voltaire an equilibrium always re-establishes itself ultimately. Whatever his first rage, it passes, and the aroused Voltaire yields to the pacified Voltaire. Then, in that deepset eye, the smile appears.

[†] Victor Hugo, "Le Centenaire de Voltaire" (30 mai, 1878), in *Œuvres* *Complètes de V.H.* ("Actes et Paroles," 1940), III, 298–306.

This smile is wisdom. This smile, I repeat, is Voltaire. This smile broadens sometimes to a laugh, but then a philosophic melancholy tempers it. Against the mighty it is mocking; in behalf of the weak, it is tender. It disturbs the oppressor and comforts the oppressed. Against the mighty, raillery; for the little people, sympathy. Ah! let us be touched by that smile. He experienced the clarities of dawn. He illuminated the true, the just, the good, and what there is of honesty in the useful. He lit up the interior of superstitions; these ugly sights are good for us to see, and he showed them. Being luminous, he was prolific. The new society, the desire for equality and justice and that first stage of brotherhood which is called toleration, mutual good will, the due proportioning of men and rights, the recognition of reason as a supreme law, the eradication of prejudices and preconceptions, the serenity of the soul, the spirit of indulgence and pardon, harmony, peace—that is what came forth from the great smile.

The day, soon to dawn no doubt, when the identity of justice and mercy will be recognized, the day when the amnesty will be declared, I tell you now, among the stars on high, Voltaire will be smiling. (*Triple salvos of applause. Cries of Long live the amnesty!*)

Gentlemen, there exists between two servants of humanity who appeared eighteen hundred years apart, a mysterious connection.

To combat the pharisees, unmask the hypocrites, humble the tyrants, usurpers, bigots, liars, and persecuters, to demolish the temple in order to rebuild it—that is, to replace the false with the true —to attack the ferocious magistrates and the bloody-minded priests, to take a whip and drive the moneychangers from the temple, to reclaim the heritage of orphans, to protect the weak, the suffering, and the humiliated, to struggle in behalf of the persecuted and the oppressed: that is the war of Jesus Christ. And who is the man who fought that war? It is Voltaire. (*Bravos.*)

The work of the evangelist is fulfilled in the work of the philosopher; what the spirit of inspiration began, the spirit of toleration continues. Let us say it in a spirit of deepest respect, Jesus wept, Voltaire smiled; and it is from this divine tear and this human smile that the glory of modern civilization is compounded. (*Prolonged applause.*)

THE GONCOURTS†

28 March. Dinner at Magny's. The new member of the circle is Renan. The conversation turns naturally to religion. Sainte-Beuve says that paganism was originally a fine thing, but then it

† *Journal of the Goncourts,* March 28, 1863.

became a rotten mess, a pox * * * And Christianity was the mercury that cured the pox, but the dose was too strong, and now humanity must be cured of the remedy * * *

And the battle is over Voltaire. Both of us, in discussing this writer, set aside his political and social influence, we challenge his literary value, we dare to repeat the sentence of the Abbé Trublet defining Voltaire's genius as "the perfection of mediocrity," we grant him only the value of a popularizer, a publicist, nothing more, a man possessed of wit if you will, but of wit no loftier than that of all the witty old women of his day. His plays can't be discussed. His history is lies, the same old pompous and stupid conventions repeated by the most conventional and antiquated historians. His science, his hypotheses, are objects of ridicule by contemporary men of learning. Finally, the only work by which he deserves to live, his famous *Candide*, is LaFontaine in prose, spoon-fed Rabelais. What are these eighty volumes of his worth, alongside *Rameau's Nephew*, alongside *This is not a Story* [both by Diderot] —this novel and this story which contain in germ all the novels and stories of the nineteenth century?

The whole company falls upon us, and Sainte-Beuve ends by saying that France will be free only when Voltaire has his statue on the Place Louis XV.

VOLTAIRE'S COHERENCE

If Voltaire, without writing an unqualifiedly great book, managed nonetheless to give the very general impression of being a great author, we should not be startled to find that without having a coherent philosophy he gave the general impression of being a systematic thinker. But this reputation faded too, and the brothers Goncourt, in their assault on the Patriarch, could toss aside his intellectual achievements with a contemptuous phrase. Yet precisely out of the ruins of his reputation as a systematic philosopher sprang the seeds of other valuations.

EMILE FAGUET†

These are petty reasons for a great reputation. There are better ones. It is much rarer than people think for a great man of letters to be the perfect expression of his native land, to represent brilliantly the spirit of his country. Neither Corneille nor Bossuet nor Pascal nor Racine nor Rousseau nor Chateaubriand nor Lamartine gives me the idea—even an enlarged, improved, and purified idea—of a Frenchman as I see and know him. What they represent, each of

† Emile Faguet, "Voltaire" in *Dix-Huitième Siècle*, pp. 286–287.

them, is an aspect of the French character, a single one of the intellectual qualities of the French race, picked out of many and carried to a point of excellence. This is why—as much because of their narrow range as because of their superiority within it—they scarcely represent us at all. But Voltaire is like us. The average spirit of France is in him. A man more witty than intelligent, and much more intelligent than artistic, is a Frenchman. A man of great practical good sense, swift in repartee, quick and brilliant with the pen, and who contradicts himself abominably as soon as he ventures on the great issues, is a Frenchman. A man impatient of minor restraints and docile under the heaviest ones is a Frenchman. A man who thinks himself an innovator and who is conservative to the bottom of his soul, who in literature and art is strictly attached to tradition as long as he has the right to be disrespectful toward it, is a Frenchman. Voltaire is light, impulsive, a fighter; he is a Frenchman. He is sincere, by intention anyway, and among all his faults he does not have those of pedantry or charlatanism; he is a Frenchman. He is almost incapable of metaphysics or poetry; he is a Frenchman. He is gracious and charming, in verse or prose, and eloquent on occasion; he is a Frenchman. He is radically incapable of understanding the idea of liberty, and knows only how to be a malicious slave or a gleeful tyrant; he is a Frenchman. At heart he loves despotism, and expects all progress from the State, from an enlightened savior; he is a Frenchman. He is not very brave; and this is not French at all, but the French have recognized so many of their other qualities in him that this one aberration they have forgiven.

DANIEL MORNET†

Voltaire outlines, with a marvellously sure hand, the architecture of an epic poem which will conform with all the rules of the most harmonious construction—and the most boring. He is just as good, or just as puerile, an architect in his tragedies. But there is no longer a question of order, or even of equilibrium, in most of his stories. What he proposes to study there is precisely the quirks of fate, the disordered complexity of existence. He will pursue this disorder, which is both picturesque and necessary, in *Zadig*, in *Candide*, and *l'Ingénu*. Accident still serves as a link in these works. But Voltaire will reach the stage of giving up linkage of every sort. In order to publish the confused body of reflections stirred up within him by the confusion of human affairs, he will have to forego writing a treatise, a discourse, or even an essay. He will jumble all his ideas into those *Questions on the Encyclopedia* which eventually

† Daniel Mornet, *Histoire de la Clarté Française* (Paris, 1929), p. 110.

become the *Philosophical Dictionary*; logical order is thus reduced to alphabetical order. Faguet said of Voltaire that he was "a chaos of clear ideas." It was a reproach. I should almost be tempted to think it a grounds for praise. The same chaos is found in a good number of his contemporaries. It is the consequence of a prodigious influx of new ideas; it results above all from a renunciation of the classic spirit, which, for fear of losing its way, was reduced to turning forever in a narrow and monotonous circle.

VOLTAIRE'S HUMANITY

Whether Voltaire laughed with the human race or at it, whether he pitied men or sneered at them, whether his famous smile was a benediction or a grimace, these were questions which centered rather closely on *Candide*.

MADAME DE STAËL †

[*After a passage explaining why serious German philosophy has trouble gaining a hearing in a flippant and worldly society*]
The philosophy of sensations is one of the principal causes of this frivolity. Since people have taken to considering the soul passive, a great number of philosophic works have fallen into contempt. The day when it was announced that there were no more mysteries in the world, that all ideas reached us through our eyes and ears, and that nothing was real which was not palpable, every individual who enjoyed the full use of his senses supposed himself a philosopher. One continually hears it said of people who have enough sense to make money when they are poor and to spend it when they are rich, that they have the only reasonable philosophy, and that only dreamers spend their time thinking of other matters. And in fact the senses can teach us nothing much more than this; if one can know nothing but what they teach, we must dismiss as madness everything which is not grounded on material evidence.

But if one should admit that the soul acts of its own accord; that it can sink into itself, and find truth there; and that this truth can be grasped only with the aid of a profound meditation, since it is not within the sphere of terrestrial experiences, then the entire direction of our thoughts would be changed. Men would no longer reject disdainfully exalted thoughts because they require careful consideration; what they would find insupportable is the superficial and the commonplace, for the void in the long run is singularly heavy.

† Madame de Staël, *De L'Allemagne*, Part III, Chapter 4, "Du Persiflage."

Voltaire had so clear a sense of the influence which metaphysical systems exert on the direction of our thinking, that he composed *Candide* to combat Leibnitz. He took a curious attitude of hostility toward final causes, optimism, free will, and in short against all those philosophic opinions which tend to raise the dignity of man; and he created *Candide*, that work of diabolic gaiety. For it seems to have been written by a creature of a nature wholly different from our own, indifferent to our lot, rejoicing in our sufferings, and laughing like a demon or an ape at the miseries of this human race with which he has nothing in common. The greatest poet of the age, the author of *Alzire*, *Tancrède*, *Mérope*, *Zaïre*, and *Brutus*, repudiated in this novel all the great moral truths which he had so worthily celebrated.

When Voltaire, as a tragic author, felt and thought in the character of another, he was admirable; but when he remained in his own character, he was a trifler and a cynic. The same mobility which allowed him to take on the lineaments of those characters he wished to depict, was only too effective in inspiring a language which, at certain moments, was appropriate to the character of Voltaire himself.

Candide sets in action this mocking philosophy, so indulgent in appearance, so ferocious in reality: it presents human nature under the most deplorable aspect, and offers us, as our only consolation, the sardonic laugh which exempts us from pity toward others by inviting us to renounce it for ourselves.

ANATOLE FRANCE†

Comedy turns sad as soon as it becomes human. Does not *Don Quixote* sometimes make you grieve? I greatly admire those few books of a serene and smiling desolation, like the incomparable *Don Quixote* or like *Candide*, which are, when properly taken, manuals of indulgence and pity, bibles of benevolence.

GUSTAVE FLAUBERT‡

As for novels, Voltaire wrote just one, which is a summary of all his works * * * His whole intelligence was an implement of war, a weapon. And what makes me cherish him is the disgust I feel for his followers, the Voltaireans, those people who laugh at great things. Did he laugh, himself? He ground his teeth.

† Anatole France, *The Garden of Epicurus*, in *Œuvres*, ed. Calmann-Levy, 1927, IX, 412.

‡ Gustave Flaubert, letter to Mme. Roger des Genettes (1859–60?).

BOURGEOIS OR NIHILIST?

Eldorado is evidently the crossing-point of a great many intellectual trails in *Candide*; but as an esthetic performance, it has not aroused a great deal of enthusiasm. Mr. William Bottiglia, in the course of his full-length study of *Candide*, comes to the defense of the episode:

WILLIAM F. BOTTIGLIA†

Few value judgments have been made on the Eldorado episode. Le Breton condemns it in a phrase: 'rien de plus froid' (André Le Breton, *Le Roman au dix-huitime siècle*, Paris, 1898, p. 212). But *Candide* is a philosophic tale, not a novel. One demands of a novel that it generate fictional incandescence; of a philosophic tale, that it irradiate a steady phosphorescence. There is well-nigh unanimous agreement on the phosphorescent effect of *Candide* as a whole. This discussion has tried to show that the same effect suffuses the Eldorado episode. Toldo ("Voltaire conteur et romancier" in *Zeitschrift für französische sprache und litteratur*, XL, 174–75) and Faguet (*Voltaire*, Paris, 1895, pp. 194–95) take a condescending view of the entire presentation because they find it more or less derivative and very deficient in imagination. Their criticism is answerable partly on the same ground as Le Breton's; partly by invoking the nature of methodical parody; partly by pointing out that neither of them takes the episode seriously enough to give it his sustained attention. A comparison of Voltaire's utopia with others would reveal that he has risen far above the merely derivative level to create an episode as imaginatively original as the character and possibilities of the philosophic tale allow.

Of course, to defend Eldorado on the grounds that it is supposed to be phosphorescent instead of incandescent is to concede pretty openly that its temperature is lower than that of the surrounding atmosphere. A more urgent question has to do with Voltaire's basic attitude toward Eldorado, whether admiring or ironic. Ludwig W. Kahn, citing the protestant and bourgeois "religion of work", urges that the "garden" which Candide tells Pangloss to cultivate, at the end of the book, is no specific horticultural enterprise, but a symbol of creative activity. Cultivating one's garden is doing creative, productive work, whatever its nature; and Eldorado, with its built-in wealth and comforts, offers no proper sphere for such activity, therefore it is no utopia but an ironically-viewed pleasure-dome.

† William F. Bottiglia, *Voltaire's Candide: Analysis of a Classic,* in *Studies on Voltaire and the Eighteenth Century,* VII, 129–30.

LUDWIG W. KAHN†

In the light of this new "religion" of activity, I would like to question those interpretations of *Candide* which maintain that Voltaire offers in Eldorado an ideal and positive utopian goal. The trouble with any "perfect" or "best" world is precisely that it does not leave any room for amelioration or for activity, social or otherwise. Between "one's garden," in the sense established by Professor Bottiglia, and Eldorado there is no possible reconciliation, the former is a sphere of creative activity, the latter a place of idle, sterile life. *Candide* is a diatribe against those mistaken philosophers who consider the actual world as incapable of further improvement; such philosophers were wrong in seventeenth-century Germany; they are wrong in eighteenth-century France; could it be that Voltaire considers them right in Eldorado? Would their philosophy not always lead to the same life of passivity? Paradise, Eden, the City of God are places of rest, not to say of otiosity, because they are perfect. As Faust knew so well, if all human needs and wants are satisfied—as they are in Eldorado—life is at a standstill. I wish to suggest that the author of *Candide* did not differ much from Goethe's opinion in this respect. There are various reasons why Candide left Eldorado, not least among them that he wanted to find his beloved Cunégonde; but the fact remains that Eldorado proved unsatisfactory and could provide neither an end nor a consummation. It is not merely Candide's unregenerate character or his unfitness for the ideal life, if he says: "Si nous restons ici, nous n'y serons que comme les autres." Voltaire makes it quite clear that it is a life without challenge, without litigations, priests, social incentives—a life pleasant, placid, and stagnant rather than ideal—which proves unattractive for any length of time. When Candide inquires how people pray to God in Eldorado, the sage answers: "Nous ne le prions point, nous n'avons rien à lui demander." Can this be an ideal? A world where there is nothing to pray for is also a world where there is nothing to work for, nothing to live for. In Eldorado science, too, in its museum-like "palais des sciences," seems to require no further work for its already existing perfection. If we are right in assigning to Voltaire a place in the process of secularization which step by step substitutes activity and life for religion, Eldorado can hardly be, in the words of Professor Bottiglia, "a philosophic ideal for human aspiration."

But Mr. Bottiglia rebuts by showing in detail that most of the characteristic features of Eldorado are things of which Voltaire, in his correspond-

† Ludwig W. Kahn, "Voltaire's *Candide* and the Problem of Secularization," *PMLA*, LXVII. 887–88.

ence and other writings, expressed frequent, emphatic approval; that he often described his own household at *Les Délices* in terms reminiscent of Eldorado; and that *Candide* contains no specific, overt satiric assault on Eldorado proper. Mr. Bottiglia defines the relation between Eldorado and the "garden" in the following terms:

WILLIAM F. BOTTIGLIA†

* * * The former offers a dream of perfection, a philosophic ideal for human aspiration. The latter depicts the optimum present reality, which calls for work illumined by a sense of social purpose, with the former as the guiding standard. Eldorado provides happiness for an entire society; the garden, for a few. Eldorado is another world sufficient unto itself, hence can have no actual connection with this world, except by way of inspiration. The garden is very much a part of this world, and is dedicated to influencing it. Such are the basic differences; but there are resemblances too, which help to clarify the author's design. Both Eldorado and the garden are *model societies* whose inhabitants have learned the value of *settling down* to *dynamic activity:* in one case for perpetuation, in the other for pursuit, of the ideal. At the very beginning of the Eldorado episode Voltaire strikes the keynote of his message, for the first thing which he has Candide notice is that the country is *cultivated* 'pour le plaisir comme pour le besoin.' He thereby subtly prefigures the cultivation of the garden. And the *vow* of the Eldoradans adumbrates, not only the decision at the end to settle down, but also *the gesture of philosophic disdain.*

But the "ideal" solution to life's problems offered by the Eldoradans involves one major unreality; they seem never to confront the problem of boredom. The problem they have triumphantly solved is one from which the chief problematic has been tacitly extracted in advance. Thus they may have our envy or our curiosity, but not our full sympathy. As for the "gesture of philosophic disdain" which Mr. Bottiglia sees alike in Candide's retirement to his garden, and the vow of the Eldoradans never to leave their hideaway—it might provide an interesting exercise for one's literary tact to seek out reasons why these two broadly parallel actions produce such different effects on the reader. (Another good question would be: What functions do the Oreillons serve in preparing the way for Eldorado that Pococurante also serves in preparing the way for Candide's garden?)

Artistically speaking, there are obvious reasons why Voltaire would not have wanted his hero to confront (let alone solve successfully) the problem of the Good Life early on in *Candide*. There are also more interesting reasons why he would not have wanted to solve the problem too successfully even at the end of the book. For he did not really think all, or even most, of life's problems were soluble; like all sensible

† William F. Bottiglia, *op. cit.,* p. 119.

men, he knew that those which cannot be solved or evaded must be endured, preferably with stoicism. The acid realism which assigns Candide his heart's desire only when she is a hideous old hag and which leaves faithful Cacambo drudging his life away on the farm without any expression of relief or compassion, could not give any very deep allegiance to the innocent paperdolls and naive moral cutouts of Eldorado. If they represent an ideal, it is a hollow and almost shamefaced ideal—but this is a way of saying that a man of Voltaire's social temper probably does not lay great weight on utopian social ideals even when he shares and indulges them. The relative "coldness" of Eldorado, compared with the "warmth" of the little farm, underlines a distinction between them which is not altogether to be defined in terms of ideas or even attitudes. Perhaps more than anything else it is a matter of tempering the reader gradually down to the character, and making acceptance of limitations a matter of earned experience rather than learned dogma. Flaubert struck an exact and brilliant balance in assessing the conclusion of the book:

GUSTAVE FLAUBERT†

Thus the end of *Candide* is for me patent proof of a genius of the first water. The claws of the lion are marked on that quiet conclusion, as stupid as life itself.

VOLTAIRE'S STYLE

Four short comments on Voltaire's style, which some find hampering, others liberating; but within which even the slightest details may be an occasion for appreciation. In the larger sense, Voltaire's stylistic influence is too immense and fluid ever to be fully accounted for. It stands wholly apart from matters of intellectual influence. Gérard de Nerval, greatest of the mystically-minded *illuministes* (i.e., visionary poets of the nineteenth century), described himself quite naturally as a "fils de Voltaire."

GEORGE SAINTSBURY‡

* * * Mademoiselle Cunégonde (nobody will ever know anything about style who does not feel what the continual repetition in Candide's mouth of the "Mademoiselle" does) * * *

† Flaubert to Louise Colet, April 24, 1852.

‡ George Saintsbury, *History of the French Novel*, I, 382.

HEINRICH HEINE[†]

You can't imagine how hard it is for a German to compress the German soul [*Geist*] into these circumscribed, defined, fixed forms [of the French language]. My own songs reach me, under these circumstances, as complete strangers. I, a German forest-bird, accustomed to build his nest from the simplest and most varied materials, I find myself nesting there in the long curly wig of Voltaire.

NOVALIS[‡]

Voltaire is one of the greatest *poètes-manqués* (*Minuspoeten*) who ever lived; *Candide* is his *Odyssey*. Too bad for him that his world was a Parisian boudoir. With less personal and national frivolity, he might have been even greater.

HIPPOLYTE TAINE[§]

And this is the most striking quality of the style, its prodigious rapidity, the dizzy, dazzling passage of things forever new—ideas, images, events, landscapes, stories, dialogues—in a series of miniature paintings, which fly past as if projected by a magic lantern, withdrawn almost as soon as they are put forward by the impatient magician, who in the wink of an eye, races around the globe, and who, now astride of history, now of fable, now truth, now fantasy, now present, now past, frames his work sometimes into a parade as grotesque as that of a fair, sometimes into a spectacle more magnificent than that of the Opera * * *

In fact, M. Taine's commentary is more acute than he could have realized; Mr. Bottiglia, in his study of *Candide* already referred to, has shown that Voltaire was passionately fond of the magic lantern (not-too-remote ancestor of the modern movie), and that one's sense of the character in Voltairean *contes* as jerkily animated cutouts may well be a deliberately contrived effect.

VOLTAIRE'S APOTHEOSIS

We conclude with a selection from the magisterial comments of Paul Valéry, in a discourse pronounced at the Sorbonne on December 10, 1944.

† Heinrich Heine quoted by Alfred Meissner, *Heinrich Heine, Erinnerungen* (Hamburg, 1856), p. 194.
‡ Novalis, *Schriften* (Berlin, 1901), II, 78.
§ Hippolyte Taine, *Les Origines de la France Contemporaine: L'Ancien Régime* (Paris, 1891), pp. 342–48.

To pronounce Voltaire a classic is no longer enough, he has become the creator of the classic standard, the measure of the measure.

PAUL VALÉRY†

Voltaire was twenty-one at the death of Louis XIV. He was eighty-four when he perished himself, a monarch of the European mind. He led the funeral cortège of an age, of which the real strangeness, the complete originality, escape us, so familiar are we from childhood with its language and imposing discipline. It is pompous and simplified, this age; it combines the arbitrary and the logical; all the rigors of thought with the ostentation of appearances; will expresses itself in all forms of art, pursuing the natural by artifice and capturing it sometimes by abstraction. The severe goes hand in hand with the theatrical. In the life of the monarch himself, a sincere devotion and an exact observance of religious duties exist side by side with a succession of passionate attachments, known to everyone, of which the illegitimate products are publicly avowed, and take their place in the highest ranks of the state.

Voltaire lowers this century into its tomb. But with what respect, in what a finely finished casket does he commend it to its glory! He gives it the name of the king. He was the first to state that Europe, under this reign, recognized in our nation, in the order of its directing ideas and its general style of intellectual accomplishment, as well as in its manners, a supremacy which could be brought into question neither by abuses nor by defeats nor by the final exhaustion of the kingdom's resources. And he had the quite new and felicitous idea of introducing within his history an account of the state of arts and letters at the period he was describing. It was he who drew up, without error or omission, so that posterity has never erased or inserted a single name, the list of those great writers whom we call our classics.

He is the unquestioned inventor of this famous and imperious notion—completely French—of the classic, he who was able in his maturity to embrace within a single perfectly lucid glance the entire corpus of a firstrate literary achievement which was just hardening into an authoritarian system of perfection. It was directly inspired by the purest models of antiquity, as far as its structure and its economy of effects were concerned; but nourished, on the other hand, in the sacred simplicity of the Vulgate; and penetrated, lastly, by a sense of logical rigor which the taste for geometry had, since the day of Descartes, communicated to more than one thoughtful citizen.

And yet Voltaire was to spend his entire life in ruining, in con-

† Paul Valéry, *Voltaire, discours prononcé le 10 Décembre, 1944, en Sorbonne* (Paris, 1945), pp. 5–16.

suming with the fire that was his being, what remained of the grand
century, of its traditions, its beliefs, its pomps—but not its works.
Between the time of his youth and that which saw him disappear,
the contrast is striking. Had he lived ten years more, this man who
could have seen Louis XIV could have seen the end of the Terror
—supposing he had not perished at its hands before Thermidor.

Thus he may make us think of that god Janus to whom the
Romans attributed two opposed faces, and who was the god of be-
ginnings and endings. The face of young Voltaire looks toward
the sumptuously melancholy evening, in the dark purple shades of
which the Sun King sank to rest, overwhelmed by his glory, and
abandoning himself to the dark like a solemn sun never to reappear.
But the other face of this Janus, old Voltaire, looks toward the
East, where some unfamiliar dawning gilds enormous cloud banks.
At the level of the horizon throb a multitude of rays * * *

No, he is no philosopher, this devil of a man, whose mobility,
whose complexity, whose contradictions make up a character which
only music, and the liveliest of music, could follow and follow to his
end.

Bibliography

I. EDITIONS OF VOLTAIRE'S WORKS

Moland (1877–85) in fifty-two volumes very largely reprinted Beuchot (1829–40) but added much *Correspondance*; this *Correspondance* is now available in much more accurate and complete form in the great Besterman edition. But all these editions are institutional in their grandeur. For the practical student both Classiques Garnier and Gallimard's Bibliothèque de la Pléiade publish editions of the *Romans et Contes*; the former publishes also the *Dictionnaire Philosophique*, the *Lettres* and *Dialogues Philosophiques*; the latter, *Œuvres Historiques* and a generous assortment of *Mélanges*, ideal for browsing.

II. BIBLIOGRAPHIES OF VOLTAIRE

Bengesco, Georges. *Voltaire, bibliographie de ses Œuvres* (Paris, 1882–1890) 4 vols.
[To be used in conjunction with Malcomb, Jean, *Table de la bibliographie de Voltaire* (Genève 1953), which makes it possible to discover something in Bengesco.]
Barr, Mary Margaret H. *A Century of Voltaire Study* (1825–1925) (New York, 1929).
[Two supplements have appeared in *Modern Language Notes* (XLVIII, 292–307, and LVI, 563–582).]
Annual bibliographies of *PMLA* and *The Year's Work in Modern Language Studies*.

III. FURTHER READING

Barber, W. H. *Voltaire: Candide* (London, 1960).
Bellessort, André. *Essai sur Voltaire* (Paris, 1925).
Bottiglia, William F. *Voltaire's Candide: Analysis of a Classic* in *Studies on Voltaire and the 18th Century* (Genève, 1959, 1964), Vols. 7 and 7A.
Brandes, Georg. *Voltaire* (2 vols.) tr. O. Kruger and P. Butler (New York, 1930 and 1964).
Champion, Edmonde. *Voltaire, Etudes critiques* (Paris, 1893).
Delattre, André. *Voltaire L'Impétueux* (Paris, 1957).
Desnoiresterres, Gustave. *Voltaire et la société française au XVIIIe siècle* (Paris, 1867–1876), 8 vols.

Faguet, Emile. *Voltaire* (Paris, 1895).

Flowers, Ruth C. *Voltaire's Stylistic Transformation of Rabelaisian Satirical Devices* (Washington, D.C.: Catholic University of America Press, 1951).

Havens, George R. ed. *Candide* (New York, 1934).

Hazard, Paul. "Le problème du mal," *Romanic Review*, XXXII, 147–170.

Lovejoy, Arthur O. "Optimism and romanticism," in *PMLA* 1927 (XLII, 921–945).

McGhee, Dorothy. *Voltairian Narrative Devices* (Menasha, Wisconsin, 1933).

Mornet, Daniel. *Histoire de la clarté française* (Paris, 1929).

La pensée française au 18e siècle (Paris, 1926).

Noyes, Alfred. *Voltaire* (New York, 1936). [The second edition of this Catholic appreciation of Voltaire was withdrawn from circulation "by order of the Supreme Congregation of the Holy See in June, 1938."]

Pellissier, Georges. *Voltaire philosophe* (Paris, 1908).

Prod'homme, J. G. *Voltaire raconté par ceux qui l'ont vu* (de Paris à Genève, i.e., de 1694 à 1754) (Paris, 1929).

Spitzer, Leo, "Pages from Voltaire," in *A Method of Interpreting Literature* (Northampton, Mass., 1949), pp. 64–101.

Torrey, Norman L. *The Spirit of Voltaire* (New York, 1938).

Finally, various "vie-et-œuvres" creampuffs, such as French scholarship too generously abounds in—Crouslé (1899), Bertault (1910), Naves (1942), and Cresson (1948).

NORTON CRITICAL EDITIONS